"Chaff fell about him like metallic confetti."

I'm looking for a nurse who works here. My fiancée. Her name is Annie Little. Do you know her?" RAF pilot Eric MacKenzie asked a doctor as he helped to push patients' cots into the safety of the hospital corridor while "Moaning Millie," the air raid siren, wailed over the city of London.

The booming pops of an antiaircraft battery interrupted him. Over the racket, Eric distinctly heard the menacing drone of German Junkers.

"Take cover!" he shouted. The terrifying scream of a bomb rent the air. Then a more terrifying silence. The doctor dove under an empty bed and Eric threw himself over a prostrate patient. A fiery blast ripped open the wall of the hospital ward, spewing bricks and mortar. Shards of glass crashed to the floor like jagged icicles.

No one at the hospital knew Annie's whereabouts. Eric had to return to duty without any word of her. Having spent most of the war flying above the city, he was unprepared for the devastation that met him on the ground as he dodged debris and shrapnel. Chaff fell about him like metallic confetti in a ticker tape parade. Bells clanged as fire engines and ambulances threaded their way through the streets. An Auxiliary Fire Serviceman dashed past him hauling buckets of sand to douse an unexploded incendiary bomb. Men scurried about uncoiling thick hoses or feverishly shooting jets of water from their stirrup pumps onto flaming buildings. Although nightfall, the city was brightly lit by fire and the skyline glowed a sinister scarlet.

The London Blitz had begun.

What Readers and Reviewers Are Saying
About Melanie Jeschke

"Step back in time and enjoy an enriching tale of Oxford, C.S. Lewis, and the characters Melanie Jeschke brings to life—you will feel as if you know them personally. Reminiscent of Jan Karon's books, you will be enchanted with the story and enriched by the truths tucked in along the way. This love story weaves around the people, places, and histories that have shaped our lives. I have loved all three books of The Oxford Chronicles and hope there is a fourth to come."

—Ruth Graham, daughter of Billy and Ruth Graham,
author of *A Legacy of Love* and *I'm Pregnant...Now What?*

"Melanie Jeschke's meticulous period research is integrated seamlessly into a gripping and delightful yarn of love, faith, and loss set during the horror and terror of war. Playing a small but important part in the central story, C.S. Lewis and his immediate circle in Oxford come to vivid life."

—Colin Duriez, author of *Tolkien and C.S. Lewis:
The Gift of Friendship* and *A Field Guide to Narnia*

"With this second book [*Expectations*] Melanie Jeschke writes about things she knows to the depths of her being: family, parenthood, loss. And it works on multiple levels, lifting it beyond the simple category of 'romance' and into the sphere of *A Grief Observed*. Anyone who has struggled with loss will find themselves touched by this story."

—Sarah Arthur, author of *Walking Through
the Wardrobe* and *Walking with Frodo*

"Once again, Melanie Jeschke brings joy to her readers! *Expectations* is every bit as enchanting as *Inklings*, with memorable characters and a warm, engaging story. If you haven't yet read a Jeschke story, 'expect' to be entertained!"

—Loree Lough, author of Heartsong Presents novels

"Melanie Jeschke's *Expectations* continues the charming treat started with *Inklings* and *Intentions*. Readers familiar with those novels, as well as new Jeschke fans, will delight in delving deeper into the loving relationship of David and Kate MacKenzie as they experience the excitement of life in Paris and the very real struggles of new marriage and possible parenthood."

—Trish Perry, author of *The Guy I'm Not Dating*

"Melanie Jeschke weaves a great love story with the fascinating Oxford world of C.S. Lewis and J.R.R. Tolkien. The Inklings fraternity was probably one of the most interesting and stimulating small groups of all time. Melanie takes you there to enjoy the greatest of fellowship and debate coupled with modern-day romance and intrigue. A delicious combination—especially for admirers of Jack and the author of *The Lord of the Rings*."

—Ron Boehme, Youth with a Mission, author of *Leadership for the 21ˢᵗ Century*

"*Expectations* is a very uplifting and fascinating book that you will not be able to put down. Mrs. Jeschke has a way of writing that will have you believing you are actually watching the story unfold. Each character truly brings this book to life. I would recommend this book to anyone wanting to read an inspirational romance."

—*The Romance Reader's Connection*

"The author has done splendid work with dialogue and narrative [in *Expectations*]...and doesn't hesitate to treat us to some beautiful writing. I highly recommend this novel to any believer who appreciates excellent literature. I guarantee that the story line and the characters will minister to your heart and soul."

—*Christian Fiction Reviewer*

EVASIONS

Melanie M. Jeschke

HARVEST HOUSE PUBLISHERS

EUGENE, OREGON

Cover by Left Coast Design, Portland, Oregon

Cover photo © George Marks / Retrofile / Getty Images

This is a work of fiction. Names, characters, places, and incidents are products of the author's imagination or are used fictitiously.

EVASIONS
Copyright © 2006 by Melanie M. Jeschke
Published by Harvest House Publishers
Eugene, Oregon 97402
www.harvesthousepublishers.com

Library of Congress Cataloging-in-Publication Data
Jeschke, Melanie M., 1953-
Evasions / Melanie M. Jeschke.
   p. cm.
ISBN-13: 978-0-7369-1678-3 (pbk.)
ISBN-10: 0-7369-1678-4 (pbk.)
1. Upper class families—England—Oxford—Fiction. 2. Oxford (England)—Fiction. I. Title.
PS3610.E83E83 2006
813'.6—dc22

                    2006005868

Printed in the United States of America

06 07 08 09 10 11 12 13 14 / BC-CF / 10 9 8 7 6 5 4 3 2 1

With gratitude to my lighthouse keepers
Bob and Marilyn White
for their vision and faithfulness

and

to the loving memory
of my father-in-law
Col. Richard Hall Jeschke Jr., USMC,
and all those of the "Greatest Generation"

*"Never in the field of human conflict
was so much owed by so many to so few."*
~Winston Churchill~

Evasions Character List

The MacKenzie Family

Annie Little MacKenzie—(b. Aug 16, 1920, Charlottesville, VA) wife of Eric, mother of seven MacKenzie children, younger sister of Jeff Little

Eric MacKenzie—the Reverend Eric Richard MacKenzie (b. July 31, 1917, Gairloch, Scotland) husband of Annie, father of seven MacKenzie children, Rector of St. Aldate's Church, Oxford

David MacKenzie—né David Lawrence (b. Dec 13, 1940) oldest son of Eric and Annie, husband of Kate, father of baby Jeffrey, Fellow of Magdalen College, Oxford

Kate MacKenzie—née Katherine Lee Hughes (b. June 26, 1944, Richmond, VA) wife of David, mother of Jeffrey, graduate of William and Mary College and the University of Oxford

Ginny MacKenzie—née Virginia Anne (b. April 10, 1944) oldest daughter of Eric and Annie, nurse at St. Bartholomew's, London, dating David's Cambridge roommate, Dr. Kevin Ryan

Natalie MacKenzie—née Natalie Marie (b. March 18, 1946) second daughter of Eric and Annie, graduate of the University of Oxford dating Lord Stuart Devereux

William MacKenzie—né William Jeffrey (b. Feb. 4, 1949) fourth child of Eric and Annie

Richard MacKenzie—né Richard Eric (b. Aug. 29, 1952) fifth child of Eric and Annie

Mark MacKenzie—né Mark Cameron (b. Aug. 8, 1954) sixth child of Eric and Annie

Hannah MacKenzie—née Hannah Joy (b. Aug 9, 1961) seventh child of Eric and Annie

Jeffrey MacKenzie—né Jeffrey Thomas (b. Feb 14, 1967) baby son of David and Kate

Davey MacKenzie—né Richard David MacKenzie, husband of Maggie, father of Eric

Maggie MacKenzie—née Margaret Cameron, wife of Davey, mother of Eric

"Fatbug" MacKenzie—né William, Eric's uncle, a fisherman and caddie at St. Andrews

"Slim" MacKenzie—née Margaret, Fatbug's wife, Eric's aunt, lives in Anstruther

Bob and Marilyn—Eric's cousin and his wife, the lighthouse keepers of Rua Reidh

Friends of the MacKenzies

Austen Holmes—(b. May 28, 1938) friend of David and husband of Yvette, Fellow of Merton College, University of Oxford

Yvette Holmes—(b. Oct. 14, 1936) née Yvette Goodman, friend of David and wife of Austen, daughter of Molly and James Goodman of London, Fellow of St. Hilda's College, University of Oxford

Kevin Ryan—Cambridge roommate of David, dating David's sister Ginny, a resident doctor at St. Bartholomew's, London

The Devereux Family

Stuart Devereux—né Lord Stuart Winston Spencer Devereux, Viscount Devereux (b. May 31, 1943) heir and son of Charles Stuart Spencer Devereux, Earl of Essex, and Elaine, Lady Devereux, Countess of Essex, graduate of the University of Oxford, dating Natalie MacKenzie

Clementine ("Clemmie")—Lady Fitzwilliam, wife of Edward, Earl of Carlisle, older sister of Stuart Devereux, mother of Teddy and Spencer, mistress of Carlisle House, Yorkshire

The Little Family

Jeff Little—né Jeffrey Lawrence Little (b. March 30, 1919) elder brother of Annie, American student at Magdalen College, Oxford

Annie Little—(see Annie MacKenzie above)

In Scotland

Laurene Kilmorey—(b. 1921) daughter of the laird, Lord Kilmorey, Earl Kellie of Kilmorey House, Kingsbarns, Scotland, loves Eric

Peter Kilmorey—(b. 1918) Laurene's older brother, later marries Catherine

Lord and Lady Kilmorey—Earl and Countess Kellie, parents of Laurene and Peter

Fiona McPherson—maid to Laurene

Mrs. McPherson—mother to Fiona, Kilmorey House cook

John—Kilmorey House butler

In Greater London

Roger L. Green—Jeff's friend from Oxford, an actor in *Peter Pan* (see historical characters below)

Peggy Myers—Annie's flatmate and a nurse whom Jeff likes

Betty Purcell—Annie's flatmate and a nurse who works with her at Dunkirk

June Brown—Annie's flatmate and a nurse who dates a doctor

Dr. Henry Benson—("Harry"), doctor who dates June and advises Annie

Ian McLeod—Eric's RAF buddy

Historical Characters

Jack Lewis—né Clive Staples Lewis (b. Nov 29, 1898, Belfast, Ireland)
   Fellow of the University of Oxford, Christian author

Warnie Lewis—né Warren Hamilton (b. June 16, 1895, Belfast, Ireland)
   elder brother of C.S. Lewis

Mrs. Moore—née Janie King (b. March 23, 1872, Ireland) "adopted mother" of C.S. Lewis mother of "Paddy" Moore (killed in WWI) and Maureen

Maureen Moore—(b. Aug 19, 1906, Ireland) daughter of Janie Moore, "adopted sister" of C.S. Lewis, married Leonard Blake on Aug 27, 1940.

Fred Paxford—faithful gardener and caretaker of the Kilns, home of C.S. Lewis

Roger Lancelyn Green—a student and later close friend of C.S. Lewis, also an Inkling (see London characters, above)

Map

Prologue

In everything you do, put God first, and he will direct you and crown your efforts with success.

PROVERBS 3:6 TLB

Our whole being by its very nature is one vast need; incomplete, preparatory, empty, yet cluttered, crying out for Him who can untie things that are now knotted together and tie up things that are dangling loose.

C.S. LEWIS
The Four Loves

July 1967
Carlisle House, Yorkshire

*R*everend MacKenzie, I would like to ask you for your
daughter Natalie's hand in marriage."

Lord Stuart Devereux anxiously watched his prospective
father-in-law for his reaction to this proposal. The two men
sat in the sumptuous library of Carlisle House, home of Stuart's sister, Lady Clementine Fitzwilliam. The French doors
of the library were flung open to the gentle summer breeze
and the distant chuckles of the fountains playing in the gardens beyond the terrace. Stuart had seized this moment of
after-dinner privacy—while the rest of the MacKenzie family
settled in their guest rooms throughout the manor house—
to initiate the request that had been burning in his heart for
months.

In celebration of the Reverend Eric MacKenzie's fiftieth birthday, he and his wife Annie, their seven children,
daughter-in-law, and new grandson were taking a holiday trip
to Scotland. Stuart's sister had graciously offered her hospitality to the MacKenzie clan as they made their journey north
from Oxford, and Stuart had conceived a plan to propose to

Natalie MacKenzie on the spectacular grounds of the York-shire estate.

But first he needed her father's approval.

In the long silence that followed, Eric MacKenzie puffed on his pipe and regarded Stuart thoughtfully but not unkindly. He observed a tall, lanky man in his mid-twenties with green eyes, short brown hair, and a pronounced widow's peak framing his heart-shaped face. Stuart's handsome features and charming manners had the unavoidable bearings of the aristocracy as befitted the eldest son of the Earl of Essex. But Eric recalled that his first introduction to the young aristo-crat had been to a boorishly behaved rival to his oldest son, David. Although only a few years older than Stuart, David, in his position as an Oxford don, had demonstrated the maturity to overlook the rivalry and act as a mentor, urging Stuart to seek help in overcoming his alcohol abuse. As a result of this intervention, Stuart had found a renewed faith, new friends and family among the MacKenzies, and new love in David's sister Natalie.

Stuart finally blurted out, "I know I'm not worthy of her—no one could hope to be—but I do love Natalie so very deeply. I am a different man than when you first met me—by the grace of God, that is—and I've been sober now for a year and a half. If you consent, I promise I will take excellent care of her. I have a sizable income from my mother's estate and, of course, when my father passes on I will inherit Clifton Manor and my father's title. Natalie would become a countess—the Lady Devereux—well, she'd be a viscountess anyway until then, not that titles matter at all to you—"

"Stuart," Eric interrupted gently, "I'm not unmindful of the great honor you are bestowing on our family by your request."

"My point wasn't to make a fuss about the title. I only mention that to assure you that I can provide well for her."

"I have no doubt of that."

"Well then, sir, can you see your way to giving us your blessing?" Stuart asked eagerly.

"Have you spoken to Natalie?"

"I haven't popped the question, if that's what you mean. I wanted to have your approval first."

"I appreciate that, Stuart." Eric smiled. "Most considerate of you, especially in this modern era. But I wondered if you know Natalie's mind and heart on the matter."

"We've talked about the possibility of marriage in a general way. I believe she loves me, but to be honest, I don't know whether or not she will agree to marry me…at least not yet."

"Then why not wait until you are certain?"

"I am certain about this, sir, but I'm afraid she is not. In any case, I wanted to know what you thought about it before I pursued it further."

"Why now?"

"Well, since Natalie just took her degree from Oxford and is looking for employment, you know she's contemplating going to London or going back to Paris to work at the British embassy. I've been out of Oxford for over a year now and working hard to make Clifton Manor financially solvent. I've made great progress by opening it to public tours in the summer months, and I hope to turn a profit this year. In any case, I've been pursuing Natalie by this long-distance courtship, and I would much prefer to be married or at least live closer to her. If she follows a job to Paris, it would make the separation even more unbearable for me."

"I see." Eric set his pipe in an ashtray. "Have you spoken to your father?"

"No. I thought it appropriate to speak to you first."

"But do you think he would agree to this? Doesn't he have plans for you? Surely he could not be pleased that you would choose someone who is neither of your class nor your wealth."

Stuart sighed. "I saw long ago what my father's marrying for money did to my mother. I'm independently wealthy now and don't need to marry for money. He knows that when my mother died, I resolved to marry for love. I don't believe he would stand in my way."

"But he could make things difficult for you and Natalie."

"He could," Stuart acknowledged, "but I don't think he would."

"Let's just say for the sake of argument that your father decides to disinherit you if you don't marry someone of his choosing—what then? If it came to that, could you lay down your title out of love for Natalie?"

Stuart regarded Eric steadily. "I could. I believe I could lay down anything for her, even my life. Certainly my old life. I've done that already. I hope, by God's grace, I could even lay down my desire to marry her if that would be best for her and would most please God. But I do desire most earnestly to marry her and have prayed and prayed for God's will to be done."

Eric nodded. "I have prayed that too and have asked Him to show you both clearly what His will is. I know you won't be happy unless you walk in His ways. Nevertheless, although times are changing, I know from sad experience that it can be difficult—for both of you—to marry across class lines."

Stuart looked at him with puzzlement. "Your own sad experience, sir?"

"Aye. When I was a lad in Scotland, I had the misfortune— or perhaps it would be more apt to say, the bitter joy—of loving a laird's daughter. That, of course, was before the war and before I met Annie."

"Would you tell me about it, sir?"

Eric hesitated while he considered this. "I suppose there would be no harm. Perhaps something in my story could be of help to you. But I don't know. After all these years, it's still difficult for me to sort through so much sadness."

"I beg your pardon if I was presumptuous or asked amiss."

"No, no—" A knock at the door interrupted Eric's reply.

"Enter," Stuart called out.

David MacKenzie, Eric's eldest son and Stuart's friend and mentor, opened the door. He held a chubby infant with black curls and bright blue eyes, very much like his father's and grandfather's. "Excuse me, gentlemen," David said as he handed the baby to Eric, "but this little lad would like a good-night kiss from his granddad before going to bed."

David's wife, Kate, along with his little sister Hannah, followed closely behind. The men rose in greeting. Six-year-old Hannah skipped up to Stuart and dropped down in a neat curtsey. "Good evening, Lord Devereux."

"Good evening, my lady," Stuart bowed slightly, enjoying their oft-played game of chivalrous courtesy. "Hello, Kate," he said, turning to her and noticing once again how much she resembled Natalie with her petite figure and dark beauty.

Since the birth of her son five months earlier, Kate had also acquired a healthy maternal glow which only enhanced her natural loveliness. "Has Clemmie made sure you're sufficiently settled?" Stuart asked. "Is everything to your satisfaction?"

"Everything is wonderful, thank you, and your sister has been most welcoming." Kate smiled warmly. She took her baby, Jeffrey, from Eric's arms, and while he resumed his seat she sat on a nearby sofa. "We feel like quite the privileged guests here," she said. "This house is amazing! I can't wait to explore it and the grounds tomorrow."

Stuart laughed softly. "You always have appreciated the beauty and history of these old houses. Perhaps I should hire you for the summer as a docent at Clifton Manor and let David spend the days reading in our library."

"Sounds like a good plan to me, old boy," David said, grinning. "A summer of studying on a country estate near Cambridge has a definite appeal. We just might take you up on it, but first we have to see my dad up to Scotland for his birthday."

Hannah, Eric's youngest daughter, stood at his knee for her goodnight kiss. Slipping her arms around her father's neck, she laid her head on his shoulder. Hannah had grown taller and slimmer since Stuart and Kate had first met her, but her blond ringlets, large blue eyes, and charming manners still exuded an angelic aura. "Goodnight, Daddy," she whispered, kissing him softly on the cheek.

"Goodnight, my darling," Eric rejoined. "Butterfly?" he asked, and then he brushed her cheek with his eyelashes.

Hannah giggled. "Nose-à-nose?" She rubbed the tip of his nose with her own.

Eric smiled. "You, my sweet girl, keep me young." He hugged her tightly. "I love you so much! Now may the Lord bless you and keep you and angels watch over you. See you in the morning!"

"Okeydokey!" Hannah sang happily and proceeded to grace each of them, including Lord Stuart Devereux, with a kiss and hug.

"Ah, here you all are!" said Natalie as she and her mother, Annie, joined the company in the library. "We've been looking for Hannah, but I can see she's being a good girl and giving everyone their goodnight kisses. Don't forget me, Hannah. Let me have a nose-à-nose."

Hannah sweetly complied.

"Now off to bed with you," Natalie said, kissing her little sister again for good measure and then nestling next to Stuart on a divan. She looked up at him and smiled when he placed his hand over hers, squeezing it gently.

"Come on, Hannah," Annie urged her youngest child. "It's time for bed, pumpkin. I'll take you up. This is a big house and we don't want you getting lost."

"Okay, Mummy. Goodnight, everyone!"

"Goodnight, Hannah!" the group chorused.

"Since we're all cozily gathered in here," Stuart interjected, "I'll ring for some coffee and biscuits. Mrs. MacKenzie, please join us when you come back down. Reverend MacKenzie, would you be willing to share that story? I'd like to hear it. Unless, of course, you'd rather not. Or we can postpone to another time if your family has heard it before."

"I always love a good story," David said as he lowered himself onto the sofa where Kate sat cuddling Jeffrey. "Which story is it?"

"Before you all came in," Eric explained, "Stuart and I were talking about relationships. I mentioned to him a little about my past before I met your mother, and he was interested in hearing more. I've shared bits and pieces with you all but never the whole saga."

Annie regarded her husband carefully. After their long years of marriage, she could read in his face and words much that was unspoken. "Perhaps this would be a good time to tell the children some of your experiences, honey. If you'd like to, that is. I'll put the baby down so Kate and David can stay to listen."

The serious tone of their parents' exchange did not go unnoticed by the family. They recognized that their father would not merely be recounting a frivolous tale of his youth, but something much more profound. When coffee had been served and Hannah and Baby Jeffrey had been put to bed, the rest of the MacKenzies and Stuart Devereux gathered in the library to hear what Eric had to share.

Part 1
Eric's Story

*Where can I go from your Spirit? Where can I flee
from your presence? If I go up to the heavens, you
are there; if I make my bed in the depths, you are
there. If I rise on the wings of the dawn, if I settle
on the far side of the sea, even there your hand will
guide me, your right hand will hold me fast.*

PSALM 139:7-10 NIV

*We may ignore, but we can nowhere evade, the pres-
ence of God. The world is crowded with Him. He
walks everywhere incognito. And the incognito is
not always hard to penetrate. The real labour is to
remember, to attend. In fact, to come awake. Still
more to remain awake.*

C.S. LEWIS
Letters to Malcolm: Chiefly on Prayer

2

Spring 1936
Kilmorey Estate
St. Andrews, Scotland

*T*he distance from St. Andrews to Oxford is but a long day's journey, yet for Eric MacKenzie it took far longer. His journey traversed national boundaries and cultural divides, and his course met many twists and bends in the road—some, the inevitable perils of war and some of his own making. The hand of Providence gently prodded and protected him along the way, but he veered recklessly into dense thickets or charged headstrong into blind alleys. Eric MacKenzie did not always choose the straight and narrow.

But Eric had little inkling of what lay before him as he poked about the gorse bushes looking for stray golf balls on a windy spring afternoon. Every caddie knew that the "lost" balls lining their pockets would easily convert into real currency. With his keen eyesight and quick mind, Eric had a particular knack for finding the hidden treasures. And this spot on the old Kingsbarns course along the rugged North Sea coast was a favorite foraging site. The drive from one green to the next sailed over a rocky inlet, and many a ball went diving into the sea or was dashed by the wind into the gorse.

Spying a glimmer of white, Eric gingerly worked his hand through the branches of the prickly shrub and then triumphantly slipped the ball into his pocket. The ringing bark of a dog caught his attention. He looked up to see a black Labrador bounding down to the pebbled beach.

"Abby!" he cried. "Did ye find one fer me, lassie?"

The dog answered by lifting her head and almost grinning with her bared teeth.

"Good girl!" Eric called. "Come!"

"What makes you think she's fetching that ball for you, Eric MacKenzie?"

The voice, rippling with laughter, took his breath away. He turned to watch a slender raven-haired girl run lightly over a footbridge and down the hill to his side.

Laurene.

He swallowed. "Hello, there."

Her brilliant blue eyes met his. She smiled boldly. "Hello, Eric." She placed a golf ball in his hand. "Here. Take this one too. I found it along the path in the woods. Somebody was way off the mark."

"Thanks." Eric pocketed the ball and they both laughed as Abby loped toward them and dropped a ball at Eric's feet. "Good girl, Abby. Ye've raised my count to five." Squatting down, he rubbed the Lab's head affectionately, and then he glanced up and grinned at Laurene. "I've got somethin' to show you."

"I don't need to see your collection. You know most of the ones you find are my father's, don't you?" Her smile undermined her chiding tone.

"Nay, 'tisna the laird's golf balls I'd be showin' ye. 'Tis this." From his jacket pocket Eric drew out an envelope.

Laurene snatched it from him excitedly. "Is it? Is it…?" She pulled out the letter and quickly scanned it.

"Aye," he replied with an undisguised hint of pride. "'Tis my acceptance letter to the University of St. Andrews."

She threw her arms around his neck. "Oh, Eric! This is wonderful! And a scholarship too?"

"Aye."

"Congratulations! I am so proud of you and Peter will be and all your family and all the caddies and all the fishermen and all the folks in Anstruther—the first of your family to go to university—oh, golly, we're all so proud!"

Eric beamed. "Thank ye." He gently pulled her hands from his neck but kept them tightly in his. "I really do mean to thank *you*, Laurene. Ye've been my inspiration."

"Nay, I can't take credit. You know it's the good Lord Himself who's been your inspiration. Now you can train for your calling at last." She smiled. "Why don't you tell me the story again, Eric? Tell me about your vision."

He laughed softly. "But ye've heard it so many times."

"I love to hear it as often as you'll tell it. It inspires *me*."

"All right, then." Still holding her hand, he led her to a towering birch tree where they settled, leaning against the smooth trunk. As they looked out over the windswept greens to the whitecaps skipping across the restless sea, Eric cleared his throat and began reciting his oft-repeated tale to his ever-enraptured audience.

"Well then, as ye know, I grew up in the western Highlands near Gairloch. In the summers I'd often go out to stay at Rua Reidh, where my uncle is the lighthouse keeper. And there—"

"Tell me about Rua Reidh," Laurene interrupted.

"Och!" Eric shook his head with amusement. "Well, the lighthouse is a fine one, built by a cousin of the great Scottish author Robert Louis Stevenson. It's tall and strong and all whitewashed so ye can see it against the sky from miles away. 'Tis a lonely spot and the land is wild. The sea is wild too with the waves crashin' against the rocks. 'Tisna usually as blue as 'tis here—more often the color of slate and sometimes black as ink. But I would love to wander over the cliffs, especially with Daisy, my little sheltie. Or I would just sit lookin' out over that vast and powerful sea and wonder about my life and where it was goin' and what God's purpose was fer me. That wild landscape would put such a longin' in my heart fer...somethin'...I never quite knew fer what. Sometimes my heart was so full, I would sing like David, the shepherd boy, out on the hillside. And the wind would roar so loudly, no one could hear me— except God—but I was singin' to Him anyway, singin' praises for this beautiful world He's created. And sometimes I would pray and ask Him to speak to me or show me what He wanted me to do, or tell me what I was longin' fer."

Eric stopped speaking for a moment and gazed east out over the North Sea. In his mind, he envisioned that other coast looking out to the western horizon of the Irish Sea.

"And did He?" Laurene prodded, though she knew the answer well enough.

"Aye," Eric answered quietly. "He did. One night, my last summer there, I was in my bed. I couldna sleep and was just lyin' awake and prayin'. The lighthouse is snug and as solid as the rock 'tis built on, so it wasna the wind that kept me up. Although as I prayed, I felt strangely like a wind was blowin' in my heart and the room suddenly seemed full of light. I sat up in my bed and I saw a vision—it was Jesus."

"And how did you know it was He?" She added, "I get the shivers whenever I hear it."

"I knew because His hands were outstretched and I could see the nail prints in them."

"Were you scared?" Laurene asked in a whisper.

"Nay, I wasna frightened. More stunned, I should say, or awestruck. I just looked at Him, not knowin' what I should do. And He smiled at me and said, 'Eric.' He said my name! And He called me His son. He said, 'Eric, My son, I want you to be My minister.' And that was all. He was gone. But I heard Him quite clearly and I'll ne'er forget it. 'Eric, My son, I want you to be My minister.' I thought about how when Samuel was a wee lad, the Lord called him in the middle of the night to be His prophet. I jumped out of bed and ran down to the kitchen to see if anyone was still up. My mither was there. She and my aunt were sippin' hot milk and talkin'. And I came in and announced, 'I'm goin' to be a minister.'

" 'That's nice,' my aunt said. But my mither knew this was important. She looked at me and asked me to explain myself. So I told her what had happened. She stood up and hugged me tightly. There were tears in her eyes. She said, 'I dinna care what it takes, we'll see that ye are.' Then she sent me on to bed. But the next mornin' she was up early writin' a letter to my Uncle Billy MacKenzie to see if I could come out here and stay with them in Anstruther and go to school to prepare for university. So ye know the rest. I did come and have been here since, studyin' and caddyin' for the Royal and Ancient Golf Club—where I met you."

"And now you've been accepted to the university!"

"Aye," he grinned. "I have. And will start in September."

Laurene sighed contentedly and nestled against him. "I'm so very happy, Eric. You can fulfill your vision right here in Fife and we can still be together. I wish my brother could stay here too. I shall miss him terribly."

"So Peter's off to Cambridge, is he?"

"Yes. All the Kilmorey sons go up to university at Cambridge. I'm so glad I'm a girl!"

Eric laughed. "Aye. So am I!"

Abby hopped up and began barking with excitement. Rising quickly, they spied a dark-haired young man strolling jauntily down the hill, swinging a golf club at the bracken along the footpath.

"Peter!" Laurene cried as she waved. "Hullo! We're down here!"

Peter raised the club in greeting and then stooped to pet Abby, who had raced up the hill to meet him. When he reached the others, his greeting was cordial and his smile, warm. "Hello, Eric."

"Hello, Peter." The two young men shook hands like old friends.

"Peter," Laurene spoke breathlessly. "You'll never guess. Eric received his acceptance letter today to St. Andrews and he's been awarded a full scholarship! Isn't that wonderful?"

"Well done, old boy! Yes, that is wonderful. Congratulations!"

Eric accepted the slap on the back with good grace. "Thank you."

Turning to his sister, Peter grimaced apologetically. "I say, I'm sorry, Laurene, but Mother's looking for you to practice your piano, so you'd best get back to the house now."

Laurene frowned. "Oh, bother. All right." She lightly touched Eric's arm. "Thanks for sharing your good news. I'll look for you on the Old Course. Bye."

"Goodbye." Eric watched her as she flitted like a sprite back up the hill, over the footbridge, and then disappeared among the trees.

Peter's eyes followed Eric's. "Well then. Want to practice putting with me?"

Eric turned back to his friend and chuckled. "Sure, if ye're not worried about my embarrassin' you."

"Me embarrassed?" Peter scoffed. "Right! I've been putting on these greens since I was in nappies."

Eric drew one of the balls from his pocket and placed it on the green for Peter. "Fine then. Show me yer stuff."

Peter's face grew grim. "Eric, before we putt there's something I need to talk to you about."

Eric had not missed the change in expression or tone. "What is it?"

"It's about…Laurene."

Sucking in his breath sharply, Eric waited.

"We've known each other for a good while now," Peter rushed on, "and I'm not blind. I can see how you fancy one another and how your feelings have gone beyond friendship. And, Eric, though it hurts me to have to say it because I respect you greatly—you may only be as a friend to her. If you have thoughts of anything else, you must put them out of your mind. You must remember that she is only fifteen! And my father is yet the laird and to him you are but the kin of fishermen and a caddie, though a fine one. He has great plans for his children to marry into money and property and he will not brook any opposition." He held up his hand as Eric mouthed a protest. "Nay, I'm thinking of Laurene too and you must as well. If my father catches wind that there's anything going on between the two of you, he will send her away to boarding school in Switzerland so fast it will make your head spin."

The protest died on Eric's lips and he visibly crumpled. "I see."

"I don't want her hurt, Eric."

Eric nodded. "Nor do I. Thank ye for the warnin', Peter."

"Thanks for taking it so well." Peter exhaled loudly as if he had just thrown off a great weight, which indeed he had. He smiled kindly.

"So then, shall we putt?"

"Aye." Eric watched Peter line up his putt, grateful for the distraction. When Abby began barking furiously again, the young men looked up to see Laurene, waving and running back over the footbridge toward them.

"What is it?" Peter called.

She shouted, "Bobby is back!"

"She's gone daft," Peter muttered and then raised his voice. "What do you mean, Laurene?"

She climbed the green and paused to catch her breath. "Bob Jones is in St. Andrews!"

"*The* Bob Jones?"

"Yes! *Our* Bobby Jones. The very same American who won the Grand Slam in 1930." Laurene, her cheeks flushed with exertion and excitement, turned to Eric. "Oh, you weren't here then. I was only ten, but I'll never forget it. He was incredible."

"I would imagine he was after winnin' the British and U.S. Amateurs and both the Opens all in one year. But how do ye know he's here now?"

"Father received a call from the captain at the Royal and Ancient. Bobby Jones is on his way to the Olympic Games in Berlin and stopped here with some friends to play again on the Old Course. The whole town is shutting down and heading to the links to watch him. Father says there are already nearly two thousand gathered and that I should run down here to get you right away so that we can drive over."

"Let's go!" Peter stooped to retrieve his ball.

"Eric, are you coming?" Laurene asked.

"Aye. I'd love to see the great Bobby Jones. I'll just fetch my bike and be along after ye."

"It will take you too long to bicycle the seven miles to town. You don't want to miss any of his play. You can ride with us. Can't he, Peter?"

"Nay, thank ye," Eric said quickly. "That's kind of ye, but I'll be fine."

"Don't be ridiculous, old boy. Laurene is right," said Peter. "Why don't you stow your bike in the stables? I'm sure there will be a carload of the servants you can hitch a ride with."

"Peter!" Laurene protested. "He should ride with us. Besides, he can give his expert commentary on Bobby's play, which I'm sure Father will appreciate. Please!"

"All right," Peter relented. "Come on with us, then. After all, it's not every day that Bobby Jones comes to play the Old Course!"

3

April 1939
St. Andrews

ow did Bobby Jones take this shot back in '36? Do you remember, lad?" grumbled Lord Kilmorey as he peered over the gorse bushes to the barely visible white flag marking the next hole.

"Aye, my lord, I do remember, but the wind was takin' a different tack that day." Eric responded respectfully as he set down the heavy bag of clubs he was carrying for the laird.

"But he was off in this gorse, if I recall," insisted Lord Kilmorey.

"Aye, to be sure. And he let the wind help him out of a tough spot. I recommend ye try it too, but since it's blowin' from the sea today, why not try loftin' yer ball a wee bit toward the sea and see if ye can hitch a ride on the back of the wind to the green."

The laird grunted but swung as instructed. He gave a shout as his ball hung in the air for a moment and then, catching the wind, sailed over the hummock and past the bunkers to the green beyond.

"Just like Bobby Jones!" The laird declared with satisfaction before striding off to reclaim his ball.

"Aye, just like Bobby," Eric affirmed with a wink to his friend Peter.

"Lucky for you he made that shot and didn't end up with his ball in that bunker or the gorse again," Peter said with a laugh.

"That's not luck. In truth, yer father is a skilled golfer. I was takin' a wee chance, but I thought he could do it." Eric hefted the bag of clubs onto his shoulder. "How have ye been, Peter?" he asked as they found the footpath through the tall grass to follow the laird. "Is Cambridge treatin' ye well?"

"Yes. I'm in the homestretch now. Back here for the Easter holidays and then I'll have to cram for my finals in June. What about you? How is university life?"

"Things are fine. Ye know St. Andrews has one more year than Cambridge, so I have a bit more to go than you. But with Hitler marchin' into Czechoslovakia, I don't know what the future holds anymore. Chamberlain's appeasement plan doesn't seem to be very effective. I'm afraid we could be at war by summer."

Peter nudged his cap off his forehead. "If it does come to war, will you join a service?"

"I don't know. What about you?"

"No. I don't want to get stuck in some trench somewhere. I saw what that did to our parents' generation. Father had wanted me to join his old regiment from the Great War. He went down to their headquarters to see about signing me up, but when he went to the bar to order a drink, the barkeep didn't salute him or say, 'Yes, sir.' Father was appalled at the lack of order and respect. He came home and told me that the army is not what it used to be and he refused to have me join such an uncivilized service!" Peter's eyes crinkled with laughter. "So I'm grateful to that derelict barkeep for saving my skin. But if it comes to war," he grew more sober, "I may ask for an appointment in the Ministry of Defense. I'm good at analyzing data and may be of some use to the poor chaps who have to slog off to the trenches."

"I wouldna want to be in the army, either," Eric said.

"Navy, then? You're a natural sailor—and swimmer. How many people have you MacKenzies pulled out of the bay?"

"More than we care to. Och, but drownin' is a terrible fate. To be sure, I've considered the navy, but what I'd really like to do is learn to fly."

"Fly? Where'd you get that notion?"

Eric nodded toward the mountains framing the northern horizon of the Old Course. "I watch the planes takin' off and landin' at the RAF base over there at Leuchars. Ye know, one thin' I love most about golf is bein' outside in the wide open spaces where I can feel the wind in my face. It's liberatin'. If I were a bird, I could stretch my wings and soar out to the sea or up to the mountains. I think it would be wonderful to fly."

"Well then," Peter said as they trudged up to the green, "join the RAF. I'm sure they would be happy for more recruits. They say if it comes to war, the air will be a crucial strategic line of defense against the Nazis."

"I'm hopin' it won't come to war. I'd rather not leave St. Andrews."

Peter shot Eric a look to ask if what he really meant was that he didn't want to leave Laurene, but Eric was purposely busy pulling the laird's putter out of the bag.

Over the last three years, Eric had managed to walk the very fine line of cultivating his relationship with Laurene without overstepping his bounds. He had worked hard at his studies while earning extra money on weekends and holidays as a caddie. Meanwhile, Laurene had grown from a slip of a girl to a lovely young woman, poised to attend the University of St. Andrews in the autumn. When they managed to meet by seeming coincidence in town or on the local golf courses, they had discussed Eric's remaining at the university as well. Laurene and Eric were exceedingly fond of each other—in truth, they were devotedly in love—and when the time was right, he intended to find a way to marry her.

Eric walked onto the green and stood quietly holding the flag while the laird sank his putt. As they followed Lord Kilmorey to the green box marking the next tee, Peter lowered his voice and uttered what seemed to be a *non sequitur* but which both young men understood was not.

"You should know, Eric, that Laurene has been taken very ill."

Eric drew his head up sharply. "What?"

"Yes." Peter nodded solemnly. "She has influenza. But don't worry. The best doctors have been called in."

"Is she recoverin'? May I see her?"

"No. She's quarantined in the west wing in my grandmother's old room. My mother is deathly afraid of the rest of us contracting it. I'm sorry not to have mentioned it sooner. She should be all right, but do say some prayers for her."

"I will." Eric's jaw clenched. "Peter, ye must promise to let me know how she's doin'."

"All right, Eric." Peter sympathetically touched his friend's arm. "I'll do that."

When several days passed with no word of Laurene, and Eric could not bear the uncertainty another day, he decided to take matters into his own hands. He pedaled his bicycle boldly up to the kitchen door of the great house and covered his audacity with an ice chest full of herring, fresh from his uncle's nets.

He rapped sharply on the door, which was cracked open by a young housemaid. Her round, ruddy face broke into a broad smile when she recognized Eric.

"Och, if 'tisna Eric MacKenzie. What are ye doin' up here at the big house, laddie?"

"Good day, Miss Fiona." Eric flashed her a winsome smile. "Here's our fresh catch of the day—straight from the North Sea. It'll make a fine supper for the laird's table."

"Och, come in, come in." The maid held the door open wide, matching her gesture with an even broader smile. "Put them over there on the washboard by the sink. Those are beauties," she said as Eric lifted the fish off the ice and onto the board. "Should we be creditin' them to Fatbug MacKenzie's account?"

Eric rinsed off his hands and wiped them on a tea towel. "Aye, tell Cook to add them to what she owes Uncle Billy."

The maid nodded. "Would ye be wantin' some tea now before ye go?"

"Aye, thank ye kindly." Eric smiled again, grateful for the opportunity, for which he had hoped, to linger and hear some news of Laurene.

"Sit down then and I'll get a cuppa for ye in a minute. I was just preparin' a tray for the young mistress." Fiona wrapped a towel around the kettle handle and carefully poured the boiling water into a china teapot.

"How is yer mistress farin'?" Eric tried rather unsuccessfully to sound casually disinterested. "Young Master Kilmorey told me she had a touch of the flu."

"Aye. She's been frightful ill, but the fever broke this mornin' and we pray she's on the mend."

Closing his eyes, Eric sighed deeply with relief and gratitude. "I am glad to hear it."

His reaction did not escape Fiona's notice. Neither had the surreptitious but, nevertheless, obviously affectionate relationship flourishing between the young mistress and her handsome friend. "Dinna worry, Eric," Fiona reassured him. "She'll be all right."

Eric stayed Fiona's arm as she reached for the tea tray. "Please, let me take that to her. I must see her, Fiona."

Fiona wavered. She knew a visit from Eric could be a powerful tonic to Laurene and yet it was against all propriety. "Och, Eric, dinna ask this o' me. If the laird were to hear of it…"

"He won't. Just tell me where her room is. Then ye go look for some biscuits in the pantry. If ye should happen to find the tea tray missin' when ye return, why then ye must suppose one of the other maids took it up, mustn't ye?"

Fiona stared wide-eyed as she considered this and then nodded. "Aye. I would suppose that." She swallowed. "In case ye be wonderin' where the sickroom is, 'tis in the west wing in the Dowager Kilmorey's old set of rooms. When I take things to Miss Laurene, I go up those back stairs yonder." She nodded toward the servants' stairs in the corridor beyond them. "I go up to the first floor and turn left to walk down a long hallway. I pass one, two, three doors on me right and where the hall ends, around the corner are a set of three more doors. The door to the old Dowager's bedroom is the first door on the right 'round the corner. I always knock before I enter." She added helpfully, "And I dinna usually see a soul about at this time o' day because they're takin' their tea in the parlor."

Eric repeated her instructions. "Right then, Fiona. Thank ye for the offer of tea but I think I should be goin'. Perhaps now ye should fetch some more biscuits."

"Aye, I will. Thank ye for the fish." She turned and without looking back, walked into the pantry.

Eric quickly picked up the tea tray and skirted out into the corridor. His heart pounding, he climbed the stairs to the old Dowager's rooms—and to Laurene.

4

Teatime, April 1939
Kilmorey House

*E*ric mounted the back staircase rapidly and paused on the first floor landing. Glancing right, he saw the open door to what he surmised was the drawing room as he glimpsed a massive chandelier and heard the clinking of teacups and hushed conversation. He headed quickly down the hall to his left, trying not to rattle the tray as he passed the billiard room and two closed doors. At the end of the corridor he turned the corner, paused to collect himself, and knocked gently on the first door on his right.

"Enter," Laurene's voice weakly called, followed by a spate of coughing.

Eric nudged open the door to a darkened room lit only by a shaft of light peeking through a partially opened shutter. "I've brought ye some tea, miss."

Laurene struggled to sit up. She resembled a tiny porcelain doll against the tall Victorian tester bed. "Eric?" she asked with surprise as she recognized his voice. Then she added with some apprehension, "What are you doing here?"

"Bringin' yer tea, miss," he said, smiling as he carefully set the tray down on her bed table.

"But how did you...? Oh, never mind!" She laughed delightedly. "I am so glad to see you! But you mustn't stay long. Father would be furious if he caught you up here. Besides, you don't want to be exposed to this flu."

"I'm not worried about that. Ye shouldn't be contagious any longer, in any case. Fiona said that yer fever broke this mornin'. I'm sorry if I startled ye, Laurene, but I simply had to see you. Peter told me ye had been quite ill. He was to let me know how ye were doin', but he has neglected to. I was nearly mad with worry, so I decided to come see ye for myself."

Laurene reached out and tenderly touched his cheek. "Poor you! I am sorry to have caused you any anxiety. I am going to be just fine, really I am. But to be honest, there were a couple of days there when I felt so bad I thought that perhaps I might die. And yet the funny thing was, I wasn't one bit afraid. I had a real peace in my heart that I would be with the Lord and it would be just like stepping into another dimension. Though it did make me sad to think I wouldn't see you again—at least until you joined me. But then again, there probably isn't time as we know it in heaven, and it would just seem like a few moments until we were together again."

"Hush, please! Don't even speak of it. I couldna bear it if somethin' were to happen to you." Eric took her hand in his and kissed it softly. "Laurene, yer illness made me realize more than ever how much I love you. Life is too short not to speak the truth and the truth is—" Still holding her hand, Eric knelt beside the bed. "The truth is that although I have nothin' to commend me but my love, I do love ye so dearly. Laurene, could ye, would ye ever consider marryin' me?"

"Oh, Eric!" she breathed.

"I know ye could have a husband with much more money or position, but I believe no one could ever love ye more than I."

"Nor you, than I."

He searched her eyes. "Truly?"

She smiled. "Truly. And yes, I do want to marry you, Eric MacKenzie, with all my heart."

"Oh, my darlin' girl!" he whispered, leaning over to kiss her.

But she pushed him gently away. "No, don't. I'm sick yet and wouldn't want to risk giving it to you, despite what you say."

He frowned. "Maybe if ye weren't ill ye would give me a different answer. I hadn't meant to ask ye now. It just popped out. Maybe later ye will think I took advantage of yer weakened state and ye'll regret yer acceptance."

"Don't be a goose, Eric. I've been hoping, dreaming, praying you would ask me—and I'm so happy!" She leaned back into her pillows. "When do you want to be married, darling? I haven't even finished senior school and what about university? Should I go? Should we wait at least until you graduate?"

"Goodness, whatever ye want to do. Certainly, if ye want to go to university, ye should. I plan to stay on for my divinity degree from St. Mary's College anyway." Eric frowned again anxiously. "Laurene, ye won't mind terribly bein' a pastor's wife, will ye?"

"No, of course not! Ever since you first told me the story of your call to ministry, I've hoped to share it with you. But sad to say, you know the Kilmoreys are Anglican, not Church of Scotland. All that English education, I'm afraid. If it would make it any easier for my father to accept our marriage, could you ever consider becoming an Anglican priest?"

He smiled. "Mother Kirk is the church, whatever the stream. I've never put much stock in denominations. If the Anglicans will have me, and if yer father will, then so be it." He leaned forward eagerly. "When may I speak to yer father? Peter warned me years ago that he would not be happy about us, but I believe I should put a bold face on and ask him for yer hand as soon as possible."

She lightly touched his arm with a tremor of anxiety. "I think perhaps it would be best if we could keep this our secret for a while. I would like to break it gently to my parents when the time is right."

"Well, whatever ye think best. Although I'll want to burst with the news, we can keep it our special secret for as long as ye think necessary. I just hope it won't be for too long."

"And I neither. We'll just pray and ask God's guidance. I'm afraid Daddy does have plans for me, and he probably won't be terribly happy with us, but I think with time and prayer we can bring him around." Her brow creased with worry. "You should probably go, Eric. It would be best for you not to be discovered here with me."

"All right," he agreed. "But is there anythin' I can do for ye before I leave?"

"Aye, there is. Would you please open the shutters? I feel positively claustrophobic shut up in this dark room all alone."

"Righto." Eric strode over to the window. It spanned the width of the room and rose to the height of the eighteen-foot ceiling. Pushing back the heavy veil of velvet drapes hanging from a thick brass rod, he then folded back the large wooden shutters into the wall recess. Light flooded the room and revealed a spacious bed chamber with a marble fireplace, round table and chairs, massive mahogany wardrobe, and the tall wood-and-shrimp-pink-upholstered bed frame looming above Laurene's small figure.

"Oh," she cried, "that's ever so much better! I can see the garden and the woods now."

" 'Tis a lovely view," Eric agreed.

"I really prefer the one from my room. It's in the wing overlooking the front lawn. This side of the house is so quiet it's almost spooky. I have been so dreadfully lonely. I—" She stopped suddenly at a sound from the corridor. "Someone's coming, Eric!"

He looked about quickly, realizing there was no time for escape. The wardrobe was his first thought but, as capacious as it was, there was no guarantee it wasn't crammed full of clothing. Putting his finger to his lips, he stepped behind the thick folds of the velvet drapes just as someone rapped on the bedroom door.

"Who is it?" Laurene called, looking about to make certain Eric had not left any sign of his presence.

"It's your mother, dear."

"Do come in, Mummy."

Lady Kilmorey entered and rushed over to the bed in a flurry of motherly concern. "How are you, my dear? Feeling better? I am so relieved the fever has broken. You do look better—there's more color in your cheeks. But you haven't even touched your tea. Shall I pour some for you? There. Please drink up. The doctor said to drink plenty of fluids. Oh," she said looking up. "Who opened the shutters? Do you want them open?" She walked toward the window. Hearing her, Eric squeezed himself as small and still as possible in the shadow of the drapes. He could see her as she stood looking out over the garden. Lady Kilmorey wore her abundant dark hair up in the old style, piled in a soft cloud framing her refined and lovely features. Her blue eyes held a hint of strain.

"Yes, Mummy." Laurene coughed to cover the tension in her voice. "Please leave them open."

"All right." Lady Kilmorey turned back to her daughter. "Perhaps the sunlight will do you good. Would you like anything else, dear?"

"No, thank you, Mummy. Unless…John could bring a wireless up here. And later, if it's allowed, could Peter come in to see me?"

"Yes, of course. Now that your fever has broken, it should be all right." She gave Laurene a kiss on the forehead. "I am so relieved you are better, dear. Now do get some rest. And I'll send John up with a wireless."

"Thank you, Mummy," Laurene replied as her mother glided out and shut the door behind her. Laurene exhaled in relief and then listened intently. "Eric," she whispered, "you'd best go quickly before someone else comes."

He peeked out behind the curtains. "Close call," he said, grinning. "I thought my heart would stop when she came over to the window."

Laurene laughed. "Me too. Now get going—no, not that way," she said as he headed across the room to the door. She pointed to a door hidden behind a screen next to the window. "Go through there. It's a dressing room and will come out closer to the servants' staircase. Now hurry." She blew him a kiss which he pretended to catch in midair and put to his lips before blowing it back to her. Then he slipped behind the screen and was gone.

5

Summer 1939
Kilmorey House

*S*omehow Eric and Laurene managed to keep their engagement a secret while quietly seeing each other whenever possible as they stayed busy with studies and exams through the end of the term. When summer vacation arrived and the days lengthened, they took long bicycle rides in the countryside or walks on the beach or along the burn in the cool woods of the Kilmorey estate. Laurene grew increasingly anxious of discovery by her parents, yet Eric did not press her into approaching them about their relationship. He hoped before the summer ended that she would find a way to bring it out in the open. With the growing Nazi threat and the possibility of war looming, he knew that their life of peace could be shattered as quickly as their season of happiness, and so for now he determined to make the most of their times together.

A highlight for them that summer proved to be the community theater production of *Romeo and Juliet* at the Hope Park Church. The Reverend Alex McIver had devised the theater as an outreach to the young people of St. Andrews, and he had encouraged Eric to hone his sermon delivery skills by cultivating his thespian talents. With his melodious voice and handsome visage, Eric seemed the perfect choice to play the role of Romeo while the vivacious and lovely Laurene easily won that of Juliet. The young couple found the rehearsals and production to be an intoxicating experience. The glorious poetry of Shakespeare completely expressed their deepest feelings, and they reveled in the opportunity to be often close together and embracing, even on an open stage. In fact, the public declaration of their private sentiment was liberating. Other than the greater threat of war, the only shadow cast on that summer idyll was the outcome of the play itself, whose inevitably tragic conclusion vaguely haunted Eric. And yet— although its themes echoed their own situation—in the end it was, after all, only a play.

When the show's run concluded to the acclaim of the town populace, the Kilmoreys toasted their daughter's success by hosting the cast party. Eric relished the novel sensation of strolling through the front hall as an invited guest rather than sneaking up to the back door as a purveyor of fish.

Kilmorey House, impressive but not spectacularly beautiful, stood as a relative newcomer to the ancient neighborhood. Although the Kilmoreys had resided on their estate for several centuries, the original manor house had been burned to the ground in Victorian times by careless servants enjoying a Christmas party while the laird's family was absent. The new house, barely more than a half century old, lacked the grandeur and architectural charm of its predecessor; however, it was compensated by its modern conveniences. The old laird had the foresight to install electricity and Fife's earliest water closets. The house also boasted some striking marble mantelpieces rescued from the fire, a gracefully carved oak staircase, and an imposing clock tower from which one could view the sea. When Eric arrived in the drawing room, he noted with interest the magnificent chandelier he had merely glimpsed on his foray to Laurene's sick quarters. He had learned that this had been a very proud purchase of the laird, who had commissioned it specifically for this large room. A London artisan had arrived in St. Andrews via train with his suitcases filled with the crystals, and after working for four days he had reassembled them to dazzling effect. The chandelier provided a splendid accent to the long room decorated with family portraits and fine tapestries.

Laurene reflected the glow of the lights in her excitement both for the success of the play and for an occasion when Eric could be an invited guest in her home.

She led him over to speak to her parents. "Mummy, Daddy, this is my Romeo!"

Eric politely bowed his head in greeting. "Good evenin', Lord Kilmorey, Lady Kilmorey."

"Good show, old boy!" boomed the laird. "Excellent job."

"You were wonderful," Lady Kilmorey concurred.

"Thank you, but I had a wonderful Juliet." Eric and Laurene exchanged smiles while her father peered at them closely, taking stock of Eric. He observed a tall, well-proportioned youth with dark wavy hair and deep blue eyes.

"You look familiar to me, lad. Have we met before?"

"Yes, my lord. At the Royal and Ancient. I've caddied for ye many times."

"Oh, right. MacKenzie, isn't it? Fatbug's lad?"

"His nephew, my lord," Eric politely corrected.

Lord Kilmorey grunted. "Well, you're multitalented aren't you, MacKenzie? A good actor and a good caddie and golfer."

"And he plays the pipes and has a lovely baritone voice. And next year he'll graduate from the university and attend St. Mary's Divinity College. He plans to be a clergyman," added Laurene helpfully.

The laird regarded his daughter with awakened curiosity. "Is that so? Well now, young MacKenzie, you *are* talented. Enjoy the party." With that he dismissed Eric and steered his wife off to mingle with the other guests.

Laurene linked her arm in Eric's. "That wasn't too bad, was it?"

Eric shrugged. "He knows of my existence, but that's about all. When may I speak to him about us?"

Laurene pulled him toward the dining room, where the tables had been pushed to the sides of the room and John had rigged up the Victrola. "Maybe later when everyone else goes home. But for now, let's dance."

They did and took turns with other cast members as well. As the party wound down, Eric attempted to excuse himself, but Laurene begged him to stay.

"I think tonight's the night," she whispered as she led him back to the drawing room and offered him a seat near the fireplace, where her parents and brother had gathered. No fire burned on this warm summer's evening, but tobacco smoke hung heavily in the air.

Peter raised an eyebrow at Eric's inclusion in the family circle but held his peace. His father stared at Eric suspiciously. "Ah, MacKenzie, you're still here. Smoke?"

Eric considered it briefly, not knowing if sharing in the indulgence would be favored or frowned upon. He decided not to risk it. "No, thank you. Wonderful party, my lord and lady. Thank ye for yer hospitality."

"Our pleasure!" Lady Kilmorey spoke up a bit too enthusiastically, as if she sensed they were on the verge of some awkward scene. "It is getting late, though. I think I'll retire. Laurene?"

Laurene shook her head. "Wait, Mummy. There's something I'd like you to hear first." She caught Eric's eye and smiled reassuringly.

So this is it. Be bold, MacKenzie. Eric sat up very straight and tried to look directly at Laurene's father, who was concentrating intently on the smoke wafting from his pipe.

"Lord Kilmorey, although I've enjoyed every minute of workin' with yer daughter on this play, I've actually been friends with her and with Peter for several years now, ever since I made their acquaintance at the R and A. Over the years my affection for Laurene has grown very deep. I love yer daughter very much and, incredible as it may seem to ye, she returns that love." He took a deep breath and then continued. "My lord, would ye consider givin' me the honor of yer daughter's hand in marriage?"

Lady Kilmorey grew very pale. In contrast Lord Kilmorey turned bright red as his face clouded. Gripping the arms of his chair, Eric braced himself for the approaching squall. Laurene held her breath. Peter took a sudden interest in petting Abby, who had curled up on the hearth.

Lord Kilmorey's silence seemed interminable to the anxious young couple, but when he finally spoke, his answer shocked them all. "Yes," he said quietly. "I'll consider it."

Laurene rose. "Oh, Daddy! You will?"

He held up his hand in warning. "However, I will not agree to a marriage until Laurene completes her university education."

"But, Daddy, Mummy didn't go to university. She was eighteen when you married."

"Women weren't expected to go to university in our day. The world is changing. Those are my terms. If you are still of the same mind once you've earned your degree, then Mr. MacKenzie may again request your hand."

"But, Daddy—"

"Thank ye, my lord," Eric interrupted as he stood to leave. "We will respect yer wishes. In the meantime, may I call on Laurene?"

The cloud passed over Lord Kilmorey's face again. "Yes, I suppose so."

Eric bowed his head. "Thank you. And thank ye again, my lady, for the lovely party. Good evening. I can show myself out."

Laurene hopped up and rushed after him. "Eric! I'll come with you."

She grabbed his arm as they walked down the great oak staircase. "Four years! How can we wait that long?"

Eric breathed a deep sigh of relief. "Laurene, darlin', he could have outright refused us. And now it's out in the open. We can't publicly announce our engagement, but we don't have to sneak around anymore, either. Really, it went much better than I expected. I was afraid after what Peter had said that he would forbid us ever to see each other again."

They had reached the front driveway. The sky had darkened to a midnight blue pierced by the pinpricks of the stars and the brightly lit clock tower. "But four years!" she protested.

"Ye need not be bound that long, Laurene. I will release ye from the engagement."

"I don't want to be released! I love you, Eric MacKenzie, and I want to marry you. But can you wait for me?"

"Aye, my love. If Jacob could wait seven years for Rachel, I can wait four for you. I can wait as long as needed. Besides, yer father is right. It would be good for ye to get yer degree. Don't fret, my love." He stroked her hair. "The time will allow me to attend seminary and then find a curacy, maybe even save some money—that should make yer father more amenable. It will also give him time to get to know me better, and he'll grow to like me so much that will make him more amenable still." He grinned and she laughed.

"It is a jolly good thing that he didn't say no or we would have to elope like Romeo and Juliet. I'm also so glad you asked permission to call on me. When can I see you again?"

"I'll be workin' at the course all week. Do ye fancy some golf?"

She smiled. "Aye, I always do with you caddying. But will you call here Thursday evening, say at eight o'clock? We can walk in the garden."

"It's a date. But please come by the course too. Meanwhile, my Juliet, '*parting is such sweet sorrow that I shall say good-night 'til it be morrow.*'"

"You stole my line!"

"How about I steal a kiss too?" He drew her into his arms and kissed her, and then reluctantly let her go. "Goodnight, my love."

Upstairs the Kilmoreys were having their own discussion about the evening's turn of events.

"Well, Father." Peter had abandoned the dog to lounge in a chair. "I must say you took me completely by surprise. Don't get me wrong. Eric MacKenzie is a fine chap and I like him very much, but I never would have expected you to agree to his marrying Laurene. In fact, I told him as much years ago when she was yet a girl."

Lord Kilmorey puffed heartily on his pipe. "I didn't agree to their marriage. I merely said I would consider it after Laurene took her degree. She may be infatuated with him now, but a lot can happen in four years. I figured that if I forbade it outright, Laurene is so headstrong she would have run off and eloped. The forbidden fruit has the most allure. This just buys time for her to change her mind."

"But she'll be at St. Andrews and so will he," protested Laurene's mother. "And you gave him permission to call on her. They may see quite a bit of each other."

"Well, I may yet enroll her in an English university. I've also been thinking that if war does break out, we may send her to America out of harm's way. I don't want to lose that daughter of mine either to the Nazis or to that young man."

6

*O*n the last day of August—the last day of peace—
business was slow at the Royal and Ancient, and the
caddies were hanging about the caddie shack discussing the
impending war. They fell silent when Laurene approached.

"Is Eric MacKenzie here?" she asked.

"Aye, my lady," Fatbug answered respectfully. "Eric!" he
hollered into the caddie shack, where some of the men were
listening to the news on the radio. "The young Lady Kilmorey
is here fer ye."

Eric quickly emerged. "What is it, Laurene?" he asked with
concern after seeing her anxious face.

"I need to talk to you. Can you go for a walk on the
beach?"

"Aye." Eric excused himself from the other caddies.

Neither of them spoke until they had reached the pebbly
shore of the West Sands and Laurene had slipped her arm in
his.

"What is it, Laurene?" Eric repeated his question. "Is it
about the war?"

"Daddy is sending me to America," she blurted out with no preamble. "He has booked a berth on the *Athenia*. It departs from Glasgow tomorrow."

Dumfounded, Eric gaped at her. "What?"

She repeated herself.

As the import of what she was saying registered, Eric felt as though he had been punched in the gut. "Why?" he gasped painfully.

"He's been on the telephone to friends in London constantly since the Nazis signed the pact with the Soviets last week. He's convinced that Hitler will invade Poland and that we will have to go to war. Even now they are preparing to evacuate children from London and the major cities."

"I've heard that," Eric acknowledged. "But evacuees are bein' sent here for safety. So why would yer father feel ye need to leave? Why would Hitler bomb St. Andrews?"

"He's worried that we'll be a target because of the RAF base at Leuchars and also because of the shipping on the firth. He wants me out of harm's way in America. In fact, he's arranged for me to attend Wellesley College near Boston. I had thought Fiona was packing my things for St. Andrews, but that's not the case. Apparently he's been planning this for some time, but he didn't tell me anything until today. I think he was afraid that I would run away if I knew—and he was right." She clung to Eric's arm. "Let's run away to Gretna Green, Eric, and be married tonight. Then he can't send me away."

"Let me think, Laurene." Eric said as he sank onto the sand and stared out to sea. Laurene quietly sat beside him, leaning her head on his shoulder. He slipped his arm around her and pulled her close.

"I can't believe this is happenin'," he finally said. "This megalomaniac Hitler is wreakin' havoc in everyone's lives. All those poor evacuees bein' separated from their families, and now you—is yer mother to go with ye?"

"No, she won't leave Kilmorey House or my father. They want to send Fiona with me. Her mother wants her to go as well. But, Eric, I don't want to leave you! Let's go to Gretna Green tonight!" she urged again.

"Laurene, yer father knows more than we do. If he's worried about yer safety, then perhaps we should listen." A suspicion began to grow in Eric's mind.

What if Lord Kilmorey is using events to orchestrate a separation between us? What if he cares more about protecting Laurene from me than he does from the Nazis? But no. Laurene said he has been talking with friends in London. He has to be privy to more information than we are. Surely he would not take such drastic measures just to separate us. After all, he could have forbidden us to see each other, but he has not. He must be very concerned about possible bombings to send Laurene to America. I should take the threats seriously as well and ensure that Laurene will be safe. Her safety is more important than my feelings.

"Laurene," he finally said, "this war is liable to tear the whole world apart. If ye stay here and somethin' were to happen to ye, I would ne'er forgive myself. I don't want to be separated from ye, but I also don't want to lose ye. I'd rather live through a temporary separation than a permanent one." He sighed heavily. "Much as I hate to say it, I think ye should sail on the *Athenia*. And I won't hold ye to our engagement. If ye meet someone else while ye're in America, then so be it. But as for me, I will wait for you."

"Eric, don't talk like this!"

"I mean it. Anythin' can happen. The war could take years and people change. I won't bind ye if ye should change yer mind."

"Eric MacKenzie, I'm a grown woman now and I know my own mind. I refuse to even entertain such talk. You are and will always be the only man for me."

"But if I should have to fight—if I should die—I will not bind ye to this promise. It should only be until death do us part. If I should die, I want ye to love someone else, be married, have children, be happy."

"Eric, please stop!"

Tilting up her chin, he looked intently into her eyes. "Promise me. If we go to war and I have to fight, I will be fightin' for Britain and for you. If I die, I don't want to die in vain. I want ye to go on to live a happy life. Promise me."

"I promise," she solemnly agreed. "But please don't fight unless you have to. You can serve in other ways. Peter is going to work in codes. You could be a chaplain. You don't have to be a big hero for me. I'd rather have you here when I return. Please stay out of combat if you can."

"All right. I'll try to stay here and wait for you."

"And, Eric," she added, "whilst we're making promises, if something were to happen to me, I would also like you to promise to go on and love someone else, have a family, and be happy—for my sake."

"But, Laurene…" he protested.

She held her hand up to silence him. "You promise too."

"Aye, I promise." He took her in his arms and they clung to one another, scarcely believing that they were making such covenants. War still seemed too surreal and distant, and yet their separation was only too real and imminent.

"Spend the day with me," she pleaded. "I don't want to spend one more moment in Scotland without you."

"All right," he agreed. "I'll just go and tell the caddie master that I'm takin' off for the afternoon. We don't have much business now anyway. Everyone's glued to the wireless and no one feels like playin' golf."

Laurene desired to visit all her favorite haunts in St. Andrews and on the Kilmorey estate, saying goodbye to her beloved woods, gardens, links, and seashore. Eric escorted her, walking arm in arm—sometimes in comfortable silence, sometimes in animated conversation as they tried to express all their thoughts and feelings in this one short and final afternoon together. As evening closed in, Laurene begged her parents to allow Eric to stay for dinner. They reluctantly agreed, sensing that their acquiescence would assuage her grief at departing. Then at her persistent importunity, the laird also extended an invitation to Eric to accompany them to Glasgow for Laurene and Fiona's embarkation on the *Athenia*.

Thus it was that Eric found himself standing bewildered on a pier in Glasgow in a rush of hugs and tears and shouts. Laurene was in his arms, crushed to his chest in a final embrace and hurried whispers of "I love you. I'll write every day. I'll wait for you. I'll pray for you. Pray for me. I love you. I love you! Remember me..." And then she was swept up in the crowd, up the gangplank, and onto the deck, a small pale figure with long black hair swirling about her face as the wind whipped around her and carried her voice with a thousand others crying, "Goodbye! Goodbye!" The massive ship trembled and rumbled and then with a blast of its deafening horns pulled away from the pier with the last faint calls of "Goodbye! Goodbye! Goodbye!"

And Laurene was gone.

7

Beginning of September 1939
Anstruther and Kilmorey House

O n the first of September, Hitler invaded Poland and everything changed for everyone. All waited anxiously for Prime Minister Neville Chamberlain to announce whether the ultimatum for peace would be met or Great Britian would join France and Poland in fighting the Nazis. Preparations for mass evacuations of children from London were finalized as the nation girded itself for the ever-growing threat of German bombing raids.

On the third of September, Great Britain declared war on Germany. The government had been given no alternative since Hitler had refused to withdraw his troops from Poland. And so after months of talk and debate and threats and compromises, they were now at war and eager for news.

The fishermen of Fife huddled around the smooth oak bar of the Smugglers' Inn in Anstruther. From a wide glass window in the centuries-old pub, one had a splendid view of the stone seawall, its protective arm encircling the small fishing craft bobbing gently in the harbor. A rainbow arced across the early evening sky, framing whitewashed buildings with their steeply pitched gabled roofs of black slate or burnished orange Dutch tiles. But the picturesque view of Anstruther harbor was lost on the weather-beaten men hunched over the bar or even the younger men, whose tanned faces were yet unlined with wind and worry. The only sounds emitting from the smoky pub were the occasional thud of a dart finding its mark, the clink of glasses being refilled, and the scraping of chairs and stools as patrons drew closer to the crackling broadcasts from the radio. For here was the focal point of the gathering: news from London and the world beyond their tiny burgh.

But the news coming now from the BBC had stunned them into shocked silence:

> *Last night the Cunard passenger liner* SS Athenia *sailing from Liverpool and Glasgow to Montreal was struck by a torpedo from a German submarine at 7:45 PM. The 13,581-ton ocean liner sank 250 miles northwest of Ireland with 112 of the passengers and crew perishing in the North Atlantic. A massive rescue operation throughout the night saved most of the 1418 people on board. The Norwegian ship* Knut Nelson *and* Southern Cross, *a Swedish yacht, were first on the scene, picking up 500 survivors. The rest were rescued by three destroyers,* Electra, Escort, *and* Fame, *as well as by a freighter,* The City of Flint. *Many of the passengers—including more than 300 Americans—were women, children, and Jews trying to escape the war. The Germans are denying responsibility for this heinous crime against defenseless civilians, doubtless hoping to avoid the entry of the United States into the war as happened in 1915 after the disastrous sinking of the* Lusitania.

Grabbing his uncle's arm, Eric rose quickly. "Laurene was on the *Athenia*! I must go to Kilmorey House to see if they've heard anythin'."

"Take my truck, lad," Fatbug MacKenzie urged, handing him the keys. "Ye'll get there much faster."

Eric nodded gratefully and rushed out of the pub. He appreciated his uncle's generosity even more when a squall blew in, spattering rain across the windshield. He hurtled the small truck along narrow country lanes bordered by hedgerows that skirted the coastline. Turning off where two stone pillars marked the entrance to the Kilmorey estate, he slowed as he followed the winding dirt-and-gravel drive through an arched canopy of tree limbs. A fox darted across the path of his headlights, and curious cows raised their doleful eyes in greeting as they lay patiently in the downpour. The lighted clock tower served as a beacon, and Eric pulled behind it into the stable yard, switched off the engine, bounded up to the back of the house, and pounded on the kitchen door.

Although he could hear muffled voices in the kitchen, where he correctly assumed the servants had gathered for news, what seemed a long minute elapsed before the door was opened by a tall, starkly bald man.

John, the butler, recognized Eric and invited him in. "Come on in, lad. We're waitin' for news. Mrs. McPherson is quite distressed about poor Fiona."

Until now, Eric had forgotten that the estate staff also had one of their own aboard the *Athenia*. He tugged off his cap and nodded to the servants gathered around the radio. Fiona's mother was seated at the kitchen table, her plump fingers running over twisted knots in a tea towel as if it were a rosary. Eric found an open spot by the sink, where the previous spring he had brought a fresh catch to Fiona to bribe his way into seeing Laurene. He leaned back against the counter and joined the vigil.

At length, the front entrance bell rang and John excused himself to answer it. The tension in the kitchen escalated until at last the door swung back open. The roomful of waiting staff collectively gasped when the laird himself entered, followed by John.

"Pardon me for intruding on you," Lord Kilmorey said, "but I just received a telegram and wanted to bring you word myself. Mrs. McPherson, your Fiona is accounted as safe in Galway, Ireland."

A murmur of relief swept around the room.

"And what of Lady Laurene?" asked Eric anxiously.

The laird sighed deeply as if repressing a sob. He merely shook his head in reply, turned, and hastily left.

A moan of dismay quickly quashed the elation over Fiona's escape. "John," Eric cried, "do ye know anythin' more?"

The butler sadly shook his head. "Nay, I'm sorry. The telegram merely listed Miss Fiona as accounted for and Lady Laurene as 'presumed lost.' Lord Kilmorey will try to ring his friends in the Admiralty to get more information, but he may not know more until tomorrow when he'll go to Glasgow to meet Miss Fiona on the return ship. Mrs. McPherson, ye should prepare to leave with him right after breakfast. Eric, lad, we have a spare room upstairs if ye want to bunk here. I'm sorry," he repeated, "I don't know what else to tell ye, but ye're welcome to stay if ye like."

Eric decided to cling to the faint hope held out by the words "*presumed* lost" and not to relinquish that hope until it was proved otherwise. The next day he threw himself into whatever occupations he could find to fill the time as he waited: chopping wood, mucking out stables, grooming horses, and running errands, all the while alternating between prayer and despair.

At last, as the dying sun shot plumes of pink and violet across the midnight blue sky, the crunch of gravel heralded the arrival of cars on the driveway. Eric dropped the armful of wood he had gathered and raced to the front of the mansion. He watched as John, stooping to open the car door, gave his hand to Lady Kilmorey. She covered her face with a handkerchief and hurried into the house, followed by Peter. Next Fiona and her mother were escorted to the kitchen and into the embrace of the household servants.

But there was no sign of the laird—or of Laurene.

Eric stood for a moment in bewildered disbelief before making his way to the kitchen. There he found Fiona already installed in the place of honor at the head of the table while the others fussed around her like courtiers. Although she had clearly survived a harrowing ordeal, there was yet an aura of excitement about her as if she enjoyed the attention showered on her. She told her tale as one who relishes sharing the dramatic scope of her reactions to an event—as if those reactions were of more import than the event itself. Eric quietly took his place, leaning against the kitchen sink to listen.

"Well," she said, "we left Glasgow on Friday evenin'. I ne'er been on such a big ship before. It was like a floatin' city, and all the men and women were dressed so fine and strollin' about all pretty like. On Sunday about noon, they posted notices that we had declared war against Germany, but none of the passengers seemed too surprised or upset about it. We had just settled down fer dinner at about 7:30 when the torpedo struck. We heard a gigantic explosion down below and that big ship shook and shuddered to a stop and all the lights went out. I let out a scream but the rest of the passengers, includin' Lady Laurene, stayed very calm. Our servin' man, that be called 'Sorbie,' told us to join hands about the table, and then he slowly led us up to the top deck. I can tell ye, I felt lucky fer sure that Lord Kilmorey bought me a ticket to share a room with Lady Laurene so I could eat in the first-class dinin' room with her. I found out later the torpedo struck right in the galley and through the third-class section o' the boat, trappin' and killin' many people who were a-lyin' in bed too seasick fer dinner."

Fiona dabbed at her eyes. "Many trapped below were children. I'll ne'er forget the pitiful sound of their cries fer help. It was horrible. But Sorbie assured us that the crew would try to save them; meanwhile, he guided our little group to the top deck to board a lifeboat. There was oil spurtin' in the air, and e'en though I tried not to look, I saw half-naked passengers runnin' around on deck and people who'd been blowed up. We had to pick our way o'er dead bodies to get to the rails and had a hard time keepin' from slippin' in the oil and filth. I almost fell to hysterics, but Lady Laurene was such a darlin'. She held my hand tightly and kept me from fallin' many times. She kept encouragin' me, sayin', 'Come on, Fiona, we're almost there' and 'Come on, lass, be brave' and such. When she got me to the side, she went back to help others and brought up a goodly number of children. She was like an angel of mercy—so calm and brave.

"And then when one of the lifeboats was lowered there be a mishap. One of the ropes must have broke, for the poor souls were flung into the sea and some sailors dived in and pulled them out and into the boat. And when that happened I began to cry. I couldna help it; I was so frightened. I was sobbin' and blubberin' and clingin' to Lady Laurene. I know she was frightened too, but she was so brave. She said, 'There now, Fiona, we'll be all right. No matter what happens, we're in God's hands. He'll take care of us.' Then I said, 'But I dinna want to die!' And she hugged me tight and said, 'Nay, but if we should, we'll be in heaven with Him.' Then she said, 'Promise if we are separated, ye'll tell my parents and brother Peter how much I love them and tell…'"

Fiona paused and looked about the room until her eyes rested on Eric, who felt his heart freeze under that gaze. "She spoke of you, Eric MacKenzie. Aye, she did. She said, 'And tell Eric that I will always love him and that I will be *there* waitin' fer him. He will understand.' That's what she said, that she will always love ye and that she will be *there* waitin' for ye. God rest her soul."

The servants followed her gaze in silent surprise. Eric crumpled in grief. He pulled his cap down over his face and slumped to the floor. Exclamations of sympathy filled the room, but they were interrupted by a hoarse croak from Eric. "Go on, Fiona. Tell us what happened then."

When all eyes returned to Fiona, she resumed her tale. "And then they were orderin' us into the lifeboat with Sorbie, our waiter, and Lady Laurene told me to get in but she dinna' follow me. She kept handin' wee children into the boat and helpin' the women. There must have been about sixty of us crowdin' into the boat. And still she was helpin' others get to safety. Finally, when the ship seemed to be sinkin', the captain ordered her off the ship, and she started to climb down a rope ladder into the lifeboat. But a wave came up and washed our boat away, leavin' her hangin' off the side of our fast-sinkin' ship. She let go and tried to swim to us, but she must have been too worn out from savin' so many others 'cause she couldna make it. Sorbie dove in after her and pulled her up into the boat. He tried to push the water out o' her and to get her breathin' again. He tried and tried, but it did no good. Then I held onto her, hopin' some warmth would restore her.

"But there was water in our boat and the women had to bail it out with their shoes, and one of the men stayed at the oar e'en though he had a broken arm and a broken leg. We spent twelve hours in that lifeboat wonderin' if we'd ever be picked up. All we had was one little torch that we tried flashin' whene'er our boat breasted a wave. The search lights o' the rescue ship kept sweepin' o'er us, but they dinna see us. But then we were luckier than one of the other boats, which was smashed like kindlin' by the propeller of a rescue ship, and another boat was swamped and many of those people drowned before they could be pulled out o' the water. We finally gave up rowin' and just kept balin' water with our shoes.

"It was the longest night of me life—'specially with tryin' to keep me lady dry, and not knowin' for certain whether she be dead or alive. Finally, at dawn a rescue ship saw us and picked us up. They hauled the children up in buckets and then the hurt ones and me lady were pulled up by ropes. I was able to climb a rope ladder. When I got on deck, I saw the last of the *Athenia* sinkin' until only the lifeboats bobbin' all empty were left as witness to the horrible crime of those wicked Nazis."

Fiona shuddered and whispered, "And as to me Lady Laurene, the doctors couldna save her. And she bein' so brave and savin' so many others...'tis terrible," she sobbed. "Terrible. But at least Sorbie pulled her out o' the sea. Lord Kilmorey be bringin' her home tomorrow. I still can't believe it, though. It all be a ghastly nightmare."

Not able to endure any more, Eric groped his way to his feet and staggered out into the black night with his heart full of anger and despair.

Laurene was buried three days later in the family crypt on the Kilmorey estate—in sight of the sea yet safe from it. At the funeral, Eric stood with the household staff at a respectful distance from the family. Peter approached him after the service. The two young men embraced briefly in their shared grief.

"Father is shattered," Peter said. "He really believed he was sending Laurene to safety. He bears tremendous guilt that he sent her to her doom instead."

"He was sendin' her away from me," Eric replied bitterly. "She wanted to run away to Gretna Green and be married. I should have listened to her. She would still be alive if I had. I told her to go. I thought she would be safe."

"Neither you nor Father could have known. And you can't live now in a world of what-ifs. It won't bring her back. You know she'd want us to carry on and fight the good fight. I told Father I would get back at those Germans by helping to crack their codes. I'm returning to Cambridge tomorrow. What will you do?"

Eric shook his head. "I don't know. I just really don't know."

He spent the remainder of the afternoon pondering that question as he walked over the Old Course, down along the West Sands, among the remains of the old castle, and finally through the graves and broken walls of the cathedral of St. Andrews. In times past, he had found the cathedral grounds to be of surpassing beauty and grandeur, but on this day they symbolized for him the corruption and evil of man—destroying all that was beautiful and good and true. And he attributed its destruction to the weakness of God, who must be impotent to allow such havoc to be perpetuated on His people and His property.

How could I serve such a God? Did He really call me into the ministry or was that the vain imagination of a suggestible and callow youth? In any case, I don't want to serve Him anymore! There's nothing to hold me here any longer, and I am not going to stick around here and play seminary student when people are dying out there. I want to kill as many of those bloody Nazis as I can get my hands on, and I don't care if they kill me. I'll just take out as many as I can when I go. I'll kill the whole bloody lot and that blasted Hitler too.

Eric's head drew up sharply at the steady drone of propellers as a squadron of Hurricane fighters from Leuchars RAF base flew overhead in a training exercise. Although he was too angry at God to acknowledge His leading, he nevertheless seized on the sudden appearance of the Hurricanes as a sign.

Eric made a grim resolution, and the next morning he left St. Andrews to join the RAF.

Interval

Whom have I in heaven but thee? And there is none upon earth that I desire besides thee. My flesh and my heart may fail, but God is the strength of my heart and my portion forever.

PSALM 73:25-26

God designed the human machine to run on Himself. He Himself is the fuel our spirits were designed to burn, or the food our spirits were designed to feed on. There is no other. That is why it is just no good asking God to make us happy in our own way without bothering about religion. God cannot give us happiness and peace apart from Himself, because it is not there. There is no such thing.

C.S. LEWIS
Mere Christianity

8

July 1967
Carlisle House, Yorkshire

*E*ric, was it difficult for you to recount all that tonight?" Annie asked as they stood on the balcony of their room overlooking the south lawn of Carlisle House and its massive, ornately carved stone fountain.

Eric put his arm around his wife and drew her close. "Aye, I suppose so. Those were such dreadful yet pivotal times. It's also rather odd to be telling our children about my first love. You didn't mind, did you?"

"No, of course not. I think they should know about Laurene and she should be remembered. She must have been a remarkable young lady—certainly very brave and selfless. Although sometimes I've felt guilty that Laurene was on the *Athenia* and I was not, and that I'm the one to have been blessed to marry you and have your children. But then there's the sovereignty of God in our lives that we may never understand, and I have to trust that. I am glad she insisted you promise that if something were to happen to her, you should go on to love again and be happy. It's hard for me to explain, but at times I feel like I'm in a sort of partnership with her and I owe it to her to make you as happy as I can."

Eric softly kissed her hair. "Aye, you've done that."

Annie leaned into his embrace. "How did you come to tell your tale tonight after all these years?"

"It came up in my conversation with Stuart. While you all were getting settled, he asked for permission to propose to Natalie."

She looked up at him in surprise. "Really? Oh, my. I'm not sure I'm ready for another child to be married."

"Me neither—of course, we should have known it was coming. He's been courting her pretty seriously since last February when David's baby was born. Guess we've been in denial that the courtship could lead to marriage. Same with Ginny and her Kevin. I expect we'll also be hearing something from them soon. Honestly, Annie, I've loved every minute we've had with these children, and I hate the thought of them growing up and leaving home. Somehow David's marrying Kate seemed easier than seeing our girls going off and getting married. Maybe it's because he's still in Oxford and Kate has had to adopt us as her family since hers is back in the States. But two daughters likely to get married soon...I can't believe it!"

"And that would mean two weddings to plan and pay for. I don't suppose they'd want a double wedding...no, they wouldn't. The girls are too different. Ginny says she wants something very small and private. But if Natalie marries Stuart—oh dear, how can we ever afford a wedding fit for a lord?"

"Well, I presume we'd have to accept the Devereuxes' help if they want a fancy affair. But let's not get ahead of ourselves here.

Stuart hasn't proposed to her yet, and she hasn't accepted. He merely asked for my blessing. He hasn't spoken to his father yet, and I warned him he may face some opposition from that quarter. And that's how we got started on my story."

"Oh. Well, I wonder what wisdom he gleaned from it."

Eric shrugged. "Perhaps nothing but a sad story. Or perhaps it will dissuade him."

"Or perhaps it will make him that much more determined not to bow to convention and throw happiness away," Annie observed. "Natalie may not be from a highborn family, but she's quite a girl and would make any man a wonderful wife."

"Aye, she would. She's like her mother."

"Well, she is headstrong, but hopefully she's turned that into a strength, not a weakness."

"I think she has. She's like David—unwavering in her commitment to the Lord and eager to do His will. She may not be confident what that will is, though. Stuart's not convinced that she'll have him, so it will be interesting to see how all this plays out. I'll just continue to pray that His will be done on earth as it is in heaven—especially regarding the spouses our children choose."

"Amen to that!" Annie sighed. "But isn't it strange to think that Natalie might one day be a countess? That she could live in a place like this? She has never cared much for material things."

"Maybe that's why God can entrust her with them. She may very well be the right one for Stuart because she will love him for himself, not because of his wealth or title."

"I guess you're right," Annie said. Then she laughed. "But if Clifton Manor is at all like Carlisle House, I know which child I'll want to visit the most when you retire!"

Eric smiled. "You're shameless." He suddenly grew more serious. "Annie, you know the children are going to want to hear the rest of our story, don't you? Only David and Ginny have heard the whole saga."

"How much of it do we have to tell?" she asked anxiously. "I don't know if I want to tell them everything."

"Well, you needn't tell them *everything*. Children don't need to know their parents' intimate lives anymore than the parents need to know theirs. I remember in the Chronicles of Narnia, when a character would ask Aslan about another character, He would answer with something like 'I am telling you your story, not hers. I tell no one any story but his own.' I should think Natalie at any rate is ready to know more of our story."

"Maybe so. I just hope that the Lord will help us to share just what is needed—what will be helpful to them and not harmful."

"Don't worry, love," Eric said, hugging Annie tightly. "You're a woman of remarkable tact and discretion."

Stuart was determined that the MacKenzie clan would have a relaxing and fun holiday on his sister's Yorkshire estate. To that end he served as the activities director. While the adults slept in or lounged and read in the library, Stuart and Natalie spent the morning rehearsing the younger MacKenzie children, as well as Clementine's two boys, in a melodramatic and comedic rendering of the "Pyramus and Thisby" play-within-a-play from *A Midsummer Night's Dream*. Stuart and Natalie took the title roles of the doomed lovers; Richard, the Prologue; Mark, the Lion; Clemmie's boys Teddy and Spencer, the Wall; and Hannah, Moonshine. William served as general prompter, stage manager, and ultimately cinematographer. At noon they loaded pony carts full of props and costumes, as well as enormous hampers packed with an elaborate picnic lunch, and trotted off to the manor "folly," a summerhouse perched on the hillside overlooking the North Lake. There the household feasted in sylvan splendor until the actors disappeared into the summerhouse to don their costumes. The children's play resulted in unbridled hilarity, and by its finale the cast had dissolved into giggles and wrestling matches on the summerhouse lawn—all of which William duly recorded on Stuart's movie camera.

Ample daylight remained for swimming, fishing, and boating on the lake as well as pony rides and races about the gardens. Since the summer weather continued to be fine and warm, Clemmie decided to serve dinner as a casual cookout on the terrace of the Garden Hall overlooking the south parterre and fountain before they assembled in the long gallery for a screening of Errol Flynn's *The Adventures of Robin Hood.* When the exhausted younger members of the party had retired to bed, Stuart invited Natalie to stroll with him in the garden.

As he had orchestrated the entire day, so Stuart had left nothing to chance this evening. Flambeaux brightened the garden paths and the jets of the great fountain were lit in a dazzling spray. A violinist softly serenaded them from the terrace. Even the moon cooperated with its gentle glow in the midnight blue sky. The ambience was perfect for romance.

Stuart toyed nervously with the small jewelry box hidden in his trouser pocket.

He led Natalie by the hand to sit on a bench near the fountain. "Darling," he said, trying to maintain his usual unflappable decorum, "there's something I'd like to ask you."

Did he detect a slight paling in her cheek? Her eyes met his—expectant but wary. "Yes, Stuart?"

His fingers closed on the box but then suddenly released it.

No, this isn't right. Perfect setting; wrong timing. She must be certain. I must be certain of her. I should talk to my father first. I should be certain of him as well.

"Blast!" he muttered.

"What's wrong, Stuart?"

"Sorry. I just remembered some business I have in London. I won't be able to go on with you to Scotland tomorrow."

She looked genuinely chagrined. "Oh, no! Can't the business wait? Everyone will be so disappointed."

"No, I'm sorry. I'm disappointed too, but there's something I must take care of."

"You will try to join us later then, won't you? At least try to come up to Gairloch for Daddy's birthday. Ginny and Kevin will be there." She grasped his hand tightly. "You will come, won't you?"

"I don't know. It will depend on how things go in London. But if you really want me to, I'll try to make it for the birthday party."

"I do, Stuart. And I know the rest of the family will as well. You've won your way into the hearts of the MacKenzie clan now, you know. It just wouldn't be the same without you."

"Is that so?" He smiled and kissed the tips of her fingers. "I'm glad to hear it. Do you think they've enjoyed their stay here?"

"Oh, yes! It's been such fun! Clemmie has been such a darling to host us all."

"She's enjoyed it too. She loves a house full of guests. And it's been delightful for her boys to have some playmates."

"I had wondered if they aren't lonely sometimes in this huge old house. If I ever lived in a house like this, I wouldn't want to waste all this space on just a few people. I would want to fill it with children."

Stuart chuckled at the thought. "So you want to have a big family too?"

"Yes, I do. But I was thinking in terms of how wonderful it would be if a place like this could be used as an orphanage or as a school for needy children."

"Hmm. You do come up with some interesting ideas. Well, what do you think of this place besides it being so huge?"

Natalie trailed her hand in the fountain as she looked back at the brightly lit baroque facade of the mansion. "It's splendid. Really, really beautiful and amazing. Is it much like Clifton Manor?"

"The grounds are similar but not the architecture. Carlisle House was designed by Vanbrugh as a forerunner to Blenheim, but Clifton Manor is much older. Although parts of it are eighteenth century, the central Hall is Elizabethan and the main building from the time of King James the First."

"Someday I should like to see it."

Stuart grasped the jewelry box in his pocket and then released it again. "Someday I should like you to."

Natalie clutched his arm. "Look!" she said, pointing to the terrace. "It's Kate and David. They're dancing!"

They watched as David twirled Kate around and caught her in his arms. Kate laughed happily and David bent to kiss her.

"I feel like a voyeur," Natalie whispered with a giggle.

"Well, let's join them," Stuart said as he drew Natalie to her feet. They walked hand in hand up to the terrace and then smiled in greeting as they joined the dance.

Later, Natalie stole up to her parents' door and rapped gently.

"Who is it?" Annie softly called from the other side.

"It's me, Mummy. Natalie. May I talk to you? I brought up some milk and biscuits for you."

Annie opened the door and invited her daughter into the sitting room. "Your father's asleep," she said, indicating the bedroom beyond. "What is it, honey?" Annie tightly tied the belt of her cotton bathrobe and settled in a plush armchair.

After placing her tray on a lamp table, Natalie pulled up another chair. "You know, Mum, I feel so stupid. I thought for certain Stuart was going to propose to me tonight."

"Oh, really? And did he?"

"No! That's why I feel stupid. He asked me to walk with him in the garden. It was such a gorgeous night with the moonlight and the fountain all lit up. There was even a violinist playing out on the terrace. And Kate and David were dancing. It couldn't have been more romantic. So I thought he had set it all up to propose to me. But he hadn't. Instead, he surprised me with the news that he has to go down to London tomorrow for business and can't go on to Scotland with us."

"I'm sorry to hear that. We thought he'd be coming for the birthday celebration."

"So did I. But he promised to try to come—if he gets the business taken care of. Anyway, I just feel rather stupid for letting myself get so carried away with the idea that he was going to propose, especially when he didn't."

Annie took a sip of milk. "If he had, would you have accepted, Nat?"

Natalie sighed. "I don't know. Maybe deep down I'm glad he didn't ask. I would hate to give him some lame answer like, 'Let me think about it.' I should know my own mind by now."

"You love Stuart, don't you, honey?"

"Yes, I love him very much, and I should like to be his wife. But I want to be sure it's God's will and that I'm marrying him for the right reasons. That's why I haven't wanted to see Clifton Manor. I don't want to be caught up in imagining myself as the mistress of a great house. I want to marry Stuart because he's the man I love and he's God's best for me, not because of his money or his earldom."

"I wouldn't expect anything less of you, Nat."

"Do you and Daddy approve of Stuart? If he asks, would Daddy give his blessing?"

"Yes, honey, I believe he would. And so would I. I think after a rough start Stuart has proven himself to be a man after God's own heart—and that's the most important qualification a husband can have."

Natalie tucked her legs up into her chair. "Is that how you knew Daddy was the one, Mummy? I mean, last night he shared how he was all bitter and angry with God after Laurene died. Had he changed by the time you met him?"

"Not exactly, dear." Annie answered cautiously. "Your father and I did not do everything right, Natalie. But by God's grace and mercy, He worked it all together for good."

"Please tell me your story, Mummy. I've only heard bits and pieces."

Annie took a deep breath. "All right, honey. I guess it's time you knew."

Part 2
Annie's Story

*I know your deeds, your hard work and persever-
ance. I know that you cannot tolerate wicked men...
You have persevered and have endured hardships for
my name and have not grown weary. Yet I hold this
against you: You have forsaken your first love.*

REVELATION 2:2-4 NIV

Innocence is carried away by the unforeseen.

C.S. LEWIS
The Allegory of Love

9

September 1939
Oxford

The summer of 1939—the last summer of peace—was warm, sunny, and idyllic in Oxford. Annie Little enjoyed every moment of her summer holiday visiting with her older brother, Jeffrey. Less than seventeen months apart in age, they were kindred spirits of the soul, so that when Jeff left the University of Virginia the previous summer to matriculate to Magdalen College in Oxford, Annie immediately began saving her earnings as a nurse's aid at UVA hospital to visit him. The summer had served as her personal reward for graduating from high school a year early and completing two years of her nurse's training. Her mother and father, a professor of religion at the University of Virginia, had trepidations about their youngest daughter gallivanting to a European nation on the brink of war, but Annie had a bit of the adventuress in her. Her parents called her "stubborn" and "headstrong." She thought of herself as "determined" and "independent."

While Jeff worked part-time in Blackwell's bookstore and stayed in his rooms at Magdalen, Annie found student lodgings vacated for the summer on nearby Holywell Street in a terrace house occupied by a kind, middle-aged couple with the Austenesque name of Bingley. Annie earned spending money as a nurse's aid at the Radcliff Infirmary and then used her free time to enjoy the fruits of the good life in Oxford—picnicking and punting; frequenting pubs and parties; and attending plays, concerts, and the cinema. While seldom availing themselves of newspapers or radio, the high-spirited Americans and their young British friends managed to isolate themselves from the dire news of the Nazis trumpeting from across the Channel. Of course, one could not live completely oblivious to the continuous speculations of war which flew about town, but some of the students did find it efficacious to live in their dreaming spires and to *carpe diem* in a last, almost desperate effort to delight in the final days of peace.

As one of the few young ladies in a predominately male environment, Annie found herself the belle of the ball. But in many respects, even had she faced competition, she would easily have conquered them. Petite and pretty with warm brown eyes and shining golden-brown hair that swept past her shoulders, Annie's brightness and gaiety won her many admirers, while her charming Southern drawl melted the coldest British reserve. Jeff's friends buzzed around her like bees to honey, and Annie thoroughly reveled in her role as the Scarlett O'Hara of Oxford.

But after she had passed her nineteenth birthday in the city of London where the news from Europe was unavoidable, Annie faced her impending departure from England with an ambivalence she could not resolve. So it was on the last day of August when Jeff arrived on Holywell Street to transport her to Liverpool, where she had a berth reserved on the SS *Athenia*.

When he entered her room, Jeff was astonished to find Annie sitting distractedly on the floor amid half-packed trunks and clothes strewn carelessly about.

"Annie, what are you doing? Why haven't you packed yet?" he chided her. "We'll be hard-pressed now to make it to Liverpool in time for the embarkation." He grabbed a few blouses off of hangers and packed feverishly for a few minutes, until he realized Annie was making no effort to help him. "What's wrong with you?" he demanded. "Why aren't you getting ready to go?"

"I don't think I should go," she answered slowly.

"Why not? I know you've had fun this summer, but you need to get back to Charlottesville so you can finish nursing school."

"It's not that."

"Is it the war?"

"Yes."

"All the more reason why you should go. If hostilities break out, you don't want to be stuck over here."

"If hostilities break out, I think I should be here. Jeff, I know this sounds crazy, but I have a feeling that I shouldn't be on that ship."

"Why? Are you afraid of sailing now? You don't think the Germans would be nuts enough to fire on a passenger liner, do you? Especially when war hasn't been declared yet?"

"No, but like I said, I have this inner voice saying to me, 'Don't go.' I don't know why, but I almost feel that I'd be disobeying God if I board that ship."

"If you don't board that ship, you'll be disobeying Mom and Dad. Good grief, Annie, your ticket has been bought already!"

"Well, maybe Cunard will give me a refund. I can phone and find out. I'll bet there are people desperately trying to get out of here who would snatch that berth right up."

"But what about Mom and Dad? They're expecting you to go back home. They'll have a fit if you stay."

"Maybe so, but there won't be much they can do about it, either. And if there's not a war, then I'll just catch another boat home."

"But if we do go to war, who knows when you'll have another chance to make it home."

"I know, but part of me feels like *this* is home. I can't explain it, but I feel such an affinity to the people here. Maybe that's why I should stay. So I can help."

In exasperation, Jeff ran his hand through his hair. In many ways the siblings looked enough alike to be twins. They shared the same coloring and fine bone structure. In fact, as a late maturer, Jeff had stood eye level with Annie for many years; but now when he pulled himself up to his full height, as he did at this moment, he towered over her.

"Annie, you've had a fun summer, but life over here is not all summer fun. When the term starts back up, we have to get to work, and the guys won't have so much time for parties and socializing. It won't be all gaiety and games anymore—not to mention that if we do go to war, it's likely to get pretty nasty. You'll be wishing to be back at UVA before you know it."

"I'm not talking about the socializing, Jeff. My affinity with this country is not limited to punts and parties. Really, I'm insulted that you think I'm that shallow. You don't know this, but I haven't been completely idle since I've been here. While working at the infirmary, I made some inquiries about finishing my nurse's training at St. Bartholomew's, a teaching hospital in London. I'm thinking that if there is war, my nursing skills could be of use."

"Gee whiz, Annie!" Jeff sank down on her bed. "I'm sorry for what I said. You know I don't think you're shallow. But golly day, if war breaks out and you go to London, you could be in the thick of it!"

"That's kind of the idea, Jeff," she said wryly.

"But Mom and Dad will really have fits then! And so will I. If those Nazis send bombers over—oh, good grief, you can't stay there!"

Annie sat beside him. "Okay, let's just take this one step at a time. We aren't at war yet. I don't know why, but I just don't feel right about leaving tonight on the *Athenia*. I really love it over here—you know you do too, and I want to go up to London to look into Barts and going there this fall for my nurse's training. I'll send a telegram to Mom and Dad after the *Athenia* departs. You won't be implicated at all. Okay?"

He sighed with resignation. "Okay, but I want you to promise me something. If war breaks out, and the Nazis start bombing London, promise me you'll come here to Oxford."

"Okay," she said, smiling. "It's a deal."

Autumn 1939
England

On September first, when Hitler invaded Poland, Warren Hamilton Lewis, a forty-four-year-old officer in the Army Reserves, was called back into active service and promptly left Oxford for a camp in Yorkshire. His brother, Clive Staples Lewis, the Oxford don and author, learned he was also eligible for service until his forty-first birthday on November twenty-ninth. Although C.S. Lewis had fought bravely in the Great War and still had shrapnel in his chest to prove it, he felt he was no longer physically fit enough for active duty. Instead he hoped to serve his country by doing what he did best—lecturing, tutoring, writing, and mentoring students. The day after delivering a lecture on Shakespeare at Stratford-upon-Avon, he also welcomed four little refugee schoolgirls to the Kilns, his home in Headington Quarry, a suburb of Oxford.

On the morning of September third, Jeff and Annie Little—while out with friends pleasure-boating on the Isis—heard over the radio Prime Minister Neville Chamberlain make his declaration of war. Lewis was met after church by his refugee children jumping up and down with exhilaration about the war and the exciting thought that they might experience an air raid that very night. The next morning, the story of the sinking of the *SS Athenia* came as a horribly sobering shock to everyone. Annie hurried to the post office to telegraph her parents that she had not been on the ill-fated liner.

By mid-September Lewis experienced a measure of compensation for the loss of his brother's companionship: his friend and fellow writer Charles Williams moved to Oxford from London with the Oxford University Press for the duration of the war. Williams became a valued addition to the group of writers known as the "Inklings," as well as to the lecturing staff of the university, which had announced that in spite of everything they would have a term and quite a number of undergraduates coming up. Lewis then learned that all the books he and "Warnie" had hand-carried down to the basement of the New Building for safekeeping had become his solitary burden to be brought back up, because the government had decided not to requisition the Magdalen College buildings after all. With happy anticipation, Jeff welcomed the Michaelmas term and his studies reading English with Lewis, while Annie traveled off to London to begin her new life, training at St. Bartholomew's Hospital.

After spending a week in a boarding house, she quickly made friends with three nurses and moved into their shared flat in Bayswater. The girls were happy to be on the Central Line of the underground, which directly led to St. Paul's, only a few blocks' walk to the hospital. It also pleased Annie that she could be close to Hyde Park as well as to Paddington Station and its frequent trains to Oxford. In addition, she knew Jeff would be thrilled to learn that around the corner from her flat stood the house once owned by Sir James Barrie, the celebrated author of *Peter Pan.*

Annie eagerly applied herself to her work and studies and also volunteered on occasion as a hostess at the YMCA, where she could meet plenty of military officers on leave. Like many young people who did not recall the horrors of the Great War, Annie and her friends found the first months of the war an exciting phase with its social whirlwind of dances and parties. As the holidays approached, however, and the days grew shorter and colder, Annie's spirits dampened along with the wet, wintry weather. She began to long for her family back in Virginia and wondered at times if she had been foolish not to return home when she had the opportunity. Then with a jolt she would recall the fate of the *Athenia.*

She and Jeff had determined to carry on the American tradition of celebrating Thanksgiving; and so on Thursday, November twenty-third, Annie took the train up to Oxford and met Jeff at the Eastgate Hotel. Conveniently located on the High Street across from the Examination Schools, the Eastgate's ambience and its proximity to both Merton and Magdalen Colleges made it a favorite dining spot of the Inklings. As it happened, they were holding their weekly Thursday evening meeting in the hotel dining room when Annie and Jeff arrived for dinner and settled at a nearby table.

Jeff nodded to the august group of authors and with lowered voice identified them to Annie.

"Some of those men are my tutors. See the dapper one with the fancy vest?"

"Yes."

"That's Tolkien. He's the author of *The Hobbit.*"

Annie looked over with more interest. "Really? I love that book!"

"Yeah, me too. And remember I read Anglo-Saxon with him last term, and that I went up to St. Andrews, Scotland, last March to hear him give a lecture on fairy stories? Well, *ecce homo*. He's an amazing guy. He invented his own languages and myths for his stories. He's supposed to be working on a sequel to *The Hobbit*, but it sounds like it'll be more of an adult fairy tale than a children's story. In fact, he may be reading some of it now. Boy, wouldn't I just love to be able to hear it! I wonder if we're really quiet if we can..."

"But, Jeff, that would be rude!"

"I suppose it would be, but still I'd give anything to be invited to listen in. These guys call themselves the 'Inklings,' and they're sort of a literary club—mostly dons, all friends, all Christians, all writers, and—"

"All male," Annie observed.

Jeff grinned. "Well, this is Oxford and there are lots of these little clubs. I've joined one that meets one afternoon a week to discuss theology."

"Theology?" Annie asked, raising an eyebrow. "Daddy would love to hear about that."

"Yeah. Well, Christian theology," Jeff said, leaning closer. "C.S. Lewis is one of our faculty sponsors, and he's also my tutor this term. Look over there when you can without being too obvious. He's the balding one with the big red face."

"The guy who's laughing so loud?"

"Yeah, that's him. But he's doesn't laugh much at tutorials, I can tell you that. I'm a little intimidated by him. He's so blinking smart. You can't put anything past him, but I really like him. He's a true Christian. Wasn't always. In fact, when he was an undergrad here and then a Fellow, he was an atheist. Some of those men sitting there were instrumental in influencing Lewis to become a Christian, like Tolkien and the other loud one with the thinning gray hair. That's Hugo Dyson. He's an English professor at Reading who sometimes gives lectures here."

"I thought most everyone over here was a Christian," Annie said as she glanced over the menu.

"Nah. You know just attending church doesn't make someone a believer."

"Well, but not all believers attend church, either."

"Speaking of which, have you been going to church since you've been in London?"

"Hmm…sometimes I've gone to Evensong at St. Paul's."

"Well, I've heard of a good church near there I think you should visit. It's called All Souls."

"But that's an Anglican church, isn't it? We're Methodists!"

"What do you think St. Paul's is, Annie?"

"Right, but I just visit there because it's convenient. I wouldn't go there regularly. I know that I should try to find a Methodist church, but I've just been so busy with school and all."

"Look, I don't think the point is to go to this denominational church or that one. The point is to gather with other believers regularly so that you can grow in your faith. I've heard good things about All Souls and I want you to check it out sometime. Definitely when I come down for Christmas."

Annie shrugged. "Okay. But since when did you get so religious? You didn't go to church much this summer."

"Well, I've been reevaluating things and trying to make my faith my own. I think it's partly the influence of Mr. Lewis and this study group I told you about. And let's not forget, we are PKs."

"I prefer to think of us as professor's kids, not pastor's kids."

"You know we're both, like it or not. Dad's an ordained minister, after all."

"Yeah, but he doesn't have a church now, so that means we're just professor's kids," Annie stubbornly insisted.

"Uh-huh. When you meet some good-looking ministerial student, you'll change that tune. You'll say," Jeff assumed a thick Southern drawl, "'Well, I declare! My daddy is a clergyman too and my mother's daddy was a pastor and so was her granddaddy—three generations of women in my family have married ministers, so I guess I will too.' Yeah, you won't deny your spiritual heritage when it'll work to your advantage."

"Stop it!" Annie laughed and threatened to throw a piece of bread at him. He was tempted to reciprocate when a waiter stopped to take their orders. Since turkey and stuffing were unavailable for a traditional Thanksgiving dinner, they settled for chicken and potatoes.

Uproarious laughter could be heard from the corner where the Inklings were eating their dinner. Annie leaned in closer to Jeff. "Tell me more about those guys. That Mr. Lewis. Has he written anything?"

"Yes. In fact, last year he published a novel about space travel."

"Space travel?" Annie wrinkled her nose. "Have you read it? Is it any good?"

"It's quite good, actually. It's called *Out of the Silent Planet* and is set on Mars—but for Mars he creates an entirely new world and calls it Malacandra. It's very enticing. And he weaves his faith into it although it's not at all obvious. The main character's name is Ransom. He's a professor of languages, a philologist. I have a hunch that Mr. Lewis based him on Professor Tolkien."

Annie smiled. "Really? I wonder what Professor Tolkien thinks of the book. Do you suppose he would tell him what he really thinks?"

"Well, that's just what they're doing now. They read to each other what they're working on and then critique it. So I suspect Mr. Tolkien had a chance to say what he thought before the book went to publication."

"What do you suppose Mr. Lewis will read to them tonight?"

"He mentioned that he had been asked to write a book on the problem of pain."

"Well, that could be a timely subject with the current state of affairs. So he doesn't write just novels?"

"No. He's written poetry, an allegory, and, of course, literary criticism."

"Not drama?"

"No, but it sounds like that is what is being read now. Some sort of play. That's Charles Williams. Lewis is very high on him. He's published quite a bit—plays, poetry, and novels. Some really interesting stuff. And rather bizarre. He works for the Oxford University Press as an editor. He's not a don, but he is a superb lecturer."

"He looks different. But nice too."

"Yes. Well, I had an opportunity to hear him read a paper last week at St. Hugh's. I went on Lewis's recommendation. Boy, am I glad I did! He's really a dynamic speaker. Didn't just stick his nose in his paper and read it in a monotone the way some dons do. He talked nonstop—quite eloquently—without reading any notes. And he quoted all these references from memory. He was fascinating. He's one of those guys who's kind of odd-looking, but his personality is so charismatic the girls just swoon over him."

"Huh. Really? Well, he does look animated when he reads. I'm beginning to understand why you'd like to eavesdrop. They do sound like they are having a lot of fun over there."

"Yeah," Jeff agreed enviously.

"So, you're still doing all right, enjoying your studies and friends and all?"

"Yeah, it's going great. How about you?"

"I love London. The girls I live with are fabulous, and I'm enjoying my work at Barts."

"What about the fellows? Anyone special?"

"Oh, I meet lots of guys at the Y, but nobody special. Any girlfriends for you?" Boyfriend-girlfriend status checking was a ritual between them.

"Are you kidding? Here in Oxford? This place is like a monastery. But, hey, I'm looking forward to getting to know those girlfriends of yours better."

Annie smiled. "Yeah, I'll bet you are. So you're coming down for Christmas, aren't you? Jeff, we have to spend Christmas together. I hate being so far from home over the holidays. I hope this war doesn't last too long."

"Me too, but I have a feeling we're in it for the long haul. In any case, after I finish up the term I have to work for a while at Blackwell's—but then nothing can stop me from spending Christmas with my little sister." He raised a glass to toast her. "Here's to you, kiddo, and here's to victory for the Brits!" They clinked their glasses together and then eagerly tackled their Thanksgiving feast.

11

December 1939
London

*J*eff kept his promise and arrived in London before Christmas for a fortnight's holiday. He slept on the couch in Annie's flat—a paradise of pretty girls in the midst of a grim London. Her flatmates, Peggy, Betty, and June, giggled and blushed when he fought his way through the clotheslines of lingerie and nylons hanging in the bathroom. But Jeff wasn't nonplussed. He had grown up in a household with three sisters and felt quite comfortably at home.

On the twenty-first of December, the shortest day of the year in what would prove to become one of the coldest winters in recent memory, Jeff and Annie decided to garner a little Christmas cheer by attending a concert of Handel's *Messiah* performed by the Royal Philharmonic Orchestra with the London Philharmonic Choir at the Royal Albert Hall in Kensington. Since the declaration of war, the Hall had been closed due to fear of bombing raids, but when these did not materialize, the decision was made to reopen for the season with a series of Christmas concerts. When Jeff and Annie arrived at the massive domed arena, they discovered themselves bereft of tickets in a sea of humanity. They waited patiently in the standing-room-only line for no-shows. Throngs of uniformed men and women filed past them.

"Dang!" muttered Jeff. "Don't these chaps look smart? Makes me want to sign up. I feel so…well, superfluous…just sitting out the war in a university. Look at that one," he said nodding toward a tall, handsome RAF pilot officer resplendent in a dark blue dress uniform, who was scanning the crowd as if searching for someone in particular. "Impressive, isn't he?"

Annie gulped. *Impressive indeed. And he's staring at me!* She felt her chest squeeze tightly as the young officer strode up to her and bowed his head in polite greeting.

"Pardon me, miss. I have an extra ticket and wondered if ye'd like to have it." He spoke with an unmistakable Scottish burr.

Annie looked up into impossibly bright blue eyes and thought, *A girl could get lost swimming in the deep pools of those eyes.*

"Miss?"

"How much are you selling it for, bud?" Jeff stepped up and asked.

"Oh, I'm not sellin' it," the pilot said without taking his eyes from Annie's. "It was given to me by a mate who took ill. So I'd like to give it to the young lady if she wants it." He held the ticket out to her. "Miss?" he repeated gently.

"Yes!" Annie quickly recovered herself and took the ticket. "Thank you."

Jeff placed his hand on the small of her back and spoke loudly. "All right, honey, you enjoy the concert and I'll meet you back here afterward."

Finally taking note of him, the officer gave a curt nod and stepped into the stream of concertgoers filing into the auditorium.

"Okay," Annie said. "I'll meet you back here."

"Don't let that guy pull anything."

"He just gave me a ticket, Jeff. He didn't even wait for me to go in with him."

"Yeah, but did you notice that out of this entire queue he picked you out to offer the ticket to? He's not stupid. He knows a pretty girl when he sees one. Just watch it! Where's your seat?" He looked at the ticket. "Okay. I'll be in the back keeping an eye on you and, like I said, see you here afterward."

"All right." Annie found her way to the stalls and her empty seat next to the handsome officer. He stood smartly until she was settled and smiled as he reseated himself.

"Thanks for the ticket," she said.

"Ye're welcome. I'm glad yer boyfriend let ye use it."

She let that one pass. "I'm Annie Little," she said, offering her hand.

"I'm Eric MacKenzie. Glad to make yer acquaintance. Ye're American?"

"Yes. Are you Scottish?"

"Aye. What are ye Yanks doin' over here durin' a war?"

The question remained unanswered for the time being as the conductor strode out to a wave of applause. Eric and Annie directed their attention to the stage and the concert.

At the interval, Eric excused himself and Annie looked about the enormous hall with its row upon row of plush crimson seats, opulent gilt gallery, and splendid pipe organ rising above the stage. She spotted Jeff in the rear of the auditorium and waved to him. When she sat back down and perused the program, she saw the notice posted at all such gatherings:

In the event of an air raid warning the audience is requested to leave the auditorium immediately and carry out the instructions of the stewards and attendants. Shelter is provided in the various corridors, but if any persons should wish to leave the building, the nearest public shelters are trenches in Kensington Gardens and trenches in Hyde Park, Knightsbridge.

Although she had read such notices before, Annie could not quite get used to the idea that Great Britain was really at war. Of course, the daily reminders were there: the requirement to carry a gas mask at all times, the taped windows and stacks of sandbags in case of bombing, the blue lightbulbs in the train stations, and the white stripes painted on lampposts to prevent accidents during the blackout. But because the city had not been bombed and events in Europe seemed at a stalemate, people had begun to call it "The Phoney War." She fervently hoped the stalemate continued and that an air raid siren would never mean anything more than a drill.

Eric soon returned holding two bottles of ginger beer. "Would ye like somethin' to drink?" he asked.

Annie nodded and took a bottle. "Thank you! I am really thirsty."

"So how is it ye're here in London?"

"I came to visit this summer, and then when the war broke out, I decided to stay and finish my nurse's training at St. Bartholomew's. How about you?"

Eric sipped his drink. "I just finished my pilot's trainin' at Cranwell and have some leave before joinin' my squadron at Kenley aerodrome just south of here."

"You didn't want to go home before you report to duty?"

"No. Too far."

"Where is home?"

"St. Andrews."

"Oh, my brother attended a lecture up there! It was given by the Oxford professor who wrote *The Hobbit*."

"Ye mean J.R.R. Tolkien. I attended that lecture too! Small world, isn't it?"

"Isn't that something? It is a small world. Were you a student at St. Andrews?"

"Aye."

"What was your major? English?"

"Aye, as a matter of fact. But I'm also readin' theology."

"Oh, my gosh! My dad is a theology professor back home in Virginia." She almost added that three generations of the women in her family had married ministers, but remembering Jeff's comment, she caught herself before it slipped out. "Do you intend to be a minister?" she asked instead.

"No." His mouth was set in a grim line that indicated there was more to this than he cared to discuss. "I'm goin' to be a pilot." He noted her empty bottle. "I say, if ye're finished with that, I'll put it in the rubbish for ye."

"Thanks." As she watched him walk away, a jumble of feelings—nervous anticipation, attraction, hopeful longing—made her queasy. Eric returned while the orchestra tuned up. He settled back in his seat and suddenly said, "Ye know, Annie, pardon me for my presumption, but if I may say so, ye have extraordinary eyes. They're—how can I say this?—*smiling* eyes."

She laughed, evidently pleased. "Smiling eyes? Why, that's the nicest compliment I've ever received."

He smiled back at her and then they returned their attention to the concert when the conductor picked up his baton. Although at first she found it difficult not to think about the young man sitting closely beside her, as the glorious strains of Handel's masterpiece enveloped them, Annie's heart and thoughts soared heavenward.

"Hallelujah! Hallelujah!" The audience rose to their feet in the traditional tribute to the majestic chorus. Annie's heart was stirred to join in praise. "And He shall reign for ever and ever. Hallelujah! Hallelujah!"

Thunderous applause greeted the finale of "Worthy is the Lamb that was slain." As the clapping died away, Annie, flushed with delight and wonder, looked up at Eric. "Wasn't that amazing? Now I'm really in the Christmas spirit! Thank you so much for the ticket."

"Ye're more than welcome. I'm very glad to have made yer acquaintance." He held her coat so that she could easily slip into it. "I'd like to meet yer boyfriend too. May I buy ye both a drink?"

Annie didn't desire to keep up the pretense any longer. "He's not my boyfriend. He's my brother. And I'm sure he'd be happy to meet you." They filed out and found Jeff anxiously searching the crowd for his sister.

"Oh, Jeff, wasn't that fantastic? I'd like you to meet the gentleman who so generously gave me the ticket. This is Eric MacKenzie. He just finished his pilot's training and is on leave before joining his squadron. Eric, this is my big brother, Jeff Little."

The two young men sized each other up as they shook hands and liked what they saw. "May I buy ye two a drink?" Eric asked.

"Nah. But you can join us for one," Jeff said, grinning. "Where are you staying? We're over in Bayswater."

"Really? Well, I am too. I'm stayin' near Leinster Square."

"Great! We're practically neighbors. Let's cut through Kensington Gardens. There's a nice pub on Bayswater Road."

As they stepped out into the pall of night made even darker by the enforced blackout, they all automatically pulled out their flashlights, covered by regulation tissue paper. Crossing the street, they entered the park gate by Gilbert Scott's gilded neo-Gothic memorial to Prince Albert.

"Boy, old Queen Victoria really must have loved her man," Jeff remarked. "The Royal Albert Hall, the Victoria and Albert Museum, this memorial, the chapel at Windsor, the mausoleum at Frogmore—it's a bit much, don't you think?"

Eric grunted in assent. "I say, Jeff, on a different subject—yer sister tells me ye came up to St. Andrews for the Andrew Lang lecture last March."

"Yeah, I did. To hear Tolkien, my Anglo-Saxon professor, give a lecture on fairy stories."

"So ye're an Oxford man. Well, the funny thin' is that I attended that lecture too. I was a student at St. Andrews."

"You don't say? Golly Ned, lucky you! That's one gorgeous town—the way it sits along the sea, the beach, that old castle, and the cathedral ruins…" Jeff whistled. "It's really something. And the golf courses—wow. Amazing. Do you golf?"

"Aye, I'm a Scot, aren't I? The truth is I caddied at the Old Course."

"Nah, you're kidding me! I'd love to golf there. Say, when this war is over, would you take me out on the Old Course?"

The American's easy familiarity with a complete stranger amused Eric. "Sure. If we all survive this war, I'll take ye golfin' on the Old Course."

Jeff beamed happily. "Neat-o. Hey, is this your first trip to London?"

"It's not only my first trip to London but my first *day* in London. I just arrived this mornin'."

"How long are you here?"

"Five days. I report for duty on Boxin' Day."

"The day after Christmas. Boy, that's a little brutal," Jeff observed.

Eric shrugged. "Someone has to mind the fort. At least I have Christmas off."

"But why are you here for Christmas? Isn't your family in Scotland?"

"Aye, but my parents live way up in the Highlands, and there's no one else closer." Eric knew this wasn't strictly true, but he was not of a mind to divulge his life story to a curious American whose acquaintance he had just made, even if he did have a pretty sister.

"Well, our folks are all back home in the States. So I came down here to spend Christmas with Annie. But she's working at the hospital a lot. I could use a sightseeing pal. Whaddya say? Would you care to bum around London with me tomorrow and visit some of the sights?"

"Sure, that'd be splendid. My mates have been here plenty of times and are only interested in seein' the inside of some dance halls."

"Well, that wouldn't be so bad either," Jeff said. "I'll tell you what. I'll take you around during the day to sightsee and at night you can take me with your friends to a dance."

"Jeff!" Annie protested.

"You can come too, Annie. And you can bring your girl-friends." In an aside to Eric he added, "She has three lovely flatmates."

"I'd be very pleased if Annie and her friends could join us at a dance," Eric said, hastening to take advantage of this opening.

Annie glanced at him. "Why, thank you."

They had wandered down the trail along the edge of the Longwater that flowed through the gardens of West Carriage Drive to the adjoining Serpentine Lake of Hyde Park.

"You know, Jeff," Annie said as she watched the interplay of the circles of light from their electric torches flit like fairies on the path ahead of them. "The Peter Pan statue is just ahead."

"Is it?" Jeff answered eagerly. "Oh, you're right! There it is!"

They stepped up to the black bronze statue of the mischievous little boy who would never grow up. After shining their flashlights over it and reading the inscription, Jeff remarked, "Barrie commissioned the statue and used Michael Davies, one of his adopted sons, as the model. He had it brought here secretly in the middle of the night so that it would appear magically on May Day morning." He chuckled. "He had such a sense of fun, didn't he?"

"I think you're Peter Pan," Annie teased.

"I am," Jeff agreed. "I wish none of us had to grow up. At least not with the world the way it is now."

"I say," interjected Eric, "the same mate who gave me tickets to tonight's concert has tickets to *Peter Pan* at the Theatre Royal in Drury Lane. But since he's really under the weather, I'll bet I can talk him into givin' me those tickets. If I can, would ye be interested?"

"Are you kidding?" Jeff's eyes gleamed with excitement. "Every year they put on the revival of *Peter Pan* and I've never seen it. I'd love to! Do you think you could get us both tickets?"

"I'll try to find tickets for all three of us. Why don't ye write down yer contact information for me and I'll give ye mine."

Annie couldn't help smiling as they exchanged cards. If Eric MacKenzie was some sort of cad, he had really pulled a number on her brother. On the other hand, nothing about him spoke of anything other than the "perfect gentleman," and she was rather pleased at her brother's sudden affinity for the "Flying Scotsman." She would be quite happy as well for the opportunity to get to know him better.

12

After a round of refreshments at the Black Lion on Bayswater Road, Jeff and Eric hit it off so well they decided they would indeed meet up the next day to tour London together. Since many museums and monuments had been closed for the duration, their treasures packed up and secreted away to safety, the young men found their sight-seeing largely restricted to outside viewing. Nevertheless, they enjoyed their camaraderie while exploring the city. They strolled through Covent Garden, gawking at street performers and sampling the wares of the vendors in the riot of shops and stalls. Eric spied a flower girl and impulsively bought a bouquet of Christmas roses.

"And whom, pray tell, are those for?" asked Jeff. "I'm flattered, but flowers are not my style."

Eric grinned. "They're for yer sister. Do ye think they'll please her?"

"My sister!" Jeff stood arms akimbo and looked bemusedly at Eric. "Have you taken a liking to Annie?"

"Would ye mind if I had?"

104

"Ha! I told her you had your eye on her."

"What do ye mean?"

"I told her you picked her out of the queue at the *Messiah* concert."

In truth, Eric had not perused the standing-room-only line with any intention other than giving away his extra ticket. But once he laid eyes on Annie, he could see no one else. In fact, he had been surprised that he had thought little of anyone or anything other than her since they had met. "Aye, I did," he admitted. "But then the way ye spoke to her, I thought at first ye were her boyfriend."

"That's what you were supposed to think. I didn't want some strange RAF officer putting the moves on my sister."

"Well, now. Do ye still think I'm strange?" Eric asked with a smile.

"Absolutely. You'd have to be to let a Yank be your London tour guide."

"Well, I won't 'put the moves' on yer sister, but would ye mind if I give her these flowers?"

"Nope." Jeff clapped him on the shoulder. "Go for it, bud. She loves flowers. What woman doesn't? Hey, maybe I should buy a bunch for Peggy." He began to pull some cash out of his wallet and then thought better of it. "Nah, I don't know when I'll see her, and I don't want to cart flowers around London for the rest of the afternoon. When are you going to give those to Annie?"

"How about now? We're only a couple of Tube stops away, and I thought perhaps we could surprise her at the hospital and take her out to lunch. She doesn't have a boyfriend now, does she?" Eric asked with a trace of anxiety.

Jeff laughed. "No, no. Don't worry about that. She has plenty of fellows asking her out and lots of friends who are boys, but no boyfriend. So you just may strike it lucky. But it's hard to say. She's a tough little cookie and has a mind of her own."

"Right. I figured that." Eric sucked in his breath and exhaled loudly. "Well, nothin' ventured, nothin' gained. So how about stopping by Barts on our way to lunch?"

They took the underground over to St. Paul's and walked the few blocks to St. Bartholomew's. Founded in the twelfth century, the hospital could have been on their list of tourist sites with its imposing Great Hall and the North Wing's impressive staircase flanked by William Hogarth's enormous paintings, *Christ at the Pool of Bethesda* and *The Good Samaritan*. But they entered in a back gate of the gigantic complex, and asking directions, found their way to the School of Nursing.

Eric hid the bouquet behind his back as they entered the building and made inquiries. They were advised that if they would take a seat and wait for ten minutes, the nursing students would be coming out for their lunch break. Jeff complied, easing himself down on a bench, but Eric paced restlessly back and forth like an expectant father in a waiting room. At last the doors flew open and a crowd of talkative young ladies streamed by wearing blue-and-white pinstriped uniforms with blue aprons and starched caps. With identical uniforms and their hair all neatly pinned up into buns, how would he distinguish her from the others? Then he spotted the petite one with hair the color of honey and warm brown eyes that were smiling—at him.

"Eric MacKenzie!" Annie called, her face flushed with pleasure. "Whatever are you doing here?"

He thrust the bouquet into her hand. "These are for you. And I thought perhaps ye might like to join me and Jeff for lunch."

"How lovely!" she said, admiring the delicate white-and-pink flowers. Her eyes met his and she smiled. "Thank you, Eric. I would be happy to join you for lunch."

"Listen, Annie," he said quietly, "I know this is presumptuous of me, but I have no idea when I'll be back to London again and I'd like very much to spend as much time as possible with ye. I wanted to ask if I may continue to see ye—often—the next few days while I'm here."

Her smile broadened. "I'd like that."

"Good." He sighed, relieved. "Well then, may I ask if ye'd like to go with me to a Christmas dance for the RAF at the Dorchester on Saturday night?"

Annie laughed and Eric, hearing a faint echo of Laurene's melodic laugh, felt his heart ache. "You aren't wasting any time, are you, Eric? I'd be happy to go with you to the dance," she replied as she caught sight of her brother. "Oh, there's Jeff! Could he come along too?"

"Aye, of course. And I'm sure the lads would be ever so glad if ye'd bring yer lovely flatmates as well."

"Sure. They'd like that."

Jeff had sauntered over to join them. "Hey, kiddo. How's it going?"

"Great! Aren't these beautiful?" Annie asked, holding the bouquet up for his approval. "I hear you're taking me to lunch. And Eric has just invited us to an RAF dance at the Dorchester Saturday night."

"Hot dog! May we bring Peggy?"

"Aye," Eric answered. "And the other girls as well. Look, I have a little surprise for ye too. I was able to acquire those tickets to *Peter Pan*."

"Are you kidding me?"

"No, but they're for tonight. Can ye make it?"

Jeff beamed. "You bet we can!"

"Then it's a date. I'll come round yer flat around half past six and we can take the underground together to the theater."

Annie glanced at her watch.

"Would that be all right?" Eric asked.

She thought a moment and then said, "Yes. I was just trying to figure out if I should meet you there or go home first. I have rounds to make here at the hospital, but I should be able to finish by four. That should give me time to get home and change. Yes, six thirty should be fine. What fun! Flowers, lunch, and *Peter Pan* all in one day. This feels like Christmas already. So where do you want to go for lunch?"

"Sorry, we don't know the area," Eric said. "Where would ye suggest? My treat."

"I know a little Italian place on Falcon Square. Would that do? It's only a few blocks away."

"Sounds perfect."

They walked briskly, saving their conversation for the restaurant, where they could be sheltered from the sharp winter winds. The trio enjoyed a hot lunch and a lively discussion before escorting Annie back to the hospital with high expectations for an evening at the theater.

After completing her rounds and attending to her patients, Annie raced home, bathed, and dressed carefully, choosing a royal blue rayon dress with a cinched waist and a narrow skirt which fell straight to a pleated flounce at mid-calf. As a professor's daughter on a tight budget, Annie had learned how to design and sew her own clothes and she was particularly proud of her stylish pleats. She wore her hair down and tightly curled with a pert little beret adorned by a single feather perched jauntily on the side of her head. Jeff looked smart in a three-piece suit, but he could barely contain his envy of Eric's uniform. The threesome chatted and laughed as they rode the Central line, transferring at Oxford Circus to Piccadilly. As they walked through crowded Piccadilly Circus to Haymarket, they couldn't help noticing how strange it was that the statue of Eros was gone, packed away for safekeeping, his pedestal covered up by boards. But for that, the war seemed rather surreal and distant to them as they enjoyed an evening out in the West End.

When they had settled in their seats in the Theatre Royal, Jeff leafed through the program, past the requisite instructions about air raid warnings, to read the cast list.

"Golly Ned!" he cried with excitement. "Look at this! Noodler, one of the pirates is played by Roger Lancelyn Green. He's a classmate of mine at Oxford! He studies with Lewis too and has worked on the fairy stories of Andrew Lang with Professor Tolkien. Isn't this a hoot? I knew he was in OUDS—the Oxford University Dramatic Society," he explained for Annie's benefit, knowing how she detested acronyms. "But I had no idea he had landed this job for the holidays. The lucky duck— for an English scholar to get the insider's view of Never Land! A pirate too! Did you know that Daphne du Maurier's father, Gerald, was an actor who played Hook during Sir James Barrie's day? She's written about her memories of attending the play as a little girl and her impressions of Barrie."

"I didn't know that," Annie said. "You're talking about the author of *Rebecca*, right?"

"Yeah, and *Jamaica Inn*, *The King's General*, *Mary Anne*, and others. Her father's sister Sylvia was the mother of the Davies boys, the 'lost boys' whom Barrie adopted when their parents died."

"So that would make Michael—the model for the statue of Peter Pan in Kensington Gardens—the cousin of Daphne du Maurier," Eric observed.

"Right!"

"Boy, Jeff," Annie teased, "you're a fountain of literary information."

"But he's forgotten the most important fact about Sir James Barrie," Eric said.

"And what would that be?" asked Jeff.

"He was a Scot," Eric said, grinning triumphantly.

Jeff laughed. "So he was, so he was."

"Maybe you should write a book about Barrie, Jeff," Annie mused, "since you're so fascinated by him."

"I'd like to, but I think Roger may be planning to. He's a real literary scholar. And now he's playing a pirate! The only thing that would beat that would be to play a 'lost boy' so you could actually fly."

"I've always wanted to fly," Annie said wistfully.

"Me too," Eric interjected, "That's why I joined the RAF."

"No, I don't mean fly airplanes," said Annie. "I'd be too chicken for that. I mean just fly—without a machine—like Peter Pan and Wendy. I used to daydream about sprinkling some fairy dust on myself and just taking off, especially if I wanted to get away from somebody. Remember, Jeff, how we used to jump from bed to bed trying to fly when we were little?"

"You mean last year?" Jeff joshed.

"Ha-ha. Maybe you've never grown up, but I'm much too dignified to jump on beds now."

They ceased their banter as the houselights dimmed and the curtain rose to the set of the Darlings' nursery. Soon they were carried off to Never Land and were able to escape for a time into a magical world without war and the threat of air raids and bombs. When the pirates appeared, Jeff eagerly searched their faces with his opera glasses until he spied his friend Roger Green. He passed the binoculars over to Annie and whispered, "There he is. The tall one with the blue coat and the black beard."

After spotting her brother's friend, Annie dutifully gave the glasses to Eric, repeating the identification. Their fingers brushed as the binoculars exchanged hands. Eric took a look through them and passed them back, but his hand caught Annie's and held it. At his touch, Annie felt as if a storm of flurries swirled around her heart. She returned the binoculars to Jeff with her right hand but kept her left in Eric's strong but gentle grip, releasing it only when applause required it.

At the interval, Eric once again anticipated her desire for refreshments and treated her with thoughtful deference. When the lights dimmed for the play to resume, she quietly slipped her hand into his. But her emotions were anything but quiet.

Can I be falling for this guy? How can I? I shouldn't. He's going off to fight a war and I may never see him again. I doubt he's falling for me. He must just be lonely and wants a little feminine attention and comfort. Never fall for a guy during a war,

Annie. Don't be a little fool. Wartime romances can't last. Can they? And besides, we're just holding hands...

Her hand stayed in his throughout the second act of the play until the curtain call. Jeff whistled loudly through his fingers when the pirates took their bows.

"Let's go back to the stage door and see if Roger comes out," he said as they gathered their coats to leave.

When they stepped out into the dark night, a voice called out, "Watch your step. Two steps down, madame. Then you'll turn right." They carefully followed the usher's directions. Since the blackout, there had been far too many accidents with people blindly bumping into signs and lampposts, which was why the painted white stripes had proved helpful. The young people switched on their flashlights and made their way to the stage door, waiting as the actors emerged—sans makeup and costumes. At length, a modestly clad, bespectacled young man, bearing little resemblance to a pirate but a great deal to that of a university undergraduate, appeared in the doorway.

"Green!" exclaimed Jeff.

The actor blinked for a moment in puzzlement, so out of context was this encounter with a fellow student. Then comprehension dawned. "Little! What are you doing here?"

"Came to see you, old boy. No, honestly, I about died from shock seeing your name in the program. You didn't tell me you were going to be a star."

"I'm hardly that," Roger Green said humbly. "The real actor got called up to duty, so I stepped into the part. I'm afraid I'm exempt from service. So here I am. What a lark, right?"

"Green, I'd like you to meet my sister Annie, and this is Eric MacKenzie. Annie and Eric, this is Roger Lancelyn Green, otherwise known as 'Noodler, the pirate.'" They exchanged greetings and handshakes. "Can we buy you a drink, old boy?" Jeff asked.

"Absolutely," said Roger. "I know a place around the corner." He led the way, chatting with Jeff, while Eric and Annie followed.

"How did you like the show?" Roger asked when they had settled in a booth in a cozy pub nearby.

"Wonderful! Fantastic! Great fun!" they all chorused in agreement.

"I guess that means you liked it."

"So tell me," Jeff spoke up. "How do you like being in *Peter Pan*? I mean, it must be so neat to be in such a famous play and bring a little joy into these dark times. Not to mention all the literary connections with it."

"Right, it is. And I've become obsessed with learning more about Sir James Barrie."

Annie sighed. "You and Jeff both. I feel like we're on a Barrie pilgrimage—his house is near my flat in Bayswater, we paid homage to the Peter Pan statue in Kensington, and now this. I think Jeff should write a biography of Barrie."

"That's what I want to do," Roger said earnestly. "I've also thought about documenting all the performances of *Peter Pan*."

"Okay, when we get our degrees and this war is over, I'll help you," Jeff said.

"Agreed." Roger smiled and Annie knew she genuinely liked this gentle friend of her brother. Roger turned to Eric. "So you're in the service."

"Aye. I've just finished my RAF trainin' and am goin' to join my squadron on Boxin' Day. By the way," Eric added, "the show was really splendid. I was recently in a production of

Romeo and Juliet up in St. Andrews, so I have a bit of an idea what goes into a show like this. Well done."

"Thank you very much. What part did you play?"

"Romeo."

"Romeo! That's impressive," Jeff chimed in, exchanging an approving look with Annie. "You are full of surprises, Eric."

"And how did a Scot like you meet up with these two Yanks?" Roger asked.

Eric explained the story while Jeff added some commentary. "So," Jeff concluded, "I owe it to my pretty baby sister that I met this guy who had a friend who had tickets to *Peter Pan.* All so I could see *my* friend play a pirate."

"God works in mysterious ways, doesn't he?" Roger mused.

"Aye," Eric answered, gazing at Annie. "He does, indeed."

13

Christmas 1939
London

On the following evening, the Saturday before Christmas, Annie, her girlfriends, Jeff, Eric, and two other pilots met for the servicemen's Christmas ball at the Dorchester Hotel in Mayfair across from Hyde Park. The Dorchester, a white stone high-rise less than a decade old, had been heralded as a triumph of the modern yet chic art deco style, although its grandeur had been somewhat diminished by taped windows and stacked sandbags. Inside, however, the ballroom literally sparkled with its paneled walls of black Spanish glass. Blue-lighted domes crowned the sixteen-foot ceilings, and blue and pink mirrors reflected the handsomely dressed dancers.

Annie looked dazzling in a sleeveless V-necked gown of rich wine-colored silk-crepe that cinched her narrow waist before falling in a straight column to flare in a swirl at her feet. No one had any inkling that she had made the elegant dress herself. Certainly Eric had only admiration for her as he carefully pinned a gardenia corsage to her shoulder and offered her his arm to escort her into the ballroom.

Jeff felt slightly out of place in his white dinner jacket among the smart dress uniforms of the officers, but he held his own on the dance floor. Since Jeff had mastered the Lambeth Walk and the jitterbug, he was in great demand as a partner—although he favored Annie's roommate Peggy. Annie also enjoyed taking a few turns with him, especially when the big band struck up "In the Mood," as they had often practiced together in the basement of their parents' home.

But it was in Eric's arms, waltzing or dancing the fox-trot, that she found herself most happily engaged for the majority of the evening. She felt quite small cradled against his chest and yet completely secure as he led her confidently about the dance floor. She delighted in dancing with him, being held so close and swaying in sync to the popular tunes of Tommy Dorsey and Glenn Miller.

After a long set of dances, he reluctantly parted from her and asked, "Are ye thirsty?"

She nodded and he tucked her hand in his arm and escorted her out to the Promenade, an airy indoor gallery of golden marble pillars lit by hanging glass lanterns. Punch and refreshments had been tastefully set out on long tables for the servicemen and their guests.

"Annie, may I ask ye a personal question?" Eric queried as he handed her a tumbler of punch.

"Of course."

"Jeff says ye aren't attached, but I want to hear it directly from you. Are ye seein' anyone in particular? Do ye have a boyfriend?"

Their eyes met. "No, I don't," she said slowly.

"Well, I'm quite glad to hear it, but I must say I find it difficult to believe a bonny lass like ye hasn't been claimed yet."

She laughed. "Well, I'm not all that old. I'm only nineteen. I've met lots of young men over here, but I haven't been drawn to anyone in particular and I haven't wanted to be claimed— yet. And what about you? Surely a handsome RAF pilot has someone special. Don't you have a girlfriend back home?"

"No." His mouth set in the grim line she had noticed the first night at the Royal Albert Hall. She knew there had to be deep waters there, yet she hesitated to pry. Seeing the unasked question in her eyes, he inwardly debated how much to divulge but decided to skirt the subject. "Are ye enjoyin' the dance?"

She played along. "Yes, very much. It's a great band, don't you think? I love the saxophone."

"It's fantastic," Eric agreed. "Say, I'm sorry I'm not much of a jitterbug. It hasn't quite caught on back in Scotland yet, so I haven't had a chance to learn. I hope ye don't mind. Ye and Jeff are certainly good."

"Jeff can make anyone look good. But it's not hard. It just takes some practice. Maybe sometime we can show you how."

"I'd like that." He hesitated, and then he finally blurted out, "Ye know, Annie, I wasn't completely honest with ye a moment ago. The truth is… there was someone special back home. We had planned to marry, but when it looked like war was inevitable, her father booked her on the *Athenia*."

Annie gasped in realization. "Oh, no! Was she…lost?"

He nodded.

"Oh, my gosh. Eric, I am so sorry!" Suddenly she felt her legs weaken.

Eric caught her and held her firmly. "Are ye all right? Do ye want to sit down?"

"I'm all right, thanks. It's just that…I was supposed to be on that ship! I had a berth reserved and decided at the last minute not to go. I'm so sorry," she repeated helplessly.

"Don't be sorry ye weren't on that ship," Eric said fiercely.

"No, no, I'm sorry about your fiancée. That's horrible."

"That's why I joined the RAF. I want to kill as many of those bloody Nazis as I possibly can."

"I can't blame you for that," Annie said. "I think you must be very brave."

"I'm not brave. I'm just mad as blazes. So there it is. Now you know my sad story." He relaxed his hold on her. "I'm sorry if I've upset you, Annie."

"Oh, Eric, don't be sorry," she replied with earnestness. "Thank you for telling me. It must be so hard for you even to talk about it."

He sighed heavily. "Aye. 'Tis." Composing himself, he finally mustered a smile. "Well now, would ye care to fox-trot some more with me?"

"Are you sure? We don't need to dance anymore if you'd rather not."

"I'm sure."

She managed to return his smile. "Okay. I'd like that."

Arm in arm, they ambled back into the ballroom and danced slowly to the poignantly romantic tunes of "Deep Purple," "Stairway to the Stars," "Blue Orchids," and "My Reverie." Annie moved dreamlike, not wanting the evening to end. When the band struck up its quiet rendition of "Heart and Soul," she silently sang the words in her head:

Heart and soul, I fell in love with you
Heart and soul, The way a fool would do

Madly
Because you held me tight...

In truth, since she had met Eric MacKenzie at the *Messiah* concert, Annie's head had been filled with little other than thoughts of the handsome Scottish officer. She found his accent and gentle sense of humor utterly charming. He treated her with such polite courtesy—even gallantry—that she felt rather like a princess with him. The only caution she had sensed was his reluctance to discuss his faith—odd for a man who had studied theology—and the grim sadness she could see from time to time reflected in his eyes and the set of his mouth. But now that had been explained. He had loved and lost, and she felt tremendous compassion for him. By the time they had strolled home through Hyde Park, she had become convinced that not only had she met someone in particular, but she was also ready to be claimed.

❧

Annie was rather disappointed when Eric declined to join them for Sunday services the next morning at All Souls Church, which Jeff had been so eager to attend. Grateful not to spend the holidays alone and enamored with his new American friends, Eric did accept their invitation to spend much of the rest of Christmas Eve with them. The occupants of their flat had dwindled to just the two of them since Annie's girlfriends, along with many of the nation's refugees, had returned to their homes for the holidays. In the afternoon, after decorating a scrawny excuse for a tree, the trio rolled back the carpet in the parlor and, with much hilarity, taught Eric how to jitterbug. Then after some gentle persuasion, he agreed to accompany them to the Christmas Eve Evensong service at St. Paul's Cathedral.

The expatriates tried to make Christmas Day as cheerful as possible, but somehow it all seemed slightly out of kilter. Annie prepared a turkey dinner as their last feast before rationing took effect in the New Year. Eric surprised them with gifts he had picked up in the flea market on Portebello Road: a nicely bound illustrated copy of *Peter Pan* for Jeff and a pair of kid gloves for Annie. She in turn surprised him with a warm woolen scarf she had made from a yard of MacKenzie dress tartan she had found in the Edinburgh Woolen Outlet on Oxford Street.

Eric, sensing the Little siblings were as homesick as he, tried to draw them into talking about their family and Christmas traditions. "So," he asked, "with ye two over here, are yer parents alone for the holidays?"

"Nope," answered Jeff, "we have two older sisters, Margie and Alice, who are married but still live in Charlottesville, so they'll be having a big Christmas dinner together."

"And don't forget our niece, Susie," added Annie. "Alice has an adorable two-year-old daughter," she explained to Eric.

"I'll warrant ye miss her," he said with a smile.

"You bet I do. I love babies, and Christmas is so much more fun with kids."

"Does yer family have any special traditions?"

"Well," replied Jeff, "One of my favorite things is laying out the Christmas garden and a train set under the tree every year. I wonder if my dad will bother with it this year…"

"Jeff has the trains," Annie said, "but we girls had dolls. We have a lovely collection of dolls and every year when we were little we would set them all out by the hearth and on Christmas morning when we ran downstairs, we would find that Santa had dressed them all in new finery. Actually, my mother sewed the new outfits for them all, but we didn't know it at the time." She sighed. "It was quite magical. And what of you? What traditions do you most enjoy?"

Eric thought for a minute trying to blot out any recollection of his years at St. Andrews by reaching back to his childhood in Gairloch. "Och, I always especially liked to go carolin'. Even the poorest people would give pennies to us and some would offer us hot chocolate and biscuits."

"People give you money when you carol?" Jeff asked.

"Aye. Don't they in America?"

"Nope. But sometimes we do get offered cookies."

"Speaking of which," Annie said, "let me get the dessert." When she returned with tea and home-baked cookies, Eric posed another question.

"Tell me about yer home. What's Virginia like?"

"Well, we live in Charlottesville, which is a small university town in the Blue Ridge mountains," Jeff answered. "It's surrounded by rolling wooded hills and beautiful green countryside—maybe a little like the lowlands of Scotland."

"It really is pretty," Annie affirmed. "And since our dad holds the department chair at the University of Virginia, we now live on the Lawn."

"Ye live on a lawn?" Eric couldn't follow this.

"What she means is, we live in one of the original houses built for the professors in what Thomas Jefferson designed and called an 'academical' village. It's a bit like a college quad at Oxford but looks more like Georgian-styled brick build-ings joined by an arcade of student rooms—if you can picture that—all opening onto a grassy quad which we call the Lawn and centered around the Rotunda, which housed the library in Mr. Jefferson's day."

"Oh, right, I've seen pictures of Jefferson's Rotunda. And that's where ye live?"

"Yep."

"It's beautiful in every season," Annie said wistfully, "but especially in the fall when the leaves turn. Then again, it really is pretty in the winter too when it snows."

Eric thoughtfully regarded her. "Say, Annie, there isn't any snow in London, but how would ye fancy goin' ice skatin'?"

"Oh, I love to skate," she answered with enthusiasm. "But where?"

"I've passed a rink at Lancaster Gate."

"You're right!" She acknowledged enthusiastically. "There is one there. Oh, let's do go, Jeff!"

"I'm game," he said affably.

Equipping themselves with coats, hats, and their new scarf and gloves, they headed out into the cold night. After lacing up their rented skates, Eric offered Annie his arm and they glided out onto the ice. They skated in silence for a while and watched with amusement the antics of Jeff and others slip-ping about or playing games. When a boy zoomed past them, causing Annie to lose her balance, Eric caught and steadied her.

"Are ye all right?"

She laughed. "Yes, I'm fine."

"Annie," he said without releasing her. "Ye know I report for duty tomorrow. I wanted to thank ye for the kindness and hospitality ye've shown me and for includin' me in yer Christmas celebration. I've had a wonderful time here in London. Meetin' ye has been the best thing that has happened to me in a long while. I wondered if it would be all right for me to write to ye while I'm gone."

"I'd like that," she answered with complete sincerity.

"That's splendid!" he said, and his warm smile swept away the sadness of the moment. "And will ye try to write back to me sometimes?"

"Of course. I'll write to you often."

"There's one more thing." He paused for a moment and then plunged ahead. "May I kiss you? I know I may be rushin' things a bit, but I don't know when I'll see ye again and…"

"Hush," she interrupted gently and lifted her face with expectation. He brushed her lips with his and then she yielded her mouth eagerly. It was not a first kiss for either of them, but it was perhaps the most ardent. Eric felt a rush of desire he could barely master. Then suddenly, their feet slipped out from under them and they tumbled in a heap on the ice.

"Oh, my dear! Are ye all right? I am so sorry!" Eric cried apologetically as he scrambled to his feet and helped Annie to her own.

But she burst into infectious laughter which he caught. "I'm fine," she said as she wiped a tear of merriment from her eye. "I guess now you could say we've truly fallen for each other."

14

January 1940
London

Heart and soul, I begged to be adored
Lost control, and tumbled overboard
Gladly
That magic night we kissed
There in the moon mist...

Annie often sang this song softly to herself as she sat in her nursing classes and went about her rounds at the hospital. After the holidays she resumed an intense routine of study and work, her courses having been accelerated so that her class could take their certification examinations early. The government had urged the hospital to train the doctors and nurses as quickly as possible in preparation for the anticipated Nazi attacks and battle for Britain. She didn't mind the overtime and extra training as they kept her busy and her thoughts from dwelling on Eric MacKenzie and what dangers he might be confronting. Yet, when she returned to her flat, she sorted anxiously through the mail hoping for a letter. She was grateful to hear from her parents and sisters back home as well as to receive breezy updates from Jeff at Oxford, but it was the small photocopied and censored letters from RAF Pilot Officer Eric MacKenzie that she secreted to the privacy of her bedroom and read again and again before crafting her own replies to be posted the following morning.

1 January 1940

Dear Annie,

  Happy New Year! I wanted to thank you again for your hospitality while I was in London and for letting me spend the Christmas holidays with you and Jeff. I had a wonderful time. I'm sorry not to have written to you sooner, but this is the first bit of free time I've had since I arrived here. They've been training us hard, but we get a little holiday today. The base sponsored a dance last night and invited in the local girls, yet all I could think of was how I wished you had been here. Then maybe I could have impressed everyone with my jitterbugging ability! Would you mind terribly sending me your picture? It would considerably brighten this dismal brown hut that is my new home. It's freezing here, but I have your lovely scarf to keep me warm and give me happy memories of you. Please write when you get a chance.

Yours truly,
Eric MacKenzie

∽

Thursday, January 4, 1940

Dear Eric,

  How nice to hear from you! Jeff and I really enjoyed meeting and getting to know you. We loved being able to attend Peter Pan *and the RAF dance*

at the Dorchester. Thank you so much for the kid
gloves for Christmas. I hadn't expected to receive a
gift so it was a very much appreciated surprise—
and believe me they've come in handy with this
bitter cold winter. The Londoners say it's the coldest
winter they can ever remember. I've begun sleeping
with a hot water bottle—otherwise my sheets are
like ice. For New Year's we all attended a dance at
the Grosvenor House close by the Dorchester. It was
very swanky but not nearly as much fun without
you there. Jeff and Peggy cut quite the couple. She
has really learned to jitterbug well with him. She's a
great girl, and I think Jeff is growing very sweet on
her. I'll bet she'll get more letters from Oxford than
I will! He returned this week to work at Blackwell's
bookstore until the winter term starts. At Barts
they are pushing us to finish our training and pass
our certification examinations. I'm studying very
hard and have become a recluse—quite a bore. I've
enclosed an old picture of me. Sorry it's not a better
one, but at least I didn't break the camera! Take care
of yourself.

> Fondly,
> Annie

∽

> Sunday, 7 January 1940

Dear Annie,

I was so happy to get your letter yesterday. Now
I have something to look forward to at mail call.
Thank you for the picture. What rubbish about
breaking the camera. You look lovely. Although
I do wish we had thought to take pictures at the

Dorchester. You were stunning in that maroon gown of yours—heavenly. It's dreadfully cold here as well. The bunks farthest from the heater are called Siberia. As one of the newest men in the squadron, I'm often banished to outer Siberia. When we stand around the heater, our front sides are nicely toasted while our rear ends are frozen stiff. When you're flying up at 22,000 to 30,000 feet, believe me, your hands and feet get numb pretty quickly. Sometimes hoarfrost forms on the canopy, and even our breath freezes on the oxygen masks. The worst thing is when the bends set in. As the atmospheric pressure drops, your muscles and joints can swell up and cause the most dreadful ache. I feel like an arthritic old man!

I've heard rumours that they may decide to start censoring our letters if we mention the weather. I don't know why because I'm certain the Nazis know it's cold. They're freezing too. That's the good thing about this cold winter—it's keeping the Jerries quiet. But enough of weather. I'm sure all that studying is quite a bore, but just like my training there'll come a day when we'll be glad for it. Right now I'm learning to fly a new plane. She's a Spitfire and smaller, lighter, and faster than the Hurricane and a very sweet machine to have in a dogfight. I do love flying—there's nothing like it—even if it is colder up there in the clouds.

The lads in my squadron are all capital, but may I say that I think of you often and very fondly?

Yours,
Eric

∼

Wed., January 10, 1940

Dear Eric,

Checking the mail is much more fun for me now as well. I do enjoy hearing from you. And yes, you may say that you think of me often—as I do of you. In fact, I find that my thoughts are often of our brief time together. What fun we had! I am missing all that—and you. Things here in London are rather boring. We've begun rationing. Each of us has been issued a book of coupons. I get hungry just thinking about the restrictions: eggs, bacon, butter, coffee, cheese, sugar—even marmalade! What I wouldn't give for a big fat Virginia ham just now. Maybe my mom will send us one! At least we get a block of chocolate, and they haven't rationed sausage yet. Still, the girls and I are going to take as many meals as we can at Barts. Are they feeding you okay? I hope you are doing well. Please take care of yourself in that little Spitfire. We're all so proud of what you men are doing and are keeping you in our thoughts and prayers.

Fondly,
Annie

⌒

Sunday, 14 January 1940

Dear Annie,

I think I shall make Sunday my official day to write to you. It's frankly the only day I have much free time—although we still take shifts for patrol. Many of the lads go to church in the morning and write letters in the afternoon. Then they'll hit the

*pubs once they open. Speaking of pubs, here's a
funny story for you. I've been flying nighttime
patrols to check on the effectiveness of the blackout.
For the most part, people have been very good about
sticking to it and all is dark. But invariably at 10:30
pm we'll see a burst of twinkling lights everywhere
below. It's the thousands of pubs opening their
doors to send their patrons home at closing time.
We get such a laugh from that! I daresay there'll
be a lot of disgruntled Brits if our beer is rationed.
That would be a true hardship! I'm always happy
to get a patrol over London because I know you are
down there studying or sleeping. I feel closer to you,
and it's almost like I'm keeping watch over you. I
hope you don't think I'm crazy for saying all this,
but I'm beginning to believe that old adage that
"absence makes the heart grow fonder." I think of
you often and wish I could be with you. When I get
some leave, may I come up to see you? Thank you
for writing back to me. Your letters mean more than
you can know.*

Truly yours,
Eric

*PS. By the way, would you please tell me your full
Christian name?*

∼

Wed., January 17, 1940

Dear Eric,

*I like the thought that you could be flying over
London and keeping watch over me. I'll think of
that from now on when the planes fly over and keep*

*a lookout for you! We've got these giant silver bar-
rage balloons tethered all over London now to keep
the Germans from flying in too low. They remind
me of pictures I've seen of the big balloons they use
in the Macy's Thanksgiving Day parade in New
York City. Do you know the ones I mean? I'll bet
from the air the balloons look like London's having
a big birthday bash. Anyway, the children love them
and it makes the rest of us feel safer. I just wanted to
let you know that I'm thinking often of you too. I'll
need to keep this brief because I should be studying
for the certification exams. God willing, I'll be a
full-fledged nurse by the end of the month! Please
say a little prayer for me—that I can retain all this
information and pass with "flying" colors. I am
praying for you as well. And yes, I would love to see
you again whenever you are able. Please stay safe
and take care.*

Very fondly,
Annie

*PS. My Christian name is just plain "Annie." Maybe
after two other daughters my parents ran out of
inspiration. They said I was too little to have a big
name, and I am often called "Little Annie."*

～

Sat., Jan. 20

Dear Annie,

*How are you, kid? It's freezing here in Oxford!
How about in London? "Carry Me Back to Ole Vir-
ginny" is my new theme song. It could get cold back
home, but nothing like this—this is bone-chilling!*

Up near the University Parks, the river has completely frozen over and people are going skating, so that's fun. But it's so cold at night it's hard to sleep. I've had to wear a jumper—sorry—sweater over my pj's and I'm using a hot water bottle to keep my tootsies warm. Mr. Lewis told me that one night he slept with two sweaters and a pair of pants over his pajamas, plus an enormous pile of blankets. For tutorials, he'll wear a dressing gown (bathrobe) over his trousers and jacket! His rooms in the New Building are freezing, but the man's heart is not. He really loves God and is a sincere Christian, which is sadly unusual among the dreaming spires. I'm really enjoying my tutorials with him as well as our little theological discussion group, which now meets on Friday afternoons. And Roger shows up often too, which makes it even better. The study group is a part of the SCM—sorry, I know how you hate acronyms, dear Annie—that's the Student Christian Movement.

By the way, if you ever need to evacuate London, I want you to contact Mr. Lewis at the Kilns in Headington. He has some refugee children staying with him now, and I'm sure he'd welcome you too if you need a place to stay. And don't worry, there are women in the household. He has a rather odd arrangement with a sort of adopted mother named Mrs. Moore and her grown daughter, Maureen. There's a long history there but a lovely story of a pact made with Mrs. Moore's son in the last war. He and Lewis agreed that if one of them died the other would take care of his family. So since the son did die, and quite bravely as the story goes, Lewis has been looking out for the Moore women ever since. Anyway, I'll speak to him about you and let you know what he says. But in the meantime, please don't hesitate to get out of town if things get too hot. I should sign off now and get my paper written for the old boy. How are your studies going? I'll pray for you as you face those dreadful exams. Give my best to Peggy, okay? And take care of yourself. When can you come for a visit? I miss you.

Lots of love,
Jeff

PS. Have you heard anything from the "Flying Scotsman"? If you write to him, say "hi" for me.

PPS. I've joined the Oxford University Air Squadron, a sort of student RAF—sorry—Royal Air Force. So maybe one day I'll be the "Flying Yank"!

∽

Sunday, 21 January 1940

Dear Annie,

Please don't feel like you need to answer this. I know you are busy studying and must be feeling swamped. I just wanted you to know that I was thinking about you and hope you are doing all right. Things here are fine except for this bitter winter. "O Wind if Winter comes, can Spring be far behind?" Trouble is, I'm sure in the spring Hitler will get serious about the war and we'll be in for it then. We're eating fine, and if you need anything, let me know as I may be able to commandeer it somewhere. We're sent out a lot now on patrol to protect the convoys and help keep the shipping lanes open. So hopefully the ships will get through and none of *us will starve this winter—although we may freeze first, anyway!*

What do you hear from that jitterbugging brother of yours up in Oxford? I'm hoping to get at least an evening of leave the end of this month so that I can come up to London and help you celebrate passing your exams. Thinking of you often—

Yours,

Eric

Wed., January 24

Dear Jeff,

Just a quick note to say I'm studying like mad for my exams, which I take next week. Please do say a prayer for me. There is so much to learn. I'm not much of a scholar but I know I'll make a good nurse. I have heard from Eric, and he may come to see me when he gets some leave. I'm a little put out by you joining up with this air squadron without any warning. I hope you don't have any grandiose ideas about fighting in this war! The Royal Air Force uniforms are swell but the chance to wear one is not a good reason to go off and get yourself killed! Peggy is doing fine—working hard at the hospital and helping me study for the exams. Come for a visit after they're done. I miss you too.

Bunches of love,

Annie

Wed., January 24

Dear Eric,

It's always so good to hear from you. Thank you
for writing and for thinking of me. I'm sorry not to
write more, but I have so much to memorize for the
exams next week. Please pray for me! And I'd love
to celebrate with you. Just let me know the day you
get leave and I'll be ready. Jeff is doing well, but he
signed up for the Oxford University Air Squad—
some sort of RAF training for the university students.
So I guess he's trying to follow your example. It all
seems very nerve-racking to me. Then I would have
two young men to worry about. I'll try to write
more next week. Meanwhile, take care.

Very fondly,
Annie

Sunday, 28 January 1940

Dear Annie,

I wouldn't count on my prayers being much
help. So far they haven't proven very effective. But
I am thinking of you and hope your exams go well
this week. I'm sure they will. You are such a bright,
capable young woman, and Barts should consider
themselves fortunate to have you in their program.
If I'm ever wounded, please come and take care
of me. The lucky men that will have you for their
nurse! It makes me jealous to even think about it.
But frankly, the lads who are shot down and survive
have a tough go of it—many are burned terribly. If I
ever were hurt, I hope I'll be like Douglas Bader. He

lost both his legs in a crash before the war, and he's back flying after being outfitted with metal legs. He's a true hero and inspiration to us all. But don't you worry about that for me. Mind you, I fully intend to keep both my legs—especially so that I can see you next weekend. I will be able to come up to London on Friday and wondered if you would like to go out to dinner and to the cinema with me. I don't know what's playing, but I'm sure we can find something over at Leicester Square. Thinking of you often—

Yours,
Eric

∼

Wed., Jan. 31

Dear Eric,

I hope you get this in time. Yes, do come on Friday. It will be a wonderful way to celebrate having the finals behind me—and hopefully I'll find out by then that I've passed! I'll be waiting for you at my flat. Safe travels.

Very fondly,
Annie

15

February 2, 1940
London

ello there!" Eric said, handing a bouquet of white roses to Annie. "These are for you—to celebrate the passin' of yer exams and exchangin' yer blue pinafore for a white one."

Annie's face flushed with delight as she took the bouquet. "Thank you, Eric! They're beautiful."

"As are you. It's so good to see ye, Annie."

She laughed lightly. "And you, Eric. Come on in while I put these in some water." He stepped into the apartment but did not remove his coat. As she bustled about the kitchen finding a vase for the flowers, he curiously perused the family photos and books lying about. Eric thought one could always tell a good deal about a person from the books they kept on their shelves, but then again he couldn't know if he was sleuthing Annie's books or one of the other girls'.

"There!" she said with evident satisfaction as she placed the arrangement in the center of the kitchen table. "Oh, they're so pretty, Eric. You really shouldn't have."

"Why not? It pleases me to please you."

"Well, I am pleased. I love flowers. One day I'd like to have a big English cottage garden."

"How about a Scottish one?"

She blushed and covered her confusion by retrieving her coat. "I didn't know there was a difference."

"Sorry, I was just joshin' ye. I really don't know if there is. So did ye decide what movie ye'd like to see tonight?"

"What about *The Wizard of Oz*? Have you seen that yet?"

"Nay, but it sounds like fun. Is it playin' at Leicester Square?"

"Yes."

"All right, then," Eric said as he helped her with her coat. "How do ye fancy havin' dinner in Chinatown and then catchin' the late show of *The Wizard of Oz*?"

"I fancy it just fine," she answered with a smile.

After taking the underground to Leicester Square, they purchased the tickets in advance and found a quiet Chinese restaurant where they chatted and laughed throughout dinner. Arm in arm, they strolled back through Chinatown to the cinema. Once they had settled in their seats in the darkened theatre, Eric took Annie's hand in his. She squeezed it tightly when the newsreels flashed up about the valiant men of the RAF escorting convoys and protecting the British Expeditionary Force in France. Then the feature began and they escaped to "somewhere over the rainbow" in the brilliant Technicolor film that had captivated the imaginations of people on both sides of the pond.

"Well, how did ye like the picture?" Eric asked as they walked back to the underground station.

"I loved it! The music, the bright colors—wasn't Judy Garland wonderful? And I adored the Cowardly Lion. And

Glenda the good witch was so beautiful. And weren't all those Munchkins a riot?"

"Aye. I thought ye might feel at home among all those midgets. I think I shall call ye 'munchkin.'"

"Ah!" Annie's mouth fell open in mock shock and she playfully shoved Eric in protest. "That was totally uncalled for. I'm not that short. You're just—"

"Tall?" he suggested helpfully.

"Yes! Definitely, at least to me. Say, by the way, just how do you fit into those little airplanes with those long legs of yours? I mean, don't they have some sort of height limitation to be a pilot?"

"Well, I think they must be rather desperate for recruits at this point so they passed me. Actually, I was a bit concerned about the height requirements. When they ran us through the physical they had us sit in a chair and they held a bar up where our head needed to be to fit under the canopy. Then I thought I might have a chance because my legs are longer than my torso. But when I got up close I didn't think I would pass. I scrunched down as low as I could in the chair and the sergeant barked, 'Sit up, MacKenzie!' So I squirmed around a bit but still tried to sink down under the bar. He barked again, 'Sit *up*, MacKenzie!' Well, I had to sit up then, and sure enou' my head shot past the bar. I thought it was all over, but wouldn't ye know, the sergeant pressed the bar down on the top o' my head and yelled, 'You pass!' And that was it, even with these long legs of mine." He chuckled. "It is a bit of a disadvantage though, especially when I'm on a long flight or up at those high altitudes where I can get those bends I wrote ye about. Still, I'm grateful I passed. I love flyin'. It's a great adventure. And I'd also hate to be on the ground if the enemy starts bombin' us. I'd much rather be able to hop in an airplane and take my chances fightin' it out in the air rather than bein' trapped on or under the ground somewhere."

"I can understand that. I hate the thought of being cooped up for hours in some shelter or down here in the underground—which some people are talking about using as a shelter. But I'm afraid I can't hop into an airplane if Hitler decides to bomb us."

Eric put his arm around Annie and drew her close to his side as they stood together on the train. "I'm sorry I didn't think of that. Listen, Annie, if they do start bombin', will ye please evacuate London? Couldn't ye go up to Oxford with Jeff?"

"That's what he said for me to do. He wrote and told me to contact one of his professors who has a house outside Oxford where he's already taken in some refugees. But, Eric, I'm here to be a nurse. I made the decision to stay over here so that I could complete my degree and be of some service. I don't want to run away from danger when I could be helping people. I might as well have gone home in September."

"No!" he said vehemently. "Thank God ye didn't."

"Oh!" She felt stricken to have reminded him of his loss. "I'm sorry I mentioned that."

"It's all right. There's no gettin' round the reminders. At least there aren't as many here in London."

"Would you like to talk about it?"

"Nay. Not now, anyway. We're supposed to be celebratin', remember?" His smile was grim.

"Yes." Annie took his arm as they stepped off the train and found their way above ground into the black night. Eric switched on his flashlight and they carefully and quietly wended their way back to her flat.

"Would you like to come in?" she asked as they reached her door.

He hesitated. "I'd love to, but it's late and I wouldn't want to disturb yer flatmates."

"It's okay. They're probably all in bed asleep. We won't bother them if we keep our voices down. Oh, my—when do you have to be back to the base?"

"Actually, my train doesn't leave London until tomorrow mornin' at six."

"Where are you staying? At Leinster Square again?"

"Nay. I didn't think it would be worth it for such a short stay. I'm just goin' to walk to Victoria or if I get tired, I'll take a taxi the rest of the way and then curl up on a bench at the station. Shouldn't be too cold in there."

"Well then, I insist that you come in and have some tea or hot chocolate. I'm not sending you out into the cold unprovided for. Besides," Annie said, smiling as she unlocked the door, "I'm not ready to have you leave just yet."

"That's fine by me if ye're sure we won't bother yer flatmates."

"No, it'll be fine as long as we're quiet." When they had entered the darkened apartment and shut the door, Annie turned on a light. "Okay," she whispered. "What would you like, tea or hot chocolate?"

"Hot chocolate, please," he answered as he removed his hat and coat. "Where did ye get the cocoa?"

"We hoarded it in anticipation of the rationing," Annie replied, pulling a tin from the cupboard and setting about lighting the stove and placing a pan of milk over the little flame of the burner. She frequently stirred the milk and, in the interval, set out two cups and saucers and a few cookies.

"Thank you," Eric said as he helped himself. "This looks great. Now, please, I want to hear all about you. Tell me more about yer family, yer mother and father and yer sisters. Tell me about yer childhood and schoolin', and what it was like to live on the Lawn at yer university. I want to know everythin' about you."

They talked long into the night and the early hours of dawn, each sharing their stories, their hopes and dreams, their discouragements and failures. Finally, after they had moved to the sofa and were snuggled together, Eric quietly told her of Laurene.

"Oh, Eric," Annie sighed sadly as his voice trailed off. "I am so very, very sorry."

"It still seems unreal to me," he spoke softly. "I'll wake up some mornin's not rememberin', and then it all hits me with this crushin' blow that sends me back to reality. In some ways it all seems part of another life now—even someone else's life—back in a distant time. Then I think of Laurene as the love of my youth and, like my youth, gone forever.

"Ye know, Annie," he said, stroking her hair as she rested her head against his chest. "I seem to have grown through a lifetime of changes in the last few months. I've become a pilot, and I've become a man. It never occurred to me that I would ever love anyone other than Laurene for the rest of my life, but here I am with you. I've been caught totally by surprise and have found that I have fallen absolutely and completely in love with you."

She looked up at him in astonishment.

"That's right," he said, smiling down at her. "I love you, Annie Little."

"Oh," she said weakly. "Oh, Eric, I love you too!"

"My darlin', darlin' girl!" He bent and kissed her, holding her tightly. "I should leave soon," he whispered, releasing her. "But I must also tell ye that I will be gone for a few weeks. A few of us in the squadron have been asked to go to France to relieve some of the pilots there who've been on duty for days on end. I leave on Monday. If ye don't hear from me very often, don't worry. I'm afraid the mail service is unpredictable." He handed her a slip of paper with his contact information.

"Oh, no!" she cried. "Not France!"

"Hush, now." He pulled her closer. "I'll be fine. Plus I'll be flyin' reconnaissance and perhaps seein' some real action, which is why I got into this war in the first place."

"But you're already flying patrols and protecting the convoys. Surely that's enough action."

"Aye, to be sure. But I'd really like to get a look at those Jerries. Now don't worry. There's not much shootin' goin' on yet. We're still fightin' a phoney war, remember?"

"Oh, Eric, I wish you didn't have to leave—and so soon!"

"Me too. But it's almost dawn, so I'd best be goin'." He stood and retrieved his hat and coat.

"When will I be able to see you again?" she asked anxiously.

He drew her into his arms and they embraced tightly. "As soon as I can. I'm hopin' to be back in March. Will ye be here for me?"

"Yes, of course. I'll be waiting and I'll write as often as I can—even if my letters don't get through, you can count on my writing to you. But, Eric," she pleaded, "please don't do anything reckless or terribly brave."

"Don't worry. I've been well trained and I'll be fine. Now, ye take care of yerself, little one, do ye hear me? I can't bear to lose anyone else."

"Oh, Eric!" She buried her face in his wool coat.

"Annie," he said gently, lifting up her chin. "I love you. Always remember that, no matter what happens." He kissed her again and held her in a long embrace. "I'm goin' to miss ye so much," he said hoarsely, nuzzling her hair and trying to imprint its texture and fragrance on his memory. "Goodbye, little one." He gave her one more gentle kiss and then reluctantly walked away.

16

Winter 1940

In Great Britain the winter of 1940 proved to be relatively quiet for the onset of a war, and for the most part the British endured little more than inconvenience with the bitter cold, rationing, and blackouts. Both C.S. Lewis and J.R.R. Tolkien bore the aggravation of water pipes bursting in their homes. In Tolkien's case, his North Oxford house at 20 Northmoor Road proved to be uninhabitable until renovations could be completed, which forced his family to stay in the attic of a hotel for nearly a term. With the frigid weather came inevitable illness, and many suffered influenza and colds. Sickness also plagued Tolkien's household: his wife, Edith, required a stay in the Acland Hospital. Likewise, Warren Lewis was hospitalized with illness while in France, which gave his brother hope that he would be discharged from active service.

In mid-January the Earl and Countess of Essex rejoiced over the birth of their firstborn son and heir Charles Spencer Devereux, only to mourn two days later when he died. Lady Devereux was left alone to grieve on their estate of Clifton Manor while her husband returned to his duties at the Admiralty Office in London. Across the country in the Cotswold village of Castle Combe, a young mother by the name of Elinor Holmes struggled to care for her rambunctious toddler twins, Austen and Dianna, while her husband served in the British Expeditionary Force in France. In the Bayswater neighborhood of London, not far from Annie's apartment, another mother by the name of Molly Goodman, whose husband also served oversees, cared alone for three small children. Families all across Britain had been similarly impacted. Through the disruptions and hardships of separation, letters kept these loved ones connected and heartened those both at home and abroad.

Sunday, February 4, 1940

Dear Eric,

It's only been two days since you left London, but I feel like it's been forever. I miss you so much! I hope you have safely arrived at your new base and all is well. Is it any warmer there? London seems so drab and dreary. It feels almost like you took all the color and excitement with you when you left. Or maybe I'm just thinking of London now in contrast to the bright colors in The Wizard of Oz. I wish we had a wizard who could grant us a wish and you could come back home! Wasn't that a delightful movie? Thank you for taking me out. I had such a wonderful time with you. I always do. I have no news to report—I wish there were something interesting to tell you. Well, one thing—I did pass my exams for certain and am now a certified registered nurse! Now I can join Peggy and the other girls working shifts at the hospital. Peggy and I are also going to talk to the Red Cross to see if they'd like us to work with the air raid wardens. I'm so glad Hitler hasn't bombed us yet. I hope he never does!

*No matter how many times we practice the drills,
I'm sure it's nothing like the reality of a bombing
raid. Now we are pretending to work on someone,
but they too are just pretending to be hurt. I can't
imagine what it will really be like when bombs are
flying and people are screaming and lying bloody on
the sidewalk instead of just quietly playacting like
we've been doing. Peggy says though that the more
we practice, the more naturally we'll respond as
we've been trained to when we're in the thick of it.
That's what you said too. I hope you're both right!
At the end of the day I don't want to be a blithering
coward. But enough of this morbid tangent. I hope
you are doing well. Please know that I think of you
all the time and whether or not you believe in the
efficacy of prayer—I am praying for you.*

*Love,
Annie*

∽

Tues., Feb. 6

Dear Annie,

*I haven't heard from you in a while, sis. I
thought once you were finished with your exams
your letters would flood my pigeonhole. But alas, it
is all too empty. Well, to be honest, Peggy has been
very kind to write me quite a bit, as have Mom and
Dad. But no letters from my kid sister—I'm quite
crushed. I'm assuming you passed your exams and
have been busy with celebrating.*

*Say, how's it going with Flyboy? Did he come
to see you? I wanted to tell you about the lecture I
heard last night. It was given by Charles Williams.*

*Remember the odd-looking fellow I pointed out to
you at the Eastgate when the Inklings were meeting?
Well, if you recall, I think I mentioned what a phe-
nomenal lecturer he is—the guy is truly amazing.
And one of the most amazing things is that he never
had a formal university education. He's self-taught,
but has whole passages of poetry memorized, and
he can spout off without notes these very erudite
literary analyses and criticisms. Remarkable! Since
he's in Oxford now with the University Press, Mr.
Lewis has been arranging some lectures for him.
On Monday nights he (Mr. Williams) is giving a
series on Milton in the Divinity School library of the
Bodleian. Not withstanding the excellent lecture, the
room alone makes it worth attending. Next time you
come for a visit, remind me to take you over there.
It's one of the oldest university structures—built
back in Henry V's time by his brother Duke Humphrey—and is one of the most exquisite rooms I've
ever been in. The stone ceiling is all beautifully
carved fan vaulting…*

*But I digress. Back to the lecture. It was on
Milton, yet seemed almost more of a sermon than a
lecture, because what Williams expounded on was
the virtue of virginity or chastity. And this to a room
full of young men and women—and the curious
thing was that no one laughed or scoffed. They
were completely silent—not a hostile silence, but
a thoughtful one. I for one was very taken with his
argument, and although I haven't had any intention
of willfully seeking to be unchaste, I frankly hadn't
given a great deal of thought to willfully seeking to
be chaste, either. This lecture has had a profound
impact on my thinking, not literarily but spiritually.
I talked about it today with Lewis at our tutorial.*

He made the comment that that beautifully carved room had probably not witnessed such an important lecture since the Reformation. He also said that he was gratified to see at last the university doing what it had been founded to do—that is, to teach wisdom. I wish you could have been there too. I know you would have been impressed. Anyway, I miss you. I'm threatening to come down and surprise you and Peggy one of these days. Write sometime!

Love,
Jeff

～

Wed., February 7, 1940

Dear Eric,

I don't have any news, but I am just writing to say that I miss you terribly. How can it be less than a week since you've been gone? You probably haven't even arrived at your camp or received my last letter. I know I shouldn't expect to hear from you yet, but I can't help hoping that somehow I will. Here's a little shorthand symbol I've learned: X is for kisses and O is for hugs. So I send to you

Lots of love,
Annie

XXXXXXXOOOOOO

～

Thurs., Feb. 8, 1940

Dear Jeff,

I'm sorry not to have written and promise to try to do better. So much has happened since I last wrote to you. Yes, I did pass the exams and am now an RN! Eric had a night of leave and he came up and took me to Chinatown for dinner and then to The Wizard of Oz. (Have you seen it yet? It's fantastic and you will love it. It's almost like going to Never Land in bright Technicolor.) Anyway, I had a wonderful time with Eric and must confess to you that I've fallen in love with him. We stayed up all night talking—don't worry, Mr. Chastity, we really just talked! Oh, Jeff, he's the most wonderful guy! But now he's off somewhere in France, and it may be weeks until I see him again or even hear from him. And isn't it just my luck finally to be in love with someone when Valentine's Day comes along and my guy is miles away in another country! I'm trying not to be too despondent, but I miss him so. Do come visit sometime. I'm certain it would make me happy and, I suspect, Peggy as well.

Love,
Annie

⌒

Sunday, February 11, 1940

Dear Eric,

It's Sunday and I can only hope that you will have a chance to write to me today like you did on the other Sundays when you were based at Kenley. I wish you were not so far away! But I am comforted that it's only a temporary assignment and hopefully you will soon be walking back through my front door and I will forget these long hours of missing you. I attended church at All Souls this morning. That's the church that Jeff had heard good things about. I worked the late night shift at Barts and walked over to All Souls. I'm getting a little more familiar with the liturgy of the Anglican service and am able to really pay attention to the words as I read them. They really are beautiful, but so different from what I'm used to in the Methodist church. If you had gone to Divinity School at St. Andrews, would you have become a Presbyterian minister? Or I guess you would say Church of Scotland. We call Anglican and Church of England "Episcopal" in the U.S.

I guess we all say Methodist, though, don't we? Anyway, Jeff says that since he's joined this Student Christian Movement, he doesn't think we should be so divided by denominations—that what's important is that we are all Christians. Do you agree with that? Eric, I'm not as religious as Jeff is now, but I'm sad to think that you are angry at God or worse, don't believe in Him anymore. I'm sorry if I sound preachy. I don't mean to. Oh, how I long to see you again and be able to talk about these things! I'm not as good at expressing myself in writing. Please write when you can. Since I don't know when you will get this, I'm going to be bold and trust that you meant what you said when you told me that you loved me and I can say again that I love you. I wasn't entirely secure with writing this before, in case you had changed your mind or I had dreamed the whole conversation. But since you may not get this letter until Valentine's Day or later, I am going to be bold and not only wish you a Happy

Valentine's Day but say that you are my Valentine, dear Eric. I love you. I love you! Please take care of yourself.

Much love,
Annie

XXXXXXXOOOOOO

17

St. Valentine's Day, 1940
London

Annie attempted to keep her spirits up, but when Valentine's Day arrived and she had not yet heard from Eric, she found it daunting neither to worry about him nor to feel a bit sorry for herself. To be at last in love but not able to see or even hear from her beloved was trying. She determined to avoid despondency by focusing on showing love to all those she cared about, and in that spirit she sent off affectionate letters to her parents and sisters back home in Virginia and to Jeff at Oxford, as well as notes of appreciation to her flatmates. In an overflow of goodwill, she cleaned their entire apartment and stood in line with her ration book at the grocery store to stock their nearly empty shelves. But by the afternoon, after she had completed her tasks and had sunk down on the sofa to rest, thoughts of dejection crept over her unbidden.

I've tried to make everyone happy for Valentine's Day, but who has tried to make me happy? I know it's selfish of me, but I would so love to be given some chocolates or a bouquet of flowers. But poor Eric is off who knows where, and he can't even write to me, let alone send me flowers. And I wonder if he will receive my letter or if he too is sitting somewhere feeling sorry for himself. But no. Men don't care about Valentine's Day. He probably doesn't even know it is Valentine's Day!

A sudden rap at the door broke into her miserable ruminations and her heart leaped. *Eric! He's come home!* As she walked quickly to answer it, she calibrated her thinking. *That's ridiculous, Annie. He's hundreds of miles away.*

She opened the door and was greeted by a sandy-haired young man holding a bouquet of red and white carnations.

"Happy Valentine's Day, sis!" Jeff said, grinning at her.

"Jeff! You rascal! What are you doing here?" Despite her fantasies about finding Eric at the door, Annie was quite delighted to see her brother.

"I thought you might be lonely, so here I am."

"Those flowers aren't for me, are they?"

"Well, not entirely. They're for all of you. I didn't want any of you to feel neglected on Valentine's Day. I also brought some chocolates." He pulled a bag out of his pocket.

Annie laughed. "You do know what girls like, don't you?"

"One of the perks of having three sisters, I guess. May I come in?"

"Of course," she said as she opened the door wider. "You know, I was just sitting here feeling sorry for myself and thinking how I wish I could have some flowers and chocolates. And then you show up. Of course, I was really hoping I'd get something from Eric, but I guess you're a good substitute."

"Gee, thanks, Annie," he said dryly.

"No really, you're a sweetheart to surprise us like this, and the girls will be very happy you came bearing gifts. Where on earth did you find this bag of chocolates?"

"I've been saving these since Christmas. I figured they'd come in handy sooner or later. Say, is Peggy around?"

"Yes, I am," Peggy answered, walking into the lounge. "Hello, Jeff. It's lovely to see you."

"No, you're the one who's lovely to see, Peggy. Wow, you get prettier every time I see you." With her shoulder-length auburn hair, green catlike eyes, and creamy skin, Peggy was a striking girl. And while a capable and skilled nurse, she also had a sweetness and gentility that won approval from doctors and patients alike.

"Thank you," she said, smiling graciously.

"I brought these carnations and chocolates for all of you to enjoy for Valentine's Day," Jeff said. "And this…" He separated a red rose from the bouquet and handed it to Peggy. "This is for you."

"Oh, how beautiful! They're all beautiful, but this one especially." She sniffed it and then gave Jeff a kiss on his cheek. "Thank you, Jeff. This is lovely of you."

He beamed and winked at Annie. "And furthermore, I'd like to escort you ladies to dinner. My treat."

"Oh, Jeff, no!" Annie protested.

"Really, I have it covered," he assured her. "And I owe you something for passing your exams. Where would you like to go—Chinese? Indian?"

"How about English?" Peggy asked sweetly.

Jeff winced. "Sorry, Peg, but you Brits are not noted for your fine cuisine. We're grateful that the Commonwealth has brought variety to your shores. But if English is what your heart desires, then pub grub it will be."

"Why don't we just walk down Queensway and see what's open and what catches our eye?" Annie suggested.

"Or our nose," Jeff added. "Sounds good to me. But where are Betty and June? Would they like to come too?"

"Betty has to work and June has gone out with a doctor friend."

"Aaah, I see." Jeff raised an eyebrow in mock tribute to June for snagging a doctor. "But poor Betty. Be sure to save some chocolates for her. Well, it will be cozier with just us anyway. Bundle up, ladies. It's bitter cold out."

In the end, they agreed on a small local Indian café where their relaxed conversation, no less than the hot curry and tea, filled them with warmth and contentment.

"So, Annie," Jeff ventured as he pushed aside his empty plate, "you said you were hoping for some gift from Eric. Have you heard from the Flying Scotsman since he flew the coop?"

Annie sighed. "No."

"She's been moping about since he left, poor dear," Peggy said.

"Have I?"

"Yes, love." Peggy leaned forward and patted Annie's arm sympathetically. "But Jeff, you were good to come. It's cheered her immensely. And me as well."

"Good. It cheers me to have dinner with two pretty girls rather than looking down a long board of young undergraduate males in Hall. I'm the old man at Magdalen now, by the way. The upperclassmen have all been called up. Only the lads under twenty are left—and the expats like me."

"It's not your war," Peggy said. "You're here to study, not fight."

"I'm glad you aren't fighting," Annie added. "Just as I'm glad that things are quiet in France."

"Things aren't quiet for the poor Finns," Jeff observed. "They're really in for it with the Soviets trying to invade."

"Yes," agreed Peggy. "But did you see that headline story last week in the *Daily Mail* about Finnish troops who saw angels?"

"No, but I heard about it."

"They saw angels?" Annie asked doubtfully.

"Yes," Peggy said. "Well, they described them as gigantic white figures in the sky above Lake Ladoga. Their arms were outstretched as if to protect the Finns against the onslaught of the Soviet attacks."

"Right," Jeff said. "Apparently the reports are similar to ones that occurred with many British soldiers at the Battle of Mons in the last war. They claimed to have seen visions of St. George with angels and cavalry in the sky."

Annie frowned. "What do you make of that?"

"Well, it's very difficult for skeptics to discount when so many troops reported the same vision. I think it's clearly miraculous—and not unbiblical in precedent. Remember the story of Elisha telling his servant not to fear when they were surrounded by an army? He prayed and the servant's eyes were opened to see that they were encircled by a mountain full of horses and chariots of fire."

"Oh, yeah," Annie murmured.

"Anyway, while so many of my Oxford friends are off fighting, I can't help but feel guilty just sitting back comfortably among the dreaming spires," Jeff said. "I hope the U.S. will get into it soon. Have you heard how the Nazis are rounding up Jews? It's sickening. This should be our war too. But for now at least, I'm trying to be content with being a student and doing the best I can with my studies."

"You know," he added while thoughtfully sipping his tea. "Back in October at the term opening, Mr. Lewis preached a sermon at Great St. Mary's Church, addressing all the younger classmen on this. He said that some of us may have to give our lives in this war, and that this is a cause worth dying for. But the war is not what we're *living* for. We need to live for God. He challenged us to give every aspect of our lives to God, including our scholarship. He's also said that the important thing is to be found at one's post—that's wherever God has called you in this life: nursing for you two, studying for me— to be at your post or on duty, if you will, as one of His children and to live each day to its fullest because it could be our last. And yet we need to plan as if we were to live another hundred years. So while I'm going about my life, working hard as a student and as an employee at the bookstore, I'm trying to do excellent work for His glory and to serve Him in every aspect of my life. But I'm also trying to prepare for the future, for the eventuality of the U.S. getting into the war and the possibility that I will be serving as well, which is one reason why I joined the University Air Squadron."

"I thought you joined so that you could wear an RAF uniform," teased Annie in an attempt to lighten the serious tone of the conversation.

"Ha-ha. That's not why I joined, although I must admit that the RAF is the most glamorous of the services. And flying is great fun."

"You've been up already?" Annie squeaked in surprise.

"Well, it is called the *air* squadron, Annie," Jeff responded in a patient tone, belied only by a hint of mockery in the twinkle of his eyes. "I'm sure it isn't a top secret that in training university men for the RAF, eventually we will learn to fly. We've spent a lot of time on the ground learning about aerodynamics and the mechanics of airplanes, but now we're taking flying lessons and it's fun. I can understand why your Eric loves it. There's nothing quite like it."

Annie groaned. "I don't want to be worrying about you too. You're not going to run off and join the RAF now, are you?"

"No, there's nothing to worry about. I'm just learning how to fly—just like I'm learning about Shakespeare and Milton in my reading. But don't worry. I'm going to stay the course and finish the year at Oxford."

This statement pacified her. "Good! I'm glad to hear it."

"Me too," Peggy said, smiling. "So long as you tear yourself from your studies once in a while to visit us."

"That I'll be happy to do." Jeff patted her hand and returned her smile. "But, I'm sorry to say that I need to be getting back to my post now. I'll walk you ladies home and then I'll have to run up to Paddington to catch the 9:30 back to Oxford."

As they headed up Queensway, Jeff urged them to switch off their flashlights for a moment. "The wonderful thing about the blackout," he explained, "is that even in London, you can see the stars. That is, if it isn't foggy out. Look up! Isn't that amazing?" They obeyed and gazed in hushed awe at the sight of the moon, Jupiter, and Venus perfectly aligned against the clear, midnight blue heavens. "Lucky Eric, to be able to fly on such a night." Jeff spoke with quiet envy. "I can't wait to get my wings!"

When they arrived at their flat, they almost stumbled over a long box in the dimly lit hallway. Jeff shined his flashlight over it while Annie stooped down to examine it. She gave a little gasp.

"What is it?" Peggy asked.

"Let's get inside," Jeff suggested, "so we can turn on the lights and get a good look."

Unlocking their door, they stepped in and made certain the drapes were tightly drawn before switching on the lights. The narrow white box in Annie's arms was unmistakably from a florist and bore her name on the address label. Annie's hands trembled as she untied the ribbons and lifted the lid.

Inside lay a dozen long-stemmed red roses resting in a spray of baby's breath. Annie fumbled with the small card. It read:

> *To my darling Annie.*
> *Happy St. Valentine's Day, sweetheart.*
> *Will you be mine? I am yours always.*
>
> > *I love you.*
> > *Eric*

Annie clutched the card to her breast and tears sprang to her eyes. "He remembered! Oh, Eric! But how could he have sent them when he's in France?"

Jeff gave a low whistle of admiration. "Got to hand it to the guy. What a master stroke. He must have ordered them from the florist before he left the country."

Peggy gave Annie a swift hug. "There, you see? He does love you. Isn't this wonderful? How romantic! And the roses are beautiful." She smiled at Jeff. "Now we have two lovely bouquets to brighten our little flat."

Jeff smiled back. "And don't forget the chocolates, ladies."

The girls laughed and said together, "We'd never forget the chocolates!"

A week later as the roses began to fade, Annie came home from work one night to find a letter in her mailbox.

Sunday, 11 February 1940

Dear Annie,

I'm now at the new base. Sorry, I have to keep the location undisclosed to avoid offending the censors. I'm afraid our letters are crossing in the mail. It certainly was easier to correspond when the letters had less distance to travel. I was delighted to receive your letter of 4 February, although I was rather alarmed at the morbidity of your thoughts. Could this be my little munchkin worrying about such dreadful things? I was also sorry not to read more effusive declarations of your love for me.

Putting aside facetiousness for a moment, let me say most sincerely and without doubt or equivocation that I meant every word I said to you on our last night together in London. I do love you, Annie Little. I love you dearly and completely and cannot wait to see you again and hold you in my arms. You are constantly in my thoughts. And every night when I go to sleep I hope I will dream of you so that I can be with you even then. So please, my darling little one, if you do indeed return these feelings, do not hesitate to write them to me. Such words will bring me comfort in the dark hours. They will sustain me until I can see you again. I'm sorry that this letter may not reach you before St. Valentine's Day, but I will be thinking of you, and although we are apart I want you to know that you are my only

Valentine and I am yours alone. I love you, Annie.
Please write as often as you can.

Yours always,
Eric

PS. You should receive a special St. Valentine's
surprise from me, sent with all my love.

After reading and rereading the message, Annie took one of the fading rose blooms, placed it inside the folded paper, and pressed them together. Then with a contented sigh, she sat down to write her own letter to Eric.

18

*T*hroughout the remainder of the winter, the correspondence continued to flow between France,
London, and Oxford, as well as back and forth across the
Atlantic to Virginia. The letters' common themes dwelt on
love, homesickness, and the bitter cold. Slowly the winter and
the frozen stalemate of the Phoney War began to thaw; and
as spring emerged, the Germans mobilized for their *Blitzkrieg*
attacks on the western front.

                                        Friday, 8 March 1940

Dear Annie,

 *I'm back in the country and glad to be home
and closer to you. I'm also glad that there's a hint
of spring in the air. I was getting weary of scraping
the ice and snow off my plane and of the impos-
sibility of ever getting warm—even indoors. Yet I
fear that with the thaw we may have subsequent
flooding and wet engines with which to contend. I
did see some action over there but can't write about
it in any detail. Anyway, I'm home safe and sound
now. I will look forward to talking to you in person*

soon. The base is sponsoring a dance next Saturday evening. Would you possibly be able to come down for it? (I'm not keen to dance with anyone else!) I will pay for the train ticket and for your accommodations. There's a nice local inn around the corner from the train station (with the same name as the base) where I could reserve a room for you. Please say you'll come. I've missed you dreadfully and love you more than I can say.

Yours forever,
Eric

∽

Tuesday, March 12, 1940

Dear Eric,

I was so happy to receive your letter and to know you are safely back in England. I'm even happier to be invited to visit you and attend the RAF dance. I have longed to see your base, the aerodrome, etc. so that I can better picture you on duty. Yes, please reserve the room for me. I will plan to take the train Saturday morning and should arrive around noon. I will go straight to the hotel and get settled, so you can leave any instructions or contact information with them. Oh, my darling, I can't wait to see you again! I love you and have missed you so much.

All my love,
Annie

Annie could not find a seat on the train from London Victoria to the Surrey parish of Kenley. Since the rationing of petrol, automobiles had become an unaffordable luxury, and everyone from troops to refugees traveled by rail. Annie sat on her valise in the corridor, letting the breeze from a cracked-open window alleviate the suffocating smells emanating from the crowded car. Above the murmurs of the passengers, a baby wailed in a rising crescendo accompanied by the staccato "hush," "hush," "hush" of his harried mother. Annie's heart went out to the young woman, but she greeted her journey's end with gratitude as the train hissed to a stop at the small Kenley station.

Although she had planned to walk by herself to the hotel, she was delighted to be greeted on the station platform by a tall handsome man who swooped her up into a warm embrace.

"Och, Annie, I'm so glad to see ye! I've been countin' the minutes for the train to arrive."

Her melodic laugh made his heart ache as he gently set her down. "Oh, Eric," she said breathlessly. "I'm so glad to see you too! Let me look at you." She inspected him and smiled broadly. "You look great! I'm so relieved that you are really back safe and sound. And believe me—" She adjusted her beret and smoothed out her straight skirt. "I've been counting the minutes too. Train travel is not as much fun as it was before the war."

"Yer journey was uncomfortable?" he asked as he picked up her suitcase and offered her his arm.

"Only if you consider sitting on your luggage and listening to babies cry incessantly uncomfortable." She wrinkled her nose. "Which, I must confess, I do. But my word, I was surprised to see you here! And that's made up for everything. Do you have some time off?"

"Yes. My flight lieutenant gave me leave until tomorrow mornin'. Wasn't that cricket of him? So ye're stuck with spendin' all yer time with me while ye're here."

Annie looked about the scattering of houses and shops that couldn't even qualify Kenley as a village. "Doesn't look like there's much to do around here, so I guess your company will have to suffice." She squeezed his arm. "I'm joking, of course. There's nothing I'd rather do than be with you. What do you have planned for us?"

"First, we check ye into the hotel, and then ye can change into somethin' more comfortable." He indicated his own khaki trousers, open-collared white shirt, and a brown leather bomber jacket. "Did ye by any chance bring some slacks?" She nodded. "Good! There are some lovely walkin' trails around here, and I thought since it's such a fine spring day, we could take a long walk through the Kenley Commons. How does that sound?"

"Lover-ly," she answered, affecting a Cockney accent.

The Kenley Hotel sat along the Godstone Road, the main thoroughfare through Kenley. A small hotel with a red brick facade, it boasted four steeply pitched gabled windows decorated by a profusion of flower boxes. Annie registered at the front desk while Eric carried her valise up to her top-floor room. He peeked in to make certain it would serve her well and—after noting a simple, clean accommodation tucked under the eaves of one of the gables—waited in the ground floor pub for her to change.

The spring day beckoned them outdoors and they wandered hand in hand on the chalk path along Riddlesdown and through woods out to the open meadows of Kenley Common. Skylarks and yellowhammers flitted overhead and brave wildflowers poked through the tall grass. Exhilarated with the joy of being out in the countryside in the warm sunshine, Annie threw herself down on the hillside and gazed happily at the wisps of clouds swirling like cotton candy across the cerulean sky.

"Oh," she exclaimed, "this is heavenly! It's so peaceful out here away from the city with no hustle and bustle. Listen! All I can hear is the singing of birds. One can believe there isn't a war at all."

Eric stretched out beside her and gazing at her, murmured, "'*And when Love speaks, the voice of all the gods make heaven drowsy with the harmony.*'"

"That's beautiful." Annie sighed. "Who said that?"

"Shakespeare. *Love's Labor's Lost.*"

Annie stretched and yawned. "I'm getting 'drowsy with the harmony.' The sun feels so good. May we lie here for a few minutes and nap?"

"Sure. I'm bushed and could use a little catnap." Eric reached for her hand before closing his eyes and they both dreamily dozed off. They awoke when a formation of planes suddenly swooped low overhead.

Startled, Annie sat up. "Oh, my! We must be close to the airfield. Are those Spitfires?"

"Hurricanes." Eric answered with his eyes closed. "Returnin' from patrol. The aerodrome is just up over the hill on that high plateau."

Annie glanced down at him. "How can you tell what kind of plane they are without looking?"

"They each have a different sound. The German planes drone with a menacin' sound while ours hum with their lovely Merlin engines. But the Spitfire—ah, the Spitfire—she sings." He opened his eyes and grinned. "But *ye're* supposed to be able to tell which is which by lookin', ye know. I should get ye some of those plane silhouette cards that come in the cigarette packages so that ye can be a better ground observer."

The sight of her tousled hair, rippling down her back, made his throat tighten with longing. Reaching up, he gingerly removed a reed of grass that had caught in her curls and placed it between his teeth.

"I've honestly tried to learn the silhouettes," she said, hugging her knees. "Especially the Spitfire—but I can't keep them straight. At least I can tell which are ours from the markings, and I hope I'll never spot a Messerschmitt."

"I hope so too," he quietly agreed. "But I'm afraid now that spring has come, the Huns will be comin' too."

"Did you see them in France?"

"Aye. And engaged some too on reconnaissance. They keep tryin' to penetrate the Maginot Line, and we keep chasin' them off."

"Did you shoot any down?"

"One."

Annie shuddered. "How did you feel about that? I mean, did you ever think that their pilots are men just like you who also have sweethearts or mothers who will never see them again?"

"Nay, I don't. They get what they deserve. They should have thought about the innocent children and sweethearts they've killed," he replied bitterly. "And then there are our fine pilots who never return from a sortie. Ye'll have a beer in the mess with a lad one day and his chair will be empty the next. Besides, Annie, ye can't think about the Jerries sympathetically or ye'll get yerself killed. It's kill or be killed, and ye have to stay focused on completin' the mission and comin' back alive."

"Yes," she said softly. "You must come back alive."

Standing suddenly, he brushed the grass from his trousers and offered her his hand to help her up. "Come on, lass. Enough gloomy talk. Let's walk up to see the airfield and then we'll stop at the Wattenden Arms for some refreshment."

Eric led Annie up the plateau to view the wide vista of the paved runways, camouflaged control tower, and massive aerodrome set above miles of open countryside.

"Used to be a golf course before the RAF built the airfield," he said.

"Do you miss golfing?"

"Aye, but I can play some here. When we're not flyin', it's a grand place to practice drives. And the lads and I found and cleared off some of the old holes where we can putt."

"Do you have your clubs with you?"

"Nay, but my squadron leader—who is also a Scot—has a set, and he lets me borrow them in return for a lesson now and then."

"That's nice. I'm glad you get a chance to play. And that you can have some fun."

"Flyin' is fun too, ye know—and so is havin' ye here with me." He drew her close as the wind blustered about them. "I wish ye could always be with me." He bent down to kiss her, ignoring the drone of Hurricanes flying in for a landing. Suddenly one broke out of its landing pattern and buzzed right over them. Eric raised his fist in mock anger and laughed. "Blasted idiot! That's McLeod, the other Scottish pilot in my squadron. He must be jealous." He glanced at his watch. "It's teatime already. Are ye hungry?"

She nodded.

"There's a pub at the bottom of the hill."

"I'll race you!" Annie set off running down the slope.

"Cheater!" he yelled. "Ye little munchkin—that was a disqualified start!" When she didn't slacken her pace or even look back, he swiftly followed, rapidly overtaking her in his arms. Laughing, they tumbled into the wildflowers. He rolled her onto her back and leaned over her. Her golden brown hair spread like a fan over the grass.

"You're the cheater," she panted.

"Nay, I caught ye, fair and square."

"So I'm your captive?" Her dark eyes sparkled with mischief.

"Nay, I'm yers."

He kissed her then. Desire washed over them in waves, and they wrestled with their yearning to be one. She broke off breathlessly, pushing him gently away.

"Annie," he whispered, caressing her cheek. "I love ye so much. I wasn't goin' to ask this before tonight, but my heart's about to burst. Will ye marry me?"

A hint of surprise flickered in her eyes, but she smiled. "Yes, oh yes, Eric, I will!" She put her arms around his neck and they kissed again. Then she abruptly sat up.

"What's wrong?" he asked.

"We're not married yet, so we'd better stop all this lovemaking before we get too carried away."

"Sorry. Ye're right," he said, standing and offering her his hand. "But if I had a few days' leave, I'd take ye off to Gretna Green and marry ye right away." He sighed heavily. "Well, now. Here's the Wattenden Arms." He pointed to a small whitewashed pub tucked away on the edge of the woods. "Let's get some refreshment and celebrate our engagement."

19

Saturday evening, March 16
Kenley

ince the Wattenden Arms served as a favorite watering hole for the neighboring RAF pilots and ground crew, Annie had an opportunity to meet some of Eric's comrades prior to the dance. After a full tea that left her with no appetite for dinner, she returned to the hotel to change for the evening. Rolling up her hair in strips of rags, she took a hot bath to allow the steam to set the curls. She dressed in a sheer white blouse accented by a navy-and-white dotted swiss bow which matched her calf-length skirt, cinching her waist and sweeping into a flared hemline for easier movement on the dance floor. She blotted her bright red lipstick, and taking one final check in the mirror, joined the other young women in the hotel lobby as they waited excitedly for the base trucks to transport them to the Officers' Mess at the Kenley Aerodrome.

A host of handsome RAF pilots greeted them on their arrival, but Annie thought her pilot the most handsome of all. Pushing through the crowd, he claimed her by putting his hands on her slender waist and lifting her from the truck.

"My, ye're the bonniest lass here," he said as he embraced her. "And ye're all mine for this evenin'."

She smiled gaily. "I'm all yours forever, Eric."

The strains of a live swing band greeted the throng of young people as they swept into the mess hall. To the envy of those untutored and less practiced, Eric and Annie easily dominated the dance floor with their seemingly effortless Lindy Hop and jitterbug moves. Then as the strains of "The Way You Look Tonight" and "Reverie" slowed the pace, they danced cheek to cheek in a quiet ecstasy of intimacy. Eric hummed along as the band singer took up a tune newly popularized by Glenn Miller and Ray Eberle:

> *Fools rush in*
> *Where angels fear to tread,*
> *And so I come to you, my love,*
> *My heart above my head.*

When they left the dance floor for refreshments, Eric was hailed by a burly redheaded fellow with a thick Scottish burr. "MacKenzie, is this the lass ye were cavortin' with in the meadow today?"

Eric laughed. "I thought it was you, McLeod, who buzzed us. Annie, this is Flying Officer Ian McLeod, the only other Scot in the outfit besides our squadron leader. Ian, Annie Little."

"Hello, lass," he said, shaking her extended hand. "Nice to make yer acquaintance. Now I can see why MacKenzie canna stop talkin' about ye." With an abrupt change in demeanor, he turned soberly to Eric. "Did ye hear about Scapa Flow, lad?"

Eric frowned and shook his head. "Nay. What happened?"

"Those bloody b——" Ian stopped and glanced at Annie. "Sorry, miss. The Nazis attacked the naval base again and one of their bombers turned tail and unloaded nineteen bombs over the village of Bridge of Waithe. Seven civilians were wounded and one was killed."

Eric sucked his breath in sharply. "A civilian killed in an air raid?"

"Aye. First one. Although I'm sure there'll be plenty more before this war is done. Shame it had to be in Scotland too. Poor man had run across the road to help his neighbor, who coincidentally was a McLeod, though no relation. Accordin' to the reports he was a young lad and leaves behind a widow and infant son."

"Blast them!" Eric slammed his fist down on a nearby table. "I wish we had been there. We would've gi'en them a run for their money."

"Aye, none of the enemy was shot down, but our lads did some damage and managed to keep them from reachin' the Forth Bridge."

"Well, that's somethin', anyway."

"Och, 'tis a bad business."

"Is Scapa Flow near St. Andrews?" Annie asked.

"Nay, it's way up north in the Orkney Islands," Eric replied. "There's a big naval base there. The Germans bombed it back in October and hit a battleship, but there weren't any civilian casualties."

"Say, MacKenzie," Ian interrupted. "Is it true ye volunteered to go back to France?"

Annie looked up sharply at this. Eric glanced at her and pressed his hand against her back in reassurance. "Aye," he said. "I leave again on Monday. I figure that until they show their faces in London, I'll go after them over there."

"Well, ye won't be alone. I'm comin' too. I reckon if we beat 'em back in France, maybe we won't have to fight 'em here. But I just wish they'd leave Scotland alone!" Ian growled.

"Aye. Well, I'll be glad for someone else along who speaks English properly. At any rate, I'll have plenty of time to talk with ye over there. But this bonny lass is only here for tonight, so if ye'll excuse us…"

"Go on!" Ian slapped Eric on the back, and then touched his forehead in a farewell salute. "Nice to meet ye, miss."

"Nice to meet you too, Ian." Annie called after him, "Good luck!"

"Now then," Eric said, "how would ye fancy walking with me back to the hotel, rather than takin' the truck with the other girls? Can ye manage in those high heels of yers?"

"Aye," Annie said, mimicking his burr. "I believe I can, as long as I can take yer arm."

Smiling, he offered his arm as they headed back toward the town. "Ye'll make a proper Scottish bride before long."

"Eric." She dropped the teasing tone along with the accent. "Are you really going back to France?"

"Just for a while to give more of those lads the chance to come home for Easter on holiday. I believe once it really warms up, Hitler will be on the march and they won't be able to return home again for a long time."

"But what of you? Don't you want to go home for Easter? And what if you get stuck over there?"

"I'm just on loan, so don't ye worry about my gettin' stuck. Anyway, I can't get enough time off to go all the way back home. Remember, my real home is Gairloch, not St. Andrews, and it's way up in the western Highlands. Too far for me to go without a fortnight's leave."

"Your poor mother. I'm sure she misses you."

"Aye, I'm sure she does, but no more than yer parents miss ye, I'll warrant. Annie, do ye think they will give ye their consent to marry me?"

"Yes, I believe so. I will write them, though, when I get back to London. And what of your parents?"

"I have already written them about ye, and they sound quite pleased. When this war is over, I'll take ye home to Gairloch to meet them. I know they'll love ye dearly."

"I'd like that and I'd love to see where you're from." They walked in silence for a few moments and then Annie asked, "Eric, what will you do when the war is over—for a living, I mean?"

"I don't rightly know. I still have a year to complete my degree. I had planned to go to divinity school, ye know, but no longer. Perhaps I'll be a teacher."

"Why don't you want to be a minister anymore? You still believe in God, don't you?"

"Och, Annie, of course I still believe. But I'd rather not talk about it—at least not now. I'd rather not think about it when I'm with you." He stopped and caressed her cheek. "Ye make me so happy. Ye're so pretty and sweet and kind. I just want to enjoy bein' with ye now—in the present—and not think about all the sadness that was or will be."

"Okay," she said softly.

They were standing near an old stone church, which gave Kenley its status as a parish despite its small size. "I say, let's go in for a minute," Eric said. "I want to show ye somethin'."

"I thought you were avoiding church."

"Not for this." He swung open the lych-gate and shined his flashlight on the path up to the church's unlocked side door. Eric pushed it open and led Annie by the hand into the small sanctuary. Striking a match, he lit enough candles to fill the darkened church with a warm glow.

"Now," he said. "Would ye come kneel with me at the communion rail?"

She did and bowed her head to pray silently. He waited. When she opened her eyes, she saw in the palm of his hand a gold ring, glinting in the candlelight.

"Ye deserve more than a plain gold band, Annie, but with rationin', all I could buy was the standard issue weddin' ring."

"Oh, Eric, I don't mind! I didn't expect a ring at all. Well, to be honest, I didn't even expect a proposal."

"I consider this more than a proposal. I wish we could be married tonight. I would drag a priest out of bed if I could, but English law says we need to have yer parents' permission since ye're only nineteen and we must wait a fortnight after postin' the notices. So if ye'd be willin', as soon as I have enough leave, I would like to take ye to Gretna Green, just over the border in Scotland, where we can be married without all the regulations."

"That would be fine. My family's not here anyway, except for Jeff, so I wouldn't care about having a fancy wedding. It would be wonderful to be married as soon as possible. I wish we could before you go back to France!"

"Well, perhaps we can't legally, but we can still make the covenant between us here in this church before God." He looked into her eyes and tenderly said, "Annie, will ye have me to be yer husband from this day forward; for better, for worse; for richer, for poorer; in sickness and in health; to love and to cherish 'til death us do part?"

"I will," she whispered.

He slid the ring on her finger and held her hands in his own. "Then I, Eric Richard MacKenzie, take thee, Annie Little, to be my wedded wife; to have and to hold, from this day forward; for better, for worse; for richer, for poorer; in sickness and in health; to love and to cherish 'til death us do part. And to you I pledge my faith. What God has joined together, let no man separate. Amen."

"Amen."

He brought her hand to his lips and then gently kissed her. "Now we are pledged to one another in a solemn covenant. And as soon as we can, we will make our vows legal." He helped her to her feet and blew out the candles. Closing the church door behind them, they walked arm in arm back to the hotel.

When Annie and Eric arrived at the hotel, they found the ground floor pub packed with servicemen and local girls having returned from the dance but reluctant to part company. As Eric made his way to the bar, some of the pilots recognized him and cried, "MacKenzie, have you asked her? What did she say?"

"She said yes!" He beamed.

"Hip, hip, hurrah!" shouted his comrades. "Champagne for the happy couple!"

The barkeep produced a bottle and two glasses. Annie blushed profusely as the men proposed toasts and raised their pint glasses in tribute. Grabbing the bottle and glasses in one hand and Annie with the other, Eric led her out of the bar, calling out his "thank-yous" and "cheers" as they left.

"Let's get out of here," he murmured in her ear, "to where we can celebrate in privacy. How about yer room?"

They climbed the stairs to the top floor. Stepping into her room, they shut the door and turned on the bedside lamp. "There," said Annie as she kicked off her shoes and sat on the bed. "Peace and quiet and all alone. How about some of that bubbly?"

Eric popped the cork, poured the foaming champagne, and offered her a glass. "To us!" he toasted.

"To us!" They clinked their glasses together and drank. Strains of big band music filtered up to the room from the radio blaring in the pub below.

"Would ye care to dance?" Eric asked, pouring her another glass.

"I'd love to." Annie came into his arms and they swayed together as they sipped the champagne. For a long while—or was it only minutes?—they slowly danced until the bottle was empty and the music faded away into silence. Annie began to feel light-headed as Eric kissed her hair and face and throat.

"I should probably go," he murmured, not wanting to.

"Don't go!" She clasped her arms around his neck. "Don't leave me. I don't know when I'll see you again."

"I should go." But his words weren't convincing and he made no move to release her.

"No, please don't! I can't bear to spend even one minute away from you. I love you so." She clung to him more tightly. "Just stay with me. Please, don't leave me."

"I can't leave you, my darlin', my wife," he whispered, kissing her fervently, and she melted into his embrace.

Annie awoke to the racket from the busy street below her hotel room window. Disoriented at first, it took her several minutes to realize where she was. Like a hazy dream, the events of the previous night floated through her mind—the dance, the walk home, the betrothal vows in the church, the champagne—Annie sat up with a start. *Eric!* She felt the impression on the bed next to her. It was still warm.

Her head pounded and her stomach churned with nausea. She sank back with a moan. *What have I done? What have we done?*

She rolled over and squeezed her eyes shut. *Oh, God. I'm so sorry! It all happened so fast. I shouldn't have had so much to drink. I shouldn't have begged him to stay. We meant those vows we said before You in the church and I felt so married last night, but we should have waited until it was legal. I'm so sorry!*

She clutched at the pillow where Eric's head had lain and heard the rustle of a piece of paper. Pushing up on her elbow, she opened it to his now familiar handwriting.

17 March 1940

My darling Annie,

I have to get back to the base to report to duty. You look so beautiful sleeping there that I don't want to wake you, even for a kiss goodbye (although I will kiss you before I leave). I just want to write this note to reassure you of how much I love you and how I meant every word I vowed to you in the church. I will consider you as my dearly betrothed wife from that moment until death us do part. But as much as I never want to leave your side, I know we shouldn't have spent the night together. I take all the responsibility for what happened last night and am very sorry not to have exercised more self-control. Please forgive me. It will not happen again until we are married in the sight of man as well as God. I love you, little one. Please remember that in the days ahead—especially as you may not hear from me again for a while. Do not worry about me. I will come back for you, and as soon as we are able, I will properly make you my wife.

Yours forever,
Eric

Annie pressed the letter to her lips with a little sob. She pulled herself out of bed, dressed mechanically, and sat down at the desk to compose her reply to Eric.

March 17, 1940

Dearest Eric,

I wish you had awakened me so that I could say goodbye to you. Oh, how I miss you already! Thank you for your loving words, but it is I who must ask forgiveness. I know it was wrong, but to be honest,

*part of me was so glad to be with you. I do worry
about what may happen to you and hanging over
me is the dread that each time we're together may
be our last time. Still, I shouldn't have asked you to
stay or tempted you like that. I promise I will try
hard not to again. Meanwhile, I don't want you to
be distracted from doing your job well, so do not be
concerned about me. I will be fine, although I will
think of you every moment until we can be together
again! I love you, my darling, my own dear husband.*

Much love,
Annie

XXXXOOOO

She folded the letter, sealed it with a kiss, and left it at the
hotel desk for delivery to the Kenley base. She realized with a
groan that since it was Sunday all the shops were closed and
she would not be able to purchase aspirin from the chemist to
alleviate her splitting headache. As she returned to London,
the crowded train lurched forward and her stomach lurched
with it. *This is penance,* she thought, *for my indiscretions last
night.*

Little did she know that her penance had just begun.

Easter Holidays 1940
London

Sunday, March 17

Dear Annie,

How are you, kiddo? Easter Vac has begun for
me and I plan to run down to London and spend
some time with you lovely girls over the Easter
weekend. Would that suit? How's it going with your
flyboy? Looking forward to hearing all the news. I've
missed you.

Your loving brother,
Jeff

Annie and Jeff spent Easter Saturday afternoon enjoying
the fine spring weather in Hyde Park. He rented a boat and
rowed out into the Serpentine, where they casually tossed
bits of stale bread crusts to the ducks. Annie had harbored
vague feelings of uneasiness about seeing Jeff. He could read
her like no one else could, particularly when she did not wish

to be read. She had tried to divert any serious conversation by affecting a gaiety she did not feel. But as she let down her guard by lying back in the boat and lifting her face to the warm sun, he innocently sent over the first salvo.

"So, kiddo, where do you want to go to Easter service tomorrow? Should we go to the big guy, St. Paul's, or back to All Souls? You know, I've also heard that Holy Trinity at Brompton is a good church, and we could actually walk there. It's on the other side of Kensington Gardens. Do you have a preference?"

"You should pick where you like," Annie replied without opening her eyes. "I don't think I'll go to church."

"Not go to church? Are you kidding? It's Easter, for goodness' sake! We always go to church on Easter. Gee whiz, everybody goes to church on Easter."

"Well, we shouldn't do something just because everyone else does."

Jeff grunted in perplexity. "Say what? You mean you shouldn't do something bad because everyone else is doing it. I don't think church attendance would fall under that category." He flicked some crusts at a row of small ducklings swimming behind their proud mother. "Are you serious about this?"

Annie sighed. "I suppose so."

"Would you mind telling me why? You aren't going through some sort of crisis of faith, are you?"

"No. It's just that…" She sat up but concentrated on feeding the ducks rather than looking her brother in the eye. "I don't think God would want me there. I didn't go to the Maundy Thursday or Good Friday services or take communion, and I don't think it would be right for me to show up at Easter like I'm the perfect Christian or something."

Jeff silently cast out bread while he considered what could be behind this statement. Finally he spoke. "Are you feeling guilty about something? Do you think that perhaps you shouldn't go to church because you've done something wrong and you don't believe God can forgive you?"

"Something like that," Annie answered quietly.

"You know, Annie, the Bible says that when we confess our sins He is faithful to forgive us and cleanse us from all unrighteousness. If you've done something wrong, you just have to confess it and God will forgive you."

"I don't know if He will."

"If He says He will—and He does say that in the Scriptures—then He will. He forgave Peter for denying Him, the woman caught in adultery, Paul for arresting and leading Christians to execution, and so on. I mean, after all, didn't Jesus die on the cross to pay the penalty for our sins?"

"Yes, I know, but I just feel so bad and I don't know if He really will forgive me."

"Annie, your feelings and thoughts on the subject can't be set on a higher level than God's Word. Do you want to tell me about it?" he asked gently. "I could serve as your confessor."

She blushed deeply and shook her head. "No, I'd rather not."

Jeff studied her.

Suddenly, he knew.

"Did you go to bed with Eric?" he asked incredulously.

She hesitated and then slowly nodded.

Jeff slammed the oar down. "I'll kill him!"

"Wait! It's not like you think. And see? When you react this way, then how can I think God will forgive us? Anyway, it's more my fault than Eric's. He proposed to me and gave me a ring. In fact, we went in a little church and we took the marriage vows together. He said if he could have, he would have taken me to Gretna Green so that we could be legal, but as far as he was concerned we were married."

"Yeah, right!"

"Really, Jeff. He meant it and so did I. It's just that we drank a lot of champagne and then I didn't want him to leave me because I didn't know when I'd see him again—or even if I'd *ever* see him again. So I asked him to stay with me." She hurried on, ignoring Jeff's grunts. "I know I shouldn't have, but I did and things just…happened." She pulled Eric's crumpled and oft-read letter from her handbag and handed it to him. "Here, read his letter and then maybe you'll believe me when I say he really does intend to marry me as soon as possible."

Jeff snatched it from her and quickly scanned it. His demeanor softened. "Well, I hope he means this. But Annie, what if he got you pregnant?"

This thought had terrified her, but she tried to answer casually. "It was only one time, Jeff, so I doubt anything happened. And we won't stay together again until we're married."

"But what if it did happen? What would you do? It would break Mom and Dad's heart."

She grabbed his arm. "Jeff!" she cried in a panic. "Promise me you won't tell Mom and Daddy anything!"

"Hey, calm down, I won't. I'm your confessor, so I'm sworn to absolute confidentiality. Anyway, that's your call to make. Besides, like you said, it probably won't happen, so we shouldn't be worrying about it. Listen, Annie. I'm sorry if I overreacted. It's just a huge shock for a big brother to hear such a revelation. But despite that, it doesn't change the fact that if you've sincerely turned away from this, God will forgive you. Would you like to pray with me now and get back on track?"

"Okay," she whispered.

He took her hands in his and bowed his head. "Father, my dear sister Annie has confessed this to me and to You, and she's sorry for disobeying You. Please forgive her and give her the assurance of Your forgiveness and Your love. And we pray for Eric that You will also forgive and bless him."

"Lord, I'm sorry," Annie said, sniffing. "Please forgive me. I haven't really been following You the way I should. Please help me to be a better person. And help Eric. Protect him from all harm."

"In Jesus' name we pray," Jeff added. "Amen."

"Amen." Annie looked up and brushed the tears out of her eyes.

"Okay then." Jeff smiled at her. "Now, where do you want to go to church for Easter?"

In the end they decided to attend Holy Trinity Brompton. They walked to the service with Annie's flatmates through Kensington Gardens and returned there afterward for a picnic lunch. Jeff stayed through Easter Monday and joined Annie, Peggy, and the crowds of Londoners celebrating the holiday in prewar style by thronging to the restaurants and theaters despite the blackout. The queues for the cinemas stretched for more than a hundred yards, and they secured a place in line for *Gone with the Wind* before Jeff headed off to buy Chinese takeout for them to eat while waiting. The West End glowed with flashlights in the festive atmosphere, and one could almost believe that the war was only an unpleasant illusion. After the film, Jeff hopped a packed train back to Oxford and found to his delight that his fellow travelers spontaneously broke into a sing-along to which he happily added his lusty baritone.

When Jeff returned to work and studies, Annie did as well, serving her ward at St. Bartholomew's Hospital and teaming with the Red Cross in preparation for air raids. The weeks passed with little word from Eric. Daily, Annie grew more anxious and nauseated. She skipped two periods, blaming it on stress. And then on a lovely day in May, she tested positive for pregnancy.

21

May 1940
London

"I think we've had just about enough momentous news for one day, don't you?" Annie's flatmate June said over a cup of tea in the staff cafeteria at Barts Hospital. "I am glad Chamberlain has resigned and Sir Winston is now at the helm, but all the news out of Europe is ghastly. Who would have thought that Hitler would go around the Maginot Line and launch invasions of Belgium, Luxembourg, and the Netherlands! Now our boys are really in for it over there. I certainly hope everyone puts up a good fight, or we'll be staring down Jerries in the Channel before you know it. Oh, Annie, you do look dreadfully pale. I'm sorry. Your Eric is over there, isn't he?"

"Yes," Annie answered quietly, staring into her teacup. Although she willed herself not to cry, tears defiantly spilled down her cheeks.

"Oh, my dear, I am so sorry to have upset you! Naturally you're worried about him. But buck up, darling. I'm sure he's an excellent pilot and will be fine."

"June, can you keep a secret?"

"Of course, my dear. You know we nurses are trained to keep confidentiality."

Annie hesitated and then leaned forward to whisper, "I just found out that I'm...I'm...expecting."

"You're...pregnant?" A look of shocked horror crossed June's face before she could squelch it. "Are you quite sure? Maybe you just missed a period because of stress. It can happen easily, you know."

"That's what I told myself. And I've blamed my fatigue on overwork. But I've missed two cycles now, so I had a blood test. I just got the results this afternoon."

June groaned. "Oh, my word!"

"Yes." Annie dashed away more tears. "I still can't believe it. We were together only one time. It was a terrible mistake and we promised it wouldn't happen again."

"I hate to say it, Annie, but the ones who get caught are the naive ones who don't plan on anything happening so they're unprepared. The others use birth control. Anyway, my dear, will you tell Eric?"

"I don't know what to do! He proposed to me that night and gave me a ring, but he's been in France for two months at an undisclosed base and I've hardly heard from him. I don't even know if he's gotten my letters. I don't want to spring this on him when he's putting his life on the line every day. He doesn't need to be worrying about this. Plus, I don't want to force him into marriage if he's changed his mind. I mean, if I tell him, I'm certain he would marry me to do the honorable thing. But I don't want this to be the reason he marries me."

"Yes, yes, I see." June aimlessly stirred her tea. "Well, at the very least, you know you should see a doctor."

"But, June, I can't see a doctor here! I would be mortified if any of them knew."

"Leave it to me. I'll set you up with my Harry. He'll make sure the test results are accurate before you get too carried away, and he'll give you sound counsel about your options. Plus, you can trust him not to breathe a word to anyone." She patted Annie's hand. "I promise. He'll take care of everything. Now go wash your face and go on back to work, and I'll stop by and speak to him."

"All right," Annie said, rising slowly, "but please remember not to tell anyone else."

"Everyone has to keep secrets in this war, darling. Don't you worry about that."

Five days later, when Holland had surrendered to the overwhelming power of the Nazi *Blitzkrieg* and Belgium was crumbling behind her, Annie sat trembling in Dr. Henry Benson's office awaiting his verdict. Being examined by her flatmate's boyfriend had been a humiliating experience, but she had been grateful that he had the propriety to handle the procedure in a professional manner, even refraining from acknowledging their acquaintance, and that he had requested that she be dressed before discussing his diagnosis. She had always believed that a doctor who addressed a patient who was still wearing a hospital gown only reinforced the vulnerability and discomfort of their situation. She felt vulnerable enough sitting there in her nurse's uniform, twisting her handkerchief aimlessly around her fingers.

"Well, Miss Little," he said in an official but not unkind tone, "my examination confirms the results of the blood test. You are indeed pregnant." He peered down at her chart and rotated a paper wheel with dates on it. "Your last menstrual period was March 6, which puts you at ten weeks and would make you due just before Christmas on—December 11, give or take two weeks. The exam indicates your uterus size is consistent with a pregnancy of two months." He looked up at her then. "Are you all right, miss?"

Annie opened her mouth and then shut it. *"No!"* she wanted to scream. She dully nodded.

"Right. Then let's discuss some options. Do you know who the father is?"

She stiffened. "Yes, of course."

"Sorry, there was no offense intended. Are you still involved with him?"

"Yes. We're engaged."

"Well, obviously the simplest option would be for you to inform him of your situation and be married as soon as possible."

Annie felt tears prickling against the back of her eyes. "He's in France now, as far as I know, with the RAF."

"Ah, yes, that could be difficult."

"And I'm not sure I want to tell him anyway. I don't want to force him into marriage. So what else would you suggest?"

"Well, your American ambassador, Mr. Joseph Kennedy, has been urging Americans to leave Britain. He is obviously concerned about a Nazi invasion here. So you could return to the United States and go to a home for unwed mothers there."

"I can't do that to my parents. And I could have gone back last September, but I decided to stay and serve here as a nurse."

"Why, that's very admirable, but you will find it difficult to continue to serve as your pregnancy progresses. We could perhaps recommend a home here in England where you could go when the time came."

"And then what?"

"These sorts of homes locate a suitable family to adopt the baby."

"Adoption?" Annie said faintly. "I don't know if I could do that—carry a baby to term and then give it up."

"Another option would be to go to such a home and keep the child, although providing for a baby alone is always difficult, and even more so during a war." He paused and then continued cautiously, "There is also another option."

"What?"

"A 'D and C.' Dilation and curettage. A simple procedure in which the patient receives anesthesia and the doctor dilates the cervix with rods that increase in diameter and then the contents of the uterus are scraped out. There is some cramping and bleeding afterward, but after about a week, the patient will return to normal."

"You mean...an abortion?"

"Yes." He lowered his voice. "But we would record it as a spontaneous abortion or miscarriage, requiring a D and C. If you decide this is the course you want to pursue, I could be available for an appointment to see you next week at this same time and we can proceed from there. But I would not recommend your waiting any longer than that since the procedure becomes more difficult as the baby...hmm...the fetus grows."

Annie blanched.

"Why don't you take a few days to think it over, Miss Little? I will block out the appointment for you and you can make a decision by then."

"All right, I will. Thank you, Dr. Benson." Annie rose slowly and extended her hand. "Thank you so much. I appreciate your candor and confidentiality."

"I'm sorry, Annie," he said, dropping the professional tone as he took her hand. "I'm afraid none of the options are good. It's rotten luck."

Annie walked out of the hospital in a numbed daze. She couldn't believe this was happening to her. A part of her wanted to stay in denial, but the nurse in her knew that was not possible. She had a week to consider and make a decision that would affect the rest of her life. When she arrived back at the flat, she searched hopefully through the pile of mail. There was no letter from Eric. She did see two letters in her brother's bold handwriting: one addressed to Peggy and one to her. Smitten with regret that she had not recently written to Jeff, she tore open the envelope and began to read.

May 18, 1940

Dear Annie,

How goes it? You've been very quiet lately. Hope all is well. So how do you like our ambassador telling all the Yanks to pack it in and go home? I think it's all a bunch of bunk! I'm ashamed he calls himself an American. Here he cozied up to Hitler all these months and assured Roosevelt he could be trusted. Right! Now he's running scared and worried that Hitler will invade Britain and arrest us all as "terrorists." Well, I can tell you I'm not going anywhere. In fact, as soon as I take my exams, I'm going to join the you-know-what for real. I've gotten my wings now from our university squadron and can't let my training go to waste. I'll show Mr. Kennedy that not all Americans are cowards or chums with the Nazis! (But honestly, Annie, I really don't want him to know or he may send me packing. We have to keep this our little secret.) Do you hear from Eric? Is he still in France? I'm afraid things are not going well for the Tommies over there. One good piece of news is that C.S. Lewis's brother is being evacuated home to England. I know that's a great relief to him, especially because his brother is well over forty and rather old to be back in the trenches fighting. Lewis, who just missed the draft, has joined the Home Guard and Prof. Tolkien is an air raid warden. It's strange to think that if it comes to an invasion, Oxford will be defended by a bunch of middle-aged professors! (Another reason why I can't wait to do my bit to keep it from coming to that.) I do hope the rest of the BEF—sorry, British Expeditionary Force—can hold out against the Huns. It would be terrible if France fell. Anyway, write sometime. I miss you but hope to get up to London before I'm off to the wild blue yonder. Now I have to write to Mom and Dad—but I'm just going to tell them that I'm helping with the war effort—no specifics, understand? Good thing I'm twenty-one and too far away for them to put up a fuss. Do be supportive of me, okay?

Love ya,
Jeff

Annie groaned when she thought of her parents. She was certain her mother would be very upset at Jeff's plans since he was their only son. She suspected that their father would be worried, but he would keep those worries to himself. She knew they would both be very proud of him.

And what of her? What would they think of her when they read the news that their youngest daughter was pregnant by a Scotsman whom they had never laid eyes on? How would they explain it to their church? What would everyone back home think? Annie couldn't bear to imagine it. Better not to tell them. Especially when there might not be anything to tell. If she did have a "miscarriage," then no one would have to know—not her parents, not Jeff, not even Eric. She could go on with her life as if nothing had happened and after the war she and Eric could be married and have other children. *Other* children…what was she thinking? If she "miscarried" in another week, then she could only consider the contents of her uterus as tissue. Nothing more. Certainly not a baby. The doctor had called it a fetus. But then she knew from her medical training that "fetus" was Latin for "young child" or "offspring." *Child.* There it was again. And she also knew that there would be more than just tissue in the bowl after the procedure. She had been in attendance once for a ruptured ectopic pregnancy of eight weeks. With amazement, she had observed floating around in the unbroken embryonic sac a tiny, perfectly formed human being with long, delicate fingers and toes. It was definitely more than tissue, and its value was confirmed by the wails of grief emanating from the bereft mother when she awoke.

How would I feel if I purposely ended this little person's life because he or she isn't convenient? What would Eric want? It's his baby too. If only he would write! How can he leave me to face this by myself? What if he doesn't want to marry me now? Or what if he's been shot down? How can I have a baby in the middle of a war? I don't know if I can stand the disgrace to carry on alone. It's too much to contemplate. But I don't have to decide now. I have another week. I'll think about it later.

Emotional and physical exhaustion overwhelmed Annie, and she did the most sensible thing she could think of. She went to bed.

Throughout the next week, Annie's mind and emotions continued to whirl around in a carousel of deliberation and denial. She spent hours alone in her room, just staring at the ceiling or sleeping. Peggy and Betty worried that she was cracking under the stress of Eric fighting in France. June kept her confidence, but she worried too.

When the day of her appointment arrived, Annie still felt confused and undecided. She thought vaguely that she should pray, but deep down she was angry at God.

How could He let this happen? I asked Him to forgive me. Hadn't He? It isn't like I'm a bad girl. I know plenty of that sort who carry on far worse and nothing ever happens. Why am I the one to get caught? And with only one slipup? It isn't fair!

She stumbled into the kitchen of their flat, looking for something to quell the queasiness in her stomach. She decided to make some tea and toast. While her tea steeped, she noticed Peggy's Bible lying on the table. *Well, let's see what God has to say to me today,* she thought bitterly as she flipped open the pages. Her eyes fell on Psalm 139:

> LORD, *thou hast searched me and known me!*
> *Thou knowest when I sit down and when I rise up;*
> > *thou discernest my thoughts from afar.*
> *Thou searchest out my path and my lying down,*
> > *and art acquainted with all my ways…*
>
> *Whither shall I go from thy Spirit?*
> > *Or whither shall I flee from thy presence?*
> *If I ascend to heaven, thou art there!*
> > *If I make my bed in Sheol, thou art there!*
> *If I take the wings of morning*
> > *And dwell in the uttermost parts of the sea,*
> *Even there thy hand shall lead me,*
> > *and thy right hand shall hold me…*
>
> *For thou didst form my inmost parts,*
> > *Thou didst knit me together in my mother's womb.*
> *I praise thee, for thou art fearful and wonderful.*
> > *Wonderful are thy works!*
> *Thou knowest me right well;*
> > *my frame was not hidden from thee,*
> > *when I was being made in secret,*
> > *intricately wrought in the depths of the earth.*
> *Thy eyes beheld my unformed substance;*
> > *in thy book were written, every one of them,*

the days that were formed for me
When as yet there was none of them.

Sobbing, Annie sank to the floor and curled up into a small ball, rocking herself back and forth as if she were the baby. The enormity of her predicament nearly crushed the breath out of her. But God had spoken to her, loud and clear. He was knitting together this child in her womb and had a plan and purpose for him. She knew that it might be easier in the short term to terminate the pregnancy, but in the end she would not be able to endure the guilt and regret. That morning, Annie decided that no matter what the cost, she would give her baby the gift of life.

Interval

*I will instruct you (says the Lord) and guide you
along the best pathway for your life; I will advise
you and watch your progress.*

PSALM 32:8 TLB

*One road leads home and a thousand
lead into the wilderness.*

C.S. LEWIS
The Pilgrim's Regress

22

July 1967
Yorkshire and Fife

O h, Mummy!" Natalie whispered, sympathetically clutching Annie's arm. "What a terrible time for you! I had no idea! What did you do?"

"Well," Annie glanced at a porcelain Empire clock gracing the mantle in the sitting room. "It's almost two. I'm afraid the rest of the story will have to wait for another time."

"All right, but please tell me one thing. David knows about all this, doesn't he?"

"Yes, and Ginny as well. I'm sorry not to have told you sooner, Nat, but even after all these years, it's still difficult for me." She noticed that Natalie was frowning. "I'm sorry too if you are disappointed in me and your dad. No parent wants their children to realize that they have feet of clay. I also don't want you to think we're hypocrites because we've harped so on the importance of purity and waiting until marriage. Part of that conviction of ours is borne from our own failings. We want to save you all from some of the heartache we went through."

"Of course you do. And I don't think you're a hypocrite. I'm sure Stuart will warn his children away from drinking, and one day when they're old enough, he'll tell them how he struggled with alcohol abuse. No, Mummy, I don't condemn you. It makes me sad, but more for you and what you must have gone through. Obviously, I know that in the end it all worked out and God turned your mistake into something good. After all, you and Daddy have a great marriage and a beautiful family. But what's puzzling me is that I thought March 16 was your anniversary. You always celebrate it then."

"Well, we have a legal anniversary, but we always felt March 16 was our true anniversary because that's the night we made our vows to each other. And we've always said it was our anniversary to avoid gossip and speculation. So that's the date we celebrate. And it's when we told your grandparents we were married so that they didn't die of shock when they found out I was pregnant."

"They still don't know the truth?"

"They know now, but during the war I wrote them that I had married an RAF officer and then later I wrote them that I was expecting. I didn't tell them the whole truth of the matter until after the war. But by then, like you say, they could see we were happily married."

Natalie shook her head. "Wow, I don't envy you having that talk with Granddad. So Mummy, when were you legally married? And what did you do? When did you tell Daddy? How did you feel?"

"My little psychologist." Annie smiled. "It's late, Nat, and we have to pack up tomorrow and leave for Anstruther. Let's save the rest of the story for another night, okay?"

"Okay, Mum." Natalie rose and collected their empty milk glasses and the plate of remaining cookies. "Thanks for sharing with me. I know it must have been hard for you." She leaned over and gently kissed her mother's cheek. "I love you and think you are the greatest. And I still want to be like you when I grow up."

Annie's eyes glistened with tears. "I appreciate your saying that, honey, but please don't make the same mistake I did. Don't deceive yourself and put yourself in a situation where you could be compromised. It can happen more easily than you think. Especially when you're in love. 'The spirit indeed is willing, but the flesh is weak.' We may have all the good intentions in the world, but one drink too many or too much time alone—"

"I know, Mum. Don't fret. Ginny and I have been well schooled by you and Daddy, and by David too. And Stuart has truly repented of his past misdeeds. You needn't be concerned on that account. Anyway, I should let you get to bed. But I do want to hear the rest of the story when we get to Anstruther."

After breakfast the MacKenzie clan packed their cars and prepared to depart Carlisle House for Scotland. Clementine's boys ran rambunctiously around the luggage in the driveway. In the shadow of the great hall's Baroque dome, they wrestled with the younger MacKenzie children, tumbling out onto the lawn like a litter of squirming puppies.

"Spencer! Teddy!" Clementine called helplessly. "Don't get Hannah's dress dirty! I'm sorry they are so excited," she apologized to Annie with a rueful smile.

"Not to worry," Annie soothed. "My boys are just as bad— look at them—and they're teenagers. They've had such a delightful time, Clemmie. All of us have. You've been a wonderful hostess. Thank you so much for a lovely stay."

"We've loved having you! And the boys have had the time of their lives. They won't know what to do with themselves when you leave. Do come back and see us again. Really. You are more than welcome to stay here on your way back from Scotland. Please consider the invitation open anytime."

Annie shook her hand warmly. "Thank you, we will."

David hefted the last suitcase into his parents' station wagon and turned to survey the chaotic scene as he wiped his forehead with the back of his hand. "Where's Stuart?" he asked Natalie.

"Um..." she hemmed awkwardly, "he said he had some pressing business in London and left early this morning."

"That's odd, isn't it? He hadn't said anything about it before. Will he be joining us in Scotland?"

"He said he would try to make it to the birthday party at Rua Reidh."

"Och," said Eric as he pushed shut the station wagon's tailgate, "I had hoped he'd play a round of golf with us at St. Andrews."

"You were just hoping to be able to boast that you had beaten a lord, even though you're an old man of fifty," David teased his father.

"Maybe so. But at any rate, as old as I am, I know I can beat the likes of both of you. Still, I was looking forward to having him with us. Is everything all right, lass?"

Natalie shrugged. "As far as I know. He acted fine. Something just came up."

"Well, I hope he gets it settled quickly and will be able to join us soon." Putting his arm around her, Eric gave Natalie a reassuring hug.

"Yeah, me too." She sighed. "Thanks, Daddy."

"Are we ready to go then? Where are Kate and the wee bairn?"

"She's inside feeding him now," David said as he carefully placed his son's car bed in the space behind the bucket seats of his MG midget. "They should be out by the time we say all our goodbyes." He smiled to himself, thinking how his father's Scottish burr had grown more pronounced the farther north they had come; in the same way his mother always regained her soft Southern drawl when she returned home to Virginia for visits. He wondered if Kate would lose hers over time. He hoped not. He found it immeasurably charming.

"Lads! Hannah!" Eric shouted above the fray on the lawn. "It's time to go. Last call for the loo."

Then, after a flurry of final preparations and farewells, the MacKenzies waved goodbye to the hospitality of Carlisle House and headed through the moors and dales of Yorkshire to Scotland and the coast of Fife.

They arrived in the fishing village of Anstruther in the late afternoon when the sun had only slightly lowered in the summer sky, casting a golden glow over the boats bobbing in the walled harbor. Eric's Aunt Margaret MacKenzie, who went by the moniker "Slim"—although she had long since outgrown that name—stood in the doorway of her whitewashed limestone cottage with her arms opened wide to embrace her great-nieces and nephews as they spilled out of the station wagon.

"Och! Look at ye now," she said reaching up to kiss William, Richard, and Mark as they dutifully bent down to offer their cheeks. "Ye're all grown so big since last summer, I'd hardly recognize ye. Soon ye'll be towerin' o'er yer pa. Come 'ere, Eric." She embraced him tightly. "I canna believe ye're turnin' fifty. That makes me an old woman, sure. Annie, how is it a young thing like ye is married to this old man?"

"Hello, Slim. How are you?" Annie asked before kissing her fondly.

"Fine. Fine. Especially now that ye're all here. Oh, Hannah!" she cried happily as the little girl threw her arms around her and hugged her tightly. "Ye darlin' lassie. Look at those flaxen curls of yers. And Natalie! Ye'er bonnier than e'er. When are ye goin' to be snatched up by some young man? Where's Ginny? And where's my David and his bride and wee bairn?"

"Here we are, Aunt Slim," David called as he opened Kate's car door and helped her with the baby. "Ginny's coming tomorrow. But here's the wee bairn." He kissed his aunt's smooth round cheek and placed Jeffrey in her open arms.

"Och. Ain't he a picture?" She covered his curly head with kisses. "We MacKenzies sure know how to make bonny babies, do na' we? Well done, Kate. How are ye, lass?"

"Fine, thank you, ma'am," Kate answered, smiling.

"Well, then. Come in, come in! Bring yer things in and then we'll have some tea out here in the garden. 'Tis such a lovely afternoon I thought we'd sit out here and enjoy the sea breezes. Och, David, before I forget—yer friend Austen Holmes rang up. Ye can use my telephone to ring him back."

"Is anything wrong? Did he leave a message?"

"Nay, he dinna' sound upset about anythin'. He sounded happy."

"Must be about the baby. Yvette was due soon. I'll give him a ring."

He quickly excused himself while the family began unloading their luggage and then came bursting out a few minutes later, exclaiming with excitement, "They're twins! They have twin girls!"

"Twins?" Kate repeated. "And here we thought she was having a big boy!"

"No, it's twins. Surprised everyone, including the doctor. One of the babies must have been hiding behind the other. Anyway, Yvette and the little girls are doing fine and Austen is ecstatic."

"Twins! How wonderful," Annie said. "What are they naming them?"

David looked at a scrap of paper. "Elinor Diane for Austen's mum and sister and Mary Anne for both Yvette's mum Molly, whose Christian name is Mary, and Austen's Marianne. They'll call them Ellie and Mary."

"How special that they're honoring Marianne," Kate said wistfully, remembering their own little Marianne. David gave her a sympathetic hug and kissed the top of her head. She smiled up at him gratefully and then released him to help his father with the luggage.

Aunt Slim bustled about her tiny kitchen preparing the tea with Natalie and Kate's assistance while the rest of the family got settled in the cottage. The boys and Hannah clambered up to the loft, unfazed that their quarters would be decidedly more modest than those they had enjoyed at Carlisle House. Eric placed his and Annie's bags in his old bedroom, which now served as the guestroom. Natalie and Ginny, when she arrived, would share Aunt Slim's room—Uncle Billy "Fatbug" having passed away years before—and David's little family would stay up the road at the Smugglers' Inn.

They passed a pleasant afternoon sipping tea and lemonade as they sat in the warm sunshine out on the terrace over-looking the harbor. As soon as the tea dishes had been washed and dried, Aunt Slim began the preparations for supper. The women laughed and chatted together in the kitchen while Eric took the boys and Hannah down to the docks to watch the fishermen bringing in their evening catch. The familiar sights and sounds of Eric's youth coupled with the rhythmic wash of the sea against the shore brought him a poignant peace. It lingered as the family gathered for the evening meal, and their conversation and laughter drifted into the night until they contentedly settled down to sleep.

But peace and contentment, as well as sleep, eluded Natalie—and not just because of the gentle snoring of her great-aunt lying in the next bed. Natalie missed Stuart. She found the charms of the day wanting without him there to share them, and she constantly caught herself thinking to tell him about this or that experience or observation. She wished to see what his reactions would be to her aunt's humble cottage and to the fishermen in the village, sensing that he would surely find it all delightful. Her thoughts lingered on him all the next day as she walked on the beach of the West Sands in St. Andrews, collecting shells and chasing waves with Hannah. She ached to share with Stuart all her family's special moments and the wonders of summer on the Scottish shore.

The MacKenzie men missed him as well when they congregated up the hill from the beach at the Royal and Ancient for a round of golf. Eric proudly showed off his four fine sons to the caddies and let the old-timers make a fuss over them. Then they hit the links with Eric's expert guidance navigating them around the bunkers and gorse patches. Thirteen-year-old Mark served as their caddie and found he shared his father's adeptness at discovering "lost" balls hiding in the brush. Eric relished being back on the Old Course, reading the familiar rolling fairways, feeling the exhilaration in the rush of the winds and the freedom of the wide open land stretching to the sea. Best of all was the opportunity of experiencing it with his sons.

After crossing back over the famous Swilcan Burn Bridge and completing their round at Tom Morris, the eighteenth hole, the MacKenzies returned to the caddie shack where Eric endured a fair amount of ribbing about his age and upcoming birthday. Overhearing the banter, a well-dressed gentleman approached them.

"Eric?"

Eric looked over at the silver-haired man and recognized an old friend. "Peter! How are you?" They shook hands warmly and smiled broadly at one another. "It's great to see you."

"And you. I just heard you talking and saying you're about to celebrate your fiftieth. Can't believe it, old boy. These must be your sons. My, they're a fine lot and so grown up now. How many children do you have? Six? I read your Christmas letters, but I'm sorry, I've lost count."

"Seven," Eric answered proudly. "These four boys and three daughters. This is my oldest, David, and this is William, Richard, and Mark. Lads, this is Lord Peter Kilmorey." The boys each shook Peter's hand and murmured their "How do you dos."

"And your wife, Annie, and your girls, are they here?"

"Yes, they're down at the beach—as well as David's wife, Kate, and our grandson, Jeffrey."

"Grandson? My word! You *are* an old man. Congratulations!" Peter thumped Eric's back. "I say, I would love to meet them all and so would Catherine. Why don't you come up to the house for dinner this evening? Say seven?"

"That's kind of you, Peter, but…" Eric hesitated. Even after nearly thirty years, the prospect of facing Laurene's parents again seemed too daunting.

"Don't worry." Peter read his thoughts. "My parents aren't at the big house anymore. Father and Mother are rather infirm now and live nearby in the Dowager House. Father passed his title and duties on to me. I'm the laird now. And I insist that you all come for a visit. It's been far too long."

"I'm sorry to hear that your parents are not well," Eric responded with polite concern.

"Thank you. You know, Eric," Peter said, lowering his voice, "Father never forgave himself about Laurene. Anyway, do say you'll come."

"All right. Thank you very much."

"Excellent. Now how many should we expect?"

"Well, my daughter Ginny should be arriving this afternoon, so all nine of us are here, plus Kate makes ten, and then the baby."

"What about that grande dame aunt of yours?"

"I doubt we would be able to talk her out of her house. She's pretty set in her ways."

"Well, don't force her, but if she'd fancy a dinner out, she's more than welcome. All right then! We'll see you at seven. Oh, and sports jackets are fine. Dinner jackets aren't necessary."

"Good thing, since we didn't bring any," Richard murmured to his brothers as Lord Kilmorey strode off.

"Well, Kate will be quite pleased to see Kilmorey House," David said. "Too bad we don't have Stuart here to give us some cachet with the laird."

"He seems like a pretty down-to-earth chap," observed William.

"He is. He's a fine man," Eric said. "Now then, let's find the ladies and inform them that we have a dinner invitation."

Following the curving driveway through the wooded Kilmorey estate on a summer evening was a far different experience for Eric than his last journey had been that black, rainy night in September of 1939. Watching his family pile out of their station wagon before the austere stone manor house and file solemnly behind the new butler up the broad oak staircase seemed surreal to Eric. They paused on the great landing to stare up at an immense oil portrait of a handsome middle-aged couple with a teenaged son and daughter. By this time, they had all been informed of the Kilmorey family's connection to their own.

"Is that Laurene?" David asked quietly.

Eric swallowed. "Yes."

"She's pretty!" Hannah exclaimed.

Annie laced her fingers with Eric's. "She was very pretty, honey."

He squeezed her hand. "Aye, she was."

"Just think," Mark said in a hushed tone. "If Dad had married her, then the laird would be our grandpa and we could live in this house."

David ruffled his hair. "If Dad hadn't married Mum, we wouldn't be here, silly."

"Oh, yeah," Mark said, grinning sheepishly. "That's right."

"Welcome!" Peter called from the doorway of the drawing room. "Come on up. We'll have drinks and hors d'oeuvres in here before dinner."

The MacKenzies complied and climbed the rest of the stairs. Catherine Kilmorey, an attractive brunette, graciously received her husband's guests, putting each one at ease.

"I'm so glad you brought all your children," Catherine said. "Ours are off on holiday with their cousins at Brighton and we miss them."

"We have only four—three sons and one daughter—so we didn't quite catch up to you," Peter said as he made certain everyone had been served a drink. "The two oldest boys are at Cambridge. Perhaps we could introduce them someday to your lovely daughters, Eric." He watched slender Ginny with her tumbling honey-colored curls and petite Natalie with her dark shoulder-length hair as they admired the Belgian tapestries adorning the drawing room walls.

"Sorry, but I think they are spoken for," Eric replied. "Ginny is seriously dating a resident physician at Barts in London, and Natalie also has a serious beau, Lord Stuart Devereux."

"Essex's son? I know him," Peter said. "To be honest, I'm not overly fond of Essex, but I've heard some good things about his son—lately. Seems he's undergone a bit of a Prince Hal to King Henry V turn. I understand that he had been rather given to drink in his Oxford days, but since taking his degree has settled down to be quite the serious businessman. In fact, I've wanted to talk with him about his work in opening Clifton Manor to the public. We're looking about for ways to increase income here and have thought of opening an animal menagerie and perhaps renting out cottages on the property for holidays, that sort of thing. Anyway, I should think he would make a fine match for your daughter."

"You wouldn't discourage him from marrying below his class?" Eric prodded.

"I'd hardly think Natalie would be below his class." Peter studied his old friend with a grim smile. "Honestly, I deserve the sting of that question from you, Eric. But you can't imagine how the war changed my outlook. I'm much more democratic now, aren't I, darling?" He directed this to his wife. She smiled and nodded. "You see, I met Catherine at Cambridge during the war when we were both working on code-breaking. Her family is not from the gentry class, but what can I say? We fell in love. And the rest is history."

"And your father approved?" Eric asked skeptically.

"No, but by the time the war was over, he was glad to have me return home, even with a wife not of his choosing. And once he and mother met Catherine, they fell in love with her too. To be perfectly frank, he always regretted interfering with you and Laurene and trying to send her away. He didn't want to make that mistake again." He patted Eric's shoulder. "So sorry, old chap, to bring all that back up."

"I still miss her," Eric said quietly, "even after all these years."

"I know. So do I. She was the best of sisters and a dear girl, wasn't she?" They exchanged a knowing look of shared sympathy. "Right, then," Peter finally said. "Let's adjourn to the next room for dinner, shall we?"

The group followed their hosts down the hallway to a grand dining room resplendent with an enormous cherry table set with fine china, crystal, and silver. Natalie had overheard Lord Peter's comments about Stuart, as well as his exchange with her father. As she looked about the faded opulence of Kilmorey House, she considered that she would feel equally at home in a manor house such as this as in a fisherman's cottage like Aunt Slim's. It seemed to her that the important thing would be to share a home—large or small, rich or humble—with someone she loved. And she knew with growing certainty that her someone was Stuart Devereux.

Later that night, after returning to the cottage, the family gathered in the small parlor to explain excitedly to Aunt Slim all they had seen and heard at Kilmorey House. When she and the younger children had been excused for bed, leaving just the young adults, Natalie turned to her parents and pleaded, "Since we're all here together and Ginny is with us now, would you please tell us the rest of your story?"

They acquiesced. Sitting side by side and holding hands like young lovers, Annie and Eric talked far into the night as they shared with their children their wartime tale of heartache and romance.

Part 3
Eric and Annie's Story

*Those whom I love, I reprove and chasten; so be
zealous and repent. Behold I stand at the door and
knock; if any one hears my voice and opens the door,
I will come in to him and eat with him, and he with me.*

REVELATION 3:19-20

*Though our feelings come and go, His Love for us
does not. It is not wearied by our sins, or our indifference; and therefore, it is quite relentless in its
determination that we shall be cured of those sins,
at whatever cost to us, at whatever cost to Him.*

C.S. LEWIS
Mere Christianity

23

End of May 1940
Dunkirk

iss Little, you missed your appointment last week," Dr. Benson said in a quietly chiding manner. They were standing on a crowded pier in Dover while people scurried about them loading medical supplies onto a white vessel painted with giant red crosses.

"Yes." Annie could not meet his eyes. "I couldn't..."

"It's all right. I understand, but what will you do?"

"I honestly don't know."

"Well then, I'll help you however I can, and we'll keep it under wraps as long as we are able. But you must come to see me next week. You need to look after yourself and be under a doctor's care."

"All right." She nodded and added, "Thanks."

"You're not planning to go on this hospital boat over to Dunkirk, are you?"

"Yes, Betty and I volunteered to help with the evacuation."

"I'm sure there's plenty of work here in Dover with all the boatloads of wounded and shell-shocked soldiers coming in by the hour. June has been working here. You can help her. Annie, I'm not sure someone in your—"

Annie held up her in hand in warning. "Harry," she lowered her voice to a whisper, "remember that is confidential." Then she spoke above the fray. "The Nazis aren't going to bomb a ship plastered with red crosses, so we'll be safe. And I want to serve where I can be most useful. I keep thinking that among the men being evacuated from France, one could be my Eric, so I want to go and do my best for all of them."

He sighed with resignation. "All right, come on board then. It looks like we'll have good weather for the Channel crossing. Thank God, it's cleared up since last night. I understand our poor chaps were dug in on the beach trying to sleep in a downpour. Must have been miserable."

"Yeah," said a seaman who had overheard this part of the conversation. "But, miserable as it was, the rain was a blessing. It kept the Jerries from being able to fly through with their bombers. Our lads stuck on the beach 'ave been raked with machine-gun fire and bombs for days. It's 'ard to believe that a fine day like this can turn to a living 'ell, but it is 'ell over there."

"So you've been to Dunkirk?" Annie asked.

"Yes, miss. This will be my fourth trip over."

"You must be exhausted."

The sailor chuckled as he helped her up the gangway. "That's an understatement. But we all 'ave to do our bit now, don't we? Anyway, it's nice to see some fresh nurses and doctors. Welcome aboard."

It was a fine spring day for sailing and Annie and Betty would have felt almost as though they were on a pleasure cruise had they been able to ignore the flotilla of ships and small craft that accompanied them out of the port. Because of the urgency of the evacuation and the difficulty the larger ships had in drawing close enough to pick up the retreating troops, the government had appealed to all available civilian vessels from motorboats to fishing trawlers to help with the effort.

Annie and Betty settled in deck chairs on their midsized converted hospital ship and took out their knitting. All over the country, women were knitting scarves, socks, and blankets to "do their bit" for the war effort. Plying their needles, the young women chatted and tried to ignore the growing knots in their stomachs as they drew closer to the French shore-line, which seemed to be completely ringed by fire. The wind carried the stench of burning oil and the sounds of bursting shells, booming explosions, and the desperate cries of men. As the captain brought the boat in as close to the shallow waters as he dared, they put their knitting aside and stood looking out over the horrific devastation.

Hordes of men crouched in the sand like piles of beetles, the dead lying next to the living. What appeared to be hundreds of densely packed logs floated in the water about the small vessels that attempted to pick up the troops queuing along the pier under intense air fire. With a shock, Annie realized they were not logs but dead soldiers. The sailor had been right: This was a scene out of Dante's *Inferno*. They were staring at a tableau of hell itself.

"Why is everything burning?" Annie asked as the smoke began to sting her eyes.

"It's a scorched earth policy," Harry answered. "Our boys have been ordered to render everything useless to the Nazis. They can't bring their equipment with them, so they're disabling and burning it. Such a shame. Must be our whole army's worth of trucks and weapons going up in smoke."

"But what will we have left to defend England now against an invasion?"

"Doesn't look like much, does it? We'll hopefully get our army out, though. I guess we'll still have the Navy and the RAF—if too many of them don't get shot down in this mess."

"Look!" cried Betty, pointing to a plane flying low toward them. "There's the RAF now!" She waved excitedly. "Hello, boys! We're glad to see you!"

Annie gasped when she realized that the insignia painted on the plane was the black cross of the Luftwaffe, not the red, white, blue, and yellow cockade of the RAF. She watched in horror as the bay doors on the plane's underbelly opened above them. "Get down!" she yelled, pulling Betty with her to the deck. They heard the terrifying scream of the bomb as the Stuka roared past. The ship rocked violently, sending the crew flying, as the bomb exploded in the water.

"Blast those Germans!" cried Harry. "They're bombing a hospital ship!"

"Get below! Get below!" the sailors shouted to the medical staff. "They're coming back!"

Annie, Betty, Harry, and the others scurried on hands and knees to the ladder well and scrambled down the steps just before hearing the bloodcurdling scream of the bombs and then the rat-a-tat-tat of machine-gun fire pelting the deck above. They gripped the steel stanchions to keep from being tossed about as the ship heaved to and fro, dodging the falling bombs. Miraculously, the captain's brave evasion methods proved to be their salvation. When the bombing ceased, they were still afloat.

Clambering up on deck to tend to the wounded crew members, Annie and Betty saw nine-inch holes piercing the area where they had sat knitting only minutes before. Among the shouting and deafening blasts, they noticed a fishing vessel unloading a score of bedraggled and soaking-wet soldiers onto their deck. Some groaned with relief to be aboard, others from their wounds. A few were nearly naked, their uniforms ripped from machine-gun fire and explosions.

For a few minutes chaos reigned on the ship as it did on the shore. The captain barked orders to his remaining able-bodied crew to pull away while Harry shouted to the medical staff to treat the direst cases first. Bloodied, broken bodies were everywhere, covered in oil, sand, and shrapnel. How was one to determine which were the worst? All seemed dire to Annie and Betty as they set to work. They had been trained in a city hospital; they had not yet been confronted with the casualties of war. Clutching each other's arms, they exchanged a terrified look and then nodded grimly.

"All right, then," Betty said determinedly. "We can do this."

Annie bent down to examine a filthy tourniquet tied around what remained of a soldier's leg. The raw flesh below looked like ground beef with splinters of bone poking through. The tourniquet had been tied too tightly for too long, and gangrene had set in where the blood had not been allowed to flow. Knowing the young man would have to face an amputation when he arrived home, Annie loosened the band and then felt her stomach heave.

"Excuse me, sir," she whispered and then ran to the ship's side, where she vomited overboard. Wiping her mouth with her handkerchief, she resolved that that would be the last time. She hurried back to the soldier and murmured what comfort she could as she gave him a shot of morphine and washed away the blood and sand while he drifted off to sleep. She groped through her pockets and retrieved her lipstick case. Gently, she drew the red letter "A" on his forehead to alert the doctors on shore that he would need an amputation.

"I still can't believe those bloody Nazis would send bombs down on a hospital ship," mutered Harry as he removed shrapnel out of a man's head and stitched it up. "So much for the Geneva Convention."

"Blasted buggers," said the soldier, wincing but willing himself to hold still for the procedure. "I was in the retreat from Belgium. Refugees clogged the roads and those bloody Stukas bombed them! Women, children, and old people—not just soldiers. They didn't care. We'd hear that terrible screaming and everyone would dive for what cover they could find in ditches along the road. They just swooped down low, dropping bombs and firing machine guns at these helpless people. I could see the blasted pilots, grinning like demons, in their cockpits. That's the honest truth! They were smiling as they gunned us down. Next to me in the ditch was a little girl, not more than seven or eight. I held that little girl in my arms as she died. That will haunt me the rest of my life. I hate those bloody Huns," he growled. "But don't you worry, miss," he added to Annie, who had grown visibly pale at his story. "We won't let them into England. We'll hold them off with pitchforks if we have to. And our RAF won't let us down."

"Just where the blazes is the RAF now?" groused another soldier. "We're getting our arses kicked back in France and we were hammered day and night by the bloody Luftwaffe back at the beach and where is our air force? That's what I want to know."

"I'm the RAF and I'm right here because one of ye buggers shot me clean out of the sky. Now me beautiful Spitty is in the drink and I'm lucky someone had the guts to pull me out." This was stated by a disgruntled pilot whose face and uniform glistened with black petrol. "We're up there all right. See all those white tracers?" He pointed to the sky. "That's us! We're doin' our bloody best up there, but it dinna help when yer own mates shoot ye down. Besides, Commander in Chief Dowding ain't goin' to send us all in. We've already lost over three hundred fighters in this campaign. We have to have some lads left to defend against the invasion. Nay, old Stuffy dinna want to lose all of us protectin' the bloody Frogs."

Annie stared at the pilot, whose unmistakable Scottish burr rose in angry protest over the accusations of the soldier. Under the oil-slicked hair she caught glints of red. "Pilot Officer McLeod? Is that you?"

Eric's friend looked up at her and grinned. "Miss Annie? Well, ye're a sight fer sore eyes!"

"Oh, Ian!" She rushed over and knelt beside him. "Are you all right? Are you hurt?"

"I'm fine. Just my pride is hurt." He looked at his blackened clothes and hands. "I could use a bath, though."

"How's Eric? Where is he? Is he all right?"

"He's up there some'eres, lass. Doin' his part to get these lads home. Don't ye worry. He's a good pilot and will be fine—as long as these blasted Tommies don't shoot at him." He glared at all the soldiers crowded on deck.

"When you saw him last, was he okay?"

"Aye, miss. We were rather busy, what with the Huns overrunnin' Europe, but he's fine and always speakin' of ye fondly."

She pressed her lips together and managed a brave smile. "Thank you, Ian. That's just what I needed to hear."

~

When their ship finally reached the harbor at Dover, kind Englishwomen greeted the grateful and war-weary servicemen with blankets, sandwiches, hot tea, cigarettes, and postcards to write their loved ones that they had returned safely. Annie and Betty gulped down some food and kept working. Dr. Benson strictly ordered them to stay put in Dover to assist the assembled medical teams in treating the wounded. They were not to return to Dunkirk.

Snatching a few hours of sleep when they could, the nurses worked feverishly for days on end tending to the unrelenting stream of casualties. Since the doctors were overwhelmed with the most critical cases, Annie often had to extract shrapnel from wounds and stitch them up by herself. By the fourth of June, the "miracle of Dunkirk," the evacuation of the majority of the British Expeditionary Force from the continent, had been successfully completed, although a small remnant of troops and the air force still fought on in pockets of France. But the intrepid Sir Winston Churchill and his government turned the apparent defeat of retreat into a moral victory by celebrating the "Dunkirk spirit" of courage in the face of impossible odds. Churchill's inspiring speech to the nation urged the British people not to give up or give in to the Nazi threat to their entire civilization. He stirred their hearts with his exhortation: "We shall fight on the beaches, we shall fight on the landing grounds, we shall fight in the fields and in the streets, we shall fight in the hills; we shall never surrender!"

The exhausted nurses traveled home to London on a train packed with the last of the returning soldiers, who were hailed as heroes at each stop. Arriving back at their flat in Bayswater, Annie took a long hot bath and slept for more than twelve hours. When she awoke, she remembered to look again through the pile of mail stacked on the kitchen table.

She ripped open a note from Jeff.

June 2

Dear Annie,

Where are you girls? I haven't heard from any of you. Makes me worried you're all involved with this evacuation effort. Have you been? I hope you're all right. I'm having a hard time concentrating on studying for my exams. Seems so inconsequential when boys are dying right across the Channel. But as soon as I can wrap things up here, I'm off to the wild blue yonder. Can you possibly come up for graduation ceremonies? If you can, it'd be nice to have some family to share the occasion with me. And bring Peggy too if she'd like to come. Let me know, okay?

Love,
Jeff

PS. Any news from Eric?

Annie sifted through the letters one more time and then sighed with deep resignation.

No. There was no news from Eric.

24

June 20, 1940
Oxford

Annie and Peggy took the train up to Oxford for Jeff's graduation ceremony, which was held in Sir Christopher Wren's picturesque Sheldonian Theatre on a lovely summer day in late June. After the requisite speeches and conferment of degrees, the dons, arrayed in brightly colored gowns and all manner of plumed hats, filed out like a flock of parrots into the brilliant sunshine. The jubilant students quickly followed and stood in the shadows of Hertford's Bridge of Sighs and the Bodleian's tower of learning while basking in the accolades of their delighted families.

"Mom and Daddy would be so proud of you, Jeff!" Annie said as she gave her brother a hug. "I know they wish they could be here."

"Congratulations, Jeff!" Peggy bestowed a kiss on his cheek.

Jeff, his sandy hair tousled from his mortarboard, beamed with satisfaction. "Well, thank ya'll so much for coming up. Boy, it's great to see you both! Say, there's a garden reception over at Magdalen, so why don't you ladies join us?" He offered an arm to each of them as they sauntered down Holy-well Street, beyond where Annie had stayed with the Bing-leys, past the walls of Magdalen College, and into the Cloister Quadrangle. Students in their black robes, looking like crows among the plumage of the dons, milled about on the rolled grass lawn. Stone arches, festooned with fragrant clusters of wisteria, enclosed the throng as the slender spires of Mag-dalen Tower hovered over the festivities.

Jeff escorted the ladies over to a large, ruddy-faced man Annie recognized from their dinner at the Eastgate Hotel back in November.

"Mr. Lewis," Jeff said, "I would like to introduce you to my sister, Annie Little, and our friend Peggy Myers."

"How do you do?" Lewis boomed as he shook their hands. It occurred to Annie that she was glad they were outdoors. A room would have difficulty containing the remarkable vitality emanating from this man.

"I'm so glad to meet you, Mr. Lewis," Annie said. "Jeff has talked so much about you. He's been thrilled to study with you here."

"And you must be the sister whom he constantly extols and frets over. Little, isn't she the one for whom you made the inquiry?"

"Yes, sir."

"A pleasure to make your acquaintance, Miss Little. Your brother has been a stellar pupil of mine and he has spoken quite affectionately of you." He lowered the decibels of his voice from a boom to a confidential rumble. "But it seems, young lady, that he is concerned for your safety should there be an invasion or bombing attacks launched on London. He's asked whether we would be willing to host another refugee in our humble abode, and I told him, 'By all means.' Until recently we had four little girls staying with us, and we'll soon have even more room when my sister marries and moves out at the end of August. So if things do get too sticky, remember that you're more than welcome to join us out at the Kilns."

"Thank you very much, sir. That's very kind of you."

"And you, miss?" He looked at Peggy. "Do you also need a place to evacuate to from London?"

"No, sir. My parents are in the Midlands near Warwick, so I can go to them if things take a bad turn. But thank you very much for the offer."

"You're welcome. You know, my brother Warren and I are the only resident males—it seems we're a household overrun by women at the moment—so a few more ladies would definitely not pose a problem." He clapped Jeff on the shoulder. "You're off to the RAF, are you?"

"Yes, sir. I pack up this weekend and then join my new squadron down at Croydon, south of London."

"Well, the RAF will be better for it, but we'll be sorry to see you go. I may run into you sometime, though. They've asked me to deliver some inspirational talks to the troops at various bases. If I'm invited to Croydon, we should meet for a drink together."

"I'd like that very much."

Mentor and pupil exchanged a warm handshake. "Stay in touch, then, and take care," Lewis said. "And may our Lord bless and keep you."

Jeff flashed a brave smile. "Thank you, sir, for...everything."

"Lovely to meet you, young ladies," Lewis said as he moved on. "And consider the invitation to the Kilns always open, Miss Little."

"Thank you, sir. A pleasure to meet you too, Mr. Lewis," Annie called after him, and then turning to Jeff she said, "He's really nice."

"Yes, he is. He's a very kind and generous fellow and has a great sense of humor. I've been very blessed to have him for a tutor, and he's had an enormous impact on my spiritual life. I am glad you were both able to meet him, and I hope you will take him up on his hospitality if things get rough."

"Well, hopefully that won't be necessary," Annie said as she linked her arm in his. "Now, why don't you take us around the college? This may be Peggy's only chance to tour this male bastion of academia."

"Okay. You're right. And since the term is over, I can let you see my rooms. I have something to give you anyway. Peggy?" He offered her his other arm. "I must say, squiring you two gals about is bound to make all the guys green with envy."

Annie laughed. "At least until you tell them I'm your kid sister."

"Mum's the word, remember?"

Jeff showed them the medieval chapel with its intricately carved choir screen and niches filled with statues, the dining hall with its Elizabethan linen-fold wood paneling, and the picturesque Addison's Walk with its flower beds and riverside meadow. He took them through a wide door of the yellow stone, eighteenth-century Palladian "New Building," up the high, twisting wooden staircase number three, past door number three on the first floor that he indicated were the set of rooms used by C.S. Lewis, and then up two more flights to his own lodgings.

Breathing heavily after the arduous climb and laughing at their exhaustion, the girls entered Jeff's room. Annie fell onto an old settee and panted, "I hope you don't have to move this furniture out!"

"No, it was already here and I'm leaving it for the next occupant. It is a trek up here, but it was rather convenient, especially in foul weather, to have Lewis right below on the same staircase. And I have a nice view of the deer grove. See?" He indicated the window.

Peggy looked out and took a deep breath. "Mm, the wisteria smells heavenly."

"Yeah, I'm going to miss this place," Jeff said with a hint of sadness. "I've loved it here. But the real world calls, and I can't stay forever in an ivory tower while there's a war on." Drawing himself up, he put on a brave smile. "I want to celebrate today. Look, girls, I have a surprise for you!" He pulled a carton the size of a shoebox out of a cupboard and handed it to Annie. Peggy joined her on the settee while she opened it. Inside, carefully wrapped in paper, were half a dozen oranges.

Annie's face flushed crimson. "Jeffrey Lawrence Little, this is not one bit funny!"

"What?" Jeff was taken aback by her vehement response. "What do you mean?"

Peggy chuckled softly. "Obviously, he didn't mean it as a joke, Annie, which does make it funny."

"I don't understand," Jeff said, still confused.

Peggy explained. "Oranges are on the ration list."

"I know. Our parents sent these in a box of goodies for graduation. I thought you all would like some too."

"But oranges *are* allowed for pregnant women. So Annie took your gift as a joke, intimating that we girls are in a family way."

"Oh, gosh! Of course not! No, I'm sorry. I hadn't bothered to read what was on the ration list for pregnant mothers." Jeff laughed with embarrassment at his faux pas.

Annie managed a chagrined smile. "I'm sorry. I overreacted. We're just sensitive to these things at the hospital and, of course, you wouldn't pay attention to them. Thanks for the oranges, Jeff. We'll enjoy them."

"Sure, no problem. And I have some chocolate for you too."

"Chocolate!" cried Peggy. "You are a sweetheart."

Jeff grinned, happy to be back in their good graces, but as they chatted, he warily observed Annie. When Peggy later excused herself, he bent closer to his sister and murmured, "I'm really sorry. I obviously hit a hot button with those oranges." He gulped. "Annie, you're not…pregnant, are you?"

Her eyes betrayed the truth by quickly brimming with tears. She nodded in confirmation.

"Oh, no!" Sighing heavily, he leaned back in his chair. "What are you going to do?"

"I don't know," she answered in a small voice.

"How far along are you?"

"I'm due around Christmas. I'm almost four months."

"Oh, my gosh! When will you start showing?"

"Maybe a little in the next month or so. I'm not sure, but I can let out my skirts and probably hide it for a while. Maybe even until the end of the summer."

"You know, I thought your face looked fuller, but it didn't occur to me that—" Jeff paused and rubbed his forehead. "What about Eric? Does he know?"

"I haven't heard any news of him since Dunkirk when we picked up a pilot friend of his. I have no idea if he's still in France or if…or if…he's been shot down."

"Golly, Annie," groaned Jeff. "This is terrible!"

"Yes," she quietly agreed. She hesitated and then added, "I was given the opportunity to have a surgical procedure by a doctor I know at Barts."

"An…abortion?"

"Yes. But I decided against it."

"Well, I'm glad for that!"

"I just couldn't do it. It's not the baby's fault, after all, so why should he or she be punished for our mistake? And it would just make things even worse if I were to have had an…if I were to have had a 'miscarriage.' I feel bad enough without compounding my guilt with that. And besides, this is Eric's child too. It wouldn't be fair to him for me to make that decision by myself. And now—I know it may be wrong to think this way, Jeff, but—I'm almost glad I'm carrying his baby." She hurried on. "I'm not glad for what we did. I know we should have waited until we were married. You remember that I did ask God to forgive me, although I still find it hard to accept that He has—especially now. But at the same time, I am growing more and more attached to this baby. And if something has happened to Eric, I'll still be carrying his child, and that brings me some comfort."

"Okay. I think I can understand how you feel about that. And certainly abortion would be the wrong way out. God's Word is pretty clear about that. And regardless of how the baby came to be, we're talking about a future niece or nephew of mine, and I would hate to lose them—particularly that way.

So I am grateful you made the decision to have the baby. But, Annie, what do you plan to do?" Jeff repeated gently.

"I really don't know. I don't even know if I want to tell Eric about the baby until we are married. I don't want to force him into a shotgun marriage."

"Are you going to tell Mom and Dad?"

"No! And don't you either! Jeff, you are sworn to secrecy about this. I'll tell whomever I think needs to know when I'm ready. So far it's only me, the doctor, June, and now you."

"Not Peggy?"

"Not Peggy, what?" Peggy asked as she glided back into the room.

Annie was grateful an answer came to her quickly. "You weren't at Dunkirk."

"Right. I missed all the action—although I think it was probably quite disturbing. You girls seemed rather traumatized and certainly exhausted by the ordeal. Well, we may all be facing it soon if the French surrender."

"Oh, they'll surrender," Jeff said, easily picking up this new thread in the conversation. "They really have no choice. Neither has anyone else in Europe. No one seems to have the military clout to stand up to Hitler."

"But we will *never* surrender," Peggy said firmly, echoing Churchill's speech.

"No, but I sure wish the U.S. would get into this war. It's going to be mighty hard for this little island to hold out alone. Still, I'll bet Hitler is sorry Britain's decided to put up a fight. He knows what a stubborn lot you are."

"Well, you're a wonderful guy to join the fight with us," Peggy said. "We're so proud of you."

"Gee, thanks, but I just have to fight. I don't see how I can sit out this war when all my buddies are going off. Besides, I have to help defend you lovely ladies from those Huns."

"And," Annie added with a gleam in her eye, "you'll look so dapper in your uniform."

"You've got that right!" Jeff laughed. "When I get some leave, I'll come visit you girls in London—wearing my uniform, of course—and take you out on the town. That's a promise."

After a celebratory dinner with Jeff in Oxford, Annie and Peggy took the train back to London and walked from Paddington Station to their flat. As soon as they opened their door, Annie checked through the mail, only to be disappointed once again.

There was still no word from Eric.

25

June 21, 1940
London

*N*ot until the day after Annie's trip up to Oxford did a crumpled postcard finally appear in her mailbox. It read:

20 June

Dear Annie,

I'm safe and home. Arrived in Liverpool.
Will come straight away.

I love you,
Eric

That same afternoon she opened the door to find him leaning in exhaustion against the doorjamb—bleary-eyed and unshaven in a filthy and torn uniform. She embraced him gratefully and promptly sent him to the bath and bed. While he slept on her couch for a full night and day, she washed, mended, and ironed his uniform and then prepared a large meal of "bangers and mash." When he awoke, they sat at the dinner table, talking late into the evening, sharing their evacuation stories. Annie told him about her experiences at Dunkirk and then in the rudimentary clinic set up at Dover.

"Those blasted Nazis! How dare they fire on a hospital ship!" Eric exclaimed. "But I am glad to hear that ye picked up McLeod." He shoveled a third helping of potatoes onto his plate. "I saw him go down and was sick with worry about what had happened to him. I thought most likely he had been killed or taken prisoner. It was bad luck our own lads shot him down, but at least they had the decency to pull him out of the drink."

"Yes," Annie said, smiling. "He was as mad as a hornet at the army for shooting him, but thank God he didn't have any serious injuries. Anyway, he was able to get home a lot earlier than you. Did you stay on in France?"

"Aye. Our base was in Brittany, and we held out there for a fortnight supportin' what remained of the BEF and the French armies until the Jerries found us and bombed our planes as they sat on the tarmac. We have a secret warnin' system here in England, but over there we had no way of knowin' the Luftwaffe was comin' until we could actually hear them, and by then it was too late. We literally had to run for our lives. Our squadron leader told us it was every man for himself and to make our way to the western coast to a port called St. Nazaire, where there would be ships to evacuate us like there were at Dunkirk. We walked a long way, which for pilots was extremely frustratin' since we covered by foot in hours what we could fly over in minutes if only we had our planes. Eventually, though, we found some trucks and then just followed all the other troops and refugees who were fleein' to the coast."

He finished eating and pushed his plate aside. "Thank ye, Annie. That surely was the best meal I can remember havin' in ages."

"It's the least I can do, Eric. I'm so relieved and happy to see you alive and well, and I'm especially glad you were able to come by here on your way back to Kenley."

"Well, since it's every man for himself, everyone who could has tried to make their way to loved ones before reportin' back to duty. I'm thankful I had to go through London anyway to get back." He reached across the table and took her hand. "I can't tell ye how good it is to see ye. Sometimes I wondered if I ever would again."

"I know. Me too." She smiled at him and squeezed his hand. "How was it after you got to St. Nazaire? Did you run into more trouble there?"

"That was the worst of it. Similar to yer experience at Dunkirk, it was complete chaos. Thousands of troops and refugees tryin' to get out to the ships and the Nazis firin' on everythin'. When my mates and I arrived in the late afternoon on the sixteenth, we saw all these uniforms lyin' across the docks, evidently meant as a decoy, and sure enou' the Nazis were pepperin' them with machine-gun fire. We sneaked down to the smaller piers and some very kind locals offered to take us out in their fishin' vessel to this enormous Cunard ocean liner called the *Lancastria*. When we got up close to it, we could see it was crawlin' with people. Some officers yelled to us that they couldn't take any more passengers. Apparently they had boarded six thousand when their limit was four. Well, we were very disappointed, to say the least, because we wanted to get the blazes out of there and wondered what harm would a handful more of RAF lads be. But they waved us away and the fisherman motored off to catch up to a destroyer named the *Highlander*, which I thought sounded more auspicious anyway."

Eric paused for a moment and then continued in a somber tone. "And wouldn't ye know it, Annie? A bomb exploded near our little craft, tossin' us all up in the air and into the water. Some of the lads scrambled back in the boat, but I decided it was safer to just take my chances and swim out to the *Highlander*. Thankfully, since I grew up on the coast, I'm a good swimmer and have helped with my fair share of rescues. The destroyer was only about a half mile off, so I yelled to my mates I'd see them there and I would swim for it. I made it—after they did, of course. And just as I was boardin' the *Highlander*, some German bombers flew in and dropped four bombs directly on the *Lancastria*. One went straight down its funnel. We were horrified to watch the ship begin listin' right away. People were jumpin' into the oil-slicked water tryin' to clear it, but it happened so fast, there was nothin' to be done for all the passengers—many civilians, includin' women and children—who were trapped below. The ship keeled over and sank in less than a quarter hour. There was one brave gunner who stayed at his post and kept shootin' his Bren until he went down with the ship. We pulled out a good number of the survivors from the water—I even dived in after some. But the Germans kept firin' on us with their machine guns! It was ghastly. Just ghastly. I kept thinkin' of…Laurene…and what she went through…I saved as many as I could…" He trailed off, grimacing with grief and Annie rose and went to his side, slipping her arms around him and laying her head on top of his.

"I'm so sorry, Eric."

He sighed heavily. "I'm haunted by their cries." Then a faint grim smile played over his face. "And then there was a group of blokes clingin' to a barrel and they were such a doughty lot. We could hear them singin' 'Roll Out the Barrel.' I don't know what happened to them. I hope they got picked up. There was another group on the ship's hull singin' hymns as they went down." He shook his head. "I doubt we'll ever know the exact number of casualties, but probably no more than fifteen hundred, maybe two thousand at most, were rescued out of six thousand souls."

"That's horrible! And we didn't hear anything about the sinking of a ship called the *Lancastria*. Not a word!"

"Ye haven't? It would have been four days ago. We received a hero's welcome when we arrived in Liverpool, but ye're right. No one seems to have heard about the *Lancastria*."

"Maybe Churchill doesn't think the British people can take any more bad news—especially a huge disaster like that."

"Perhaps not. But I think all those poor souls who lost their lives should be honored and remembered. I know I'll always remember those kind and brave French fishermen. I owe them my life. If they hadn't taken us, I might still be there—or else lyin' dead on the beach."

"You know, if you had gotten to the docks earlier, you might have made it on board the *Lancastria*. I'm so glad you didn't!" she cried, hugging him more tightly."

"Aye. It's a bit like ye not boardin' the *Athenia,* even though ye had a ticket. I know ye can see the hand of Providence in it, but it's hard for me to wrap my mind around why we were spared and others weren't. War is a strange, tragic business. And I'm afraid things are only goin' to get worse. With France fallin' to the Nazis, we Brits are facin' this darkness all alone. We really are in for the fight of our lives."

He took her hands in his and pressed them to his lips. Looking deeply into her eyes, he said, "I still very much want to marry ye, Annie, as soon as we can get some time off together, but I'm not sure when that will be, what with the imminent threat of an invasion to ward off. Anyway, my love," he said with sad resignation, "I should be goin'. I need to report back to my squadron and see what's left of us. I'll try to see ye again as soon as I can get some leave."

"Well, I don't think I'll be able to get more than one day off a month—for the duration, anyway," she observed dejectedly.

"Aye, me neither, and who knows when that'll next be. But let's write often. And as soon as I can, I'll come up here to see ye again. Do ye have some paper and a pen?"

She nodded and fetched it for him, and he wrote a name and address in neat letters.

"This is my parents' name and address in Gairloch," he said, handing it to her as he stood. "If somethin' should happen to me, please go to see them when ye're able. It would be a comfort to my mother. And if the Jerries start bombin' London, I want ye to go to them right away. I can't imagine they'll have much interest in a sleepy Highland village, so ye should be safe there."

"Jeff wants me to go to Oxford and stay with his English professor if London is bombed."

"Aye, that would be fine too and it's certainly closer—as long as the Huns don't start bombin' the dreamin' spires as well. The main thing is that ye get to safety, all right?"

"But, Eric," she said, clutching his arms, "I don't want to be any farther away from you than I need to be, and like I've said before, I decided to stay here in England to help with the war effort, not run away."

"Annie, I can't lose someone else I love in this war. Please—" He cupped her face in his hands. "If London is bombed, please promise me that ye'll get out. Besides, I'm sure they can use a nurse in lots of places. Ye don't have to serve right here in London."

"All right, I'll try. But hopefully you won't let the Nazis come near London, anyway. You do your job so I can do mine, okay?"

"Aye. I will do everythin' in my power to protect ye from those barbarians." Holding her close, he kissed her softly.

As they embraced, she inwardly debated whether or not this was the time to tell him all of her news. But he had clearly come through so much; she couldn't burden him with more.

She decided to wait.

26

July 1940
Greater London

*E*ric was prescient in his observation that it might be a very long while before he and Annie could coordinate time off together. Reeling from the nearly disastrous retreat from France and expecting to be attacked every day, Great Britain geared up to fight for its very survival. To the country's relieved astonishment and to the appalled frustration of the German generals, Hitler waited. He felt confident that the British would come to their senses and capitulate to his terms without having to fight. But Hitler was wrong. His delay only enabled the embattled Brits to rearm and refortify.

While the Germans rested, the British worked around the clock, seven days a week, to replace the several hundred fighter planes lost in France. Housewives contributed their aluminum pots, pans, and sundry household wares to provide enough metal to build a new fleet of planes in factories, garages, and workshops all over the country. One month after Dunkirk, four hundred forty-six new Hurricanes, Spitfires, and Defiants rolled off the assembly lines and out to the grateful RAF crews.

When it became evident that the British would never negotiate terms with them, the Germans polished their plans for Operation Sea Lion, which called for the Luftwaffe to destroy the RAF during the month of August and pave the way for the invasion by Nazi troops in mid-September. Although Germans regarded August 10 as "Eagle Day," the date to commence the Battle of Britain, the men in the RAF had, in truth, never stopped fighting. For them, there had been no lull after the French surrender on June 22.

There was certainly none for Eric and the men in his squadron, which he rejoined at Kenley. While few civilians were aware of their exploits, they suffered continual casualties. But they had their fair share of successes as well, and Eric and some of his fellow pilots edged closer to the five kills needed for ace status. Daily they patrolled the southern coastline and protected convoys in the Channel from attack, and by early July the air battles had escalated in earnest.

Annie went about her work at the hospital and assisted the Red Cross in training nurse's aides for air raids. Although aware of the danger Eric faced each day, his more frequent, albeit often shorter, letters brought her a measure of comfort. Notes from Jeff were sporadic, but nonetheless welcome. Whenever she received mail, she could more readily believe that the men she loved were still alive and well.

2 July 1940

Dear Annie,

 *It was so wonderful to see you again. The
thought of you is what kept me going through
France and the ordeal of the evacuation. It keeps
me going still. I was happy to find McLeod fit and*

raring to go when I returned to our squadron's home base. He spoke glowingly of you and your care at Dunkirk and described you as an "angel of mercy." I knew I would be jealous of any servicemen who were nursed by you, even if they had been shot down by their own mates! But seriously, I hope we will not ever have to meet under those circumstances. Sad to say, of the men from this base who went to France, McLeod and I are the only ones who have returned. RAF losses there were close to catastrophic. But enough of that. Please write when you have a chance. Your letters are life to me.

All my love,
Eric

July 6, 1940

Dear Eric,

I can't tell you how relieved I was to see you standing on my doorstep! It was agonizing not to hear anything at all for so long except for Ian's assurance that you were up there flying over Dunkirk. I will always treasure that little postcard you sent from Liverpool telling me you had returned to England safely. I'm truly sorry more of our brave men didn't come home. It's very hard for all of us. Betty and I are currently training some nurse's aides to assist the Air Raid Patrol. It's strange that after only a few weeks of first aid training the Red Cross treats them like full-fledged nurses when we went to school for years! Oh well, everyone is needed to help, and I guess the victims won't mind as long as

*someone is coming to their aid. I suppose our feel-
ings are like what you more experienced pilots feel
when unseasoned newcomers like Jeff come along.
With new recruits needed in every area of service,
they'll all just have to learn quickly how to do their
jobs. Anyway, staying busy keeps me from moping
around missing you. I wish you could have stayed
longer, but I am grateful for every minute we had
together. I love you so much!*

*All my love,
Annie*

July 9

Dear Annie,

*Thanks so much for coming up to my gradu-
ation. It was really swell of you and Peggy; you
two made the day very special. (Sorry about the
oranges—hope you enjoyed them anyway.) I'm set-
tling in now and have been up on some training sorties. There won't be much practice, though, until I'm
in the real battle. Sadly, the RAF lost so many pilots
in France that they're having to put us rookies right
to work. My squadron, mostly Canadian, was deci-
mated in France, and it's been refilled with green-
horns like me. But check this out: I'm in Squadron
1! I always wanted to be numero uno. We're flying
Hurricanes. They aren't as glamorous as Eric's
Spitfire, but they're reliable and actually fun to
fly—well, honestly, I don't know about in battle yet.
They aren't supposed to be as easy to maneuver as
the Spitfire. For that reason, our job is to go after*

the Junkers or Stukas, the Kraut bombers—before they can drop their payloads, of course. The Messerschmitts are the fighter planes that escort their bombers, and they pair up with our Spitfires. I'm afraid they have a lot more planes than we do, but we have some mighty fine pilots and will give them a run for their money. Hope you're doing okay. Take care.

Love,
Jeff

PS. Does Eric know yet?

11 July 1940

Dear Annie,

Yesterday we saw a lot of action despite all the rain, and it looks like today we'll be busy too. The Jerries have sent their bombers over in earnest, and I believe their battle for air supremacy has truly begun. Fortunately, we've held up to their challenge very well, and yesterday their losses were twice what ours were. Our squadron got in on things late in the afternoon, but we sent those Krauts packing. It was a bit of a thrill to be engaged in real dogfights again, but I won't lie to you, it was frightening too. I try not to dwell on it too much—just concentrate on getting the job done. The trap most to avoid is thinking too much about it once you're back on the ground. So I just try to think about you instead and that keeps me quite happy.

I do love you so,
Eric

July 13, 1940

Dear Eric,

    I am sorry to hear that the Nazis are attacking now in earnest. Everyone is scared to death that an invasion is coming anytime. Betty came home last night with a pistol from one of her servicemen boyfriends. Not that she knows anything about shooting it, but she swears she will blow away any Jerry who tries to come in our flat! I rather imagine she will too. From the city we can only occasionally see the tracers from the planes going over when the weather is very fine. Usually there's a big heavy cloud lying like a blanket over us. I just trust you all are up there doing your job. We're all so grateful and know that you brave few are standing between us and the Nazis. Thank you, my darling, for risking all every day for us—for me. I couldn't be more proud and more in love. I'm glad thinking of me helps keep your mind off of the danger. I think of you all the time!

Forever yours,
Annie

17 July 1940

Dear Annie,

    I'm sorry not to have written more often. Things have been very hectic with little time for anything—even sleep. Forgive me if this note is cut short like the last one. I never know when the telephone will ring and we'll be ordered to scramble. But it's raining today and the weather isn't good for flying, so maybe we'll get a bit of a break. We are being sent up on about three, four, or more sorties a day now and grab what time we can in between to try to relax, write our letters, read, play chess or cards, or, most often, catch a catnap. We're all pretty exhausted and running on adrenaline. We've fallen into a routine of sorts over the last few weeks. I thought you'd like to know what my "typical" day is like.

We get up at 3:30 AM, grab some breakfast (although it's difficult to eat that early), and ride out to the dispersal point. Our ground crews work all night making repairs and preparing our aircraft, and have already started warming up the engines by the time we arrive. We pilots put on our "Mae Wests"—that's what we call our life jackets—collect all our gear, and check the chalkboard for our assignments, and then we make sure all our equipment is ready. Then we sit in the huts, or outside if the weather is fine, and wait for the telephone to ring. Sometimes it's a false alarm and just someone at the base calling about some administrative detail. More often, however, the orderly answers and then starts yelling at us and ringing the bell to scramble. We never know which it will be, so the jangle of the telephone has become rather nerve-racking. It may be a sound that I'll loathe hearing for the rest of my life! Once the order is given to scramble, we race out to our planes and are airborne in less than five minutes. We can't stay up very long before we run out of ammo or fuel, so after shooting as many Huns as we can, we return to base. There our ground crews "turn our kites round quick," and we start all over again waiting for that blasted telephone. Well, that's what my days are like. Nights are too short. I hate being awakened so early, especially when I'm dreaming about you! Take care of yourself, little one. I love you dearly.

Yours forever,
Eric

19 July 1940

Dear Annie,

The weather turned fine today, but it's been a black day for us. A large number of convoys to protect and a good number of planes lost, including some from our own squadron. The ground crews wait for the return of their planes with such expectation. It's hard to look at their faces when their pilots don't return. Almost as hard as it is to walk into the dispersal hut to check the boards and find out which fine fellows will never share a pint with us again. We're trying to keep our spirits up. Hope you are, my darling, and that you're not over-working yourself. How is Jeff making out in his new squadron? I miss you so much and love you more and more each day.

Yours forever,
Eric

July 21, 1940

Dear Eric,

I'm always so happy to hear from you, even if it's just a short note. It comforts me to know you are well. I was interested in hearing what your daily routine is. Now I can better picture you in my mind as I pray for you. But I must confess, I am never up at 3:30 in the morning! Unless, of course, there's an air-raid warning. So far, as you know, Hitler hasn't dared to hit London, so we've been quite safe. But we have had false alarms and practice runs. We're all equipped now. June brought home a Morrison shelter—one of those heavy table contraptions you're supposed to sleep under. None of us do, of course, and it would only hold two or three of us anyway, but she says it's "just in case." Our land-lord put up an Anderson shelter in the back garden. It has the corrugated aluminum sheeting over the arched steel rods. He and his son dug a big hole in the garden and then erected the shelter, putting in benches and a table. He told us we could use it "just in case" all else fails, but there's really not room in it for anybody but his family. Some of the local hotels are opening up shelters in their basements, and a few public shelters have been put up on some of the streets, as well as those already in Hyde Park and Kensington Gardens. That's where I think I should like to go if I have sufficient warning. I've always liked the park, and I think there's less chance of being trapped there by falling debris. Besides, that's where we walked the first night we met at the Royal Albert Hall. So if I should have to be hit, I'd like it to be there. I really can't abide the thought of being trapped underground. Many people are planning to head to the underground stations, and if things get really bad they will probably spend all night down there. I may have to help with Red Cross work, but boy, I dread it! But when you and Jeff and all the others are being so brave every day, I suppose I can buck up and be brave underground. I'm so proud of you both. Jeff, by the way, really likes his unit. They're mostly Canadians and they fly Hurricanes. It's Squadron 1 at Croydon, so maybe you can drive over and see him sometime—that is, if you ever get some free time. I hope you are being very careful. I miss you terribly and think of you constantly. Please try to get some leave so that we can be married soon. I love you!

All my love,
Annie

XXXXXOOOOO

ℰ↝

July 24

Dear Annie,

   How are you, kiddo? My squadron is really swell, and guess what? I'm not the only Yank after all. There are two others. But all the Canadians sound like Yanks too. I guess we're all really "Americans," or North Americans, anyway. It's a good thing, because not only do we understand each other but we also push each other not to lose face with the Brits. I'll admit this only to you—I love flying, but now that I've actually been in some dogfights, I must confess that it can be a very scary experience. To tell you the truth, I think everyone is scared, but it's not really something you talk about or admit. Between sorties we all sit around nonchalantly, like we're waiting for a bus or something, but inside I'll bet everyone is just as sick to their stomachs as I am. So far I've been able to fight through the fear and complete my missions. I've done all right—no confirmed kills yet, but I've chased off some bad guys and kept them from dropping their payloads. I would appreciate your prayers, though—not just to stay safe but to conduct myself well. I don't want to ever embarrass myself or the other Americans by being chicken. Now that I've gotten that off my chest, I hope I don't sound like a scared little crybaby. Please keep this to yourself. I don't want Peggy thinking I'm not a big hero!

Love,
Jeff

PS. Did you hear the news that the Reds took over Lithuania, Latvia, and Estonia? They're as bad as the Krauts!

PPS. Any word from Eric?

July 28, 1940

Dear Jeff,

I'm glad you like your unit and are enjoying the challenges of flying the Hurricane. Don't worry about your confession. I'm glad you can share things like that with me. Surely my confession to you was far worse. No, I have not told Eric yet. I don't know when I will. I'm hoping he can get some time off and we can be married—then I will tell him. Meanwhile, June beat me to the altar with her doctor. I can't help being very jealous that she's a married woman and I'm not. So now it's just Peggy, Betty, and me. I guess we could lie sideways and all fit in that hideous Morrison shelter if need be. Right now it's serving as a catchall for our mail and clutter. The irony is that June got it for us, and I think her doctor-husband may want to send her out of London anyway to get her away from a possible bombing attack. I know you want me to do the same, but so far Jerry hasn't made much of a ruckus here and I still have plenty to keep me busy. Plus, I'm closer to you and to Eric if you are able to get some time off. Don't do anything too brave and foolhardy!

Love,
Annie

PS. Dover really has borne the brunt of the Führer's fury. How often is he going to bomb that little town? Boy, I hope he doesn't ever have the nerve to bomb London!

27

Friday and Saturday, August 16-17, 1940
London

Coming home from work on a fine summer evening, Annie and Betty emerged from the Bayswater subway station just as an air raid warning began to wail. In seconds the streets filled with people running frantically to the closest shelter.

"We might as well go back down," Betty said sensibly as they tried to move against the crowd pushing toward the station.

"Oh, you're right," Annie replied, sighing with resignation and contemplating how she dreaded being trapped underground with this teaming throng. "But perhaps the Air-Raid Patrol will need our help." Just then she spotted a grey-haired gentleman wearing Wellingtons, overalls, and a round tin helmet emblazoned ARP. He was shepherding a group of young mothers and children toward them. "Hullo, sir!" she called out. "We're nurses. May we be of service?"

"You need to get underground quickly, miss. But you can help these people get down the stairs. And when the 'all clear' sounds, check back with us to see if there are any casualties. There now, don't shove, young man!" He cautioned a ruddy-faced youth who tried to barrel through the turnstiles. "Everyone stay calm. We can all get to safety if we keep order. Follow these nurses with the white hats. That's it. Everyone stay calm."

"Right!" Betty said. "This way please. Careful on the stairs!"

In the crowd, Annie noticed a young woman struggling to keep hold of two squirming boys and a dark curly-haired girl about three years old, who loudly protested the clamor of the sirens.

"Stop, stop, stop!" the little girl shouted, covering her ears and bursting into a wail of her own.

"Hush, now," the mother soothed. Then she barked at the boys, "Lads, hold on to my skirt! Do not let go of me. I have to carry your baby sister and we can't be separated. Ben! Hold on!" she repeated as the crowd threatened to part them.

"May I help?" Annie asked. "I can carry her for you."

The mother looked down at Annie. Taking in the white cap and apron, her broad round face broke into a relieved smile. "Thank ye, miss. That's ever so kind of ye." She transferred the child into Annie's arms and grabbed up the boys' hands. "Come on, lads. I've got ye now."

"Their dad is off fightin' in the war," the mother said by way of explanation as they filed down the stairs. "And they've gotten very naughty. It's hard to manage them by meself—but we all have to do our part, I suppose."

"They're your children?" Annie asked with a hint of surprise. They had much darker skin than their obviously Irish mother.

"Aye," she said with a good-natured laugh. "Although on days like this, I could be tempted to say no."

"Mummy? Will we have to go to school tomorrow if the raid lasts long?" the younger boy asked.

"Of course not, you idiot," the elder answered. "This is Friday, remember?"

"Oh. Why couldn't they have an air raid on a Monday?"

"Lads, hush! And watch your step," their mother cautioned.

Annie carried the little girl down, down, down into the depths of the underground station. When they arrived on the platform, it was already filling up with people.

"Come over 'ere, lads." The young woman staked out a space next to the tiled wall. "Thank ye so much, miss. I can take her now."

"Here you go, sweetie." Annie passed the child over to her mother and waved goodbye. The curly-haired girl waved back and rewarded her with a cute gap-toothed smile.

Annie worked her way along the platform, helping other mothers with their babies and assisting elderly citizens to more comfortable places on the benches lining the walls. As long as she stayed occupied, she could keep her mind from dwelling on the thought that she was deep underground with deadly bombs falling above. When it seemed as though the shelter would hold no more, Annie edged toward the tunnel entrance, where she could ostensibly assist the ARP wardens, but she also hoped to catch a bit of a breeze. On this warm summer evening, the odor of stale sweat and soiled diapers soon emanated from the human bodies packed densely on the narrow platform. She hoped with everyone else that the air raid would not last long.

"Rather inconvenient of the Jerries to hit us right before we could get our suppers, don't you think?" The gray-haired warden confided to Annie, who nodded, wishing he hadn't reminded her of food.

"Here, dear," Betty said as she joined them. "I took some sandwiches from the hospital canteen before we left, just in case." Reaching into her shoulder bag, she pulled out a bundle wrapped in oilcloth and offered it to Annie. "Not much of a birthday dinner, is it? At least we had a cake for you. But you really should eat something now so you don't faint."

Annie looked guiltily at the warden.

"Is it your birthday, love?" he asked kindly.

She nodded. "I'm twenty today."

"Well, happy birthday. Rotten way to spend it, ain't it? You girls go ahead and eat up. You may have more work to do before this night is over. Don't worry," he said. "I've got me own. Me wife always packs me satchel full of sandwiches."

Annie nibbled self-consciously but gratefully on her sandwich. Someone played a mournful tune on a harmonica.

"Play something more cheery, mate!" A voice called above the hubbub. After a slight pause, the harmonica picked up with a jaunty version of "Rule Britannia!"

And then the "all clear" sounded, causing a collective sigh of relief to pass over the crowd.

"Blimey, that wasn't too bad, was it? We can all get home to our suppers," the warden declared cheerfully. "Maybe it was a false alarm." He called out to the crowd as they rose to exit from the shelter, "Come along, now! No shoving. Take your time. Easy, now! There are lots of steps ahead."

Annie and Betty helped some children, although Annie did not attempt to carry anyone back up the long flights of stairs. When they finally emerged into the fresh air, she had to catch her breath. "Oh, boy," she panted. "I hope we don't get stuck in the Tube again."

"There aren't very many other places for all us common folk to go," Betty said. "The upper classes have all fled to their country homes or they'll hole up in the posh hotel basements."

"What about the public shelters? I think I'd rather run to Kensington Gardens."

"I don't think you can realistically expect to run several blocks in the few minutes you'll have. Besides, those shelters don't look very safe to me. They look like they'd blow over in a stiff breeze—not to mention a bombing raid."

"Well, I loathe being stuck down in the Tube," Annie insisted as she smoothed out her apron and adjusted her nurse's cap. "Those poor people. What if they have to stay down there all night next time?"

Betty shrugged. "People have to do what they have to do. And you will as well."

"Thanks for the sandwich, by the way. That was very thoughtful of you."

Smoothing back her blond hair under her cap, Betty smiled. "All those years in the Girl Guides paid off. They drilled into me the motto, 'Be prepared.' Besides, with June married now, I feel it is my duty to look after you—your circumstances require a bit of extra care."

Although Annie hoped her apron sufficiently hid her condition from the rest of the hospital staff, she had at last confided in her flatmates. Betty's devotion to her was called upon again later that night around one o'clock in the morning when the sirens wailed again.

"Annie, wake up!" Betty shook her. "It's another air raid. You need to get up."

Annie groaned and pulled her blanket over her head. "No, I won't go back to the Tube."

"Get up and crawl into June's contraption. That's better than nothing. I'll go out and check to see if there's any room in the shelter in the garden. Come on, Annie, hurry!"

"Okay, okay." Annie rolled over and pulled herself up. At least it wasn't the dead of winter. That was something to be grateful for. She couldn't conceive of anything much colder than sitting out in a garden under a heap of steel and sod on a winter's night. But she was grateful just to crawl under the Morrison shelter in the living room. As the sirens wailed on, she put a pillow over her ears.

In a few moments Betty was crawling in beside her. "No room out there. I figured as much. If these attacks continue, we should probably come up with a different plan. I can't imagine this box would do much good if we're hit directly."

"No. It's only supposed to keep debris and shrapnel off us, remember? If we're hit directly, we won't know anyway."

"At least we're both small. I don't know how Peggy could fit comfortably in here too."

Annie giggled. "We could all crawl in sideways and lie side by side like spoons." She added soberly, "I hope Peggy is all right. I wonder if they have sirens down in Wimbledon. It would be terrible for her friend's wedding to be disrupted by an air raid."

"Yes, it would," Betty agreed. "I do wish our phone lines were working so that we could ring her, but she's supposed to be back tomorrow afternoon, isn't she?"

Annie yawned. "Yes. You know, I'm so tired, I think I can sleep through this. The antiaircraft guns sound like popcorn popping…just as long as the noise doesn't get any closer, we'll be all right…" She drifted off to sleep, and when the "all clear" sounded and she hadn't budged, Betty thought it best to let her sleep on under the shelter. After all, one couldn't know when the sirens would begin wailing again.

The following morning seemed positively pacific after all the racket and excitement of the previous evening. Perhaps the Germans had decided to lay low. The girls heard on the radio that the RAF had warded off several rather large forays of enemy planes, but not before bombs had been dropped as close as the London docks and in the southern suburbs. That explained the two red alerts in London proper. A number of air bases had also been bombed, and Annie froze with fear wondering which ones. Sixteen RAF personnel and scores of civilians had perished. They waited anxiously throughout the morning, staring at the wireless radio, hoping for further details, and dreading to hear if someone they loved could be among the casualties.

Then around noon they heard the front door lock rattle and the door creak open.

But instead of Peggy, June stood before them, supported by her new husband, Dr. Henry Benson. "Oh, girls!" she exclaimed and ran to the sofa where they sat in astonishment. "I have the most dreadful news. It's horrible. It's about Peggy—our dear Peggy." Putting her arms around them both, she began to sob,

"She's…she's…dead! She was killed last night! I can't believe it. Of all of us—dear Peggy!"

"Oh, no! Not Peggy!" The girls hugged one another in shocked disbelief. "It can't be! What happened?"

Harry had stood back awkwardly, twisting his hat in his hands. Now he cleared his throat and ventured to speak. "That air raid last night bombed Wimbledon. The wedding party had gathered in a neighborhood pub. It took a direct hit and the bride and most of the family died. We heard the news at the hospital."

"What's all this?" a familiar baritone suddenly boomed from the doorway.

"Jeff!" Annie rose and threw herself into her brother's arms. "You're all right! I'm so glad to see you." Then her voice broke. "Oh, Jeff, we've just heard the most terrible news. It's about Peggy. Last night…she was…in Wimbledon…in the air raid. She…she was…killed." When she spoke of Peggy's fate, the full force of its reality suddenly hit her, and the weight of it nearly crushed her with grief. Tears splashed unhindered down her cheeks.

Jeff's ruddy face drained of color. Clasping Annie to his chest, he groaned, "No! It can't be. Merciful Lord, not Peggy!"

Annie clung to him, shaking with silent sobs. June and Betty dissolved into tears. Together they wept for their lovely friend.

When the wave of grief had at last subsided, Jeff released his sister. "Are you okay?"

She covered her face with her hands and nodded.

Jeff turned soberly to Harry. "What can we do?"

"Well—" Harry pressed a handkerchief to his eyes and composed himself. "June and I thought we should pack up Peggy's things and have them taken to her family in Warwick. Look, girls, I know this comes as a great shock to you. We all dearly loved Peggy, but she of all people would want us to carry on. I was wondering if perhaps you, Annie, shouldn't be the one to take her things up there."

"You know, I'm from Warwick," Betty volunteered. "I know Peggy's family, and it might be easier for them if I were the messenger."

"Why, that's fine, Betty," Harry said, "but frankly, I was also hoping we could encourage Annie to leave town. It's really not safe for her here anymore, especially..." He hesitated, not knowing if he were violating patient confidentiality.

Annie blushed deeply. "It's all right. Everyone here knows. But I don't want to leave London. I want to stay at Barts and help."

"Annie," Harry tried to keep his tone soothing. "Children and women in your condition were supposed to evacuate a long time ago."

"I can't leave!" Annie protested. "I need to be where Eric and Jeff can contact me."

"I agree with you, Harry," Jeff said. "It's not safe in London anymore, especially for her. In fact, that's why I'm here. Croydon was bombed last night and is temporarily unserviceable, so my squadron is moving up to Northholt today and I'm just passing through. But I came to tell Annie that I have finalized arrangements for her to go to Oxford to stay with one of my professors. I'm here to help her pack up so she can leave tonight. Sadly, I had planned to urge Peggy to go to her family, but now it's too late. But it's not too late for these girls to get out. Things are only going to get worse. Now that Germany has hit London, Churchill will likely retaliate by bombing Berlin, and then Hitler will bomb London with a real vengeance. Everything can only escalate from now on. Betty, I think you should go home too for a while, but I would like Annie to go to Oxford."

"Well, I agree with you that the girls should evacuate," Harry said. "June and I will be staying up at my parents' house north of the city when we're off duty. But, Jeff, do you really think Oxford is any safer with those motor works at Cowley? I heard they were hit last night too."

"Well, to be honest, so was Warwick. The truth is, it isn't really safe anywhere because when we chase the Nazis off, they turn tail and have to unload their bombs—regrettably often on nontargeted areas. We try to chase them off into the countryside or over the Channel, but sometimes they'll still drop their payloads on inhabited areas. In general, though, I believe Oxford is much safer than London. The rumor is that Hitler fancies making Oxford his British capital, so he doesn't want to bomb it."

"I heard the same thing about Cambridge," Harry said.

Jeff grinned. "Maybe like a lot of people he can't distinguish between the two. Anyway, the other more credible rumor is that Hitler won't bomb Oxbridge if we will leave their university towns alone. As long as Sir Winston doesn't bomb Heidelberg, Oxford should be okay. And Warwick, despite its proximity to Birmingham, should be a lot safer than London right now."

"But, I don't know that I want to stay up in Warwick for the duration," Betty interjected. "I would like to continue to serve at Barts."

"Well, you can decide that after you go home and spend some time with your family," said Harry. "I'll see that you're authorized for a week's leave. You certainly deserve it. Look, we're reordering at Barts and there will only be a skeletal staff left here, anyway. Most of us are relocating to Hillend Hospital in St. Albans. You should come with us there. We have a good bomb shelter close by. It should be safer there than here by yourself." Harry kicked the Morrison shelter. "This old thing is meant only for emergencies."

"But I don't want to stay away for good, either," Annie objected. "I could stay over in the nurses' quarters at Barts."

Her brother and three friends exchanged glances.

"You have more than yourself to think of, Annie," Harry said firmly. "I'm giving you doctor's orders to leave London."

"But—"

"No buts. Doctor's orders!"

"But…I mean…what will I do about Eric?"

An awkward silence hung in the room. Then Jeff broke it. "Haven't you told him yet about the baby?"

"No," Annie whispered. "I just couldn't burden him with this when he's flying missions every day. I've been hoping he'd have some leave and we could get married, but I don't want to force him into marrying me."

"Annie," Jeff said, "I'm sorry to say that it doesn't look like any RAF personnel will have any time off for the foreseeable future. You need to let him know anyway. You should sit down and write him right now, and then tell him that you're staying in Oxford. I'll run out and post the letter for you this afternoon."

"He's right," Harry agreed.

Clenching her fists, Annie looked at them all in exasperation. She felt as though they were ganging up on her. Then she relaxed and sighed with resignation. "All right. I'll write the letter and I'll go to Oxford."

"Good girl. That's my little sis." Jeff gave her a hug. "Why don't you sit in your room to write while I help you pack."

"And Harry and I will take care of Peggy's belongings," June said, "while Betty gets hers ready. But there's no time to waste. You all should try to catch the evening trains out."

They each hurried to their tasks. Annie went to her desk and pulled out a piece of stationery, but before she could begin writing, Jeff surreptitiously closed her door and sat down on her bed.

Annie looked at him in surprise. "What is it?"

"I can't tell you much; only this: My unit is going to Northolt tonight, but I am not. Because, according to the U.S. government, I'm officially barred from fighting in this war, my enlistment in the RAF is really a bit of a secret from them anyway. Remember, the RAF let me sign up as an Oxford student, not as an American. I'm a man without a country, as it were, so I think that's why I've been recruited for a secret assignment."

"A secret assignment?"

"Yes." He tried to lighten his news. "Or maybe they picked me because I'm so incredibly handsome and intelligent."

"Oh, stop! What do you mean by secret assignment? Can't you tell me?"

Jeff grinned. "Of course not, my dear. If I did I'd have to kill you."

"Jeff, that's not funny! Is it dangerous?"

He laughed. "I don't know. It's a secret, remember? Anyway, it can't be any more dangerous than flying a Hurricane in a dogfight. But the reason I'm telling you this is that I've given your name and Mr. Lewis's—as well as his address and telephone number—to my superiors in case anything does happen to me. You are my official next of kin contact here in Britain. And I sent Lewis's address to Mom and Dad. Now, Annie, they are not to know I'm on this assignment any more than they should know I joined the RAF. Until the U.S. gets into this war, anyway, they can't know or I could be in a heap of trouble with Mr. Kennedy and our embassy. I told Mom and Dad that I'm working for the war effort just as you are, but they think it's in a civilian capacity. Please don't write them anything different." He paused. "By the way, have you told them about the baby?"

Annie blushed. "Oh, Jeff, I've felt so guilty about all this. I couldn't just come out with the whole truth—it would kill them. I wrote them that Eric and I had gotten married back in March. I know it's not true, but I couldn't think what else I could do. I'll write them about the baby before too long. I was waiting until I reached the third trimester."

"That will be soon, won't it? How far along are you?"

"I'm almost six months."

"Annie, you really need to tell Eric."

"That's what I was about to do just now when you interrupted me."

Jeff pulled a slip of paper out of his pocket. "Look. This is the base where my squadron is relocating. If you need to contact me, you can write to me here in care of my squad and they'll see that I get the letter." He handed her the paper. "And that's the address for the Kilns, the Lewis home, so you can tell Eric where you'll be staying. Say, Annie..." Jeff's tone grew subdued and his jaw tightened with emotion. "I...I can't believe Peggy is gone, can you? I'll miss her so much. I know you will too. She was such a great girl, and I thought the world of her. I'm so sorry. I don't know what to say."

Annie nodded, her eyes welling up again with tears.

Jeff sighed. "The reality is that we're going to lose a lot of good people before this war is over. But it helps me to remember two things. One is that Hitler is very evil and has to be stopped—even at the cost of good people's lives. The other thing is that there is a God and such a thing as eternal life. I know that Peggy truly believed in Him and that she's with Him now. Oh, we'll miss her, all right. We'll miss her incredibly. And it's a terrible tragedy for us. But not for her. Not for her. Do you know what I mean?"

"I think so. But I still wish she hadn't died. It seems so unfair. It's like Eric's Laurene."

"I know and that's what's so ugly about war. It is a horribly unfair and wicked business. But we need to keep our own hearts right before God, and trust Him with the outcome. Certainly with our ultimate destination. And I believe without a shadow of a doubt that Eric's girl and our Peggy both stepped out of this troubled world into the glorious new dimension which we call heaven."

"I wish I had your faith, Jeff."

"You can. Just ask for it, Annie. 'Ask, and it will be given to you; seek, and you will find; knock, and it will be opened to you.'"

Annie smiled. "Okay, maybe I will. But meanwhile, let me write this letter to Eric. And you keep your part of this bargain and start packing."

"Right!" Hopping up, Jeff pulled a suitcase out from under the bed and began folding clothes. "And like I said, when you're finished I'll run down and mail it for you."

After several false starts resulting in balled up pieces of stationery tossed into the wastebasket, Annie finally managed to write to Eric about the baby and her move to the Kilns. Jeff posted the letter later that afternoon.

Neither of them could know that, due to the unforeseen circumstances of war, Eric would never receive Annie's letter.

28

Sunday, August 18, 1940
The Kilns

Annie awoke to the cheerful sound of birds singing and the delicious smell of eggs and sausage cooking. *A cooked breakfast! How heavenly!* She yawned and stretched. Reluctant to leave her snug bed, she looked about the small room where she was quartered. Above her bed, a broad window stretched across the width of the room. She drew back the heavy black wool curtain and peered through the early morning fog drifting over the lawn and driveway, beyond which lay the narrow lane where the taxi had brought her the night before. With the trains overcrowded and delayed, she had arrived close to midnight and had fretted that the Lewis household would be in bed. Stepping back from the darkened tradesman's entrance, she had noticed an outside metal stairway leading up to a door and a window where a tiny sliver of light peeked out from the blackout curtains. Perhaps someone was still up. She had stood uncertainly at the back door to the house and then rapped as quietly as she could.

A few moments later the door at the top of the steps cracked open.

"Miss Little, is that you?" came a booming stage whisper.

"Yes!"

"I'll be right down."

She heard heavy clumping and then a large, portly man wrapped in a flannel bathrobe stood before her. Mr. Clive Staples Lewis.

He switched on a flashlight. "Don't be alarmed. It's only I, Jack Lewis. Welcome to the Kilns. I apologize for your reception."

"No, I'm sorry to arrive so late. The trains…"

"Understood. Travel is so difficult these days, and we must give deference to our troops. Come right through this door," he said opening it, "and I'll show you to your room. Here, let me take your bags. Is this all you have?"

"Yes, thank you."

"Quick note. There's a toilet right here." He indicated a closed door in the narrow passage. "And here's the scullery and the kitchen. Now if you'll excuse me, I'll go ahead of you and lead the way." Slipping around her, he carried her luggage through the kitchen and out to the hall. "Here," he said tipping his head to the right, "is the bathroom and another toilet."

They passed by a large, carved wooden wardrobe at the foot of a staircase.

"Upstairs we have rooms and those of my adopted mother, Mrs. Moore, and her daughter, Maureen—although you can tell I use the outside staircase, not this one. You'll be here in the music room for now," he said as he nudged open the door and switched on the light. "Two of our last refugee guests slept here." Annie could see tightly wedged in the room a set of twin beds in an L-shaped configuration and a piano, which gave the room its name. "I'm sorry you don't have your own wash basin in here, but you are the closest to the bathroom. Maureen is to be married on the twenty-seventh, so you can move up to her room after that. I suspect if the attacks on London intensify, we will be receiving more visitors here at the Kilns."

"Mr. Lewis, thank you so much for taking me in. I'm sorry to be arriving when you are in the middle of wedding preparations. I didn't expect to leave London, but after Friday's bombing, my brother insisted."

"Not a problem. You just make yourself at home. Now, can I get anything for you before you turn in? Are you hungry?"

"No, thank you. I'm just fine."

"Well, if you should need anything, you can just sneak out and throw pebbles at my window. I'll be up reading a bit longer. Oh, and to orient you—do you see the front door right across the hall here? The room on the left is the dining room and the one on the right is the common room. Down the hall there to the right and around the corner is a spare room, our little study, and my brother's bedroom. So don't be concerned if you hear someone shuffling by your room during the night. It will only be my brother, Warnie. Although the floorboards creak and the pipes gurgle, you need not worry that the Kilns is haunted, Miss Little. Or, as I like to say, if it is, there are only blithe spirits here. I think you'll find it a pleasant enough house."

"I'm sure I will, Mr. Lewis."

"You can call me Jack. Everyone else here does, Miss Little."

"It's—Mrs. MacKenzie now," Annie lied self-consciously, glancing at Eric's ring, which she had begun wearing. "But please call me by my Christian name—Annie."

"Of course, Annie. Congratulations on your marriage. Your brother neglected to tell me about that, but, of course, men tend to overlook such important things. Is your husband in the service?"

"Yes, sir. The RAF."

"Excellent. A brave lot. Well, if there's nothing else you need, I'll be saying goodnight. Oh, breakfast is usually served around eight, and we attend church on Sundays. Since we're up late tonight, we'll go to the 10:30 service tomorrow rather than the early one. You're welcome to join us."

"Thank you, sir. Goodnight."

A gentle rap on the door and a woman's voice calling, "Breakfast is ready when you are!" brought Annie back from her recollections of her arrival to the present.

"Thank you. I'll be right there!" she answered as she rose quickly and slipped into a loose shirtwaist housedress.

Ducking past the dining room, Annie used the washroom and then entered the kitchen. A large workman sat by the counter, calmly eating with one hand and petting a black cat with the other.

"Excuse me, I'm Annie. I was called to breakfast."

"I'm Paxford. Fred Paxford, but everyone calls me plain ole Paxford. And this 'ere ole sweetheart's Kitty-Koo. The frisky, young gray one around 'ere somewhere is Pushkin. But you, miss, should be in the dinin' room with the family."

"Are you sure? I'm an evacuee from London."

Paxford nodded solemnly. "Terrible times, ain't they? Whole world fallin' apart. But you belong in the dinin' room," he repeated, "with the family."

Annie smiled. "Okay. Nice to meet you...Paxford." She hurried back down the hall to the dining room. An empty seat was indeed set for her next to a younger woman she decided must be Maureen. The two gentlemen of the house rose from their seats to greet her.

"Ah, everyone, this is Miss, pardon me, *Mrs.* Annie MacKenzie," said Jack Lewis. "Come in, Annie. We're just getting started. Let me introduce my mother, Mrs. Janie Moore; my sister, Maureen, soon-to-be Mrs. Leonard Blake; and my brother, Major Warren Lewis."

"How do you do?" Annie said. "Excuse me for coming in late. I went back to the kitchen, but Mr. Paxford directed me here."

"Please join us," Lewis's brother said, pulling out her chair and helping her get settled at the table.

"Thank you, Major Lewis," she said, smiling at him.

His broad face, adorned with a thick bristly moustache, flushed with pleasure. "No ceremony, please. Just call me Warnie."

When Warnie returned to his seat, Lewis offered a simple grace and then they all began eating.

"Well now, Annie," the elderly Mrs. Moore said with a distinctly Irish brogue, "welcome to the Kilns. Everything all right?"

"Yes, ma'am. Thank you. I really appreciate y'all letting me stay here." She turned to Maureen and was surprised to face not a girl like herself but a mature woman in her thirties. "I am sorry for the inconvenience this must be, so close to your wedding."

Maureen smiled kindly. "Not to worry. I'm sure it must be inconvenient for you to leave London. You know, you sound a bit like Olivia de Havilland in *Gone with the Wind*. Are you a Southerner?"

"Yes. I'm from Virginia. My brother Jeff was here at Oxford—he was a student of Mr. Lewis's—and I came over last summer to visit him. Anyway, when war broke out I decided to stay and I finished up my nursing certification at St. Bartholomew's in London."

"So were you a nurse there?" Mrs. Moore asked.

"Yes, but my brother wanted me to get out of London because of the bombing, so he asked Mr. Lewis—"

"Jack," Lewis prompted.

"Jack. He asked—Jack—if I could stay here for a while, and y'all are so very gracious to welcome me."

"So London was actually bombed, was it?" asked Maureen.

"Yes. Not where I live, but along the docks and down in Wimbledon. In fact—" Annie swallowed. The thought of Peggy's death remained a fresh wound. "One of my flatmates was…killed."

Sympathetic groans met this revelation.

"How dreadful!" exclaimed Mrs. Moore.

"Oh, my dear, we are so sorry," murmured Warnie.

"Yes, we are," agreed Jack. "You must still be in shock from such terrible news. It's no wonder Jeff wanted to get you out of London as quickly as possible."

"He didn't even know about it when he came to get me," Annie said. "He was as shocked as I. He was very fond of Peggy."

"Peggy? Your lovely friend I met at the graduation party?" Jack shook his head sadly. "Oh, my dear, I am truly grieved."

"Thank you." Annie stared down at her plate to control her emotions. "You're very kind."

"But your husband?" Maureen said, with a glance at Annie's wedding band. "Where is he? Is he all right?"

Annie blushed profusely. "Yes…as far as I know. He's a pilot in the RAF. He's stationed at a base south of London."

Warnie spoke up. "Those lads are really doing the job for us. Every day and night they are up there defending us against the Germans. I've just retired from the Army, you know. Just got back from Wales and am serving now in the Home Guard. But I was in France with the BEF before that and evacuated from Dunkirk the beginning of May—although, thankfully, my unit got out before the large-scale retreat and evacuation. Those pilots of ours really deserve high marks. You must be quite proud of him."

"Yes," Annie said softly. "I am."

Mrs. Moore suddenly wailed, "I can hardly believe we're still fightin' those blasted Germans. And more young people dyin' every day. It's as if it were the same war all over again and my poor Paddy's death was in vain!"

"Now, Minto," Jack said soothingly as he patted her hand. "You know Paddy fought bravely and saved many other fine men. He did not die in vain."

Maureen nudged Annie and rose from the table. "Help me clear, will you?"

They collected the dishes and carried them back to the kitchen.

"I'll wash," Annie volunteered, filling a basin with hot, soapy water. Standing at the sink, she could look out over the front lawn, past flowering gardens and fruit trees and down a gentle hill to a large pond. "What a lovely view!" she exclaimed. "Oh, my goodness, that's Virginia creeper growing on the walls outside! I didn't know it grew in England. Now I do really feel at home!" After scrubbing a few dishes and placing them in the drying rack, she ventured to ask, "Maureen, Paddy was your brother, wasn't he?"

"Yes," Maureen answered as she plunked some dishes into the basin. "He died in the Great War. He and Jack were roommates here at Keble College when they were in training. They became fast friends, and when Jack had some leave before being sent to France, he visited us in Bristol where we were living at the time. I actually overheard the pact Jack and Paddy made with each other then. They promised that if one of them should die, the survivor would look after the other's family. Well, Jack was true to his word, and after he was wounded and discharged from the Army, he adopted Mother and me as his own family and he's taken care of us ever since."

"That says a lot for him, doesn't it?"

"Yes, it does. Jack is the dearest, most generous man I've ever known...well, except perhaps for Warnie. I will miss them both very much. But—" Maureen lowered her voice to a conspiratorial whisper, "not my mother so much. It'll be nice to get out from under her thumb. Yes, it's time this old maid got hitched and flew the coop." She smiled. "And I'm truly blessed to have found a wonderful husband. But you would know all about that—and you're so young and all. You look like a teenager. If you don't mind my asking, how old are you, Annie?"

"I just turned twenty—on Friday, as a matter of fact. But I got to celebrate by being underground in the Tube during an air raid."

"Twenty! You're just a baby. I turn thirty-four tomorrow. Well, we should have a double celebration to make up for your air-raid party."

"That's very kind of you, but I already feel like a chump barging in here when you're preparing for a wedding."

"Nonsense."

Jack Lewis carried in the last of the dishes. "Ladies, if you'd like to come to church, Warnie and I are leaving at a quarter past ten. Annie, you're welcome to join us. We attend our local parish church, Holy Trinity. It's only about a ten- or fifteen-minute walk away. It's a fine day, by the way, for a walk, Maureen."

"All right, Jack. I'm coming."

Annie hesitated. She still felt unworthy to attend church and had avoided it in London even after Jeff had convinced her to accompany him at Easter. Yet as a guest in the home of the renowned Christian writer C.S. Lewis, she thought it would be insulting to her host to decline. "Thank you," she said, "I'll come too."

After changing into their Sunday best, the Lewis brothers, Maureen, and Annie set off down Kilns Lane to Holy Trinity Church, an unassuming stone country church surrounded by a well-kept cemetery. The Lewis brothers timed their arrival to slip unobtrusively into the back of the church before the service started. Annie followed them to what she presumed to be their customary seats in a pew on the left side of the church abutting a stone pillar. The pillar blocked some of her view, but she realized it was an ideal spot to see the service without being seen and must have been chosen to protect the Lewis brothers' privacy. She looked about, delighted at the small but elegant church in its early neo-Gothic style. The whitewashed walls reflected warmth and light. With its stained glass windows, rounded stone arches, and vaulted roof of wooden rafters, the church seemed a world away from her father's clapboard Methodist country parish church, and yet she felt strangely at home.

Even so, she could not bring herself to file up to the altar rail to receive communion. She still felt undeserving and separated from God. Nevertheless, in her private prayers she implored Him to have mercy on her and to protect Eric and Jeff from all harm. During the final hymn, Maureen tugged her arm to indicate they were leaving. Annie obediently followed them out of the church but cringed when Warnie let the heavy oak door slam behind them. Their early exit had not been quite so surreptitious after all.

"How did you like our little church, Annie?" Jack asked as they headed back to the Kilns.

"It's quite lovely."

"Yes, it is. Sorry our dear old priest is not a more enthralling preacher. I confess I find it a struggle not to let my mind wander at times. You know, the most inspired ideas can occur quite inconveniently in church. A few weeks ago, I was sitting there trying to pay attention to the sermon when an idea for a new book popped into my head."

"That would be the one you wrote to me about?" Warnie asked. "The letters from one devil to another?"

"Yes. The idea, you see, is to write about the psychology of temptation from the other point of view. I think it has the potential of being both helpful and entertaining."

"Sounds very intriguing," Annie said.

"Yes, well, I've piqued the interest of the *Guardian* and will be providing them with weekly installments. So we'll see how the public responds. I imagine there'll be some sort of brouhaha when people realize that an Oxford don believes in the supernatural and a real devil."

"Or," Warnie speculated, "they'll take it as a big joke. After all, it is satire, isn't it?"

"Right. But I think that poking fun at the Enemy probably galls him the most. My conjecture is that Satan would much prefer people either to be terribly afraid of him or to think he's just a fantasy."

"Laughing at him hurts his pride, doesn't it?" Warnie chuckled.

"Precisely."

They returned to the Kilns to find dinner still under preparation. The Lewis brothers and Maureen offered to show Annie about the property while Mrs. Moore urged them all to take her large sheepdog, Bruce, with them. The early morning fog had burned off to reveal a glorious summer sky, and they ambled happily past the gardens and a tennis court toward the pond.

"Should you ever hear the air-raid siren, Annie, our shelter is down this path here to the left. Can you see it?" Lewis pointed through the woods to a concrete bunker.

"Oh, yes. I do. That looks like a much nicer hideaway than the Tube in London."

"Paxford and Jack built it," Warnie said with a hint of pride. "And, Jack, it seems that your public works have paid off. The pond is looking quite clean again and the paths are all raked. Well done, Smallpiggiebotham."

"Thank you, Master Pigibuddie. I did work rather hard at it while you were gone. And I think you'll find the pond once again delightful for a swim."

"Is this your pond?" Annie asked, smiling at the brothers' nicknames.

"Yes. Lovely, isn't it? Some people call this Shelley's Pond. You see, according to local lore, the poet Percy Bysshe Shelley, when he was a student at Oxford, used to walk in these woods and meditate on the beautiful surroundings. Of course, you probably know that he wasn't at Oxford long because he was expelled from my alma mater, University College, for his treatise on atheism. Ironically, I too was a self-proclaimed atheist when I matriculated. Anyway, we don't know the truth about Shelley and this pond, but it does make a delicious story and adds a bit of romantic mystique to the place, don't you think?"

"Yes, but it's quite peaceful and beautiful on its own merit. How nice that you have all this in your own backyard. How much property do you have altogether?"

"We have about nine acres, including that steep slope of Shotover Hill on the other side of the pond. The pond, by the way, was formed when clay was dug out to make bricks. They were fired in those kilns by the house which is, of course, where the Kilns got its name. Now, we just use them to store our coal in, but they do add a rather unique dimension to the property."

"I say, Jack," interjected Warnie. "Let's take a quick trip up *le grand escalier* so that I can inspect your public works."

"Would you ladies care to join us on a walk up the hill?" Lewis asked politely.

Maureen was struggling with the dog, who was pulling on his leash. "I think I'd rather not take Bruce up there. You know how he likes to squabble with the neighbor's bulldog. Annie, why don't you come with me and I'll show you the barn and the chicken coops? I'm afraid once I leave, Mother will want you to help tend the hens and collect the eggs."

"Oh, I don't mind," Annie said in all sincerity. "I grew up on a little farm outside Charlottesville, Virginia, so I'm used to chickens. I've also had a lot of practice with gardening. I'd be very happy to help out however I can."

"Good," Maureen said as she headed back toward the house and outbuildings. "Because once you've settled in, my mother won't give you much of a choice. She keeps everyone hopping around here, including poor Jack."

As the daughter of a college professor who had lived in the country for many years, Annie seemed uniquely qualified to blend happily into the Lewis ménage at the Kilns. After eating an ample dinner of chicken, potatoes, and fresh vegetables, laughing heartily at the witty and often hilarious conversation of the Lewis brothers, and spending the rest of the day reading and writing letters in the common room while listening to a Beethoven symphony on Warnie's gramophone, Annie realized that her brother could not have chosen a more ideal haven for her. She felt safer and more at ease than she had in months. Indeed, once she heard from Eric and could plan her own wedding day, she believed confidently that everything would be perfect.

29

Now this is what I call a real Sunday dinner!" Ian McLeod exclaimed, attacking a generous helping of roast beef and potatoes.

"A fitting reward for all our labors," Pilot Officer Robert White agreed.

Eric ate quietly but quickly. One never knew when the alarm bell would call the officers away from the table. He liked to be sure he finished his meal, particularly when the menu included roast beef.

"It's been kind of old Stuffy Dowding to let us lie low yesterday," McLeod observed, his mouth full of potatoes, after they had made considerable headway with their dinners.

"Righto," said White. "We've had a downright Sabbath."

"Especially after all the action we saw Thursday and Friday," Eric interjected, "but I'm not so sure yesterday's quiet was Stuffy's doin'. Although we lost a lot of planes this week, the Luftwaffe lost more. I think they're the ones lyin' low."

"What was the final tally, anyone know?" asked a doctor from farther down the table.

"Thursday was a bad day for us," Eric answered. "We lost thirty planes and seventeen pilots, with sixteen more wounded. But it was far worse for the Jerries, with some seventy-five planes down."

McLeod whistled. "Good for us. But then Stuffy did say we'd have to win two-to-one, dinna he?"

"Actually, I think it's more like four-to-one. We're turnin' out more aircraft, but our pilots are still vastly outnumbered."

"What was Friday's final tally?" the doctor asked.

"RAF: twenty-two; Luftwaffe: forty-five. Terrible, but the odds are still goin' in our favor nearly two-to-one."

White shook his head. "Fifty-two planes lost in two days. We're taking a real beating, aren't we? Plus they hit Croydon's airfield, not to mention eight or nine other bases. We're lucky they didn't come after us."

"They probably had targeted us and hit Croydon instead," Eric conjectured.

"Yer lass's brother is there, ain't he?" asked McLeod.

"Aye, but thankfully he wasn't on the casualty list. To be honest, I've been more worried about her. On Friday some bombs fell on the London docks and the environs and there were civilian casualties."

"I'm sure she's fine," McLeod reassured him. "What would the likes of her be doin' down at the docks, anyway?"

"Ye're probably right, but I sure would like to hear from her."

"Does she have a telephone?"

"Nay. And the lines are down, anyway."

"Maybe they'll get the phones back workin' with this current lull in the action. It's been nice for us to have a bit of a break. Unless ye consider that we're on alert round the clock.

Still, not havin' to scramble three or four times a day has been a real holiday. So how shall we spend the afternoon?" Ian asked. "It's such a fine day. Anyone fancy some bowls? Or, MacKenzie, would ye care to challenge me to a puttin' tournament?"

Eric mopped up the last of his gravy with a crust of bread. "Aye, I'll take ye. I don't have to be out at dispersal until three."

"May I join you?" White asked. "I'm keen for some golf."

"Ye're both on then," Ian McLeod pushed back from the table. "But first I'll enjoy a smoke."

Before he could light his cigarette, the air-raid siren began wailing its increasingly louder alarm, and the bell to scramble clamored shrilly.

The men instinctively abandoned their Sunday dinner and sprinted to their stations. What only moments before had been a quiet, lazy summer afternoon on base had suddenly turned into a frenzy of running, shouting people. Medical and service staff dove for cover in shelters, antiaircraft gunners took up positions, and airmen dashed to ready their planes. Eric and Ian jumped aboard a truck that roared off to the dispersal point, where some planes were already taking off and the ground crew had started the motors of others.

"We're under attack!" a crewman shouted as they raced to their aircraft. "Take your planes up—get them out of here! That's an order!"

"Thanks, mate!" Eric yelled back. "Now you take cover!" In a matter of minutes his Spitfire was airborne. On the radio traffic he could hear that Croydon was sending over a squadron of Hurricanes to defend Kenley's aerodrome from low-flying attackers. The Germans were unaware that besides its enormous aerodrome and five airplane hangars, Kenley also housed the entire sector operations headquarters for the southwest quadrant of England. Their target was even more crucial to the air war than they knew.

Eric stared in horror as a squadron of nine German Dornier bombers sailed just above the treetops but below radar detection toward the base. From the radio chatter, he could tell they had been visually spotted by an Observer Corps post.

"Let us take 'em on!" he shouted. But it was too late. They could not move quickly enough and Croydon's Hurricanes were circling around to attack the invaders from the rear. One or two Dorniers fell either to the antiaircraft guns or to the accuracy of the Hurricanes on their tails. Others became entangled in the cable defense situated on the perimeter of the airfield, but not before they had unloaded their bombs onto the fuel depot, control tower, and hangars. In a few hellish, chaotic seconds, the air was filled with antiaircraft flak and explosions as the bombs found their targets and fireballs shot skyward with ignited gasoline.

"I've been hit!" screamed a Hurricane pilot over the radio. "Mayday! Mayday!" Eric helplessly watched the flaming plane spin out of control and crash into the ground. Radio communication from the base was silenced, and all that came over the airwaves were the curses of the RAF pilots. A funnel of thick, black smoke billowed up like a tornado over the base. The pilots circled round and round like vultures waiting to swoop down. They were actually searching frantically for a place to land, but even the grassy fields had been cratered and pockmarked by bombs and machine-gun fire.

The radio crackled back to life. Orders were coming from another sector. "Hello, Hawkeye. This is Big Dog calling.

Vector one-five-two. Twenty-one angels. Bandits, six o'clock. Fifteen miles. Do you read? Over to you."

Eric switched his speaker on. "Big Dog, this is Hawkeye one-zero. We read you. Listening out."

So, he thought soberly, *they aren't finished with us yet. That was only the first wave and more are coming in to complete the job. They need only to follow the smoke and fire to find us. It's like an Indian smoke signal. But they're twenty thousand feet up. Just in our range.*

"Let's go, mates!' he cried as he banked his plane toward the coordinates being cited on the radio. Peering through his windshield, he spotted tiny black dots in the distance and flew straight for them. Flying at three hundred sixty miles per hour, Eric patiently stayed the course as the black specks loomed larger and larger. If they could break up the escort formation, then perhaps the Hurricanes five thousand feet lower could ward off the Dornier bombers before they closed in on the base. "Steady! Steady," Eric spoke quietly to himself as well as to his comrades. *If they want to play chicken, they'll lose. We are not going to let them near our base.*

"Tallyho!" Eric could hear other pilots shouting into their speakers as they held a constant course right into the formation of Bf Messerschmitt fighters. "Tallyho!" Eric yelled as he picked out his opponent and flew straight at him. He could see the grimace of the German pilot, who suddenly banked sharply and pulled away. Eric dove after him with guns blazing. A hit! Satisfied with the smoke spewing out of the damaged plane as it spiraled downward, Eric circled round and chose his next target. Although they were vastly outnumbered, the Spitfires and the courage of their pilots succeeded in harassing the Messerschmitt fighters into abandoning their formation.

Below them, the Hurricanes scattered the Dorniers, chasing them back toward the coast. Most dropped their payloads as they turned tail, but thankfully not on their designated targets. Kenley and the base nearby at Biggin Hill had been saved from further damage.

But the airfield at Kenley had been horribly savaged in the ninety seconds of bombing it had endured. Fires raged uncontrollably in four of the five hangars as petrol in the parked aircraft ignited and exploded. The hospital and the officers' mess, where they had been casually enjoying their roast beef dinner only minutes before, were reduced to heaps of smoldering rubble. The runways had been destroyed and the pilots still circled, hunting for a place to land before their fuel ran out. Orders came over the radio: Any Hurricanes still flying were to go to Croydon; the Spitfires, to Nutfield.

On arrival they took stock of their casualties: four Hurricanes lost and one pilot killed. They had no idea how many aircraft had been destroyed on the ground at Kenley. Although not demolished, the operations room had been rendered unserviceable and for many hours the refugee pilots waited anxiously for some word on the fate of their comrades. To pass the time, Eric and Ian McLeod halfheartedly joined a poker game in the officers' mess at Nutfield.

"Ye know, me friend," Ian said, looking up suddenly from his hand of cards, "I just realized ye had yer fifth kill this afternoon."

The other pilots looked up with interest at this revelation.

Eric nodded grimly. "Aye, I suppose ye're right."

"Disna tha' make ye an ace, laddie?"

"Aye. It does indeed."

"A round of drinks for our new ace!" Ian called out.

"Here! Here!" The other pilots gladly toasted Eric and clapped him on the back in a more subdued show of respect, and then they returned to concentrate on their game.

Eric's moment of glory faded quickly as the reports from airfields all over southern Britain came trickling in. Many had suffered extensive bombing that day: including bases in Kent, Sussex, Hampshire, Surrey, and Essex. They learned that at Kenley four Hurricanes and a Blenheim had been destroyed with several more Hurricanes and a Spitfire badly damaged. Many of the ground personnel had been wounded in the attack and twelve had been killed, including the doctor who had shared their dinner.

"Poor old chap," Ian muttered. "He was such a nice lad."

Then more bad news: The airfield would take weeks to repair; therefore, their squadron would be moved north to Leconfield in Lincolnshire in the morning. Eric withdrew to a quiet corner of the mess and quickly wrote a letter to Annie with the news of his reassignment. He carefully penned her Bayswater address and then, closing his weary eyes to rest them for just a brief moment, slumped over in exhaustion. He awoke to Ian's prodding.

"Come on, MacKenzie. We're off to the North Country. At least it's closer to home. Maybe we'll be back to bonny Scotland before this is all o'er."

30

Saturday, September 7, 1940
London

The Germans relentlessly continued their bombing raids throughout August. Day after day, night after night, sortie after sortie, the Luftwaffe pounded the British defenses and airfields, many of which had been attacked several times a day and were deemed unserviceable. Casualties among the RAF ran high, and the remaining pilots flew past the point of exhaustion. The average life expectancy of a pilot ran to only eighty-seven flying hours. The brave few held a tenuous command of the airspace over southern England, but they were close to being overwhelmed by the superior numbers of an enemy who gave them no time to lick their wounds and regroup. Then in early September, the air bases were handed an unexpected reprieve by Hitler, who screamed for revenge for the bombing of Berlin. To the relief of the airfields—but the detriment of the civilian population of England—the Führer unleashed his fury against London and other urban centers with a fierce determination to break the British will to resist.

The men and women of the Royal Air Force held the enemy at bay, toiling around the clock for days and weeks on end, snatching sleep when and where they could. Aware of the exhaustion of his pilots, Air Chief Marshall Sir Hugh Dowding ordered each squadron to take off one day a week—although this often proved to be impossible. Promoted to flying officer, Eric worked as feverishly as anyone. But when his squadron was finally granted a day of rest in early September, he took a morning train to London.

Although he had continued to mail numerous letters to Annie, he had not heard a word from her in weeks. Initially, he had reacted to the absence of mail as had the other men— with resigned disappointment. The Kenley post office had been reduced to rubble and their squadron's sudden move to Leconfield had further confused the forwarding process. The men bore their empty mailbags with self-deprecating British humor and the traditional stiff upper lip. In truth, Eric had been so consumed with the tasks at hand that he had little time or energy to dwell on it. Then the mail began trickling into their new base and the days turned to weeks without his hearing from Annie. Finally, when his letters were returned to him unopened, his concern turned into a deep apprehension. He determined to go to London at the first opportunity.

On the train trip, he mulled over all the reasons why she may not have written to him. *Could she have grown tired of waiting for him and found someone else? Could she have decided to return to America? What if she had been injured in an air raid? What if she had been killed?* His anxiety increased with each passing mile.

With the inexorable delays in travel, he did not find his way to Bayswater and the familiar flat until midafternoon. He bounded up the stairs of the terrace house and knocked lightly on her door. A pause. Silence. He knocked more forcefully. Silence again.

"Annie?" he called. "Are ye home? Peggy? It's me, Eric! Please let me in." *Maybe they're all at the hospital. Why didn't I go there first? But surely someone must be here. It's nearly tea-time.* "Annie? Betty? June? Annie! Anybody home?" *They can't all be working. Why doesn't someone answer?*

In frustration, he pounded on the door. "Annie!"

The door across the hall cracked open. An elderly woman peeked out.

Eric whipped around. "Ma'am, do ye know where Annie Little is?"

The woman shook her head and moved to shut her door.

"Wait!" He nearly sprang across the hallway. "Please, ma'am, where are the young ladies, the nurses? Are they out? Are they at work?"

"No, they're gone."

"Gone? Where?"

She shrugged. "They're all gone away. Ask him." She nodded toward the stairwell and then ducked back behind her door. A custodian, whistling under his breath, was climbing the stairs.

"What seems to be the problem, mate?" he asked when he reached the landing. "Sounded like you were goin' to break the door right down."

"I'm sorry. I'm lookin' for the young ladies who lived in this flat. The woman across the hall said they'd all gone. Is that true? Do ye know where?"

"That's right. They moved out about a month ago. No, it would have been the middle of August when those first bombin' raids 'it London. I 'eard that one of the girls was killed in that air raid."

"Killed?"

"Yeah. Bloody shame, ain't it?

Eric's chest tightened. He nearly choked, "Who? Which one was...killed?"

The man shook his head. "Sorry. Don't know."

"Was it the little one with the light brown hair? Or the tall one? The brunette? The redhead?"

"Sorry, mate. I don't know. All I know is that the others packed up and left after that."

"Where did they go?"

He grimly shook his head again.

"Didn't they leave forwardin' addresses?"

"They might 'ave done. But the landlord and his family up and left as well. In the mad scamble, everything slipped through the cracks. I've just been returnin' the nurses' mail to the post office. Sorry not to be of more 'elp. You're RAF, ain't ye? I can tell from your uniform. You lads are doin' a brilliant job. Ah, but the young ladies...a sad business...was one of them your girl?"

"Yes."

"Ah. I'm so sorry."

Eric pulled a matchbook out of his pocket and wrote in it. "Here," he said handing it to the custodian. "Here's my name and squadron number. Right now we're in Leconfield, but we're likely to be transferred again soon. If ye get any word from Miss Annie Little, would ye please let me know? Or if she or one of the other girls shows up again, would ye please tell them where I am?"

"To be sure. I am sorry, mate. Wish I could be of more 'elp. I hope she's all right. I 'ope you find 'er."

"Thanks. If ye don't mind, I'll stay here for a few minutes to think."

"Sure, sure. Take your time. Good luck, mate. Cheers." He took up whistling under his breath again and clomped back down the stairs.

Eric slumped to the floor, his back against Annie's door. Where had they gone? How could he find her? And one was killed? Which one of those lovely girls could be dead? He hoped against hope it wasn't Annie and then felt guilty at the thought it would then be one of the others. The tragedy of it overwhelmed him, washing over him in a wave of grief.

He hunched over his knees and silently wept.

When Eric had collected himself, he decided the only sensible thing to do would be to make his way across London to Barts Hospital and inquire there after the nurses. This turned out to be no small task.

When he emerged at last from the underground by St. Paul's Cathedral into the brilliant, late afternoon sunshine, the now familiar siren of "Moaning Millie" began wailing up and down over the city. Immediately, people rushed toward the subway and public shelters. Eric wended his way through the crowds and then sprinted the few blocks toward the back entrance of the hospital grounds. Once inside the nurses' gate, he ducked into the closest ward. Doctors and nurses were quickly but calmly pushing patients' cots out into the corridors and away from the windows. Eric, perceiving their objective, assisted them.

As he shoved one cot into the hallway, to the gratitude of the bedridden patient, a doctor spoke to him. "Thank you, officer. We appreciate the help. But you're off duty, aren't you?"

"Aye, but then, how can any of us ever be truly off duty durin' a war?"

"To be sure. But what are you here for? Did you come to visit someone? The burn ward for pilots is across the square."

"I'm actually lookin' for a nurse. My fiancée. Her name is Annie Little. Do ye know her?"

"No, sorry," the doctor said as they continued to haul cots out into the corridor. "But this is a big hospital. Do you know what ward she worked in?"

"Nay, but she's American, petite—"

"No, I am sorry. But, you know, most of our staff has been transferred out to St. Albans. We're running only a skeletal staff here and trying to send all but short-term patients out to the country. But if you could come back later, when things have quieted down, maybe someone could help you sort through the files to see where she might be."

"My leave's only twenty-four hours and I—"

The booming pops of an antiaircraft battery interrupted him. Over the racket, Eric distinctly heard the menacing drone of German Junkers.

"Take cover!" he shouted to the doctor as he pushed another cot through the door. The terrifying scream of a bomb rent the air. Then a more terrifying silence. The doctor dove under an empty bed and Eric threw himself over the last prostrate patient, heaving the cot away from the windows. A fiery blast ripped open the wall of the ward, spewing bricks and mortar. Shards of glass crashed to the floor like jagged icicles.

The clamor of sirens, whistles, flak, bombers, and deadly explosions rose unabated in a dreadful cacophony.

Eric lifted himself from the frightened patient lying beneath him. "Sorry about that. Are ye all right?"

"Yes," piped up the elderly man. "Thanks, mate. Are you?"

"Aye." Standing upright, he brushed some splinters of glass off his uniform and then looked around for the doctor, who was crawling out from his spontaneous shelter.

"Are ye all right, doctor?"

"Yes, just a few cuts, I think, but that's all." He dabbed at his scalp with his handkerchief. "Let's get these patients to safer quarters."

Another screaming whistle and *Boom!* The building rocked as the bomb hurtled through the glass roof of the main staircase and shot down the stairwell to explode in the basement. Smoke wafted through the corridor.

"Everybody stay calm!" a doctor called down the hallway. "We'll get you out as quickly as we can. Staff, we'll need to carry the patients to the north wing."

The stoically serene nurses turned to comfort their patients as the doctors and medical students set to the task of transferring the infirm to safety. Eric assisted until everyone had been properly settled in an undamaged ward. As he worked, he kept a lookout for Annie among the nurses and even made inquiries when he could, but to no avail. With little hope for success, he left his contact information with the doctor he had aided.

As the day deepened to dusk, Eric knew he had to return to his base. The beleaguered RAF would only be running on fumes of exhaustion if this barrage continued. "Well," he said to no one in particular as he stepped back out into the darkening streets of London, "I'd best be on my way. My squadron will be needin' me."

Having spent most of the war flying above the city, Eric was unprepared for the devastation that met him on the ground as he dodged debris and shrapnel en route back to the underground. Chaff fell about him like metallic confetti in a ticker tape parade. Bells clanged as fire engines and ambulances threaded their way through the streets. An Auxiliary Fire Serviceman dashed past him hauling buckets of sand to douse an unexploded incendiary bomb. Men scurried about uncoiling thick hoses or feverishly shooting jets of water from their stirrup pumps onto flaming buildings.

Sick at heart, Eric made his way back through the underground, crowded with frightened women and children huddling in the tunnels. Relieved to find the subway trains still stalwartly running, he boarded the northern line to King's Cross railway station. After an apprehensive wait, the blessed "all clear" siren heralded a respite in the bombing, and he found space on a train heading north toward Lincolnshire. In his brief brush with the plight of civilians, Eric had witnessed untold suffering and destruction, reigniting his determination to risk everything to bring defeat to the Nazis.

As the train carried him farther away, he looked back toward London. Although nightfall, the city was brightly lit by fire and the skyline glowed a sinister scarlet.

The London Blitz had begun.

October 1940
Oxford

The Nazis rained terror down on the cities of Britain night after night for weeks and then months. Valiantly the British "bulldogs" awoke each morning to dig out of the rubble and carry on. The courageous crewmen and pilots of the RAF struggled against the odds of exhaustion and attrition to defend the homeland from the vicious attacks, while the Luftwaffe suffered their own surprising losses and demoralization. Hitler indefinitely postponed Operation Sea Lion as his grandiose plans for conquering Britain were stymied. He did not, however, relent in his punishment of the Brits with his nightly bombing raids, concentrating on the cities of London, Birmingham, Manchester, Liverpool, Coventry, and even Belfast. While the urban civilians bravely forged the habit of spending their nights in bomb shelters and Tube stations, Annie Little settled into her own routine in the largely untouched haven of Oxford and the Kilns.

She rose early every morning to let the chickens out of their coops and to collect their eggs before assisting Mrs. Moore or Paxford in preparing and serving breakfast. With the shortage of nurses, she had no difficulty finding employment again at the Radford Infirmary, to which she caught the bus every day. In September, sympathetic Americans sent a staff of surgeons, physicians, and nurses to open a clinic for servicemen in the Headington suburb of Oxford. Corrugated iron Nissan huts were quickly constructed on the site of what would become the Churchill Hospital, and Annie was promptly hired. She could then often return to the Kilns for lunch or tea.

Although Mrs. Moore did not keep a rigid schedule for mealtimes, especially during the long summer vacation, Annie found that the Lewis brothers tried to maintain their own routine of breakfast, answering correspondence or reading, lunch, a lengthy walk, tea, writing and study, supper, more writing or reading or engaging conversation, and then bed. Their rhythm would often be interrupted, however, by household crises or demands from Mrs. Moore. While Warnie would most often ignore these and carry on with his work, Annie observed with growing respect that Jack would always selflessly lay down his pen or book and attend to whatever Minto required without one word of complaint. His devotion extended to filling her hot water bottle and bringing her warm drinks at bedtime when the nights turned cold. His Christlike servant's heart inspired Annie, and she strove to imitate it both at the hospital and at home as she also labored for Mrs. Moore.

Although demanding, Mrs. Moore was not unkind. As soon as her daughter had been wedded and moved to Nottinghamshire, she invited Annie to move upstairs to the spacious dormered room across the hallway from her own. Without too much prying, she inquired when Annie's baby was due and offered the use of Maureen's discarded frocks and trousers, as well as a sewing machine to remake them into proper maternity clothes. She made certain that Annie benefited from a diet as nutritious as they could provide, and as her pregnancy progressed, assigned more of the gardening and livestock chores to Paxford.

They even shared some adventures together. On one memorable evening when the brothers were in town attending one of their Inklings meetings, Mrs. Moore heard noises in the garden. Suspecting German invaders, she grabbed Jack's Great War service pistol from the desk in the common room and threw open the front door, bellowing for them to surrender. Two sheepish British infantrymen stepped out from the bushes and apologized for trespassing. When Minto heard their Irish brogues, she warmly welcomed them into the kitchen for some stout. They had such a rousing time reminiscing about dear old County Down that they returned the following evening for more Old Country hospitality.

In September, as the London Blitz began, more evacuees arrived at the Kilns. Two schoolgirls, Patricia and Marie, took up residence in the first floor music room vacated by Annie. Although often reduced to helpless fits of giggles, the girls had scholarly aspirations and in the evenings during term time, Patricia would seek tutoring from Jack, while Marie—or "Microbe," as she was quickly dubbed because of her desire to become a nurse—would ask Annie for help. For a time, they also housed a young man named Ronnie, who was mentally challenged. In the daytime he would assist Paxford with his chores, but several evenings a week Jack would patiently teach him his letters, coaching him in learning to read.

Without any show of piety, if there was good to be done, Jack set himself to do it. He daily demonstrated the depth of his Christian faith, not by preaching at his charges, but by his care and concern for them, and by the consistency of his charitable conduct he made a lasting impression on Annie. She began to understand more than ever before that a Christian was not one who merely espoused the common creeds or attended church on Sunday; rather, a true Christian was one who had committed his life unreservedly to following Jesus as his Messiah and Lord. She was simultaneously convicted by and drawn to this knowledge.

Annie's conflicted feelings were in no small part due to the circumstances in which she found herself. Simply put, she was expecting a baby and was unmarried, despite her charade of wearing a wedding band and assuming Eric's name. When she finally had the courage to send off the letter confessing all to him, she half-expected him to rush to her side at the Kilns and carry her off to Gretna Green right then and there. And then, when he did not magically appear, she began to count the days until she could reasonably expect to hear from him by post. As she waited anxiously for some word, the time doubled and redoubled again and again until she came to the dreadful but erroneous conclusion that either he had been killed or he did not truly love her and would never marry her or acknowledge the baby as his. Her anger and shame at this rejection caused her to feel even more distant from God, even while drawn to the faith of the Lewis brothers and that of her own brother, Jeff. Annie emotionally survived this journey through her own personal purgatory by shutting off her feelings as much as possible and directing all her energy into the tasks at hand.

But one autumn evening, when the household had gathered after dinner in the common room of the Kilns, Jack again took up a story he had begun to keep them entertained on the cold, dark nights. The tale had actually been told in its first rendition to the previous group of evacuees: four very much younger little girls. But owing to the more simple understanding of Ronnie, Jack offered it again, to this older group's immense delight. The tale began aptly enough with four children who had been evacuated from the bombing blitz out to the country house of a professor, but from there the story took a great departure from their own reality as the children stepped through a magical wardrobe into a fantasy world called Narnia, populated with talking animals and mythical creatures.

In his sonorous bass, Jack spun the tale this evening around the demand of the evil witch that one of the children must pay the penalty of death for an act of treachery he had committed. Jack held them spellbound as he described how Aslan, the great lion and king of Narnia, agreed that the crime must be punished and the penalty of death must stand—only Aslan would take the punishment on himself and die in the boy's place.

Jack related the tale so vividly that when he concluded, they were all brushing tears from their eyes.

"Well, that's enough for tonight," he said, rising and offering his hand to Mrs. Moore to help her up. "Minto, you look ready for bed. I'll fetch your hot water bottle for you."

"Thank you, Jack. That was a lovely story."

"You really should write it down, Jack," said Warnie. "Since Tollers still hasn't finished his new Hobbit book, I'd wager his publishers would be interested in some good children's stories from you."

"Well, perhaps I will write it all down one of these days. But don't forget that the chaplain in chief for the RAF has asked me to give some talks about faith to the lads on the bases, so I must prepare those. And you know I must first finish these blasted letters from old Screwtape," he said with a glint of merriment in his large brown eyes, "although writing fairy tales for children does sound like much more fun than letters from a devil."

"More stories tomorrow?" asked Ronnie eagerly.

"Certainly, old chap," Lewis said with warm kindness. "I'll tell you some more stories tomorrow night after we practice your alphabet. Goodnight, Ronnie."

"Night!"

After a great deal of bustle, most of the household retired. Annie remained in the common room in a shabby but cozy winged chair near the coal fire. She had requested to read Jack's copy of his newly published book, *The Problem of Pain,* and so he found her when he returned later to write for a while. As Jack sat at his desk engrossed in his own project, Annie found it difficult to concentrate on her reading. The story he had told had touched her profoundly. The picture of the innocent and blameless king, Aslan, taking the penalty of death on himself in place of the guilty boy, had made her understand Jesus' sacrifice when He had gone to the cross. She felt as if the blinders had been lifted from her eyes and that she could now clearly see what the Bible meant when it said that Jesus had died for her sins. But she felt horribly burdened by her own form of treachery. She had been living a lie with these good people, pretending to be married to protect her reputation with them. She wanted to come clean and confess, but she didn't know how to broach the subject. She sat quietly pretending to read, while in reality her thoughts and emotions roiled within her.

Then Jack put down his pen and turned to her.

"Well, I guess that's all for me tonight. But before I turn in, I wanted to ask you how things are going for you, Annie. We haven't had much time to talk recently. Is everything all right?"

"Yes, sir." She found herself lying again. "I've been fine."

"And all's well with the baby?"

"Yes. They've been looking out for me at the hospital."

"Have you had any word from your husband, Annie? Minto couldn't help noticing that you haven't received any letters. Do you know if he's all right?"

Annie flushed deeply as her stomach knotted. "No, sir. I don't know. I haven't heard anything."

"Well, I am sorry. This must be extremely difficult for you. Minto is especially sensitive to these things because there was a period of about three weeks when she was in limbo, knowing only that her son Paddy had been reported as missing. But surely the authorities would contact you if there were anything wrong—"

"No, they wouldn't!' she suddenly blurted out. "They wouldn't contact me because they don't know to. Oh, Jack!" she cried. "The truth is…I'm not married! I've lied to you all. The ring, the name, it's all a terrible charade." She covered her face with her hands. "I'm so sorry. You've all been so wonderful to me, and all along I've been lying to you. At first I was so ashamed and worried you wouldn't take me in if you knew I was unmarried, and then I didn't know how to tell you. So there it is. The truth at last. You can turn me out if you like. I wouldn't blame you."

"There now," he said gently. "No more talk of that. Minto, Warnie, and I have all agreed that you are to stay on here with the baby as long as you need to. The truth is, I've suspected this for a while now. Jeff hadn't mentioned to me anything about your being married or pregnant, and it did seem rather odd that you hadn't received any letters. But I felt you needed to own up to it in your own time. Confession is good for the soul, you know, Annie. You've been carrying a terrible burden."

"You suspected and yet you let me stay?" She shook her head in wonder. "Can you find it in your heart to forgive me, then?"

"We can. We have. I think probably the more important question is—can you forgive yourself?"

"I honestly don't know. I've let everyone down—you, my brother, my family, myself. And God. I don't know how anyone can forgive me if God hasn't."

"What makes you think God hasn't forgiven you? God is in the business of forgiving sins. That is one of the basic tenets of our Christian faith. If we confess our sins or failings to Him and repent or turn away from them, He has promised to forgive us."

"That's what Jeff said to me, and we even prayed together, but I don't feel forgiven. I still feel like God has turned away from me."

"It's a matter of faith, not feelings. We believe in His promises by faith. Sometimes He is gracious to give us feelings; but if He doesn't, we need to trust that He knows best. The lack of feelings doesn't mean that our forgiveness is any less real. Just as when a man has a cold and can't taste his food—the food won't be any less beneficial to him because he can't taste it. But I suspect that your feeling that God has turned away from you has more to do with your having turned away from Him. If you can believe He has forgiven you, and He has, then there is nothing to keep you from Him. If you ask, you will receive; if you seek, you will find Him."

"I want to know God the way you do, Jack," Annie said fervently.

"I'm nothing special, Annie. I'm just a man who about a decade ago finally realized that the God of the universe was real and that He was pursuing me. Once I stopped running from Him and made the decision to serve and obey Him, He was ready to welcome me into His kingdom."

"But how can I do that?"

"Jesus said, 'Behold, I stand at the door and knock; if any one hears my voice and opens the door, I will come in to him and eat with him, and he with me.' He wants to live in and through you. He wants to be your Savior and Lord. All you have to do is come to Him with the faith of a little child."

"I want to believe, but I don't know if I feel like—"

"There you go with your feelings again. Your feelings or moods can change from one minute to the next, especially when they're influenced by circumstances like the weather or how much sleep you've gotten or even if you have a case of indigestion. Remember the man who said, 'Lord, I believe; help my unbelief'? You can take that initial step of faith and let Him do the rest in you."

"Lord, I believe; help my unbelief," she repeated.

"Yes, that's right. Then you can help your faith to grow by putting before yourself reminders of what you believe: through prayer, reading the Scriptures, going to church, and so forth. And Warnie and I will be here to help you along. If it would be all right, Annie, I should like to pray for you now."

"I would like that very much, Jack."

"All right then. We can just talk to Him as if He's right here with us—because He is," Lewis said, bowing his head.

Annie likewise bowed her head and closed her eyes. Although later she could not remember the exact words of Jack's prayer for her, she would remember forever after the sense of peace that poured over her like a healing balm. When he concluded with "in Jesus' name, Amen," she tentatively ventured her own prayer.

"Father," Annie whispered quietly, as she dabbed at the tears coursing down her cheeks, "please forgive me for all my sins. I am so sorry. I have strayed far from You. Forgive me. Help me to believe. Help me to be the kind of person You would like me to be. Help me to grow to be more like Your Son, Jesus. And please bless and keep this little baby. And wherever Eric is, please bless and keep him. And Jeff—please bless and keep my brother, Jeff, too. Amen."

"Amen," Lewis repeated. He looked up at her. "So, is this Eric the baby's father?"

"Yes. Eric MacKenzie. He is in the RAF, and he did give me this ring. So that part was true. We planned to be married, but I haven't seen him since after Dunkirk. And I haven't heard from him since I wrote to him to tell him about the baby and that I was coming here."

"And you've interpreted his silence to mean indifference or rejection?"

"Yes. I think if he had really wanted to marry me, he would have come as soon as he could. I can only imagine that he doesn't want this baby or me now."

"There is the possibility that he never received your letter, isn't there?"

"I doubt that. All my other mail got through to him just fine. No, it can only mean that he doesn't want to marry me anymore."

"And yet, Annie, I hate to even mention it, but he could be missing in action or shot down. If, as you said, the RAF doesn't know of your relationship to him, you would not be notified if something happened to him. Do you know who his next of kin is? Are his parents living?"

"His parents live in the Scottish Highlands. He gave me their address. I've thought about writing to ask if they've heard from him, but I didn't want to presume upon them. And what if he is all right but he hasn't written me because of the baby? Then I'm right back where I was before."

"Well, at least then you'll know better where you stand. I think you should give it a try. And you might even consider writing him another letter in case he never received the first one. As you are undoubtedly aware, most of the air bases have been under attack. In wartime I don't think you can logically assume that failing to hear from someone means that they don't care about you." He rose stiffly. "But it's late now, and we should both be abed. Do you need your hot water bottle filled?"

"No, thank you," she said as she began to tidy up the room. "I'll take care of it."

"All right then, I guess I'll say goodnight."

"Goodnight, Jack." She straightened up from plumping a pillow. "And, Jack—thank you. Thank you for everything. For talking with me and straightening out my thinking and praying with me, and for accepting me and being so kind. Thank you."

He smiled and his eyes sparkled. "You're most welcome. But I should thank you. I find that one of the greatest joys in this life is to help a fellow immortal—and none of us are mere mortals, you know, as we were all created to live forever either with God in splendor or separated from Him in eternal misery. Anyway, one of life's greatest joys is to help another immortal along the path to grow closer to God. And the Bible says that all the angels in heaven rejoice when a lost child returns to the Father. So I can imagine that they are having quite a celebration over you right now, young lady."

"That's a lovely thought." Annie smiled too. "Do you really think so?"

"I do. I not only think it, but I believe it!"

32

Saturday afternoon, November 2, 1940
Biggin Hill Airfield

From July through October, relentless bombing raids
had terrorized the populace of Great Britain, and
yet Hitler proved unable to break the resistance of the people
or the defense of their armed forces. Churchill's rousing
tribute to the RAF, "Never in the field of human conflict was
so much owed by so many to so few," echoed as a taunt to the
demoralized and oft-defeated Luftwaffe. Although the Germans continued to rain down their destructive fire upon the
British for another four and a half years, by early November,
the Battle of Britain was effectively over. To the immense relief
of the stalwart but weary Brits, the Nazis cancelled their plans
for the invasion of England, and in an astounding betrayal of
their former ally, the Soviet Union, turned their attention to
attacking the USSR's western front.

Early in the war, the Dean of St. Paul's, the Very Reverend Robert Matthews, had written to the Reverend Maurice Edwards, chaplain in chief of the RAF, to recommend
C.S. Lewis as a traveling lecturer. After *The Problem of Pain*
had been released to well-deserved acclaim in October,
the Reverend Edwards contacted Lewis. They met in his

Magdalen rooms to discuss his giving speeches on the Christian faith to the various air force stations scattered throughout the country. Although cautious in his expectations for success, Lewis, who had been called up for monthly night watches as a member of the Home Guard, was eager to serve both God and country in this new venture. He spent many long weekends traveling away from home, but he was compensated by having the opportunity to explore without expense much of his adopted homeland.

The first weekend in November, he spoke to a small gathering of about two dozen RAF pilots and crewmen at the airfield of Biggin Hill in Surrey, south of London. As a sector headquarters for Fighter Command Group 11, Biggin Hill, like Kenley, had borne the brunt of bombing attacks and air raids. Squadrons had been transferred in and out as reinforcements for the battered base. Lewis knew that these men had been facing the possibility of their own deaths every single day for months. Many of their friends and comrades had not returned home. Having served in the horrible trenches of the Great War, he knew their exhaustion, their fear, and their courage—and that there truly were no atheists in foxholes and probably none under the canopies of Spitfires and Hurricanes, either.

Although initially rather nervous with the enormity of his responsibility, Lewis quickly grew in confidence as he connected with his audience on the deep level of shared wartime experience. He based his message on John 3:16-17:

> *For God so loved the world that he gave his only*
> *Son, that whoever believes in him should not perish*
> *but have eternal life. For God sent the Son into the*

world, not to condemn the world, but that the world might be saved through him.

With those verses as his springboard, Lewis vigorously expounded to them the basic tenets of the Christian faith and its promise of eternal life in heaven to those who believe.

After his talk and some discussion, a few men queued up to speak personally to him.

The first pilot spoke vehemently. "You know, I believe in God. I have met Him sometimes in the beauty of a sunset or flying high in the heavens. But I have no patience with the church and its talk of Christian doctrine and theology. Why do I need to go to church when I can experience God on my own?"

Nonplussed, Lewis responded politely. "I have no doubt you have experienced God through the splendors of nature. I have as well. But isn't it possible that God has given you these glimpses of His glory because He desires you to seek Him and truly know Him?"

The pilot pushed his cap off his forehead and shrugged.

"Just as we need a map and a guide to learn about an unknown country," Lewis continued, "we need the Holy Scriptures and other believers to help us learn more about God. God wants to offer you life eternal as well as a personal relationship with Him. You shouldn't be satisfied with a few isolated experiences that have left you with good feelings when you could have so much more. You're selling God and yourself short. Think of a man who is content with a few glimpses of a beautiful woman when he could learn to love her and have her for his wife. You're content with a few moments of beauty when He is offering you infinite splendors."

The pilot grunted. "I never thought of it that way. I'll give that some consideration. Thanks for speaking today, sir."

Several other men and a few ladies from the Women's Auxiliary Force stopped to thank Lewis or ask him a question. At the end of the queue stood a tall pilot whose demeanor was very solicitous. "Mr. Lewis?" He stepped forward when the others had left. "Thank ye for makin' the trip from Oxford to speak to us. We really need the encouragement. And I wanted to say that yer talk really inspired me."

"Why, thank you."

"Ye know, sir, I'm a Christian too, but I must confess that I haven't been actin' much like one recently—well, since the war started, actually."

Lewis listened attentively, so the pilot went on. "The truth is that as a young lad I had a vision of Jesus and He called me to be His minister. I completed three years at the University of St. Andrews and was in line to attend their School of Divinity for ordination. But then the war intervened. And, well..."

He took a deep breath and exhaled heavily. "I was in love with a local girl, the laird's daughter. We planned to be married, but when the Nazis invaded Poland, her father put her on a boat for America. It was the *Athenia,* which, if ye remember, was torpedoed on the first day of the war. She did not survive. I was so angry at the Nazis and at God Himself for takin' her that I joined the RAF with the determination to kill as many Germans as I possibly could. And I suppose ye could say that ever since I've been runnin' from God. So here I am. When ye spoke of eternal life, it reminded me that Laurene is with God now. She was a devout believer, but perhaps that's why it seems so unfair that she would die and so many nasty and truly evil people live on. I don't know. But when ye talked of heaven, it seemed more real than this life. I liked what ye said about this world bein' merely a shadow of the splendors awaitin' us. I miss Laurene. But while ye were speakin', I realized that she really is in a better place now and she probably wouldn't want to come back if she could, especially to this war. So I suppose that my anger at God is really only hurtin' me, isn't it?"

Lewis nodded.

"I guess I'm findin' out that I can run from God, but He won't let me evade Him for too long. I think He sent ye here, even if it was just so this particular pilot would turn around and fly home. Thanks again, sir, for listenin' and for sharin' today."

"You're most welcome." Lewis extended his hand, which the pilot warmly shook. "And I am very sorry about your loss."

"Thanks, but to be honest, I didn't come to hear ye today because ye were goin' to talk about faith, but because the poster said ye're an Oxford don."

Lewis raised an eyebrow with interest. "Really?"

"Well, ye see after I joined up, I met another wonderful young lady in London and we became engaged. But I haven't heard from her since the Blitz started. I went to London to look for her but couldn't find her. Then I tried to contact her brother who had joined the RAF, but he's on a secret mission. So I've been at a complete loss. Anyway, she had said that if London were bombed, her brother had told her to go to Oxford to stay with one of his professors. I thought maybe that's where she is, but I don't know the name of the professor. I know it's a long shot, but I wondered if there's any chance ye knew an American student by the name of Jeff Little or if ye're acquainted with any professor who might have tutored an American student."

Lewis sucked his breath in sharply. "What's your name, son?"

"MacKenzie. Eric MacKenzie."

"And the girl?"

"Annie Little."

A smile of wonder spread over Lewis's broad face. "Praise be to God!"

"Do ye know her?"

"Ha-ha!" Lewis clasped the stunned pilot. "Yes! I'm Jeff's professor! Annie is living at my house outside of Oxford!"

Eric grabbed Lewis's arms. "She's with you? Is she all right?"

"Yes, yes, she's fine. She's just fine."

Eric closed his eyes and breathed, "Amen. Praise be to God!" Then another thought overshadowed his joy. "But if Annie is safe, then that means one of the other girls…there were four nurses livin' together…I was told one of them had been killed in a bombin' raid. Do ye know which one?"

"Yes. Her name was Peggy. I'm very sorry."

"Peggy." Eric shook his head sorrowfully and sighed. "Well, that is bad news. She was a very special young lady." Pressing his lips together, he looked up at the horizon while he mastered his emotions. "But then, like Laurene, she was a believer. So I suppose she was the one most ready to go to God, and there's some comfort in that."

"Yes." They stood together in silence for a few moments of refection. Then Lewis spoke up. "When you said you had not heard from Annie since the Blitz, MacKenzie, did you mean that you never received a letter from her indicating her move to Oxford?"

"That's right. I haven't heard from her in a long time, and then my letters to her in London have been returned. So in

September I went to London for the day to try to find her, but all the girls had moved out and the custodian didn't have their forwardin' addresses."

"I see. So you didn't receive any news from her about her change in circumstances?"

"No…what do ye mean?"

Lewis ignored this question. "And is it still your intention to marry Annie?"

"Aye, to be sure."

"You know, MacKenzie, Annie hasn't heard from you in a long time, either. I would love to be the bearer of good news, but it may come as a shock to her. I think if there were any way that you could acquire some leave, it would be best if you could come to see her in person. I don't know if it's possible for you to come with me, but I'm returning to Oxford this afternoon."

"Ye mean, ye'd invite me to go with ye today?"

"Yes, if you were granted the leave."

"Upon my word, Mr. Lewis! That would be too good to be true! Let me speak to my squadron leader. He might say yes. I haven't taken any leave since that day I went to London in September."

"All right. I'll wait right here in the mess." Lewis settled down in a leather chair and took a packet of cigarettes from his jacket pocket.

Eric bolted from the hall and returned before Lewis had finished his smoke. "Mr. Lewis! He said I may go! He gave me forty-eight hours leave! Thank ye so much, sir. Oh, I can't wait to see my Annie!"

33

Saturday evening, November 2, 1940
The Kilns

The phone rang at the Kilns as Annie was cleaning up the kitchen after supper. She dried her hand on her apron and answered it.

"Hello? This is the Lewis residence."

"Hello, there! Jack speaking." His voice boomed above the din of what sounded like a train station. "Is this Annie?"

"Yes, sir. How are you, Jack?"

"Fine! Fine! And you're just the person I wish to speak to. I'm calling to let you know that I'm bringing a guest back with me tonight. Could you see that the spare bed in Ronnie's room is prepared?"

"Yes, I'd be happy to. When should we expect you?"

"Well, with the way the trains are running, probably not until late—around eleven, perhaps? Tell the family not to wait up for us. But since you're our little night owl, would you mind staying up to help me make sure our guest is properly settled?"

"No, sir. I don't mind at all. It will give me an excuse to keep the fire going."

"All right, then. I'll see you later. Goodbye!"

"Goodbye." Annie hung up the phone, untied her apron, and went to inform the rest of the family that Jack would be returning late and bringing a guest with him. As she put sheets on the spare bed, she wondered if this would be another evacuee who would add to the growing household at the Kilns.

After everyone else had retired, Annie sat reading in the winged chair in the common room, her foot gently rubbing Bruce the sheepdog as he lolled on the braided carpet, basking in the warmth from the coal fire. Close to midnight, Bruce's ears perked up and he yipped a greeting.

"Are they here, old boy?" Annie asked and her own ears confirmed it when she heard rumblings from the kitchen. She closed her book and rose from the chair.

Jack's ruddy face appeared in the doorway. "Hello there! Thanks for waiting up, Annie. There's someone here to see you. Excuse me. I need to check on Minto." He ducked away from the door and made way for a tall handsome man in uniform.

Startled by the familiar but completely unexpected face, Annie blanched and gripped the arm of the chair. "Eric!" she gasped. "I can't believe it!"

"Annie!" He smiled as he stepped into the room. Then he froze and his smile faded. "Ye're pregnant!"

"Yes," she said faintly.

"Oh, my word! Why didn't ye tell me?"

"Didn't you get my letter?"

"No! No, I had no idea."

"Oh, dear. This must be quite a shock. I wrote to you back in August, and when I didn't hear from you, I—"

"But—" he interrupted as he stared at the plain gold wedding band on her hand. "Whose baby is it?"

"What do you mean?"

"I mean, who is the father? Oh, Annie, please tell me you didn't go off and marry someone else!"

"No!" she cried. "Of course, I didn't marry anyone else! This is the ring you gave me the night we said our vows. Eric, you are the only man I have ever loved. You're the only man I have pledged myself to. You're the only man I have known. There has been no other. You are this baby's father, Eric. You! This is your baby, Eric. Yours and mine." She covered her mouth with her hand and said, sobbing, "And when I didn't hear from you for so long…I thought…I thought…you were dead…or that you…didn't care…I thought…you had…abandoned us!"

"Oh, my darling, what have I done?" Rushing to her, he took her in his arms. "I'm so sorry! Please forgive me. I am so sorry. I shouldn't have doubted ye. And I would never abandon ye. I have always loved ye. There, there now." He stroked her hair and gently kissed her. "Don't cry," he said as his own eyes brimmed with tears. "My poor, brave, darlin' girl. To go through this all alone. How dreadful. I'm here now. I'm so sorry!"

She nestled her head against his chest and wept over all the frustration and fear, disappointment and despair that had been pent up within her for months. He held her close and his heart wept with her. When at last her sobs slowed, he pulled a handkerchief from his pocket. "Here, darlin', take this."

She wiped her eyes and nose and then said with a little laughing sob, "I'm sorry. I've messed up your jacket." She brushed her fingers across his leather bomber jacket.

"No matter. It's been through a war. It will stand up to yer tears. Here, may I take it off? May I stay?"

"Yes, of course. I'm sorry."

He slipped it off. "Will ye sit up with me a while longer? We have much to talk about."

"Yes," she said as she sat close beside him on the sofa. "But can I get you anything? Are you hungry or thirsty?"

"I'm fine. Let me just look at ye for a moment. Ye're still so pretty, even after all those tears." He caressed her cheek. "Oh, Annie, I'm so glad to see ye and know ye're all right."

"I was so worried about you too, Eric. But why didn't you write to me?"

"I did, but my letters were returned to me. I didn't know where ye were."

"I sent you a letter back in August before we left London."

"Aye, but I never got it. Kenley was bombed, ye know, in August. And then we've been transferred several times. I went up to London to look for ye at the beginnin' of September, but no one was there. It was the night of the first major bombin' attack on London. I went to Barts, by the way, and helped them move patients around durin' the air raid, but I couldn't find anyone who knew yer whereabouts."

"So how did you find me? Was it Jack?"

"Aye. We're stationed now at Biggin Hill and he came today to speak to us."

"God be praised!" Annie breathed, clutching his hands.

"Amen to that. But, my dear, when ye didn't hear from me, why didn't ye write me again? Surely the RAF would have forwarded yer letters to me eventually."

"I did finally write to your parents just to find out if you were alive, but I haven't heard back from them yet. I just couldn't bring myself to write to you again. I was so afraid that you had decided you didn't want me anymore. I didn't know what to do."

"Oh, darlin', how could ye doubt me?"

"How could you doubt *me?*"

"Aye, ye're right. I'm so sorry. '*Our doubts are traitors, and make us lose the good we oft might win by fearing to attempt.*'"

"You sound like Jack now, talking in quotations."

He smiled and slipped his arm around her shoulders. "Well, I know ye're in good hands here. And he spoke so highly of ye that I know ye've been a blessin' to them as well. But he didn't breathe a word to me about yer bein' pregnant. I suppose he thought that was yer news to tell. So do tell me about it. How far along are ye? When are ye due?"

"I'm eight and a half months and due in mid-December."

"That's not long now. And ye're all right? And the baby? The pregnancy has gone well?"

"Yes. Everything, except for the stress, has gone fine. And since I've been working as a nurse, I'm well looked after by all the hospital staff."

"Well, I am glad. God forgive us—" Clasping her hands, he gazed at her intently. "And, Annie, please forgive me. I was wrong to take things so far. I am so sorry. Will ye forgive me?"

"Yes. But will you forgive me? I shouldn't have asked you to stay. I shouldn't have tempted you."

"I do forgive ye, Annie." He kissed her hand. "Now, my darlin', we need to discuss what we're goin' to do. Do ye think ye're up for a little train trip? I have forty-eight hours of leave and I had hoped to take ye up to Gretna Green tomorrow."

"Gretna Green? To be married?"

"Yes! To be officially married in the eyes of God and king. I wish we could be properly married here, but we'd need to wait the three Sundays for the bans, and ye're still too young. Unless…did ye by any chance write to yer parents and ask permission to marry?"

"No." She blushed deeply. "I wrote to tell them we were already married, back in March, the night you proposed and we said the vows in church."

"Ah…the night this baby was conceived then."

"Yes." She stared at the ring she still wore. "Everyone here—except Jack and Warnie and Minto—thinks we were married then."

"I understand. But go with me to Gretna Green tomorrow and we'll make ye an honest woman, as they say."

She hesitated. "Eric, I cannot marry you just because of the baby. I do love you; it's not that. But, you see, in the last few weeks I've come to realize that I love someone even more than you."

"Who?" He frowned.

She smiled sympathetically. "God. I love God more than I love you. When I thought I was abandoned, I finally turned to Him and completely gave Him my life to use as He wills. He is now my first love and He must always be. I don't know if we can have a successful marriage if we are at odds on this."

"Why should we be at odds? I don't understand. I—"

"Let's be honest, Eric. Ever since Laurene died, you've turned away from God. You once wanted to be a minister, and now you don't even want to go to church. I don't see how we can walk together as one if we are not agreed on the most important thing in life. I'm so sorry. I wish things were different."

"So ye would be willin' to have this baby alone?"

"If I have to, yes. But I wouldn't be alone. I would have the Lord with me. But without Him, I would have nothing."

Eric sat silently for a moment, rubbing his forehead. "Well, ye know what I think? I think that's very admirable."

"You do?"

"Yes. But I'm also happy to tell ye that ye're wrong about me. If I had found ye a few weeks ago or even yesterday, ye'd be perfectly right. But I had my own Damascus Road experience just today. I went to hear Mr. Lewis speak because he was from Oxford and I hoped he might lead me to you. And though that was the case, it was not the only thing that happened. I am done with runnin' away from God. He really spoke to me today and called this prodigal son to come home to Him. He led me back to Himself and to you. I'm sure it would have been better for us and this baby if we had not stepped out of God's will for so long, but He can work all things together for good, especially now, as we repent and turn back to Him."

Annie looked at him in amazement. "All this change of heart happened today?"

"Aye. And although Mr. Lewis did not tell me about the baby or even much about you, we talked for many hours about the Lord and my life. He helped me straighten out my thinkin' about a lot of things."

"Do you suppose the Lord kept us apart until we could each get our hearts right with Him?" Annie asked quietly.

"I think that seems more than likely."

"And do you think that you might want to become a minister after all?"

"Well, I can't deny that vision I had at the lighthouse when I was a young lad. But we cannot know what the future holds.

We still have a war to fight and win. So it may be a long time until I can go back to university and follow that dream…but as God guides and provides. If down the road that is where He leads me, do ye think that ye could serve alongside me? Could ye be a pastor's wife?"

She smiled. "I'm a PK, remember? Three generations of women in my family have married pastors. I always thought I was destined to follow the family tradition."

"Really? Ye ne'er told me that."

Annie laughed. "I was so tempted to when we first met, but Jeff would not have let me live it down."

"Is that a yes then? Will ye marry me, Annie Little?"

"Yes, Eric, I will marry you with all my heart!"

He lifted her chin and kissed her very gently. "I love ye so much, Annie. And I am a very blessed man indeed."

34

December 1940
The Kilns

On Sunday morning, November 3, Annie and Eric accompanied Jack and Warnie to the 8:00 Matins service at Holy Trinity, where they received the sacrament of Holy Communion as an outward symbol of the grace within their hearts. Before they boarded the train to Scotland, Jack slipped Eric a generous wad of cash as a wedding gift to provide proper food and lodging for their honeymoon. Annie and Eric were quietly married just over the border in Gretna Green. After a brief but loving night together at the Hazeldene Guesthouse, they traveled back to Oxford, where Eric kissed a tearful Annie goodbye before returning to duty and his fighter squadron at Biggin Hill.

On Friday, December 13, Annie, who was not the least bit superstitious, went into labor in the small hours of the morning and called for a taxi after light dawned to take her to the Radcliffe Infirmary. Her labor was long and difficult, but one of her nursing friends stayed with her throughout the ordeal and her solicitous doctor ensured that the delivery went smoothly. Back at the Kilns, the Lewis household prayed and waited anxiously for some word. When it finally arrived late that afternoon, they promptly rushed to the telegraph office to pass along the happy news.

Near dinnertime, Eric was summoned into the office of his squadron leader, Don McDonnell, and handed a telegram. It read:

```
CONGRATULATIONS STOP YOU HAVE A BABY BOY
7 LBS 8 OZ STOP MOTHER AND BABY ARE FINE
STOP CSL
```

Eric beamed as he read the message over and over.

"Good news, MacKenzie?"

"Yes, sir. I'm a father! I have a son!"

"Well, congratulations, old boy! And newly married too, aren't ye?" He winked slyly. "This calls for a toast, don't ye think? Don't tell the other lads about this, but I have hidden away just the thing for such an occasion." He opened the bottom drawer of his desk and pulled out a flask of amber liquid.

Eric blinked at the scarce commodity. "Scotch, sir?"

"Scotch. Just between us Scots." He carefully poured a small amount into two shot glasses and handed one to Eric. "To yer son. What's his name, MacKenzie?"

"We decided to call him David Lawrence, sir, after both our fathers."

"To David Lawrence MacKenzie, then."

"To David," Eric held up his glass, "and to my wife, Annie." They clinked their glasses together in a glow of camaraderie. "Thank ye, sir. Cheers."

"Cheers. Ahhh!" McDonnell savored the warmth of the drink as he wiped his mouth with the back of his hand. "Now,

MacKenzie, congratulations are in fact in order for something else."

"Sir?"

"You've been promoted again. Congratulations, Flight Lieutenant."

Eric couldn't help smiling. "Why, thank ye, sir!"

"You've been an exemplary pilot and great model of courage under fire to all the new recruits coming in. I'm proud to serve with you, MacKenzie."

"Thank ye, sir. And I with you."

"So, along with the added responsibility and second blue band on your uniform, this will give you a little bit of extra pay to send home to your new family."

"That would be excellent, sir."

"And I suppose ye will be needin' some leave to see this son of yers." He rifled through some papers. "Let me see...I can't give ye Christmas, but how would the twenty-second and twenty-third suit ye?"

"Forty-eight hours? That's most considerate, sir. Thank ye, sir."

"All right, Flight Lieutenant MacKenzie. Well done! Ye're dismissed."

❧

The first time Eric laid eyes on his son, David, was at the Kilns. Warnie greeted him at the front door with a hearty congratulatory pat on the back and ushered him into the household gathering in the common room. Annie sat on the sofa in front of the fireplace, holding a tiny bundle wrapped in a pale blue blanket crocheted by Mrs. Moore.

Annie's face lit up when she saw him. "Hello, darling!" she exclaimed. "Come see your beautiful baby boy."

Eric rushed to her side and gazed with a sense of wonder at the newborn infant.

"Oh, my goodness! Look at him. He's so little!"

"Well, he is half *Little*," quipped Jack, and he and Warnie chuckled.

Eric looked at them and grinned. "I suppose he is. I hope he won't take after his mother in her diminutive size, though, although it would be nice if he favored her looks."

"I think he looks like you, Eric," Annie said softly. "Look at all this dark hair. And he has your bright blue eyes."

"He certainly is an alert little fellow, isn't he?" Eric held his finger out for the baby to grasp. "And look at that grip! Strong too. He'll make a great athlete."

"Would you like to hold him?"

"I'm not sure I should." Eric laughed nervously. "I don't have much experience with wee ones."

"Here. He's your son. You don't need experience." Annie carefully placed David in his father's arms. "Just keep his head supported. That's right. See? You're a natural dad."

"Will ye look at that, now?" Eric beamed. "I've never seen such a fine lad. I wonder what he'll grow up to be."

"I hope he'll grow up to be a Christian and a good man like his father," Annie said.

"Maybe he'll be a pilot," Mrs. Moore conjectured.

"Or a poet?" Warnie added playfully.

"If my soul is at all prophetic," Jack boomed with merriment, "he is destined to be a scholar! Any baby born into this house and growing up among all these books can hardly be anything else."

"Here, here!" agreed Warnie, raising his glass in a toast. "Here's to our first Kiln's infant, David Lawrence MacKenzie, Esquire: Christian, gentleman, athlete, and scholar extraordinaire! And perhaps a pilot or poet as well. And here's to our happy couple! May they live a long, joyful, prosperous life together and may they be blessed with many more children!"

"Amen to that," Jack jovially exclaimed.

Embracing his wife and son, Eric echoed with all his heart, "Amen and amen!"

Epilogue

The Lᴏʀᴅ blessed the latter days of Job
more than his beginning.

Jᴏʙ 42:12

Oh, that they would always have such a heart for
me, wanting to obey my commandments. Then all
would go well with them in the future, and with
their children throughout all generations!

Dᴇᴜᴛᴇʀᴏɴᴏᴍʏ 5:29 ᴛʟʙ

All Joy reminds. It is never a possession, always a
desire for something longer ago or further away or
still "about to be."

C.S. Lᴇᴡɪs
Surprised by Joy

35

July 1967
Rua Reidh Lighthouse
Northwest Highlands of Scotland

The MacKenzie family left St. Andrews and the eastern coast of Fife to caravan across Scotland and up into the Highlands of Wester Ross on their way to Eric's boyhood home of Gairloch and the lighthouse of Rua Reidh. Little Jeffrey was safely carried in his grandparents' vehicle while Kate and David drove in their MG with the top down. As they left the fertile lowlands and climbed higher up into the mountains, Kate gazed in amazement at the otherworldly landscape of stark but majestic vistas. They drove along narrow, winding roads clinging to the hillsides, past solitary lochs and tumbling waterfalls. Only stalwart gorse and a faintly brushed pink-and-purple mantle of heather, not quite ready to bloom, covered the treeless peaks.

"This land is unlike any I've ever seen!" Kate exclaimed. "It's beautiful but seems so inhospitable. We've driven miles and miles without seeing anything but a few doughty sheep and some deserted crofts. I can't imagine what it's like in the winter. It must be terribly bleak."

David concurred. "When you consider how one could barely scratch out an existence on this rocky soil and the high rents the English landlords extorted, it's easy to understand why so many Highlanders were forced to abandon their homes and try their luck in Ireland or America. And I agree. It's beautiful up here but so different from what we're used to. By the way, you're not sorry we're taking our summer holiday here rather than in Virginia, are you?"

"Not at all. I've always wanted to see more of Scotland and learn more about your father's family," she reassured him.

"And don't forget, I did promise to take you back to the States for the Christmas Vac."

"I know. I'm looking forward to spending the holidays with my family this year. And Timmy is always so much fun at Christmas. He will get such a kick out of the baby! And we'll be able to show Jeff off to all the Littles in Charlottesville too. So it's only fair that we bring him up here to visit with the MacKenzie side of the family. It's a shame your grandparents can't travel very far, and that they couldn't come to our wedding."

"Right. I know they felt sad about it. But at least Aunt Slim made it. Did you remember to bring the wedding photos?"

"Yes, I've got them."

"Good. They'll enjoy seeing them."

"I know it sounds silly, David," Kate confessed, "but as much as I'm looking forward to meeting your grandparents, I'm always a little nervous when I'm first introduced to people in your family."

He glanced at her and smiled. "Remember the inquisition I faced with your parents?"

"Yes. That was dreadful. Maybe that's why I'm nervous."

"Well, you needn't worry. Grandma and Grandpa Mac-Kenzie aren't scary people and they'll absolutely adore you, Kate. And they'll go crackers over Jeff."

"I wonder how your mom felt when she first met them."

"I'll bet she was extremely nervous. But not nearly as much as my dad must have felt meeting the Littles. So tell me, what did you think of Mum and Dad's saga?"

"It's quite a story, isn't it? I really have a better appreciation of what our parents' generation went through during the war. We've grown up in such affluence and privilege. It's hard to fathom all the sacrifices they made for us."

"Right. Freedom isn't free, as they say. It comes at a high cost. And now you can probably better appreciate why every village in England has a war monument. But I was wondering what you thought of their personal story."

"Well, what struck me is how we can know someone, even well, and yet have no idea what they've gone through or suffered in their lives. I think I can better understand why your folks are such compassionate people and why they have such a zeal for sharing their faith with others, especially those who are going through tough times. And now I also have a better perspective on why you were so insistent on maintaining purity in our courtship. But, David, you've heard the story before. I was curious about how you reacted when you first heard the truth."

"I'm ashamed to say that at first I was angry at them. Frankly, I felt rather betrayed initially, like they had misrepresented to me who they really were. I felt they had deceived me, although I'm not sure why I thought they should have had a heart-to-heart with a mere child about their personal conduct. Now I see how complex people's lives can be and why we can't judge one another. I can also understand why they've been so passionate about purity and marriage. They've known the heartache of not walking in God's perfect will, and they've wanted to save others, especially their children, from making the mistakes they did. Sadly, when I was at Cambridge, I used my parents' mistakes as an excuse for my own. I rationalized that since they had messed up, then I had free license to do so as well."

"I've done that too. The old ruse, 'If they can get away with that, then why shouldn't I?'"

"Right. And as you know all too well, darling, I didn't decide to follow the straight and narrow until after Jack's funeral. It wasn't until then that I determined to try to walk in purity. I've come to realize that we are all responsible for our own relationship with the Lord. We can't blame others for our conduct or the decisions we make. In the end, each of us will stand alone before God. What ultimately matters most is our relationship with Him."

"Your parents seemed to have learned that lesson too. Anyway, I'm so glad that everything worked out for them. They have such a great marriage and a wonderful family. And I'm certainly glad your mom didn't go through with an abortion and that she decided to keep her baby, even if it meant being a single mother."

"Right! Believe me, I'm really glad about that too!"

"Just think, if she hadn't, not only would you not be here, but neither would Jeff. It makes you realize how your decisions can have ramifications that affect generations."

"That's right. They certainly do."

They pulled into the small but picturesque town of Gairloch, which clung to the rugged western coastline. After receiving a warm welcome from the locals and picking up groceries and supplies, the MacKenzies continued their journey, the final three miles of which followed a one-lane track along a lonely peninsula jutting out from Loch Ewe. The road skirted the cliffs as it twisted over narrow bridges and deep ravines. At times they would come around a blind curve to find sheep nestling in the banks of the road or a shaggy Highland cow sunning herself. The drivers progressed slowly and carefully while the passengers relished the spectacular scenery of the cliffs and sea. Then the lighthouse suddenly loomed before them tall and strong, a white symbol of safety and hope against the wild solitude of Rua Reidh.

They drove into the compound and tumbled out of their cars, the boys laughing and shouting with their liberation. The lighthouse keepers, Eric's cousin Bob and his wife, Marilyn, stood in the doorway in welcome. After exchanging greetings and hugs with them and Eric's parents, Davey and Maggie MacKenzie, the family brought their luggage into the large whitewashed concrete house and settled in for their week of holiday.

ᘓᕒ

The MacKenzies enjoyed a carefree week in Gairloch, golfing on the challenging nine-hole links course, swimming along the sandy beaches, fishing in the lochs and rivers, and hiking in the Torridon mountains and among the hills and woods of Flowerdale, the gleaming white ancestral home of the MacKenzie clan. Eric and Bob liked to boast that in a single day in Gairloch, one could golf in all four seasons, since a sudden squall could blot out the summer sun and beat them with a wintry blast of hail within minutes. The unpredictable shifts in weather added to the adventure of the family hikes as well, when trickling streams could quickly become rushing torrents. The sunshine, peeking through the storm clouds, transformed the rugged landscape into a glittering fairyland; while the branches of brooding Douglas firs, heavily bowed with rain, sparkled like jewel-clad giants, dripping with diamonds and wrapped in rainbows.

In the evenings they watched spectacular sunsets over the turbulent sea and gathered in the snug safety of the lighthouse to play board games, swap stories, or sing songs. Marilyn and Bob kept everyone well-fed and comfortable, and Davey and Maggie reveled in having a great-grand bairn to fuss over. In this remote spot hundreds of miles from the cares of his parish, Eric was finally able to relax completely and enjoy his family.

Only Natalie felt unsettled. As the week unfolded, there had been no word from Stuart. She often found herself thinking of him, wondering where he could be and what he could be doing. In the warmth of her family circle, she realized there was an empty place beside her only he could fill.

When the actual day of Eric's fiftieth birthday arrived and Stuart had not, Natalie wandered off to the tip of the peninsula to spend some time alone to think and pray. She walked beyond grazing sheep and goats to a rocky perch looking out over the Irish Sea to the Isle of Skye, faint in the distance. She hugged her knees against the whipping winds and prayed while gazing in awe at the powerful waves crashing against the rocks below. The sea often reflected the moods of the sky—some days, a melancholy black or a serene silver; on this day, a glorious aquamarine. Her heart lifted and in her clear alto, she sang a psalm of thanksgiving and praise.

> *Sing to the Lord a new song;*
> *Sing to the Lord, all the earth!*
> *Sing to the Lord, bless His name;*
> *And tell of His salvation from day to day…*
> *Let the heavens be glad, and let the earth rejoice;*
> *Let the sea roar, and all that fills it!*

Then she sang:

> *Whom have I in heaven but thee?*
> *And there is none upon the earth that I desire besides thee.*
> *My flesh and my heart faileth,*
> *But God is the strength of my heart,*
> *and my portion forever.*

On this windy cliff where only the gulls and God Himself could hear her, she could sing her heart out unself-consciously. But she had been overheard. Sensing someone's approach, she whipped her head around.

"Please, Natalie, don't stop!" Stuart called out as he clambered over the rocks to her side. "It was lovely."

"Stuart!" she exclaimed, throwing her arms around his neck. "I'm so glad to see you! I've missed you so much!"

He laughed with delight. "I missed you too, dear girl, and would have come sooner if I could have, especially for such a welcome."

"Where have you been? Why were you away so long? You've barely made it in time for Daddy's party."

"I've been fine, I had business to settle with my father, and I did make it in time for the party, didn't I?"

"Yes, but I was very concerned you wouldn't. Is everything all right with your father? Can you tell me about it?"

"I will in a minute. First, if I may, I would like to drop all the preliminaries and cut to the chase. Could you sit down again please, Natalie?"

Finding a suitable rock, she promptly complied and looked at him with curious expectation. This time Stuart read no wariness in her eyes.

He dropped on one knee. "Dearest Natalie, I love you more than I can possibly express. I would like to ask you if you would do me the honor of…if you would…Natalie…will you marry me?"

She looked at him in astonishment as if not fully comprehending this unanticipated question. Then she burst out, "Yes! Yes, Stuart, I will!"

Now he seemed astonished. "You will?"

She laughed and threw her arms around his neck again. "Yes! I love you, Stuart! I can't imagine anyone I'd rather spend my life with. So, yes! The answer is yes!"

He picked her up in his arms and laughing with her, twirled her around. When he set her back down, they were both breathless.

"You fooled me, you know," Natalie said. "I never expected you to propose to me out here. In fact, I had thought that perhaps you would ask me that night in the gardens at Carlisle House."

"I almost did, but somehow the timing didn't seem right. I was afraid you would turn me down. Would you have?"

"To be honest, I don't really know. I admit I wasn't sure what I should do. I wanted to marry you, but I also wanted to be as certain as I could that we were meant to be, that it was God's will, and not just yours or mine, that we should be married."

"What happened to convince you?"

She smiled mischievously. "Maybe absence does make the heart grow fonder. I missed you terribly, Stuart. But I've also had some time here by myself to reflect and pray and really seek the Lord's will. And my parents shared the rest of their story with us. I will tell you all about it sometime. Anyway, they gave me a lot to think about. You know, they were separated from each other for much of the war, and God used those circumstances to draw each of them to Himself. They had to learn to put God first in their lives, to keep Him as their first love, before they could come together in a true marriage."

"Seek first His kingdom and His righteousness, and all these things shall be yours as well?"

"Exactly."

"Right. I believe God has brought me to that place too."

"Well, I think it's honest to say in my case that my desire has long been to put Him first in my life. But I also believe that He has drawn us together, just as He had my parents, and that together we can serve Him in greater ways than we could apart. Just before you came up, I had been praying, and I declared to the Lord that I would follow Him either alone or with you. I just desired His will to be done. I told Him that if it were His will for us to be together and if He prompted you to propose to me, then I would say yes!"

"I confess that I am very glad to hear it! I was afraid that for those same reasons you would say no. I too have had plenty of time to talk things over with God, and I had struck a similar bargain. I told Him that if it were not His will and you said no, then I would carry on. I suppose I could live without you, my dear, but I would certainly rather be with you!"

They both laughed happily.

"Oh, I almost forgot something!" Stuart pulled a jewelry box from his pocket and sprung it open. Nestled in blue velvet, a brilliant marquise-cut diamond sparkled on a platinum ring. "This is for you, Natalie. Do you like it?"

"Oh!" she cried. "It's beautiful!"

"Here, try it on." He slipped it on her ring finger. "I thought it would be a fitting ring for you. Not too fancy or flashy, but like you, elegant and simply...dazzling."

Natalie held up her hand and let the diamond catch the sunlight. "It's perfect! Thank you, Stuart. I love it!"

"And I love you, my darling." He caught her hand and kissed her fingers. "May I have one little kiss to seal our engagement?"

She answered by brushing her lips against his. "I love you too, Stuart. And I'm the happiest girl in the world." She snuggled contentedly against his chest. "But tell me, why did you stay away so long?"

"Ah, well, that was at the counsel of your father."

She looked up at him. "You've already spoken to my father?"

"Yes, at Clemmie's."

"And?"

"And he seemed supportive of my suit, but he thought I should seek the agreement of my father. Based on his experience with the Kilmorey family, he was concerned that my father would not agree to our marriage and might even disinherit me."

"So you went to London to speak to your father."

"Yes."

"And what did he say?"

"Well, I must be honest. He was not very pleased. He had high hopes that I would tie the knot with my old friend Lady Lucy Bertram. She is not only titled but exceedingly rich. We had quite a few rather heated discussions on the matter."

"How did it end?"

"Natalie, how would you feel about marrying me if I told you I was disinherited?"

She swallowed. "I truly don't care, Stuart. Not for my sake. I wasn't born a lady, so I wouldn't be giving up anything if you were disinherited. But you...you would be giving up everything. I wouldn't ask that of you. But he shouldn't either. It's not fair. What will you do?"

"Your father asked me that, so I will give you the same answer I gave him. I love you, Natalie, more than anyone but God Himself. What's in a title? In the light of eternity, it means nothing. I can lay that down for you quite willingly. I would lay down my life for you, my darling."

"Oh, Stuart, I—"

"But don't fret, my dear," he said with a smile. "That isn't literally required of me yet and neither is the title. My father eventually came around."

"He did?"

"Yes. In the end he remembered you and your family from my graduation party at Blenheim. Seems like you all made quite a charming impression on the old boy. And I suspect that Clemmie weighed in with a word or two in your favor as well. So, after he was able to relinquish the idea of my marrying for wealth, he seemed quite pleased with my choice of a bride."

She playfully shoved him. "You cad, you had me there for a minute."

He laughed. "Well, I sincerely meant it. I think we should seriously consider our vows to pledge ourselves to one another for better or worse, for richer or poorer."

"For noble or no-account?"

"Something like that." He grinned. "Anyway, the old boy has offered to help with wedding expenses as well as giving us the run of Clifton Manor."

"Clifton Manor," Natalie repeated softly. "I should like to see it now."

"And so you shall. Perhaps I can convince your family to make a long detour around to Essex on their way home."

Natalie jumped up, pulling him with her. "Stuart! We need to tell them about our engagement!"

"I think…since they directed me down here…that they suspect what I came to ask you."

Hand in hand, they strolled back to the lighthouse compound, which had been strung with streamers and balloons for a *ceilidh* in honor of Eric's fiftieth birthday. The MacKenzie women had prepared a feast, which they were spreading out on picnic tables. David and his brothers were kicking around a soccer ball while Eric and his father, with his great-grandson, Jeff, in his arms, cheered them on. As Natalie and Stuart approached, the boisterous family activity ceased in anticipation of an announcement.

Stuart held up Natalie's left hand to flash her diamond and cried, "She said yes!"

A roar of approval greeted them and they were quickly enveloped by the family.

"Congratulations, old boy!" David exclaimed, thumping Stuart on the back.

"Hurrah!" shouted Hannah. "May I be a flower girl, Natalie?"

Eric shook Stuart's hand and kissed Natalie, while Annie embraced them both and Kate and Ginny admired the ring. Then with his arm around Annie, Eric turned to address his clan.

"Quiet, everyone!" David called out and was quickly obeyed. "Dad would like a word."

"Well, I won't bore you with a long sermon," Eric said, smiling. "First, I'd just like to say how pleased your mother and I are to welcome Stuart into our family."

"Here! Here!" The boys clamored and then, playfully shoving each other, settled down.

"And I'd like to thank you all," Eric continued, "for helping me turn fifty with such a grand celebration. A man couldn't ask for a more wonderful party or a more wonderful family. I'm truly grateful to the Lord for His grace to me. He has blessed me with so much: my loving parents—" he nodded toward them. "My beautiful wife, Annie," he added, giving her a hug. "And *all* of you, my beautiful children—my daughters and sons and my grandson—I love you all so much. I am... so...very...blessed." Eric paused, pressing his lips together as his eyes welled up. Annie, tears filling her own eyes, patted his arm in support.

Eric collected himself and declared, "God has shed His grace on me, and I am truly the most blessed of men! I pray that we will all continue to live for His glory and that our family will be a blessing for generations to come." He looked on each of them and smiled broadly. "Now, let's celebrate!"

Anglo-Oxford/American Glossary

bairn: Scots for baby or child

bird: slang term for a young woman, as in the American term "chick"

Bird and Baby: nickname for the Eagle and Child, the pub frequented by C.S. Lewis and the Inklings

biscuit: cookie

Blackwell's: the largest bookshop in Oxford, located on Broad Street

bloke: a guy

Blue: award of colors for representing the University in a sport. Oxford Blues are a dark blue; Cambridge Blues are light blue.

boater: hard, flat-topped straw hat worn in summer, especially when boating and during "Eights"

the Bod, or Bodleian: main library at Oxford University; receives a copy of every book published in England

boot: car trunk

Carfax: the center of the city of Oxford where Cornmarket, The High Street, St. Aldate's, and Queen Street meet. The tower there affords a great view.

ceilidh: (kay-lee) informal evening of song and fun

cheerio: goodbye

the Cherwell (pronounced "charwell"): one of two rivers in Oxford (see Isis)

chips: French fries

Christ Church: the largest and perhaps richest and most prestigious college at Oxford (nicknamed: "The House"). The college chapel is Oxford's cathedral.

coach: long-distance bus

college: one of about forty institutions that make up the University of Oxford

come up: to arrive as a student at Oxford, as in, "Has he come up yet?"

crack or *craic* : (Irish) talk, conversation, gossip, chat; a tale, a good story or joke

cuppa: cup of tea

daft: crazy

dear: expensive

dinner: lunch or dinner

dinner jacket, or DJ : tuxedo or dark suit with black bow tie and fancy shirt worn for formal dinners and college balls

don: college tutor, from the Latin *"dominus,"* or lord

the Eagle and Child: pub on St. Giles Street that was the meeting place for the Inklings

eight: rowing boat with eight oarsman and a coxswain to steer

Eights Week: intercollegiate rowing regatta held in Fifth Week of the Trinity, or summer term

Exam Schools, or Examination Schools: building on the High Street where exams and some lectures are held

Fellow: member of the governing board of a college. Many of the college tutors are Fellows.

first floor: second floor

flat: apartment

football: soccer

fortnight: two weeks

fresher: first-year student

Fresher's Fair: stalls for all the University clubs and societies held at the beginning of each academic year in the Exam Schools

go down: leave as a student at Oxford either temporarily or permanently

ground floor: first floor

Hall: communal eating place in (a) college. One eats "in Hall" and lives "in college."

Head of the River: winning crew or college in Eights Week. Also the name of the pub near the finishing line at Folly Bridge.

Hilary Term: Oxford's spring term. Americans would call it a winter term, as the eight-week term lasts from mid-January to mid-March.

holiday: vacation

The House: another name for Christ Church

The Inklings: perhaps the most important literary club of the twentieth century, which met informally for more than thirty years on Thursday evenings in C.S. Lewis's Magdalen rooms and Tuesday mornings in the Eagle and Child pub. When Lewis commuted from Cambridge on weekends, they continued to meet on Monday mornings at the Lamb and Flag until Lewis's death in 1963. One had to be invited, normally by C.S. ("Jack") Lewis; members included his brother, Major Warren ("Warnie") Lewis;

J.R.R. Tolkien; Charles Williams; Owen Barfield; Hugo Dyson; Dr. Robert (Humphrey) Havard; and Nevill Coghill. The friends read aloud their works in progress (including Tolkien's *The Lord of the Rings* and Lewis's *The Chronicles of Narnia*) for the others to critique and discuss, but the meetings often had no agenda other than good conversation and rich fellowship.

interval: intermission

Isis: a tributary of the Thames River in Oxford

Jack: the name with which C.S. Lewis christened himself when he was four

JCR, or Junior Common Room: club and lounge for Oxford undergraduates

the King's Arms, or the KA: possibly the pub most frequented by Oxford students, at the corner of Parks Road and Holywell Street

let: rent

lift: elevator

loo: toilet, or bathroom

mackintosh, or mac: raincoat

Magdalen College (pronounced "maudlin"): the college in Oxford where C.S. Lewis was a Fellow from 1925 to 1954. When Lewis took a Chair in Medieval and Renaissance literature at Cambridge in 1955, his rooms there were in **Magdalene College** (also pronounced "maudlin").

mate: friend (male or female)

May Morning: May 1. A carol is sung at sunrise from the top of Magdalen Tower and students welcome May with all manner of frivolity.

MCR, or Middle Common Room: club and lounge for Oxford graduate students

Merton College: where J.R.R. Tolkien was Merton Professor of English

Michaelmas: the eight-week autumn term, October–December

nappies: diapers

nought: zero. Nought Week is the week before the term officially begins.

the other place: Cambridge. At Cambridge, "the other place" is Oxford.

Oxbridge: Oxford and Cambridge Universities

paralytic: drunk

porter: guard at the front gate of each college. The porters serve as concierges, confidants, and bulldogs (policemen).

Porters' Lodge: building for the porters by the front gate that also serves as the mailroom for students

the pond: the Atlantic Ocean. The "other side of the pond" is the U.S.A.

pitch: playing field

punting: boating in a flat-bottomed boat (punt), using a long pole to steer

quad: short for **quadrangle**, a rectangular courtyard inside a college. Only dons are allowed to walk on the grass. Called "courts" at "the other place."

queue: line

queue up: line up

Radcliffe Camera, or Rad Cam: distinctive domed library in Oxford

ring up: call, telephone

St. Hilda's College: a women's college in Oxford, located along the Cherwell River. Home of the Jacqueline du Pré Music Building.

scout: person who cleans college rooms, more like a servant in Lewis's times

SCR, or Senior Common Room: club for Oxford Fellows

sent down: expelled

the Sheldonian: the Sheldonian Theatre, where matriculation and degree ceremonies, as well as concerts, are held

solicitor: lawyer

Somerville College: formerly a women's college (now coed) at Oxford; college of Margaret Thatcher and unofficial Inkling Dorothy L. Sayers

sporting the oak: in college rooms with two doors, if the outer door is open the occupant is receiving visitors. If the outer door is closed, the occupant does not wish to be disturbed and is "sporting the oak."

stalls: Orchestra section of a theatre

toff: someone with money or from the upper class

Trinity Term: eight-week "summer" term, from April to June

Tube: subway

tutor: college teacher. In term time, a student meets with his tutor at least once a week for a tutorial, or "tut," to read aloud and discuss an eight-page essay on the subject he is "reading," or studying.

underground: subway

Wellingtons, wellies: boots

Compiled with assistance from Rick Steve's *Great Britain and Ireland 2001*, Emeryville, California; Avalon Travel Publishing by John Muir Publications; and the University of Oxford website's "Glossary of Terms."

Author's Notes and Acknowledgments

Although *Evasions* is a work of fiction, the historical events in this book—from the day-to-day air battles and raids to the weather—are as accurate as I could make them after scouring letters of Lewis and Tolkien, interviewing and reading accounts of eyewitnesses of the period, and watching numerous documentaries, etc. Real people experienced much of what my fictional characters go through in these pages—with the exception of the romance, which likely also occurred somewhere to someone!

In England today the age of consent for marriage is eighteen; however up until 1977 it was twenty-one. For that reason, many young couples eloped to Scotland, where the age of consent is sixteen, and particularly to Gretna Green, the first Scottish town over the border. Today one can still be married there by merely giving fifteen working days' notice to the Gretna Registration Office. Only after I had submitted the manuscript of *Evasions* to my publisher was I able to learn—thanks to documents sent by Lynda Denton of Gretna Green—that this was not the case in 1940. Apparently, one member of the bridal party had to reside in Gretna Green for twenty-one days prior to the ceremony. I beg my readers' indulgence for my omitting this requirement for Eric and Annie's elopement. I have, however, read of instances where British clergymen did waive the waiting period for servicemen because of their limited leave during the war years, so let's assume this was the case for our young couple.

For the purposes of the story, I also rearranged some chronology of actual events as noted here:

The well-known Inklings meeting at the Eastgate in November of 1939—at which Dyson was "a roaring cataract of nonsense," according to a letter Lewis wrote to his brother—occurred on Thursday, November 9, not as I describe two weeks later on November twenty-third, the American Thanksgiving Day. The Inklings did indeed also meet the night of the twenty-third (but not at the Eastgate) when they read *Irene Iddesleigh* to much laughter.

The Royal Albert Hall was not reopened for Christmas concerts in 1939. Although many theatres stayed open throughout the Phoney War and even through the Blitz, the Royal Albert was closed from July 1939 until May 31, 1941.

Roger Lancelyn Green, a student of Lewis's and later good friend and an Inkling, was actually an actor in a London production of *Peter Pan* which initiated his interest in Sir James Barrie and the play, resulting in a biography as well as a book *50 Years of Peter Pan*. However, he was not in the play in 1939 but three years later in 1942. In his lifetime, Green was the world's leading authority on Victorian children's books and authors, including Sir Arthur Conan Doyle (*Sherlock Holmes*), Sir James Barrie (*Peter Pan*), and Lewis Carroll (*Alice in Wonderland*). His "retelling" of myths and fairy tales for children are still in print today, including *King Arthur and the Knights of the Round Table, The Adventures of Robin Hood, Myths of the Norsemen,* and *The Heroes of Greece and Troy.*

I have written Maj. Warren Lewis into the chapter at the Kilns on August 18, 1940. However, Jack actually wrote him a letter on that date, so we know Warnie was still in the Army. However, he was discharged shortly after receiving the letter and would have returned to the Kilns the following week. I chose that date for Annie to appear at the Kilns based on the first air raids on London, including the one in Wimbledon that killed several members of a wedding party (and my Peggy) gathered in a local pub.

Lewis did tell stories to entertain his young evacuees during WWII and began writing one which was the genesis of *The Lion, the Witch and the Wardrobe.* However, the great lion Aslan did not come "bounding in," as Lewis put it, until several years later (probably around 1949) when he took up the story again.

At the instigation of the dean of St. Paul's, the Very Reverend Walter Robert Mathews, Lewis was invited by the chaplain in chief of the RAF, the Reverend Maurice Edwards, to give lectures on the Christian faith to various RAF bases throughout England. The first one was at the base in Abingdon, near Oxford, in April 1941. For the sake of my story, I date these lectures about six months earlier in the autumn of 1940.

The Morrison shelter, in which I have Annie and Betty sleep during an air raid in August of 1940, was not actually introduced for household use in Britain until 1941.

Throughout the novel, I base the movements of Eric's squadron—with the notable exception of his tours of duty in France—on RAF Squadron 64, and Jeff's on Squadron 1 (Canadian).

I loosely based Carlisle House on Castle Howard in York and Kilmorey House on Cambo Estate in Kingsbarns near St. Andrews, Scotland. Today Peter and Catherine Erskine graciously open their beautiful home to guests, and I occupied the impressive Blue Room where my Laurene recuperates from influenza. I was also blessed with the unique experience of staying in the guesthouse of Rua Reidh lighthouse near Gairloch in the western Scottish Highlands.

Doubtless there are instances of chronological changes, as well as mistakes, of which I am unaware but my gentle readers will point out to me. These errors are my own. And yet I was so thrilled to discover that many times fact intersected with fiction. Some may call them coincidences, but I believe they are providences. First of all, after thinking that American Annie would possibly work near the Kilns at the Churchill Hospital in Headington, I discovered the hospital had been built by the Americans in WWII to care for soldiers. I already had this basic storyline in my mind when I came across a letter C.S. Lewis had written a little girl stating that they had a number of evacuees staying at the Kilns and one was a six-week-old baby boy! I also learned that the Reverend Peter Bide—who had married Jack and Joy Lewis, the role I had given to my fictional Eric Mackenzie—had served in WWII and after the war decided to become an Anglican clergyman. He had a wife and children, and Lewis helped him finance his return to his studies at Oxford and then seminary—just as I had envisioned for Eric. And finally, after I had decided that Eric would be a caddie at St. Andrews, I was given a book about the caddies of the Royal and Ancient golf course called *A Wee Nip at the 19th Hole*. The author, the caddie manager at St. Andrew's, is Richard MacKenzie. On my recent trip to Scotland, I was able to meet him, and not only was he very kind and willing to help, but he is also a believer.

I owe a debt of gratitude to many who helped with this project in some way. Great thanks to Colin Duriez, who has graciously shared his vast knowledge of Lewis and the Inklings and provided me the article "With Girls at Home," the wartime remembrances of evacuees staying at the Kilns. Colin guided me to producer David McCasland and his assistant Beth Guthrie of RBC Ministries, who sent me a copy of Day of Discovery's excellent documentary *The Life of C.S. Lewis,* which contains an interview of evacuee Jill Freud. Thanks to Kilns expert Kim Gilnett of Seattle Pacific University for answering questions on the Kilns during the war years, and to Dr. and Mrs. Stanley Mattson and the staff of the C.S. Lewis Foundation for their inspiration, support, and the wonderful opportunity of staying in Lewis's rooms at the Kilns. Also thanks to Kim Cameron and George Johnston of Merton College for their hospitality and making it possible for me to stay again on Holywell Street—most recently in number 12. In another fun providential connection, I learned later from reading Warren's diaries that the Lewis brothers dined in this same house exactly fifty-nine years earlier when it had been the home of Inklings Hugo Dyson and his wife, Margaret.

Many thanks to Ron and Joan Borzoni and Manfred Kory for sharing with me their reminiscences of the Battle of Britain and for checking over the manuscript. The Borzonis were children living in London during the Blitz and met during the war years. An Anglo-Italian, Mr. Borzoni's family lost several restaurants close to St. Paul's. Mr. Kory escaped from Nazi Germany as a small child with his Jewish family to England and then was evacuated from the Blitz to Stratford-upon-Avon. He is now an American citizen and a born-again believer. Also thanks to Miss Pamela Allen for sharing her recollections of her teen years during the Battle of Britain. Now in her eighties and with a still-thriving ministry to internationals in the DC area, Miss Allen worked at Barts Hospital in London and served under Dr. John Stott at All Souls. In another of those wonderful providential connections, I noticed a portrait on her wall of her great-grandfather. He was none other than George Allen of George Allen and Unwin, the publishers of J.R.R. Tolkien's books.

Thanks to Lt. Col. and Mrs. Robert White (USAF), to whom I've dedicated this book, for checking over the manuscript and most of all for sharing adventures with me in Oxford, York, and Scotland. Bob, a pilot and caddie-turned-expert golfer, was the inspiration for young Eric. He patiently walked me around the St. Andrews Old Course, drove us around the Highlands, and corrected my golfing and flying references. Marilyn has shared the vision for these novels since before their inception and has prayed them through to completion.

Thanks to all my church family at The King's Chapel and my friends who have cheered me on and supported me with prayers; especially my readers Diane De Mark and Dianna White, and Stacey Ipsan for excellent suggestions on the manuscript, and Elizabeth Sheridan for once again checking my Brit-speak. Thanks to Inece Yvette Bryant, my sister in Christ and dear friend, for everything.

Thanks to my family: my husband, Bill, and all our children for enduring my living part-time in another era and an imaginary world; and to my parents, Earl and Betty Morey, for constant encouragement, enthusiasm, and invaluable editorial suggestions.

Thanks to my wonderful Harvest House editor, Kim Moore, and to my first publisher, Tom Freiling of Xulon Press, who gave me the idea of The Oxford Chronicles in the first place.

And finally, thank you, dear readers. I hope you've enjoyed this story and have gained an appreciation for the brave men and women of "the greatest generation" who endured so much for the cause of liberty. I am so grateful for the notes and letters you have taken the time to write. I love hearing from you, so please drop me an e-mail at *inklingsauthor@yahoo.com* or visit my website at www.inklingsauthor.com.

Soli Deo Gloria.
Melanie Morey Jeschke
Vienna, Virginia
March 2006

List of References

Books on or by C.S. Lewis

Carpenter, Humphrey. *The Inklings: C.S. Lewis, J.R.R. Tolkien, Charles Williams, and Their Friends.* London: Allen & Unwin, 1979.

Como, James T., ed. *C.S. Lewis at the Breakfast Table and Other Reminiscences.* New York: MacMillan, 1979. Contains Walter Hooper's exhaustive bibliography.

Duncan, John Ryan. *The Magic Never Ends: The Life and Work of C.S. Lewis.* Nashville, TN: W. Publishing Group, a Division of Thomas Nelson, Inc., 2001.

Duriez, Colin. *The C.S. Lewis Chronicles: The Indispensable Biography of the Creator of Narnia Full of Little-Known Facts, Events, and Miscellany.* Bluebridge, 2005.

_____. *The C.S. Lewis Encyclopedia.* Wheaton, IL: Crossway Books, 2000.

_____. *Tolkien and C.S. Lewis: The Gift of Friendship,* Mahwah, New Jersey: HiddenSpring, 2003.

_____, and Porter, David. *The Inklings Handbook.* St. Louis, MO: Chalice Press, 2001.

Green, Roger Lancelyn, and Hooper, Walter. *C.S. Lewis: A Biography.* London: Collins, 1974; New York: Harcourt Brace Jovanovich, 1974. Revised British Edition: HarperCollins, 2002.

Gresham, Douglas. *Jack's Life: The Life Story of C.S. Lewis.* Nashville, TN: Broadman and Holman, 2005.

Hooper, Walter. *Through Joy and Beyond: A Pictorial Biography of C.S. Lewis.* New York: Macmillan, 1982.

Lewis, C.S. *The Collected Letters of C.S Lewis Volume II: Books, Broadcasts, and the War 1931–1949.* Edited by Walter Hooper. San Francisco, CA: HarpersSanFrancisco, a division of HarperCollins Publishers, 2004.

_____. *Letters of C.S. Lewis.* Edited and with a memoir by W.H. Lewis. London: Harcourt, Inc., 1966.

_____. *Letters to Children.* Edited by Lyle W. Dorsett and Marjorie Lamp Meade. New York: Touchstone, Simon & Schuster Inc., 1985.

_____. *The Lion, the Witch and the Wardrobe.* London: Geoffrey Bles, 1950.

_____. *Mere Christianity.* New York: Macmillan Publishing Co., Inc., 1943.

_____. *The Problem of Pain.* London: Geoffrey Bles, Centenary Press,1940.

_____. *The Screwtape Letters.* London: Geoffrey Bles, 1942.

_____. *The Weight of Glory.* Little Books on Religion 189. London: SPCK, 1942.

Lewis, Warren H. *Brothers and Friends: The Diaries of Major Warren Hamilton Lewis.* Edited by Clyde S. Kilby and Marjorie Lamp Mead. San Francisco, CA: Harper and Row Publishers, 1982.

Sayer, George. *Jack: A Life of C.S. Lewis.* Wheaton, IL: Crossway Books, 1994. First edition titled *Jack: C.S. Lewis and His Times.* Harper & Row, 1988.

Books on or by J.R.R. Tolkien

Carpenter, Humphrey. *Tolkien: A Biography.* Boston: Houghton Mifflin Company, 1977.

Coren, Michael. *J.R.R. Tolkien: The Man Who Created the Lord of the Rings.* New York: Scholastic, Inc., 2001.

Duriez, Colin. *The J.R.R. Tolkien Handbook.* Grand Rapids, MI: Baker Books, 1992, reprinted 2002.

Tolkien, J.R.R. *The Hobbit or There and Back Again.* London: George Allen and Unwin, 1937.

_____. *The Letters of J.R.R. Tolkien.* Edited by Humphrey Carpenter and Christopher Tolkien. Boston–NewYork: Houghton Mifflin Co., 2000.

_____. *The Lord of the Rings.* London: George Allen and Unwin, 1954–1956.

Books on WWII and the Battle of Britain

Barker, Ralph. *The RAF at War: The Epic of Flight.* Alexandria, VA: Time-Life Books, Inc. 1981.

The Battle of Britain, World War II. Edited by Leonard Mosley. Alexandria: Time- Life Books, 1977, 1998.

Bickers, Richard Townshend. *The Battle of Britain.* New York: Prentice Hall Press, 1990.

de la Bédoyère, Guy. *The Home Front.* Buckingham Shire, UK: Shire Publications Ltd., 2002.

The Experience of World War II. Edited by John Campbell. New York: Oxford University Press, 1989.

Hill, Maureen. *The London Blitz.* London: Chapmans Publishers Ltd., 1990.

Lang, Vera A.C. *From Britain with Love: World War II Pilgrim Brides Sail to America.* New Market, VA: Denecroft Publishing, 1988, 1999.

McCuthcheon, Marc. *The Writers' Guide to Everyday Life from Prohibition Through World War II.* Cincinnati, OH: Writer's Digest Books, an imprint of F & W Publication, Inc., 1995.

World War II: A 50ᵗʰ Anniversary History by the Writers and Photographers of the Associated Press. New York: Henry Holt and Company, 1989.

World War Two: WW2 People's War Archives (BBC). www.bbc.co.uk/history

Other References

On crisis pregnancy: Graham, Ruth and Dormon, Sara R. *I'm Pregnant...Now What?* Regal Books, 2004.

On St. Andrews' Old Course: MacKenzie, Richard. *A Wee Nip at the 19ᵗʰ Hole.* Great Britain: CollinsWillow, an imprint of HarperCollins Publishers, 1998.

On Rua Reidh Lighthouse: www.ruareidh.co.uk/ruareidh.htm

Other Books by Melanie Jeschke

Inklings

*A captivating tale of passion and purity
under the dreaming spires of Oxford*

American Kate Hughes is swept into her first year at prestigious Oxford University on the wings of adventure and romance. Lord Stuart Devereux, a fellow student, hopes to win Kate's affections with his charm and wealth. In stark contrast, her tutor, David MacKenzie—a handsome young Oxford don and leader of the Inklings Society—takes a different approach as he contends for Kate with convictions of propriety and courtship.

This engaging tale of love and purity—wrapped in a colorful sixties setting—brings alive the university world of C.S. Lewis, J.R.R. Tolkien, and the Inklings and matches the charm of old-fashioned chivalry against flirtatious contemporary indulgence. Whether you're a C.S. Lewis devotee or simply a hopeless romantic, this story will certainly delight you.

Expectations

*An unforgettable tale of dreams pursued
in Tolkien's Oxford and romantic Paris*

Autumn 1965—on a beautiful October afternoon, four members of the Oxford University Inklings Society each face different challenges as they hurry to their agreed-upon rendezvous at the Eastgate Hotel. Newlywed Kate MacKenzie has just learned that her constant nausea is due to pregnancy— an unplanned one that arouses all sorts of misgivings in the young student. Her husband, David, is bursting with the good news that he has been invited to spend a semester as a visiting lecturer at the American College in Paris. Yvette Goodman, though a successful scholar, is struggling with her disappointment in her single status as her twenty-ninth birthday looms ahead. Oxford don Austen Holmes makes a detour to the St. Cross cemetery, where he pays a brief visit to the grave of his young wife.

They all believe they have a glimpse into what their futures hold. They all have longings, hopes, and dreams as well as disappointments, fears, and sorrows. Will God provide for Kate, David, Austen, and Yvette as they trust He will, or is His plan for each of them something far beyond their expectations?

About the Author

Melanie Morey Jeschke is a pastor's wife, homeschooling mother of nine children, and former high school English teacher who writes travel articles and fiction. She graduated with an honors degree in English literature from the University of Virginia, where she also studied European and English history. Melanie has made a number of trips to England and Oxford, where she has attended several conferences on C.S. Lewis. She resides in Northern Virginia with her children and husband, Bill Jeschke, senior pastor of The King's Chapel.